SAGE ALEXANDER

AND THE
HALL OF NIGHTMARES

SAGE ALEXANDER

AND THE
HALL OF NIGHTMARES

STEVE COPLING

BROWN BOOKS
PUBLISHING GROUP

Sage Alexander and the Hall of Nightmares

Brown Books Publishing Group
16250 Knoll Trail Drive, Suite 205
Dallas, Texas 75248
www.BrownBooks.com
(972) 381-0009

A New Era in Publishing®

ISBN 978-1-61254-942-2
Library of Congress Control Number 2016953593

Printed in the United States
10 9 8 7 6 5 4 3 2 1

For more information or to contact the author, please go to www.SageAlexander.net.

This book is dedicated to the original Sage Alexander, my oldest grandson, Sage Alexander Copling. Sage, your adventurous spirit inspires me, and your love for reading thrills me. May your life be enriched by quests aplenty, great books, and countless escapades with family and friends. Your sweet nature, constant pursuit of knowledge, love of family, and fierce determination to succeed are the building blocks I used to create the Sage character for this book. You were the perfect template upon which to build a fictional character possessing supernatural powers. May God bless you and the life that lies ahead.

ACKNOWLEDGMENTS

The crafting of a novel is a team effort, and what a team I had for this one!

First, the boy who planted the seed, Sage Alexander Copling, who asked for an adventure story as a Christmas gift. I was so moved by his request, I knew I couldn't let him down and began writing the very next day. From that short story grew an entire mythology of good versus evil. Sage's younger brother, Nikhil, also inspired me. Both boys are avid readers and provided great suggestions for plot points, angelic gifts, and creatures from Greek folklore.

My oldest son, Jason Copling, who shares my love of reading, also encouraged me to continue, insisting upon reading early drafts and bouncing ideas. My middle son, Justin Copling, was my biblical expert. He kept me between the lines to ensure I didn't stray too far afield in all things religious. My youngest son, Joel Copling, listened patiently while I read segments to him for dialogue authenticity.

The biggest thanks to those in my immediately family goes to my wife, Sonora. Her patience as she sifted through page after page of grammatical errors, passive voice, redundancies, useless words, and punctuation problems left me spellbound. She encouraged me and nudged me forward but never shied away from pointing out things that might be inappropriate for my target reading audience.

Much thanks also goes to Carolyn Johnston, CEO of Innersight Pictures, who might be the most bullheaded, never-give-up woman I've ever known. Her vision for this book and the series/franchise has been steadfast and never-ending. We hope big things are in store for the Sage Alexander franchise, and if it hits, most of it will be because of her doggedness.

I must also mention the folks at Brown Books Publishing Group—Milli Brown, Tom Reale, and Abby Thrift—and The Agency at Brown Books—Cathy and Alicia—for all of their help in making this a reality. Special thanks to Sally Kemp of Brown Books, an editor who was unafraid to point out some ugly truths in the manuscript. Sally did a marvelous job of improving the story and teaching me writing tips that will carry forward to future books. And finally, the wonderful line editor at Brown Books, Rachel Felts, who must have wondered just what she'd gotten herself into after the first few chapters.

1

Sage crossed his arms and glared at Leah across the small table in the corner of his bedroom. He was sick of her questions, her demands, and her endless claims of global destruction. Well, not immediate destruction, but still, doom and gloom, the fall of mankind, the end of humanity. That's all he'd heard from her his entire life. He'd just turned fourteen, and from the moment he could understand the meaning of her words, she'd painted visions of a looming cataclysmic war between a race of special humans—people like him—and creatures that had haunted mankind since the fallen angels were expelled from heaven.

Global warfare. Monstrous mutations. Supernatural powers of unimaginable complexity. Yep, that was his life with Leah, an apparition only he could see and hear—a spirit who had caused him more issues than any two schizophrenics combined and who wanted him to study some book about people who'd been missing for centuries but might still be alive.

"Sage, did you hear me?" Leah asked a third time. She edged the book a few inches closer. "It is important that you commit their faces to memory. That you familiarize yourself with the abilities each of them possessed."

He rubbed his eyes and blew out a hard breath. "Why?" he whispered.

"Because your family is under attack and you will soon need the information."

Sage turned away. He didn't care to face her right then.

"Look at me," Leah said softly, her voice more patient than he knew he deserved. "Sage. Please. Look at me."

So he did, for what must have been the ten millionth time. Her radiant, golden hair, pulled back into a ponytail, ran to the middle of her back. Her clothes—best described as female Roman gladiator—glowed and reflected light from the corner lamp and sparkled as though studded with diamonds and rubies. Her short sword, sheathed in a scabbard crafted from some ancient bluish animal hide, had a bone-white pommel and cross guard that appeared polished with wax.

She looked like a sixteen-year-old in a Halloween costume, yet her piercing blue eyes appeared ancient; a bottomless well of knowledge, most of which she'd kept from him.

Her wings were brilliantly white along the edges, three sets layered one atop another. Translucent in the center, they absorbed light in a way that made them blend with the environment. He rarely saw them fully extended but was left speechless each time he did. She most often kept them folded tightly against her back, like now, where they nearly disappeared within the folds of her clothes.

"OK, I'm looking," he whispered. It was evening, and his parents and younger brother, Nick, were in the living room putting a puzzle together. He didn't want them overhearing because he'd gone almost three years without talking about her.

"Since the day of your birth, I have done my best to prepare you for—"

"My destiny, yes," Sage said. "I wish that word didn't exist."

"Yes," Leah said, "I am certain that is true." Her face softened. "For your benefit, I will no longer use that term, yet the meaning still sits heavily upon your shoulders. You have resisted, at every turn, my attempts to prepare you, and you are *years* behind schedule."

He'd long ago gotten used to how she often floated in front of him, her pattern of speech, and her sermons of evil beasts out to conquer mankind. Yes, he could see other angels. And demons—Darks, he called them—but he'd seen no monsters or creatures she'd preached about over the years.

Leah tapped the book in front of him. "We believe one of the Seven Princes of Hell has a special place, a kind of prison where he has taken the missing Council Members."

Sage glanced at the book, which was invisible to anyone else but had the same bluish glow emanating from it as all the others she'd given him. Most of the angelic books dealt with the formation and history of the Angelic Response Council, an organization created six hundred years after Noah's flood and comprised of angel-blooded humans like himself. The others were to teach him Adamic, the language of angels.

He hadn't whispered *a word* of any of that to his family.

"We believe they are being held," Leah continued. "That some may yet be alive. You must memorize their faces, familiarize yourself with their gifts. Learn where they came from and under what circumstances they disappeared."

The Seven Princes of Hell? This was new. Well . . . mostly. Sure, she'd mentioned the Princes through the years: Pride, Greed, Lust, Envy, Gluttony, Wrath, and Sloth. They were of the Rephaim race, one of the three evil races descended from the Watchers, the fallen angels.

Leah reached over and opened the heavy leather cover of the book. The face of a man stared back at him.

Leif Erickson, the caption read, *gifted with Pathfinding, gone missing in the Year of our Lord 1000.*

Despite his irritation, Sage did a double take on the name. He looked up at Leah, and she seemed to read his mind.

"Yes," she said. "*That* Leif Erickson."

The portrait on the page changed, as Leif frowned, glanced to the side, and then smiled just a little. Sage felt some of the blood drain from his face. "How did—"

"We angels possess some intrigue of our own," Leah said. "Leif was the first to disappear. Then, over the centuries, thirty-one others vanished without a trace. The book is chronological. The most recent disappearance, a girl near your age, Elsbeth Brown from New Orleans, gifted with Teleportation and Persuasion, has been gone nearly a month. Hers is the final page."

Sage turned the book to the back. Like Leif, she blinked, angled for a side view, then smiled, her eyes sparkling.

Wow! Cute. Really cute! Brown hair, chiseled cheeks, wide, round eyes. Sage's age, or close. She wore a mischievous grin and possessed an air of confidence that actually gave him a sliver of strength. *How was that possible?* He found himself staring at the picture.

"It is imperative that you commit all of the Angelic Response Council members to memory," Leah said again. "Your attitude these past years might well cost the lives of your family. It *might* cost your own. Begin studying this book tonight after the rest of your family has gone to bed."

Sage stole one last glimpse of Elsbeth before closing the book. This was all very interesting but not that much different than what he'd heard from Leah for more than a decade. Just another lesson. More preaching. A different spin on her you-will-not-survive-without-training blather. He wished he could disappear some-where, but he'd learned ages ago that wasn't possible. Except for trips to the bathroom, Leah never let him rest.

They sat in silence for several moments. Then Leah leaned forward slightly and slapped the desk. It sounded like a gunshot.

He flinched to attention.

"Your family is already under attack," she said. "Your scales of doubt restrict your Clarity."

Clarity? She thinks I have Clarity? She was referring to the ability to see the manifestations of the Seven Deadly Sins on the human body in those who had fully succumbed to one or more of the Sins. Those gifted with Clarity saw physical transformations take place—and those transformations matched the physical characteristics of the corresponding Prince of Hell.

A chill crept across the back of his neck. Unlike humans, Leah never joked or told tales or exaggerated stuff. She had one purpose:

to protect and train him until it was time for him to begin his journey, whenever that might be. Sage knew he was unique; Leah had told him that no less than ten thousand times. And his destiny, something she'd never fully revealed, was the last thing she would lie about, even if she was capable of lying, which she wasn't because she was a Guardian. Nor was it something she would joke about, which, again, she'd never do.

"So . . ." he said, "I'm supposed to learn about these missing Council members, who might be held somewhere by one of the Seven Princes of Hell. OK. Got it. Why? Am I going in there or something? Wherever it is? Is that what you're telling me? For real? I'm only fourteen. A small-town kid from Norris, Oklahoma."

Sure, he was big for his age; nearly five-ten, broad shouldered, with natural strength beyond guys much older, but she was talking about fighting immortal beasts—quasi-spiritual creatures of legendary viciousness that controlled millions of humans. If he weren't already numb from a lifetime of listening to Leah's claims, he might have actually freaked out at the prospect of it all.

"You are angelic-human. You are Sage the Warrior," Leah said. "The second to ever possess more than one gift, and the only one possessing more than two."

Leah had a tendency to repeat things. She did it all the time. She'd told him that so often over the years it made him wonder if angels forgot stuff.

"Well," he said, "I don't think I've developed enough of my gifts to go waltzing in somewhere to orchestrate a massive jailbreak."

"You are not ready for such a mission because you have refused to train as you should. I only instruct you to memorize the Council members in this book for the benefit of a future, yet undetermined date."

"Sage," his mother shouted from the living room, "are you talking to someone?"

"No," he shouted back. "Just reading out loud." He grabbed a regular book off the desk and opened it in case his mom walked in unannounced. He scooted Leah's book off to the side.

"I have guarded you every second of your life," Leah said softly. "I know and understand your weaknesses and fears. But do not doubt those who craft the future of mankind."

He knew she couldn't read his mind, but sometimes it seemed as though she could. Yep, fear is what he had. Loads of it. Barrels full. Maybe it showed in his face or his body language. Did his lower lip quiver? Did his eyes wiggle?

"Worthless gifts, Leah," he whispered. "Worthless. Pathfinding, which so far hasn't done squat for me. And Fighting Arts, which I'm no good at using." He waved a hand in the air. "Yeah, yeah, I know, I'm no good because I stopped training. But still. What's the point?"

"Your Markings have been visible for many years," she said. "You have three gifts. Not two."

His Markings—hieroglyphic-like angelic symbols, deeply golden in color, on the back of his shoulders that only others like him could see. Each symbol represented a gift, and she was right, he had three.

He'd never met any others like himself, but glancing at the book made him realize they were out there somewhere. "I just . . . I just wanna be normal." His voice caught. "I don't wanna see Darks. Or angels. I want the gifts to go away."

"You think if you refuse to use them, they will go away?" Leah stood and looked down at him, her voice gentle but firm. "I am afraid you only delay the inevitable. You failed to mention your greatest gift of all. A gift no other has ever possessed."

"Oh, that?" He almost laughed. "Memory Sharing?" He held up his hands and made a spooky sound. "Oooohhhhh, Memory Sharing. Like I'll defeat a bunch of Darks with *that*. I can see myself now. Hey, hold still while I press my fingertips against your forehead! I mean really, Leah. Fine, three. Three gifts."

"As I have explained many times, your mission is not to defeat Darks, as you call them, but the evil races descended from the Watchers. Regarding the rest of your gifts, they will manifest at the appropriate time. Doubt blinds you. Fear suppresses your natural course of development."

"I know, I know." He knew he'd eventually have all the gifts, but he was just so weary of the entire conversation. He knew about Bell Making, Clarity, Chains, Sight, Voice, and Persuasion. What else? Teleportation, Transformation, Might. There were others. Honestly, if he hadn't tuned her out for a big chunk of his life, he'd know all twenty-two. He wasn't about to ask her about it now. Really, he just wanted her away from him.

He was so tired of secrets, of not being able to tell anyone of his special blood, that in the past two years his injuries had begun healing at least a hundred times faster than anyone else's, that he could swing a sword so fast it resembled a lawnmower blade, and that he could read the most ancient language in all of creation. His life was one giant secret.

Before turning eleven, his mom had taken him to five different psychiatrists to discuss the "imaginary friend" he'd talked to, and about, his entire life. By then he was viewed as a freak at school, never invited anywhere, and laughed at behind his back. Until he learned to play the game and keep his mouth shut, his life was a huge disaster. Once he started telling everybody it was just a long phase he'd gone through, things got a little better, though he still didn't have any real friends. He'd been "Invisible-Friend Free" for almost three years now, and his mom couldn't be happier. His reality hadn't changed—despite how he'd learned to act normal—because he still saw Leah all the time and still had to listen to all the doom-and-gloom stuff.

He sighed. "Anything else you want to tell me? I promised Mom I would help with the puzzle."

She shook her head. "No. Just study this book. Review the many things we have gone over in training. Time is becoming critical."

Sage nodded and tried to hide the panic growing in his gut. Leah didn't exaggerate. Or tell tales. Or give him information he didn't need. Her urgency was growing. She'd been in near-panic mode for the past month; well, as much as angels actually panicked. Anyway, something was about to happen, and it was making him nervous.

His family sat around a game table where a thousand-piece puzzle lay half constructed. A big-screen television had the St. Louis Cardinals baseball game muted. Even though it was only the first weekend of summer vacation, the Redbirds were already five games up on the Cubs in the division.

"Hey, Dog Breath," Nick said as Sage walked in.

Nick was twelve, just eighteen months younger than Sage. His dark brown hair matched Sage's own, as did his lanky but solid build. Both had piercing brown eyes and dark complexions. Twins, some often commented, even though Sage couldn't really see it.

"We need you to start on Lincoln's face," his mom said. She pointed to the puzzle of Mount Rushmore and lipped "nice to see you" before going back to studying President Washington. She'd been an athlete in college, a point guard, and she still worked out religiously. Her auburn hair shaded more brown than red, and she kept it short. She had the brightest green eyes of anyone he knew. Sage sat in the chair directly across from his dad, who gave his full attention to something on his phone.

"Kevin, would you put that thing away?" Mom said.

Dad waved a hand at her, but didn't, his eyes glued to the screen. Sage and Nick got their build and hair color from their dad.

"Earth to Kevin," Mom said. "Family time."

"Just a second, Jenna!"

Nick was about to place a puzzle piece when he sucked in a little breath and his hand froze. After his eyes went wide, he cut them from Mom to Dad to Sage.

The top of his mom's ears went red, then her entire face. She glanced at Sage and Nick, then pushed her chair back. "Excuse me."

Sage couldn't believe Dad didn't look up when Mom's feet stomped out of the room.

Leah floated behind Sage's dad and hovered there. "Can you not see, Sage?" she asked. "Is your veil of doubt so thick that you are blinded to the attack occurring in front of you?"

Sage didn't respond. He couldn't. Not in front of his family. The last thing he needed was to feed the "Sage-the-Craze and His Invisible Friend" monster again. So although he said nothing, he stared at his dad.

"The attack has only just begun, but you cannot ignore it." Leah rose into the air to a spot just behind his dad's head. She bent over and inspected his neck and face.

What attack?

"The signs are there," Leah said. She floated over the top of the table and stopped next to Sage's right ear. "Soon you will be unable to ignore what is occurring. You must train. You must study. Time grows near, and there are few others available to help you."

It took every ounce of self-discipline not to jump from his chair and shout at her. Sage was up to his earlobes with her catastrophic prophecies.

"OK." His dad finally put his phone down. "Where are we?"

Nick chuckled. "Sage and I are in the living room. But you're in the doghouse."

His dad frowned. "How so?"

"Clueless," Nick sang. He stretched the word into five syllables.

Sage frowned at Nick, but didn't say anything. Neither did Dad as he pushed away from the table and headed to the back of the house.

When he was out of earshot, Nick looked at Sage and whispered, "Have you noticed how much they fight lately?"

Sage shrugged. Most of the time it was Dad that caused the fights. Work stress, Sage suspected, although he really wasn't sure. Money, maybe, or the big corporate merger he was trying to arrange with their Uncle Duncan. Sage tried ignoring all that stuff, but something was eating at him. It had been more than a year since they'd had any significant father-son time.

"This puzzle is lame, anyway," Nick said. "Wanna play me in a game of *Batman: Arkham Asylum?*"

"And lose again?" Sage was no match for Nick at gaming. Nick could probably compete in tournaments if he wanted. "Wouldn't mind a hike in the woods though."

"You're making a big deal out of nothing!" his dad shouted from the back of the house. "I mean, really, Jenna! So what? It was an article about the pitfalls of major mergers."

"I don't care what the article was," their mom shouted back.

Then their bedroom door slammed, and their shouting shrank to a low roar. Nick sprang from his chair.

"Let's get out of here," he said. "Our family time just got hijacked by Dad's hostile takeover."

They hit the front door to the sound of more shouting. Sage wondered what attack against his dad Leah could see that he couldn't. He also wondered if he'd ever be able to do anything about it.

2

Sage awoke with a start. Eyes blurry, he couldn't tell if Leah was sitting on his chest or floating horizontally just above his body. He glanced at the clock on his bedside table—2:06 a.m. Rain slapped against his bedroom windows; thunder rumbled in the distant sky.

He wasn't sure what woke him. It was dark, but he could see well enough to know that Leah stared intently into his eyes.

"What?" he whispered.

"Memory Sharing," she said. "It is time. You must learn it."

Sage rubbed his eyes. *She wants to have a training session at two in the morning?* "What? Now?" He rolled over and clamped a pillow over his head. "Let me sleep."

"I have explained how you will one day use Memory Sharing on other angelic-blooded beings," Leah said. "Other Council members, certainly, but also on the evil creatures the Council battles. I have explained all of this to you many times, but your refusal to learn requires that I explain it again."

"Leave me alone!" Sage hissed his reply with unmistakable vengeance.

She didn't. "Whomever you Memory Share with must be in an unconscious state, as you have been taught. This gift can also be used on spiritual entities such as myself, if they allow it. Since I am allowing it, it is time now to learn and experience it. We will travel to the Tomb of Ancient Documents."

"But I'm half asleep."

"Please move the pillow." Leah's voice was quiet but firm. They had often spoken in the middle of the night, and she kept her voice down as a reminder for Sage to do the same. Nick's room was right next to his, and he'd ratted him out more than once about Sage's talking to someone while everyone else slept.

He knew it was hopeless to argue with Leah when she was that determined. She would never let him go back to sleep until he complied, so he moved the pillow. Her face glowing like it did when she communicated with other angels, Leah raised her hands toward his head.

"The correct method," she told him, "is to place your thumbs in the eye sockets, near the bridge of the nose. Place your pinky fingers on the temples. Place the rest of your fingers on the very top of the forehead, near the hairline." Leah placed her hands in position.

"What if they're bald?" He'd asked her that once, years before, when she explained the general concept, and he'd laughed at his own cleverness for five minutes afterward.

Since Leah didn't really have a sense of humor, she answered him as though he'd meant it seriously and was asking for the first time. "Place your fingers where the hairline would be if the person had hair. Afterward, focus on the center of the forehead and open your mind. You will join with him or her. This gift is already fully developed and requires no training on your part. It will come naturally for you." She removed her hands. "Now, place your hands against my head the way I showed you."

Sage watched wide-eyed as Leah lowered herself slightly. He carefully placed his fingertips on her face. Her forehead was cool, and his fingers tingled just a little.

Leah continued. "As I have explained before, when you arrive inside someone's memory, you will not be able to communicate with them. Others will not see or hear you. You will be there as an observer only."

Sage nodded but said nothing. She had repeated this information many times before. He almost laughed out loud at the thought of Nick walking in right then and seeing him with his eyes wide open and his hands raised in the air, mumbling to an invisible friend.

"Now, open your mind," Leah said softly. "Think of a blank canvas. Let the image build and grow from a slate of nothingness."

He closed his eyes and focused only on the coolness of his fingers against her forehead.

"The Tomb of Ancient Documents is the depository of sacred writings chronicling the historical account of the Angelic Response Council," Leah said.

Sage heard her words but felt nothing. He saw nothing. This was just too weird. She'd explained it to him dozens of times over the years but had never attempted to teach him exactly how to perform the action needed to produce his gift.

Why now, all of a sudden?

"Relax, Sage. Tension grips you. Fear controls your mind. Your gift will do the work, but only if you allow it."

Sage let out a breath and relaxed, then felt some tightness fall away from his shoulders and arms.

"My words are pictures." Leah's voice sounded as soft as cotton candy, just a whisper on a cool breeze. "Let your mind drift. Allow it to rise and fall at the sound of my voice. Listen carefully to what I tell you. The Council sometimes holds meetings within the primary chamber of the Tomb. My memory is vivid, there for your exploration. Free yourself."

Images slowly formed from the white canvas in his mind: bookshelves, tables, library ladders reaching to the ceiling.

"The Tomb's location is a closely held secret, known only to Council members who have . . ." Leah's voice suddenly cut off, replaced by a male's voice at the far end of a large room.

Sage opened his eyes, and his breath caught. Spread out before him was a room nearly as big as his house. A black-granite, domed ceiling rose more than sixty feet high. Angel statues of every size and shape, constructed of white stone, were mounted along the bottom rim of the dome. They held swords and shields ready for battle, as if guarding the collection of ancient writings. The chamber measured a hundred feet long and almost that wide. Bookshelves lined every wall—floor to ceiling—with rolling ladders to help reach the higher books.

Several people sat in chairs around a long table. At the far end of the room, a man stood, a small notebook in his hand. An old woman with thick glasses and hair stacked a foot high sat at the head of the table. She raised a hand and cut the speaker off in mid-sentence.

Sage's point of view suddenly rose into the air and floated toward the group. He gasped before remembering that he was inside Leah's memory.

"Hello, Leah," the woman said. "I was told to expect you this evening."

"Good evening, Abigail Vaughn," Sage heard Leah answer. "I will observe this evening's discussion if you will permit."

Abigail nodded and turned to the seven others at the table. Not all of them were as old as Abigail, but they were close.

"We welcome Leah, Guardian to Sage the Warrior." The old woman smiled, but it was clear that whatever topic the group was about to discuss had her deeply concerned. "Proceed, Grigor," Abigail said.

Grigor, a professor type straight out of the 1800s era of England's Oxford University, complete with little round glasses, smoking pipe, and tweed jacket, glanced at the notebook in his hand and cleared his throat. "Last night, Elsbeth Brown and her father Calvin were involved in an undercover operation in New Orleans against a Rephaim offspring named Rupert. Rupert and a DNA expert named Pieter Baltic believe they have found a way to convert normal humans into human hybrids, which would give the humans extreme longevity, accelerated healing capabilities, and otherworldly speed."

"Using Rephaim blood?" one of the men at the table asked.

"Precisely," Grigor said. "Specifically, Rupert's blood."

Another man at the table looked at Abigail. "Does this sound familiar?"

Abigail's face darkened. "Yes, Roberto. They are trying to create super soldiers. The first time they tried this, they created vampires, of which they've totally lost control. The next time, they created werewolves, and we all know how that's turned out."

Leah had told Sage things like this his entire life, but seeing other people talk about it put everything in a new light. *Vampires and werewolves are real?*

Abigail Vaughn, evidently a leader in the Council, nodded at Grigor. "Any idea what monster they've created this time?"

Grigor glanced at his notepad. "We're not certain, but they most closely resemble zombies. Something happens to a human brain after death that can't be fixed with the properties of the Rephaim blood. Though they're snatching bodies before burial, something about their resurrection process accelerates the aging process of the brain. Calvin reports the Undead last less than forty-eight hours before collapsing." He flipped another page in his notebook before continuing. "Last night's operation involved live subjects, homeless snatched off the streets. We don't know the effects on living humans."

"How did they get Elsbeth?" one of the men asked.

"Her father is gifted with Transformation. He'd infiltrated this group some weeks ago. We suspect now that Rupert's group actually targeted Calvin and Elsbeth from the beginning. They were lured to an abandoned warehouse where a lab had been set up. They probably knew Calvin and Elsbeth would move against Rupert."

"How is Calvin?" Abigail asked.

"Recovering. He says a six-armed monster cut his way into the laboratory, from the Dark realm, probably, and took Elsbeth.

Wrapped her in some kind of lizard skin." Grigor placed his notebook on the counter and sat down.

"Thank you, Grigor." Abigail gazed off for a moment before speaking. "The count is thirty-two now. In the thousand and sixteen years since Leif Erickson's disappearance, Elsbeth Brown marks the thirty-second Council member taken. Does everyone here understand how important she is?"

The men at the table all nodded but said nothing. Several fidgeted with papers or shrugged.

"The gift of Persuasion is the greatest and most effective weapon we have against the Dark Beasts," Abigail said. "Elsbeth is the first Council member in five hundred years to have it. Combined with Teleportation, she is our most lethal weapon, at least until Sage the Warrior develops fully." She turned to Leah. "Speaking of Sage, how is his training progressing?"

Sage felt ashamed of the report Leah was about to give.

"He remains resistant," Leah said. "But some progress is forthcoming."

Abigail stared at Leah, her eyes narrowing. She frowned as though doubting Leah's word.

Sage's sense of relief made him lightheaded. Should he really care about what a group of old people thought about him? No. He'd never met them before, and might not ever. But the look in the old woman's eyes as she talked about Elsbeth's disappearance and her importance to the Council had shamed him much more deeply than he would have ever suspected was possible. Leah could have been much harsher, but she hadn't been.

"Given your past reports at how deeply the boy has resisted, I guess we should be overjoyed at the prospect of forthcoming progress." Abigail didn't sound as if she believed a word of what she'd just said, yet she said no more about it. She turned to Grigor. "Have we sent a Pathfinder to New Orleans to discover the entrance into the Dark spiritual realm through which they escaped with Elsbeth?"

"We have. Like all the others, he found no evidence of a breach."

Sage tried to remember what Leah had taught him about entrances into the Dark realm. He knew Pathfinders were the only Council members who could see them, but he also knew that a Pathfinder had been sent to each disappearance location for the past thousand years and found no evidence of an opening. What else had Leah said? What was it about those openings that were important? *Why hadn't he paid more attention over the years?*

"Will Sage the Warrior's Pathfinding skills be more precise?" one of the men at the table asked Abigail.

"In theory," Abigail said. She looked at Leah. "Is that correct? Will not each of his gifts be enhanced beyond all others?"

"It is prophesized," Leah said. "He now bears the Pathfinding Marking on the back of his shoulder, along with Memory Share and Fighting Arts, evidence that those gifts have manifested."

"Prophesy says the purity of Sage the Warrior's blood is unique in all the Council," another man at the table said. "It might be worth the effort to take him to New Orleans and have him search for the breach."

Sage flinched at the absurdity of such a suggestion. Everyone at the table began talking at once, and he couldn't understand anything being said.

Abigail finally raised a hand, and one by one the voices fell silent. "Leah will advise when he is ready. She has reported often that he is years behind schedule. Carrying through with such a suggestion would be the death of the boy, so let's table that topic." She turned to Leah. "You are the closest to the Pathfinder we sent to New Orleans. Have you discussed with him the idea of using the boy?"

"We have spoken. He is violently opposed. Sage is not ready."

Abigail nodded and slowly climbed to her feet but held Leah's attention. Because Sage was seeing this memory through Leah's eyes, it appeared Abigail was speaking directly to him. "You must impress upon the boy that the Council has entered its darkest days. The Seven Princes have stolen some of our greatest warriors. We are fighting a global war with fewer resources than we've ever had. He *must* get ready."

Sage swallowed hard as Leah promised that she would deliver the message. No need for that. Not after seeing for himself Abigail's plea.

Then Sage was back in his bedroom, hands frozen in front of him, slick with sweat, Leah standing near the little round table in the corner of his room. The rain still slapped against the window; the wind howled through the eaves; thunder rumbled in the distance.

"It was time to give you more than just words," Leah said.

Sage pulled off his pajama top and dried his face with it. He started shaking all over and sat heavily on his bed. "Who were those people?" he whispered.

"They are members of the Council," Leah said. "I traveled to the Tomb a month ago while you slept. Elsbeth Brown has not yet been found."

Sage frowned. "I thought you never left my side. Ever."

"There have been occasions, when you were sleeping, that I have been sent on short missions. That was one. You have never been left alone, however. Other Guardians were there in the room during my absence."

He'd always wondered how sometimes when he awoke there'd be a new book sitting on his table. He glanced at the table now and saw the book of missing Council members lying there. It glowed blue in the darkness. Then he noticed a second book, one Leah was resting her hand upon. "What's that?"

"Come. See for yourself." Leah floated away.

Sage walked over, sat down, and saw a thick, leather-bound tome that looked as old as time itself. *Encyclopedia of Dark Creatures*, by Fredrick Urbain. The cover had a picture of a huge, winged demon scored into the leather. He opened the book to somewhere in the middle and saw a drawing of a beast with a lion's body and the head of a gorilla. It had black wings sprouting from its back and a sleek tail tipped with two large spikes. A Midnight Raider. "I've never . . ." he whispered.

He flipped to a page containing a drawing of something called a Deep Sea Demon. The monster had arms and legs and a head and neck, but any resemblance to a human stopped there. Scales covered its entire body. Gills framed its neck; huge eyes sat deep within a basketball-sized head. Its mouth stretched from ear to ear with four-inch teeth protruding like miniature steak knives. Sage read the caption:

Deep Sea Demons were designed by Emim scientists in the early sixteenth century for the purpose of ruling the seafaring trade between coastal countries in Europe. Though largely extinct now, remnants of the species can still be found in all five oceans and in many of the world's deepest lakes.

"Is the stuff in here true?" Sage asked the question without taking his eyes off the book.

"Most certainly," Leah said. "Many of the world's mysteries, legends, and myths are explained within the pages of this book. Those joining the Council are required to study this book before being sent out on their life's work."

Sage saw a chimera—a monstrous, fire-breathing, female creature with the body of a lion, the head of a goat arising from its back, and a tail that ended in a snake's head—and a minotaur, a half-man, half-bull that he recognized from Greek mythology. There were giants in the book, several species of trolls, and even a picture of a cyclops. All of the giants were members of the Nephilim race and included many pages dedicated to bigfoot-type creatures—large, hairy beasts called by different names around the world. The drawing of Cerberus, the multiheaded demon dog, made him shiver. On and on the book went, listing creatures and legends and myths galore, from one scary page to another.

Flipping pages, the book fell open to the middle, and a great water beast stared back at him. *Leviathan—She-Beast of the Deep.* It looked like a dinosaur, not a creature patched together by evil scientists. Long legs, thick, spiked tail, webbed feet with claws that matched its razor teeth. Sage couldn't tell how big it was, but it looked vicious and dangerous. The artist had captured a look in its eyes unlike any other monster in the book. Leviathan's scaly hide was diamond shaped with sharp, barbed hooks covering every inch of its body.

Sage looked at Leah. "Why is this in here?"

"There is disagreement about the true nature of Leviathan. Some believe the She-Beast protected Council members, others believe she hunted them. She has been missing for many centuries."

Sage turned a few more pages before exhaustion overtook him. He stood and practically staggered back to his bed. His sweat had dried, and he pulled his pajama top back on. Years of Leah's words echoed inside his head. Words he thought he'd blocked out and forgotten rushed back to him in waves.

And then a memory broadsided him. "I remember one time when I was about eight years old. Dad, Grandpa Alexander, his friend Ronan and I were somewhere outside of London. Do you remember?"

Leah had settled on top of his blankets at the end of his bed. "I can recall every second of your life." As usual, her expression didn't change when she said it. It wasn't bragging; it was fact. Sage felt silly for asking.

"Well, anyway. We were driving, headed to visit some remote castle or something, when our car broke down. We were on a narrow road with thick woods on each side." Based on what he'd just seen in the book of weird creatures, he suspected the worst.

"It was dark. I was in the back seat by myself while Dad, Grandpa, and Ronan checked out the battery under the hood. You were beside me. To my right I saw several pairs of glowing eyes in the midst of the trees."

Leah stared at him, her face expressionless. She gave no hint of remembering the event. Sage knew she wouldn't comment until he asked a question.

"There were Darks flying around, of course. And Archs. You didn't really seem that worried about anything until I saw those eyes. I pointed to them, but you had already seen them. You drew your sword. Am I remembering it right?"

"Yes," Leah said.

"You told me I had nothing to fear. Was that true?"

"Yes," she repeated.

"I didn't ask you then, and you didn't volunteer any information. Do you know what it was?"

"Yes," she said a third time.

Sage waited for her to offer the information, but she didn't. She simply waited for him to ask. "What was it?" He held his breath.

"A typhon."

"That's from Greek mythology," he told Leah as though she wouldn't have known it already. "It's a half-man, half-snake. Mythology says it was summoned by Gaia—Mother Earth—to avenge the defeat of the Titans by the Olympians. Some describe it as having a hundred heads." He looked at Leah. "So they're real?"

"Yes. Everything you saw in that book is real."

"But . . . who knows about all of this? I mean . . . these are legends. Stories. Stuff you scare people with around campfires." His voice rose, but he couldn't help it.

They sat in silence for several moments. "You've told me the history of the Council," he said, "about their battles against the evil forces. Those creatures are what they're battling, isn't it? A bunch of monsters that regular humans write stories about? Make movies about?"

"Long ago, floods destroyed Earth because of what the fallen angels—the Watchers—did to humanity when they mixed with humans and created the three evil races—the Nephilim, the Emim, and the Rephaim," Leah said. "The Seven Princes of Hell are of the Rephaim race.

"The Emim corrupted the animal kingdom," she continued. "They experimented, crossbred, and manipulated living organisms by mixing human and evil angelic blood. The flood destroyed everything on the surface except for a handful of humans. But not everything died. Your Elioudian ancestors thrived in Tartarus by moving into the vast caverns left empty when the waters spewed onto the surface during the flood. The three evil races and their abominations also fled underground and lived in the great spaces where the Elioudians had made their temporary home prior to the flood. They fought their way out of the underworld after the waters receded and again began their assault against the human race. The Elioudians responded by sending the first Council to the surface to battle them." Leah lowered her voice even more. "The myths and legends and stories you speak of are based on what humans have seen but not understood. They rationalized their horror by telling stories, while ignoring the truth. For you see, Sage, the truth is too terrifying for them to face."

Leah's words echoed in Sage's head before he was finally able to speak. "So you battle the Dark Angels, and the Council battles the three evil races and the creatures they created?"

"That is mostly true," she said. "Your kind can also battle Darks directly, if they are in possession of the correct tools."

"What kind of tools?"

"Tools tempered with their own blood. You will learn more soon."

"Why show me all this tonight?" he asked. "Why not years ago?"

"Time grows short," Leah said softly. "Your family is under attack. You have resisted. Fought me at every step. You have refused to adjust to who and what you are. Because of your internal battle, you have few friends and are ridiculed and laughed at by your peers. You used to find solace within your Fighting Arts training, but you have abandoned that to the point of negligence. You are not emotionally ready for such revelations even now, but circumstances require that we proceed nonetheless."

Sage pulled his covers up to his chin. He wished he could stop shivering. "Tell me," he said, "about the typhon that night. Was it there to kill me?"

"Yes." Leah never told tales or exaggerated. She always spoke the simple truth. Always.

"What happened? I only saw the eyes for a second." He held his breath and wondered how many other times he'd been that close to death.

"The Archs drove it away until a nearby Council Member was able to mortally wound it."

"Who? Who killed it?" Sage clamped his hand over his mouth, because he'd almost shouted it.

"I cannot reveal that information at this time. Eventually you will learn of his existence."

"But . . ."

His bedroom door opened and his dad stuck in his head. "Sage," he whispered, "are you awake?"

It took him a second to control his voice before answering in a low voice. "Yeah, why?"

"It's two-thirty. We thought we heard talking. Did you have a bad dream? You shouted out."

Leah floated into his line of vision. "I cannot instruct you to lie," she said softly. "Tell him the truth."

"Uh . . . I saw monsters in a thick, leather book and a group of creepy old people inside a library somewhere on the other side of the world were talking about the destruction of the human race."

His dad chuckled. "Nightmare, huh? Well . . . it sounded as if you said, 'Who killed it?' Very intense. Are you OK?"

"I . . . I think so." Sage glanced at the digital clock on his nightstand and did a double take. It showed 2:31 a.m. All that time in the Tomb, all the time looking at the monster book and talking to Leah, and only twenty-five minutes had passed? Maybe he *was* losing his mind.

His dad walked into the room, sat down on the edge of Sage's bed. He looked at him for several moments. "You OK, son? Really OK?"

Sage shrugged. "Yeah. Sure. Never better."

"Hmmm. Well, I wonder. You remember a few years ago, right after you confessed that seeing and talking to your invisible friend was just a phase you'd been going through?" Dad smiled and squeezed his leg through the blankets.

"Yeah, I remember."

Where is this going?

Dad shrugged. "Tough time. Full of evasions, avoiding answering direct questions, furtive glances to spots where nothing was there. You got better, but you've slipped back. So I need to know. Are you all right?"

Sage held his breath, then slowly eased it out. "I'm really OK. What about you?" He watched his dad and waited for an answer. His dad said nothing. "When's the last time we went hunting or fishing? You've been a ghost lately."

Dad's smile turned into a frown. "Work's been . . . this merger . . . yeah, I know. Just . . . I've always got time to talk. You know that, right?"

"Sure."

"Remember our great talks?"

Sage did remember. He wondered how he ever would have made it through all the mess without his dad's strength. "Best things ever," Sage said.

Dad yawned and squeezed Sage's leg again. "If you're OK, then get some sleep. See you in the morning."

After his dad closed the door, Sage laid his head back, his mind racing. Would Dad tell Mom that Sage was faking it? Would they send him to a shrink again? Now? After Leah had just dumped all this stuff on him?

Monsters. Creatures. Myths. Dark Angel abominations. Trying to kill him since the day he was born. He knew the Archs were outside standing guard and that Leah now floated silently near the foot of his bed. Despite such reassurances, he didn't know if he would sleep again that night.

3

The pastor was on fire this morning, Sage thought, as his words about the evil of money echoed through the congregation. "'The greedy bring ruin to their households, but the one who hates bribes will live.' Proverbs 15:27." Pastor Young took a breath and pointed to his flock. "'But his sons did not follow his ways. They turned aside after dishonest gain and accepted bribes and perverted justice.' 1 Samuel 8:3."

Sage glanced at Nick, who sat at full attention, probably focused on the preacher's toupee, which looked as though some of it had come unglued. Sage almost burst out laughing the first time the hairpiece flipped up and waved to the crowd.

Mom sat next to Grandpa and Grandma, not Dad, and Sage wondered if his parents had made up from their fight the day before. As for him, he couldn't keep his mind on the sermon. Even when Ronan, Grandpa's ever-present personal assistant, cleared his throat and motioned for Sage to pay attention, he just nodded and went through the motions of worship.

He hadn't slept much after his dad checked on him. The storm had raged afterward, thunder and lightning, rain hammering the windows. But that wasn't it. Memory Sharing with Leah had done something to him, opened a world he hadn't fully realized existed. Well, not totally true. He'd known such a world existed by what Leah had been telling him his entire life. To see it like that . . . he just hadn't been prepared for it.

"Greed isn't just about money," Pastor Young belted from the pulpit, "although money is what we think about when someone accuses another of being greedy. The more dangerous type of greed is power—an unquenchable thirst for control." He stepped out from behind the lectern and raised his Bible in the air. "All of you are familiar with the seven deadly sins, of which greed is one. While I think pride is the most destructive, greed walks hand-in-hand with pride and might be the most apparent and influential in our day-to-day lives."

Sage's dad sat at the far end of their family pew. From his viewpoint, Sage could see his dad's right hand, hidden behind his right knee. And the phone in that hand. It looked as if he were reading an article on the Internet.

It wasn't unusual nowadays for folks to have their smartphones out during the sermon, given that so many people had a Bible app. His dad had stopped carrying a Bible to church years ago. Bible apps didn't have pop-up advertisements to invade the scriptures, yet Sage saw two ads in the few seconds he'd been watching the images on his father's phone.

Sage glanced at his dad's face. He wondered if his dad cared whether anyone knew he was ignoring the sermon.

He did a double take. What was wrong with Dad's face?

His skin looked golden. Not like the Midas man in the commercials, not so deep and dark that he looked yellow, but definitely a hint of gold, especially along his hairline, the top of his ears, and the side of his neck.

Maybe it was the way light reflected through the stained-glass windows. He looked at Nick, who was sitting beside Dad, but his brother looked normal. Sage glanced at both the man sitting in front of his dad and the woman sitting behind. Nothing. Normal. Nor was there a golden tint on Dad's clothes or the pew cushion.

Sage looked at the ceiling, where Leah was hanging out with a group of Archs. As soon as Sage looked at her, she locked eyes with him. "Look at Dad's skin," he mouthed covertly.

Leah ran her hands slowly across her own face. "The attack has begun," she said during one of Pastor Young's strategically placed pauses.

As the preacher read a verse about it being easier for a camel to go through the eye of a needle than for a rich man to enter heaven, Sage took another look at his dad. The golden hue also appeared on his hands. His lips were red and slightly swollen. Sage stared so long at him he didn't even notice that the preacher had ended the sermon and started a closing prayer until Ronan's elbow nudged him in the ribs.

Fear as sharp as a knife ran down the middle of Sage's back. Leah must have seen something last night, right after Mom stormed off.

Five minutes later, the service was over. Everyone lined up to shake the preacher's hand before leaving the church. By the time Sage's family got to the door, Sage had wiggled his way past Nick, his mom, and grandparents and stood behind his dad as the preacher gripped his hand.

"Hello, Kevin. Always great to see you and your family." Pastor Young's hairpiece sat kind of cockeyed.

"Thanks," Kevin said. "Good sermon today."

This close to the front door, nearer the bright summer sun, his dad's skin looked even more golden than before. Sage found it difficult not to stare.

"I appreciate it." Pastor Young said. "Might be a timely topic for you, given the merger you're working on, huh?"

His dad gave the minister a little chuckle but said nothing. Then he passed him and went out the door. Sage shook the preacher's hand, nodded, and chased his dad outside.

Everybody in town knew about the merger of Alexander Enterprises and McCormick Distribution. His dad's company, Alexander Enterprises, owned real estate, a Dr Pepper distribution plant, a string of laundromats, a dozen Subway franchises, and a small chain of computer retail stores.

However, the company was only a quarter of the size of McCormick Distribution, a five-state, multibrand automobile dealership that sold cars, trucks, Humvees, and motorcycles. His dad had somehow arranged financing through New York investors to buy up massive amounts of their stock and launch a hostile takeover. Sage didn't begin to understand the inner workings of the deal or what kind of impact it would have on their small town. What he did know was that dozens of jobs were on the line, because rumor was that the first thing his dad would do was close the local Chevrolet dealership and merge it with a dealership in Oklahoma City. That meant salesmen, mechanics, parts-department employees, secretaries, and the cleaning crew would all lose their jobs. Dozens. Sage and Nick both had several friends whose parents might soon be out of a job, meaning they might then lose their homes.

Sundays were family-lunch-at-a-restaurant days. "I'm riding with Grandpa," Sage shouted to his mom and dad, who both waved at him.

"Then I'll ride with your parents," Grandma ruffled Sage's hair as she walked by.

Grandma Alexander was a classic beauty. Her silver hair had the pageboy flip, something his mom told him because otherwise he would've had no clue. She was trim and fit, wore stylish wire-framed glasses, and had the warmest smile he'd ever seen.

Then there was Grandpa Alexander, a man of many looks. Sage had often wondered if his grandfather suffered from an identity crisis. He shaved his head for several years, then grew his hair out and colored it black. He had a full beard, then no beard at all, then just a moustache, and then a Van Dyke. He'd gained weight through the middle, lost it, then pumped iron and grew through the chest and arms. Currently, dressed in jeans and a polo shirt, he wore his silver hair long and his moustache short.

Grandpa drove a full-sized, four-wheel-drive Dodge pickup, loaded to the hilt with all the latest features. Sage climbed into the back seat so that Ronan could sit up front.

Sage had never understood the relationship between Grandpa and Ronan Barrister. Grandpa was retired from a forty-year career at the US State Department, through which he had spent a lot of time traveling. Ronan had been some kind of government contractor, assigned specifically to assist Grandpa with everything.

Ronan was huge—well over six feet tall—with shoulders as thick and wide as an NFL defensive lineman's. His hair, always pulled into a ponytail, hung to the middle of his back. Sage didn't know how old he was, somewhere between Dad and Grandpa, but he was probably the strongest man Sage knew.

Norris, Oklahoma, was a town of thirty thousand, twenty-five miles east of Oklahoma City. There weren't a lot of restaurants to choose from, which is why they went to the same place every week—Henry's Diner—a home-cooking, hole-in-the-wall joint with awesome food and free ice cream after every meal.

Sage waited until Grandpa's truck was out of the church parking lot before speaking. "I think something's wrong with Dad." He looked at Leah on the seat beside him. Maybe she'd give him advice on how to continue this conversation. She stared back at him, her face completely blank. He'd get no advice from her.

Grandpa glanced back. "Like what?"

Sage couldn't tell him everything he knew without sounding crazy, so he settled for subtle. "Stress or something. Business related. About the merger. He's changing."

Ronan turned around in his seat. "Changing? Have you talked with him about it?"

"And say what?" Sage didn't mean to sound defensive, but he had.

"Tell your dad what you've told us," Ronan said. "It might have an impact coming from you."

Sage just might try that. He wanted to probe the "your dad's under attack" angle Leah had suggested last night. "Does he look different to you?" he asked. "Like . . . maybe . . . pale or waxy or just different?"

Grandpa glanced quickly at Ronan, and Sage saw some kind of unspoken message pass between them. They were silent for several moments, his grandpa focusing on the road ahead.

"I think he's looking really stressed because of the business deal," Ronan said. "Old beyond his years."

There'd been something weird in Ronan's voice. Grandpa hadn't answered at all. He knew his grandpa wouldn't lie to him. Ever. "I'm not talking about him being stressed, Ronan. I'm talking about his complexion. Answer me. Does he look different this morning?"

Again they glanced at each other. "Can't really say," Ronan said. "Didn't really look at him much."

Sage looked at Leah. She raised an eyebrow and nodded, almost as if she approved this line of questioning. He cleared his throat. "His skin looks gold," he blurted before he lost his courage. "Gold. It wasn't that color when we were driving to church, but I saw it turning during the service. It was still golden when he walked outside. I'm asking both of you if you saw it."

Sage held his breath. They'd either think he was nuts, which would open up his entire past about his "invisible friend" thing, or they would humor him. They were only a few blocks from the diner, and so they didn't have a lot of time to talk about it.

"Let's assume I did notice that," Grandpa said. "What would it mean?"

Sage flinched. "Well . . . um . . . I don't know." He looked at Leah, panic rising in his throat. *What would it mean?* Leah offered nothing.

"Is it possible you saw some light trick through the stained-glass window?" Ronan asked. "I've seen that before."

For a fleeting moment, Sage thought about telling them to forget it. He glanced at Leah and decided to continue.

"No. Reflected light would have covered his clothes, the pew, maybe some of Nick. That wasn't it. It was only his skin. Darkest around his hairline and neck. Gold. I saw it. I'm not nuts." The last three words came out shaky and made him feel as if he were six years old.

"I'd never think that," Grandpa said. "Never."

Sage wasn't so sure.

"Here we are," Grandpa said. They turned into the diner.

Sage saw his mom, dad, and Nick walking in. He couldn't tell from this distance if his dad's skin was still gold.

"Do not lose faith, Sage," Leah said softly. "The scales are slowly falling from your eyes. Clarity begins."

He gave her a quick glance just before climbing from the truck. Ronan was joking about ordering two triple cheeseburgers and three chocolate shakes when Sage realized that neither of them had answered his question.

Sage took a seat directly across the table from his dad. Even more than before, his skin glowed under the bright lights of the diner, like a bar of gold bullion from Ft. Knox. Sage was careful not to stare. Instead, he watched Grandpa and Ronan as they sat in chairs at the far end of the table. He saw Ronan look at

Dad, his eyes visually inspecting every inch of his face, before looking away without expression. Grandpa also stared for a few moments but, like Ronan, didn't give any indication of anything being amiss.

Leah floated near the ceiling and watched over the group, but she mostly paid attention to Sage's dad.

"Kevin, tell us the latest and greatest on the merger," Grandpa said.

Nick groaned at the same time that Sage's mom held up a hand. "No," Jenna said, with a hardness that couldn't be ignored. "No business talk."

Grandpa held up both hands. "Hey, forgive me. Just making conversation."

"Touchy subject," Kevin said. "Not bringing work home at the moment." He grinned, his golden skin even more pronounced against his brilliant white teeth.

Sage went lightheaded when black worms the size of pencils poked out from both sides of his dad's neck.

"I'm getting it done, though," Dad told Grandpa. "This deal will create generational wealth for our family."

"Kevin," Mom warned under her breath. "Please."

Dad held up both hands in surrender. "Sorry."

The worms grew until they were about three inches in length. They wiggled around for several seconds, and then sprouted little roots—hundreds of hair-sized threads, which grew two inches long themselves. The wet and slimy tentacles then plastered themselves against the sides of his neck, their roots disappearing into his hair.

Sage felt bile rising into his throat and he fought against puking all over the table. Then he noticed his dad's hands, and he stopped breathing altogether: the skin on his palms was now black and leathery, and his fingers were twice as thick as they had been twenty minutes before. His fingernails had become spike-like claws that a grizzly bear would be proud to have.

"Sage, you OK?" Dad asked. "Something wrong?"

Sage tried answering, but his mouth wouldn't work. Dad's eyes were almost completely red, like some freaky, B-rated horror flick where the makeup guy had tried too hard to make the actors look creepy.

"He's white as a sheet." His mom put a hand on Sage's forehead. "He looks sick. Honey, are you all right?"

"Uh . . . I . . . not, I'm not sure." Sage tried taking his eyes off his dad but couldn't. He felt lightheaded. *Does nobody see this?*

"The attack worsens," Leah whispered into his ear. She'd moved behind him and placed both hands on the top of his head.

Her contact broke the spell, and he tore his eyes away. He glanced at Grandpa who, like most of the others at the table, was staring at him. He looked at Ronan, whose eyes were glued on Dad's face.

He sees it. Sage was sure of it. *Ronan sees it!*

"He's thinking Dad's gonna order him the liver and onions," Nick said. "They aren't that bad, Sage."

Sage rose to his feet, his legs wobbly. He stuck his hands in his pockets to hide the shaking. "I've gotta go to the bathroom." He walked away before anybody could stop him.

"Sage, are you sure you're all right?" his mom asked from her chair. "Kevin, you should go with him."

"No!" Sage spun around. "I'm fine. Really." He kept his eyes on Mom. "I don't need Dad to take me to the bathroom."

Almost everybody in the diner—nearly all of them from his church—turned to stare at him. His face heated up when he realized how loudly he'd spoken.

The men's bathroom had a urinal, two stalls, and a mirror above the only sink. He pulled the collar of his shirt down to expose his back right shoulder and saw the three Markings he'd had for years. Nothing new. He checked his left shoulder and found a faint symbol beginning to show.

Clarity. He'd memorized all the symbols years ago. Clarity, for sure, barely visible, meaning the gift hadn't fully manifested yet. Tears blurred his vision as he locked himself in one of the stalls, sat down, and took several deep breaths.

Chills slithered across his body like an army of runaway ants.

Maybe I'm schizophrenic. Truly. Maybe the five shrinks were right.

Maybe all of this was inside his head, even the Memory Sharing with Leah last night. Maybe the doctors should put him on antipsychotic medication and see what happens.

"Keep the faith," Leah said from the other side of the stall door. "Clarity has begun to manifest. Do not fear. The attack is real and accelerating at an alarming rate."

Sage closed his eyes, clamped his hands over his ears, and hummed quietly, drowning out Leah's words.

Then a man's voice filled the small bathroom. "Sage. We need to talk."

Ronan.

He jumped up and threw open the stall door. "What?" he said. "Did you see it? Did you?"

The big man put his hands up. "Whoa, slow down." Ronan stepped over to the door and put his body against it. "Keep your voice down. This door is as thin as cardboard."

"Did you see it?" Sage asked again. His words spilled out of his mouth in a rush.

"I don't know what I saw," Ronan said. "It wasn't clear to me."

"What's that mean?"

"The stuff you mentioned in the truck. About your dad looking different. I believe you. So does your grandfather."

That wasn't good enough. Not nearly. "You were staring at his face," Sage said. "I saw you. What did you see? Tell me." He held his breath. There was no way Sage would reveal what he saw. Not happening. If Ronan couldn't describe it, it meant he didn't see it. Sage had no interest in being patronized by the same people who hadn't taken him seriously when he tried convincing them he could see angels and demons.

Ronan raked both fingers through his long hair and pulled it behind his shoulders. "Sage. Listen." He sighed and looked at the ceiling.

Right at Leah. Or maybe not. Sage couldn't tell. He waited for Ronan to continue and crammed his trembling hands into his pockets again.

"I think it's possible you can see things nobody else can see." Ronan said. "Your Grandfather Steven and I have talked about it for years. It was actually your grandpa who convinced me of that. You know Steven. He's very convincing."

"You didn't see anything different, did you? Just now?"

"Something is different," Ronan said, "but it's gonna sound weird."

"What?"

"His face is blurry." Ronan chuckled but then immediately got serious. "Steven said the same thing. In the truck after you climbed out."

"Grandpa said that?" Sage asked. "That Dad's face looked blurry?"

"It's even blurrier just now. At the table. It was why I was staring at him. I thought something was wrong with my eyes."

Someone tried opening the bathroom door, but it didn't budge against Ronan's back. "Just a minute," Ronan shouted. "Be out in a sec." He looked hard at Sage and lowered his voice. "Look, we believe something's going on with your dad. Trust me. We just can't see what you can. That's the bottom line. We'll figure it out. OK?"

A lump formed in Sage's throat. *They believe me! For real?* He nodded, momentarily speechless.

"Just talk to us," Ronan said. "It's finally time to talk to us." He turned and opened the bathroom door and smiled at the young boy waiting outside. "Sorry, young man. Come right on in."

Sage followed Ronan back to the table and sat down. Grandpa gave him a little nod and smiled.

"We ordered you liver and onions," Nick said. "With a slice of coconut cream pie. Your favorite foods. So be happy about it."

"Then I hope you'll be happy when I blow chunks all over the table," Sage said. He glanced at his brother and avoided looking at his dad. He smiled weakly at his mom, who rubbed the back of his neck.

"You OK, honey?" she asked.

"Yeah. I'm good. Just a bit of an upset stomach. OK now."

Sage saw Ronan lean over and say something to Grandpa. After a few seconds, everyone at the table seemed to return to normal. Sage took a sip of water and finally glanced at his dad, who stared at him, his eyes glowing like a demon's, his teeth stark white against his red lips and deep golden skin.

"Train," Leah whispered into his ear. "You must resume your training. Time runs short."

Sage broke eye contact with his dad and fought the urge to flee from the diner. He had never felt so alone.

4

The next day, Sage woke up determined to accomplish several things. First was to determine if his dad's face had really looked blurry to Ronan and Grandpa like Ronan had said. If so, why? Were they angelic-human? Were they also able to see the spiritual world? If they could, why hadn't they told him before now? He'd asked Leah about them, but she said she wasn't authorized to reveal such information about others. He hadn't expected her to tell him anything, but it hadn't prevented him from pestering her for an hour about it last night before he went to sleep.

He also needed to go to his hideout, an old bomb shelter, a place he'd titled the Dungeon, and start practicing his sword-fighting skills with Leah. Whatever was going on with his dad, wherever the attack against him was leading, Sage knew he needed Leah's instruction, especially after seeing the look of disbelief on Abigail Vaughn's face at the Council meeting when Leah told her that progress was forthcoming.

Finally, he needed to study the two new books Leah had given him and refresh his memory on reading Adamic, the language of angels.

Basically, he needed to train like he had up until his eleventh birthday, when he'd grown tired of it all. Fighting Arts, Pathfinding, and Memory Share—he needed to practice all three. He'd lain awake for almost two hours the night before after he caught a glimpse through his parent's bedroom door of his dad's bare chest. Dad hadn't gotten any worse, but Sage had confirmed that golden skin covered his entire body.

Sage also planned to spend some time down at Beowulf's Loft, an oddities shop where he'd killed more summer afternoons than any other place in town. The owner, a Greek man named Theophylaktos Alastair—Theo for short—was the oldest guy Sage knew—or at least the oldest looking. The shop was a virtual museum of historical artifacts and odd merchandise from around the world. As interesting as the retail part of the store was, it was Theo's storeroom, the place where he kept his privately owned collection, that fascinated Sage the most. The old shopkeeper had been talking for three weeks about the delivery of a one-of-a-kind purchase he'd made in Europe that should have arrived last Friday. Sage promised he'd come in to see it.

After showering and dressing in jeans and a T-shirt, Sage walked into his bedroom to grab Leah's two books from his desk. He noticed a third one lying next to them. He could tell by the bluish glow that it also came from Leah. *Angelic Response Council—A Primer of ARC Histories for Young Readers* by Imogene Felton. He picked it up and flipped through the pages. It was small—four by six inches—and thin—a quarter inch at most—but crammed with information.

"Where did this come from?" he whispered.

"You need a better understanding of the basic history of your people," she said. "I had it delivered from the Tomb of Ancient Documents."

Like the others, the book tingled in his hands and sent waves of warmth through his wrists and arms. The table of contents listed eight chapters. One entitled *Gifts* began on page twenty-four.

Gifts manifest themselves in either the physical or mental arenas. Twenty-two different gifts have been recorded throughout history. Some potential Council members died early in life, before their abilities could be chronicled, which leaves the exact number of gifts unknown.

The physical gifts: Fighting Arts, Teleportation, Might, Absorption, Mimicry, Bell Making, Animation, Transformation, Elemental Transmutation, Chains, and Voice are naturally occurring yet sometimes take years of training and perfection to be effective in battle. Some physical gifts are accessible as soon as they are bestowed and take little training to master.

The mental gifts: Persuasion, Sensing, Echolocation, Projection, Sight, Possession, Summoning, Clarity, Illusion, Pathfinding, and Memory Sharing can sometimes cross into the physical realm but are all executed by focus, concentration, and training. Persuasion occurs singularly, meaning only one may possess it at any given time. Memory Sharing is cited in the Prophecy of Seth as an exclusive gift set aside for fulfillment. To date, no one has ever possessed this particular gift.

The Prophecy of Seth foretells of the birth of a male child who will eventually possess all gifts, some of which might not be listed in this publication.

Sage suddenly felt lightheaded, knowing that *he* was the one to whom it referred. He looked at the list of gifts—all twenty-two—and wondered how each of them worked. He turned the page and found the definitions for each. Great! Then he had a thought and turned toward Leah.

"You've told me all this for years. Why give me the book now?" He kept his voice low because he could hear Nick in his room next door.

"The Thrones have instructed me to accelerate the timetable for your training," she answered. "I follow directions. Always."

Unlike you, she probably wanted to say. That the Thrones—the angels guarding the throne of God—had taken notice of him probably wasn't a good thing.

"The timetable of events about to occur was put into place centuries before your birth," she continued. "Your refusal to follow directions has left you totally inadequate to repel the attack being waged against your father. Soon it will be too late."

"Sage!" his mother yelled from the kitchen. "Your oatmeal is turning into a block of concrete!"

Sage swallowed hard, the visions of his dad's transformation playing over and over in his mind. "What's the attack? What's happening to him? How can I do anything about it?" Yes, he sounded desperate, but it didn't matter. Not in front of Leah.

"The influence of the Seven Princes runs deep within the human realm, and one of them has singled out your father." Leah said.

"Which one?" he asked. "Wrath? Pride? Greed? Envy? How can we tell? Which one has singled him out?"

She stared at him for several moments. "You must determine that and destroy him. *You* must eventually destroy them all."

Her words felt like small explosions inside his chest. *What! I must destroy the Seven Princes of Hell!*

He almost laughed, but the look on Leah's face killed that idea. "Well . . . I . . . you've never . . . so this is . . . all these years . . ." He couldn't even compose a sentence. He sat down on his bed, hands shaking. All these years of her talking about his destiny, and it boiled down to six words: *Destroy the Seven Princes of Hell.* She'd never some close to telling him this. She'd hinted a few times with words so vague and disjointed that his own confusion was the only thing he understood.

He rubbed his temples and took several deep breaths. So . . . his dad was somehow being influenced by one of the Seven Princes, and to stop it, he had to kill that Prince?

Leah floated in front of his door, her hand on her sword. "I was instructed to reveal your desti . . ." She stopped and smiled. "I promised not to use that word, didn't I? I am to reveal the mission you were born to fulfill. Time runs short for your father. It is unfortunate that you are inadequately prepared to save him."

Sage wanted to scream. Why hadn't she told him this would happen? Instead, she waited until his dad turned into a freak? Once again, he took several deep breaths. "OK," he told himself. "Calm down."

"You must train," Leah told him. "In all things."

"Sage Alexander!" his mom shouted again. "I'm about to throw your breakfast down the garbage disposal."

"Coming," he shouted back. "Just a second."

OK. Train. That's what I'll do.

He dumped the contents of his school backpack onto the floor of his closet and crammed everything behind a row of clothes. Then he put the newest three of Leah's books inside. "Who can help me train?" Sage asked Leah. "Besides you?"

"I will train you in all you need to know." Leah floated over to the window and gazed out.

"When will I be ready?" Sage slung his backpack over his shoulders, determined to get his attitude right.

The blank expression on Leah's face made his stomach do a flip. "That is impossible to know," she said after several moments. "Because you have refused to train for nearly three years . . ." She looked away and shook her head.

He walked across the room but stopped before opening the door. "Are there no Council members who can help me?"

Again she paused, but this time she didn't answer the question. "The Thrones insist that you train. Time grows short. You are the key to defeating the Seven Princes."

They stared at each other and Sage knew that was all he'd get out of her. He finally nodded, fear twisting his gut. "Train. Got it."

His oatmeal *was* cold, but at least it matched his hard toast and greasy bacon. Maybe his mom *should* have flushed it down the garbage disposal. The only thing warm was his orange juice.

"I was wondering if you'd decided to skip breakfast," Mom said. She gave him a kiss on the cheek. "Nick ate an hour ago."

"Overachiever," Sage said. "Always hated that about him." He smiled and dropped his backpack on the floor.

"What's that for?" She put her palm against his forehead. "You have a fever? Carrying a book bag around on the first Monday of summer vacation?" She laughed and reached over to pick up his bowl. "I'll heat this up."

Sage scooted the bag under the table, well out of reach. If she got too curious and decided to open it, what she found there would be the biggest mystery of her lifetime—figuring out how an apparently empty bag could weigh that much. Carrying around three books invisible to regular humans was a pretty stupid idea. What was he thinking?

"Remember those old books Theo loaned me about ancient weapons?" Sage said. "The ones with all the creepy torture stuff?"

"I can't believe you're interested in that," Mom said. "Are you finally taking them back?"

"I'm heading to his shop right after I eat." He felt bad about making her think one thing when the truth was something else, but he hadn't lied.

"I still don't understand why you're so interested in all those old weapons." She lifted the oatmeal out of the microwave and set it in front of him. "Honestly, Sage, what's the point in—"

The phone rang and saved Sage from another medieval weapons inquisition. Mom picked up the phone and switched it on.

"Oh, hi, Sally," Mom said into the phone. "So glad you called. Still on for Saturday, right?" She carried the cordless out of the kitchen and wandered toward the back door.

Sage sighed with the mention of Saturday's get-together with his aunt, her new husband, and his cousin Addison. The annual early-summer family BBQ bash at Grandpa's hadn't happened the past two years because of Uncle Mike's death nearly three years before. This would be the first time Aunt Sally's new husband, Duncan Pitt, would attend.

"Everything is OK here," Mom said. She lowered her voice. "I'm getting so much grief." She sighed and lowered her voice even more. "Kevin's going to evict the private school if this deal goes through."

Sage jerked to attention and stopped chewing. What?

The back door opened and closed, and his mom's voice faded away. She had stepped into the backyard to finish her conversation.

"Did you hear that?" Sage whispered to Leah. "Dad's gonna evict the private school?"

Leah didn't say anything. Her face remained blank.

Both Sage and Nick had attended that school for preschool and kindergarten. It was the only preschool in town, and it struggled financially to make ends meet. Mom and Aunt Sally had gone there when they were kids. So had Dad. Would his business deal close it?

He jumped from his chair and went to the back door. Mom was in a chair that faced the yard, her back to the house. As carefully as he could, he pulled the door open an inch. Then he sat down and put his ear to the opening.

"That's what I told him," Mom said to her sister. "He claimed he didn't know the Chevy dealership owned the school building."

She paused and Sage edged the door open another couple of inches.

"See, that's the thing," Mom said. "The reason he's closing the Chevy dealership is so he can sell the land for an office park. The school building will be plowed under. I'm so mad I could just spit!"

"Hey, what's going on?" Nick asked Sage as he came into the room.

Sage put a finger to his lips and shook his head.

"I *can't* talk him out of it," Mom said. "I've tried. It's useless. It's like he's possessed with this merger. I'm not sure I know who he *is* anymore."

Sage swallowed hard and eased the door closed. He stood and motioned Nick into the kitchen and told him what he'd heard.

"I knew that," Nick said. "Well, knew the rumor. Also heard it's gonna crush the Food Pantry."

"How?" Three of Sage's classmates got most of their family food from the Pantry.

"The manager of the Chevy dealership donates a couple hundred dollars from each car sale for food purchases for the Pantry." Nick shook his head. "About ninety-five percent of the food they get comes from there." He shrugged. "Maybe the churches can pick up the slack."

Sage got a queasy feeling in his gut. "Does Dad know that?"

"Yeah, he knows. I heard him and Mom arguing about it the other day. He blew her off. Said this deal is bigger than a Chevy dealership." Nick lowered his voice. "Mom tried to get him to commit to replacing the food donations when he closes the dealership, but he only promised to consider it."

Leah floated near Nick. Sage cut his eyes at her, but he couldn't tell if this news surprised her.

"Gonna make us rich, though," Nick said. "At least that's what Dad keeps talking about, but he might be a rich divorcé, as mad as Mom is about the whole thing."

Sage looked at his breakfast. He wasn't hungry anymore. He scraped the dried food into the trash and set his dishes in the sink. "I'm headed to Theo's," he told Nick. "Let Mom know I'll be there most of the day."

"Yep. I'm headed over to Brian's for a minigaming tourney." Nick started toward his bedroom, then looked back. "How bad is their marriage gonna get over this merger thing?"

If Nick could see Dad through Sage's eyes, that wasn't the question he'd be asking. "Don't know. Any ideas about how to stop it?"

Nick laughed. "You're funny. Stop it? Fat chance."

Sage watched him walk away. He knew how much truth there was in that statement.

Sage stepped outside and looked up. The ever-present squad of Archangels—Archs, he called them—was strategically positioned around his house, swords in a constant state of battle readiness. He could see Darks in the distance, flying back and forth, a never-ending search for a momentary lapse in security.

It was like that everywhere he went and had been so his entire life: the Dark side stalking the side of Light. Leah once told him he was the most protected person in history. That prophecy of his birth was the most anticipated event in the annals of the Council. Sage was so used to the Darks, he never thought about how terrifying they looked. Humanoid and solid black, with rippling muscles and wings that stretched at least six feet across when fully expanded. Their heads were sleek and narrow and bald, their eyes three times the size of a human's. Their pointy ears were the envy of any Vulcan, with teeth that reminded Sage of a picture he'd once seen of a vampire's fangs on an oversized movie poster. Each of the

Darks carried a sword they wielded as effortlessly as Sage wielded a dinner fork.

The spookiest things about them were their oversized eyes. Completely and utterly black, they drew Sage toward them. "Do not look directly into their eyes. They are a looking glass into Hell," Leah often warned. Since they were always hovering in the distance, waiting for a time to strike, Sage mostly ignored them.

As impressively evil as the Darks were, the Archs were impressively magnificent. Like the Darks, they were identical to each other. Eight feet tall with muscular bodies that looked powerful enough to bench-press a fully loaded SUV. They wore gleaming breastplates, matching shin and forearm guards, and white gloves that extended several inches past their wrists. Their swords were as long as the Archs were tall, sleek and shiny, and came to needle-sharp points. Blonde hair flowed past their shoulders, held in place by diamond-studded headbands. As amazing as they were to gaze upon, their wings were the most spectacular of all. Unlike the Darks, who had a single set of wings, the Archs had three sets. The top set, thick and powerful, stretched eight feet across. Just below were a set only half that size, and the bottom set was smaller still.

Sage had seen no fewer than a thousand angel fights in his lifetime. The Darks attacked so often—nearly every time he stepped outside his house—that as a small boy he'd realized the vast differences in the flying abilities of the two. Wing structure was the key. The Archs maneuvered their three sets of wings in ways the Darks could only dream of. The fights were usually short lived.

He grabbed his bike from the side of the house and took off. Their house was three miles from town and sat on the edge of a huge piece of property owned by Grandpa Alexander. With over two thousand acres, the Alexander estate encompassed more than three square miles of Oklahoma hardwoods, pastures, ponds, and river bottoms. Thick woods, small cliffs, and rolling hills overlooked the river. A rugged trail snaked through the vast property and linked Sage's house to his grandpa's.

Once a pig, dairy, and sod farm, the property had been passed down through multiple generations. For the past fifty years, his grandfather had let nature do its thing. Sage thought it was the greatest place to grow up in the entire world because there were so many places to hunt, fish, hike, and—before he'd lost interest—practice his sword fighting.

His grandparents' house was a mile through the woods heading north, while Sage's house sat on the tip of the property on the south, nearest the main road leading to town. Sage headed that way but changed his mind at the last second. He whipped his bike north, peddled through the side yard, and cut around the back of the shed to hit the trail to Grandpa's. It would take him just under six minutes to get to his dungeon. He wanted to put his newest books with all of the others before he went to town.

The dungeon was a fully equipped bomb shelter his great-grandfather built not long after World War II ended. In the 1950s, during the time Senator McCarthy's communist hunt was in full swing, when school children all over America practiced atomic-bomb drills on a regular basis, Great-Grandpa Alexander spent more than ten thousand dollars—a lot of money in those days—to build a place for his family to hide if America got hit with the "Big One."

The Alexander family never used it, and after his great-grandparents died, everybody forgot about it. One afternoon when he was ten, Sage had found a massive, rusting door stuck in the side of a hill behind some overgrown bushes and asked his grandpa about it. It took more than a week of searching, but Grandpa finally found a key for the door. They went inside together.

Behind the outer door, down thirty steps, and through a second door as thick and solid as the first, they found a twenty-by-twenty room containing shelves of food and water; blankets, pillows, and cots; fuel for gas lanterns and stoves; matches and candles; and flashlights, portable radios, and batteries to operate them. Bags of beans and rice and dried pasta were stacked in a small kitchen alcove equipped with pots and pans, dishes and utensils, and lots of other things that would allow several people to wait out a war raging overhead. They even found portable toilets and chemicals to dissolve the waste.

On the far end of the primary room were two doors, both leading to bedrooms. On the other side of the largest bedroom was a door leading to a workshop that was empty except for shelving and a few hand tools. His grandpa showed him the bomb shelter's air filtering system, designed to keep everyone alive after the bombs went off. It was cutting-edge stuff at the time, his grandpa said, but was worthless now.

Right after one of the worst shrink visits Sage ever had, and the day after a group of older punks at school had beat him up, Grandpa Alexander secretly offered Sage exclusive access to the bomb shelter as a getaway place. Sage's dad didn't know about the shelter, and neither did his mom. As far as Sage knew, only he, his grandpa, and Ronan were privy to this secret hideout.

Sage rode the trail hard. Just before the woods opened up to a clearing leading to the back of his grandparents' house, he cut right and headed toward a creek that fed into the small river that flowed through the property. He skidded his bike to a stop in front of a stand of bushes and jumped off.

He'd seen only a few Darks flying overhead during the ride, but they had stayed away from him. Twice as many Archs flew in the middle distance, their swords drawn and ready. Leah didn't say anything on the trip; she just floated alongside, watching the sky.

He ducked behind the bushes and rolled his bike out of view, dug his hand down under the top of his shirt, and grabbed the key hanging on a chain around his neck. His grandpa had oiled the locks and hinges on both doors, and so it never took Sage long to disappear inside.

His grandpa had helped him out in other ways, too. He mounted battery-operated lamps just inside the door, down the stairs, and all over the rooms. He told Sage that if he used the lamps carefully when inside and turned them off before leaving, they would last months before needing to be recharged. It had turned out to be true.

Sage was in a hurry. He headed through the main room, which he hadn't touched since discovering the shelter, through the master bedroom, and into the room he referred to as his dungeon.

The numerous hand tools of long ago had been replaced by weapons and books and battery-operated lamps. All of his special books were here, almost a dozen, all dealing with Adamic. Their bluish glow gave the room a spooky feel, which never failed to give him the creeps. Having already studied those books in depth, Sage didn't care if he ever opened them again.

He kept the rest of the room reserved for his growing antique-weapons collection, all of which were gifts from Theo—some centuries old. There was an arbalest, a caltrop and hunga munga, a francisca and suriken, two katanas, and a ninjato.

There were throwing stars, a bagh nakh, a pair of gauntlets too big for his hands, a harpe, a macana, and a horseman's pick. All were hand-fighting weapons from various parts of the world, and he loved looking at them. His Fighting Arts training with Leah had gone so well for so long that he'd mastered most of these old weapons right here in this dungeon. Or at least he'd thought so. Until he quit. He had no idea what his skills would be now.

He turned on one of the battery-powered lamps and pulled the newest books from his backpack. He looked at them and was tempted to stay and read some more. However, he really wanted to visit Theo, who, besides having some historical prize to show him, supposedly had a pristine patu made from a whale bone waiting for him.

He was about to turn off the lamp when he saw his sword leaning in the corner. It was authentic samurai and the first weapon Theo had given him. Every one of the tens of thousands of swings had come against Leah. When he had quit, she'd insisted that his skills were years beyond any Fighting Arts–gifted Council member his age. He had to admit a sense of excitement in finding out how quickly his skills would return.

He also had a buzz about the prospect of studying the new books Leah had given him. After flipping to the last page of the book of missing Council members, he looked at Elsbeth Brown's picture for a long time. Her smile, her confidence, her raw beauty—he found himself grinning back at her picture—an endless video loop of her smiling and turning slightly sideways. He knew her photograph couldn't see him returning her smile, but he wished she could.

Sage looked at Leah. "She's been gone for a month?"

"Yes." Leah said nothing else, then deliberately glanced at his sword in the corner.

He got her message. Train.

As much as he wanted to stay and ogle over Elsbeth, he slid all the books onto the shelf with the others, turned out the lamp, locked up, and left. He'd come back later today to get started. He just wished he had somebody else besides Leah he could confide in. Too bad it couldn't be his dad.

5

Sage leaned his bike against the wall outside Theo's shop less than
twenty minutes later. The shop was in the middle of the block in
the downtown square in the shadow of a big, red-stone courthouse
that loomed over the surrounding streets, dominating an entire city
block. The lettering on the sign above Theo's front door—Beowulf's
Loft—was done in twisting swords, with bright red highlighting the
edges of each blade. Sage always believed the red was the blood of
Grendel, the giant monster Beowulf famously slew.

He pulled the door open and went inside. As usual, several
people browsed through the shelves of oddities from around the
world. Theo sold old coins and books; curious hand tools and toys;
old bones and small animals stuffed by taxidermists; weird clothing from everywhere—hats, shoes, and belt buckles; jewelry and
trinkets; and knickknacks galore. And hand bells.

His grandpa brought him here as a seven-year-old and
introduced him to Theo. The old man had given Sage a hand

bell with some ornate engraving written in a language Sage still hadn't figured out. The bell was gathering dust on a shelf in his bedroom. When Sage learned about Angelic Bells from Leah, he jokingly told her he had one already, pointing to the one Theo had given him.

"Master Sage!" Theo said from behind the counter. "I expected you early today." Although his heavy Greek accent still coated every word, Sage had no problem understanding him. Theo had no hair and wore thick glasses that magnified his eyes to twice their normal size. He was deathly thin, and his wrinkled skin sagged and jiggled in multiple places. Though he was stooped and bent and moved slowly, his voice was strong and powerful.

Helen, a small lady in her early forties, sat beside Theo at the cash register. She had been born mute but was otherwise as smart as anybody Sage knew. She smiled at Sage and waved, giving him the sign for hello. Helen wasn't deaf, but she'd learned sign language so that she could communicate with her family. Sage signed hello back to her.

"Had a late night," Sage said to Theo. He walked over to give him a high five and wished he could tell him about the Memory Share with Leah to the Tomb of Ancient Documents. He also wanted to talk about the changes in his dad. He couldn't. "And I stopped by my dungeon."

"Ah, your collection. Much to admire."

Sage wasn't sure where Theo had gotten all the old weapons he'd given him, but he told Sage he didn't want them in his store in case of a burglary. Theo said he would rather someone have them who could appreciate their value.

"Yeah, I did look them over." Sage lowered his voice. "So, do you have the patu?"

Theo flicked his head toward the back. "The bone as white as bleached paper."

Leah perched herself on top of the cash register, an antique that towered above everything else on the counter.

"How your father? No time yet for you and Nick?" Theo asked him gently. It was a topic they'd talked about many times over the past year.

"Naw, not yet," Sage said.

"Not even theater movie? Or romp at park?"

Despite their age differences, Theo was the only one who really knew how much Sage was hurting, and that was *before* Dad's golden skin and neck worms. "I don't want to talk about it. OK?"

"Well, things work out," Theo said. "You see." He slapped the counter and stood. "Now, patu. Let us look." He glanced at Helen. "Be in the back for a time."

Helen signed a reply Sage didn't understand.

Sage followed Theo through the crowded aisles of the shop. With everyone they passed asking Theo about whatever item they were looking at, and with Theo stopping to give them a complete historical dissertation about it, Sage didn't know if they would ever make it. Finally, they pushed through the door leading into the storeroom.

Theo pointed to the far wall. "You get, Sage. On a table next to alleyway door. We will inspect under light." The old man sat down on a stool facing a work bench and yanked a string to turn on an overhead florescent.

The storeroom was primarily used to house items that would replace things sold in the front. But to the far left, partitioned off from everything else, stood a locked steel door protecting a small room where Theo kept his historical treasures. Books, photographs, ancient writings, little pieces of history as varied as anything found in a museum. The room had a top-notch security system, and its walls were constructed with concrete and steel.

Sage saw the whalebone patu and jogged over to get it. He handed it to Theo when he got to the bench. It was bleached white and about twelve inches long, with one end flat and rounded like a Ping-Pong paddle. The handle was engraved with intricate markings resembling those on the bell Theo had given him. The weapon was smooth and slick and looked lethal. Sage wondered what part of a whale it had come from.

"What are those markings?" Sage asked him. "The letters on the handle?"

Theo held it closer to his eyes and studied it. "I not sure, but I have seen such markings before."

"Yeah, on that bell you gave me. Don't you remember?" Surely he remembered, because Sage had asked him about those letters too.

"You probably correct." Theo said.

"So . . . did this come from the same place as the bell? Was it made by the same people?"

"Maybe yes, maybe no," Theo said. "I get much merchandise mixed together from many countries. This from Istanbul, Turkey. Maybe that where bell came from. Strange writing possible from anything. Istanbul old city with abundant history, many people travel there." He shrugged. "Possible you solve writing someday."

"Well, it's a pretty cool weapon," Sage said. "I guess you could pound somebody on the head or something." He held it up and looked at it. It was hard and solid but didn't weigh much. "Sure wouldn't want my opponent to get that close to me, though. I think I'll stick with my sword."

Theo looked surprised. "You train again?"

Sage glanced at Leah, who, as usual, offered no expression. Theo knew Sage had trained for several years and had given it up. Only Theo, Grandpa, and Ronan knew he'd had any interest in swords at all.

"I think I'll start again," Sage said. "If nothing else, it'll get my shoulders and arms in shape again." He paused. "Not a big deal. I miss it a little."

Theo chuckled and slapped him on the shoulder. "I think that brilliant idea, young man." He stood on shaky legs and nodded toward the secure room. "OK, time to see latest acquisition. You will *love* it."

Sage followed him to the steel door. "Where Steven of late?" Theo asked. "Been many weeks not to see him."

"Grandpa's doing OK," Sage said. "He and Ronan have been out of town a few times over the past month. We've got a big family thing at his house on Saturday."

"Well, he must come visit. Hard sneeze could kill old man like me." Theo punched in a code, which shut off the alarm and un-clicked an electronic lock.

"Just how old are you?" Sage asked. It was a question he'd asked at least a hundred times.

"Old enough. The moment I brag, Grim Reaper will overhear and pay visit." He chuckled, pulled the door open, and turned on the lights. "Lock door please."

Sage locked the door behind him. Shelves from floor to ceiling lined every wall. At least fifteen feet wide, the room stretched to the back of the building, nearly twenty-five feet deep. Most of Theo's treasure trove of artifacts was crated up or sealed in airtight containers. Sage had seen much of the collection already, and he expected to see yet another box shipped from overseas that waited his inspection on the stainless steel table in the middle of the room.

"This you will like," Theo said. He pointed to a contraption unlike anything Sage had ever seen.

Theo clicked on a lamp in the corner, then killed the overhead lights. Leah floated over to the corner and watched Theo with an unusual amount of interest. At least it seemed so to Sage.

"You hear of Kodak?" Theo asked. "Company that invented Instamatic camera?"

Sage nodded. "They used to make digital cameras. And photo books, some computer printers and stuff like that. Not much of a company now."

"True. However, in 1923 they becoming strong," Theo said. "Kodak buy Nagel Camera Company in Stuttgart, Germany. All became Kodak AG. They manufacture for decades. This well before World War II, when many factories destroyed. You aware of this?"

Sage shook his head. "Nope."

Theo dragged a stool over to the table and sat down, then reached over and tenderly touched his new prize. "Kodak need factories to produce equipment wide scale. Why? Because they invent way to make amateur motion pictures. They invent 16 mm reversal film on cellulose acetate." He smiled wide. "The Cine-Kodak Motion Picture Camera. All for three hundred thirtyfive dollars." He smiled even wider. "I sound like advertisement."

The cast aluminum box measured approximately eight inches square. Sage touched the hand crank on the side.

"This is camera," Theo said. He got up and waved Sage over to another table at the back of the room. Sage hadn't noticed it because the weak light from the corner lamp didn't reach that far. "This is projector and original screen sold with package." It was a small screen, six-foot square and dingy white.

"Pretty cool equipment," Sage said. He was amazed at the old projector. "Thanks for letting me see it."

Theo laughed. "Master Sage, I own this equipment for fifty years. I show you something else."

"What?"

"Film. In projector. Came past Friday."

Sage squinted closer in the dim light. Only then did he see the film loaded and ready to show.

"Drag stools here," Theo said. "I tell you story."

Sage did as ordered. Theo began once they were both settled.

"Adolf Hitler was crazy man. Maybe most evil ever. He join German Worker's Party in 1919. Next year they change name to National Socialist German Worker's Party. Nazi Party. In 1923, Hitler, inspired by Mussolini's March on Rome, thought *coup d'état* was way to seize Germany. In November of 23, Hitler led Beer Hall Putsch, which failed. He was arrested and tried for high treason."

Sage remembered some of this from his World History class the previous year, but Theo made it sound a lot more interesting.

"Hitler desperate to become famous. Greedy for power. His trial was twenty-four days. Big spectacle. Near end of trial, Hitler confidant smuggled Kodak motion picture camera into courtroom. Hoped to film verdict of not guilty. Hitler to be Phoenix rising from ashes. Victory!" Theo chuckled. "Did not work out so well for them. Six minutes of film in my projector now."

Sage's jaw dropped.

Theo pointed a shaky hand at the projector and appeared ready to burst with excitement. "You will see Hitler. He sits at table, noble and proud. Presidential, one might say."

"Nobody knows this film exists?" Sage asked. "How come it's not in a museum?"

"There was early rumor of smuggled camera, but once Hitler sentenced to prison, footage meant nothing. Film worthless. Then, Hitler released after nine months and rose to power. People forgot film because Hitler not need it."

"Wow." Sage took a quick peek at Leah, who'd floated up over the table. "How did you get it?"

"I cannot reveal technique of buying history pieces. Must keep trade secrets private." Theo smiled. "Ready to see?"

"Sure!"

Theo reached over and flicked a switch on the projector. "Remember, Hitler thirty-five years old in film, nine years before full power in 1933. No sound."

"OK." Sage leaned closer. He wished history class was this cool.

The projector bulb took a while to heat up, but after it burned its brightest, Theo flipped another switch, and the black-and-white film flickered onto the screen. Sage saw the back of several heads at first, then the ceiling of a large chamber. The camera jerked so much it made Sage dizzy. Then the photographer finally found a good vantage point. Sage picked out the judge, and then a man pacing in front of the room, who gestured and spoke fervently to a jury box full of white men, all dressed in suits. Next the film image scanned the overflowing crowd that pushed against a sturdy wooden rail behind large tables for the prosecution and defense teams.

At last the camera found Hitler, who was sitting near another man—his lawyer, probably. Hitler's shoulders were pulled back, his head defiantly postured, jaw set, eyes hard.

Three-inch worms with hairy tentacles stuck out the sides of Hitler's neck and disappeared into his hair. Just like Sage's dad.

Sage jerked backward so hard he nearly toppled from his stool. Hitler stared at the judge. His hands were below the top of the table, apparently resting in his lap. The image jerked hard, as though the cameraman was suddenly jostled, then it stabilized just as Hitler raised his right hand and scratched the side of his neck.

A claw. Like his dad's hand.

"Master Sage, what is wrong?" Theo reached over and touched his shoulder.

Sage tried talking, but he couldn't get his breathing under control. "I . . . I . . . oh, no!"

His dad was turning into a Hitler!

Leah placed a hand on top of his head and spoke into his ear. "Clarity can sometimes be a horrible gift."

Sage covered his mouth as the film continued rolling. Again the cameraman panned the room and captured the frantic atmosphere of the event. Finally, the proceeding ended. Everyone suddenly stood, including Hitler, and faced the judge, who mouthed something as he waved his arms and the crowd moved toward the door to leave. Hitler turned his head to the left, and Sage noticed the back of the man's head was misshapen, almost as if it were growing into a point. The distortion wasn't particularly obvious, but since Sage could see Hitler's profile now, it was definitely there. Then Hitler turned fully to speak to his attorney, which put his back to the cameraman. Sage noticed the two stubby knobs protruding from his back.

"Wings," Sage whispered. "The beginning of wings!"

"What?" Theo asked. "I could not hear. The projector too loud."

Sage didn't answer. He waved him off, his eyes glued to the screen. The black-and-white film couldn't capture Hitler's golden skin, but Sage knew Hitler had it.

The Seven! Hitler had fallen under the influence of one of the Seven Princes of Hell. The same one now had his dad. Which Prince? Greed? Pride? Wrath? Sage looked at Leah, desperate to ask her opinion. Could you be controlled by more than one? His thoughts were all scrambled.

Theo clicked the machine off. "Want to watch again?"

Sage shook his head weakly, his stomach flip-flopping in rhythm with his hammering heart. He needed air. Sunshine.

"I think I'm about to be sick." He slid off the stool. "Need to use the bathroom."

He raced from the room and hit the door to the men's room just as bile rose in his throat.

6

Theo was waiting for Sage when he came out of the bathroom. Leah was in the far corner, in the shadows, arms crossed. Sage left the bathroom, shaken and still woozy but able to face them both. He looked first at Leah and immediately understood her body language: he was to choose how much to tell Theo. She wanted no part of that decision.

Sage trusted Theo. Although Grandpa had probably told him about Sage's history with his "invisible friend," Sage wasn't sure he had the strength to dredge all of that up again. And it *would* come up—no way it wouldn't.

"Tell me. What upset you?" Theo asked. "Something on film."

After wiping his mouth again with a damp paper towel, Sage considered how to answer and decided to use the same strategy he'd used with Ronan yesterday. "What did *you* see?"

Theo frowned and cocked his head. "What you mean? I see Hitler."

"I know that," Sage said, "but tell me what he looked like. Give me the little details."

Theo folded his hands in front of him. "Everything or just Hitler?"

"Just Hitler." Sage leaned his back against the bathroom door and waited.

"Well . . . something odd. Footage grainy, we know that, but overall good condition, mostly sharp. However, I would like Hitler's face more clear."

Sage's heart quickened. "What do you mean?"

"Blurry to me," Theo said. "I can tell Hitler's face, but blurry. Just out of focus." He paused, thought about something, and then continued. "That make no sense. All footage good, and only face blurry?"

Sage knew immediately what he had to do. "I want you to call Grandpa and have him come here. Ronan too. I want both of them to see the film. Will you do that?" He'd tried not to plead but knew he hadn't succeeded.

"I can phone them." Theo stood. "It will help you if they join us?"

He almost laughed at the question. Would it help him? Ha! It might be the biggest mistake of his life. It might send him back to a shrink who'd put him on medication that would turn him into a zombie. But maybe not.

"It's what I have to do," Sage said.

For the sake of my sanity.

Theo nodded. "I will make call."

Sage waited in the back room while Theo piddled around in the front of the store and Helen helped with customers. Sage inspected his patu and wondered about the ancient writing on the handle. He noticed that Leah kept her distance, and he wondered about that too. It was rare that she didn't offer her opinion about things, and he was certain she knew what he was about to do. He was strangely calm about her lack of involvement. It was his decision, and he'd have to live with the consequences.

Grandpa and Ronan arrived after twenty minutes, and Theo must have filled them in before the three of them walked into the storeroom. They headed straight to Theo's Treasure Room without saying anything. Theo motioned Sage to follow.

Grandpa was wearing grass-stained denim overalls, a T-shirt, and work boots, Ronan a pair of black jeans, cowboy boots, and a shirt that said, *With a body like this, it's OK that I'm ugly.* His long hair was loose, flowing in waves to the middle of his back.

"Please lock door," Theo told Ronan after all of them were inside the secure room.

Sage fought hard to appear normal. The moment of truth had arrived. This was it. Crazy? Or not.

Theo gathered them around the table in the back and fired up the projector. Sage stood in the middle, between Grandpa and Ronan, and watched the six minutes again. Nothing changed for him. He still saw Hitler in the early stages of a transformation that must have looked horrific by the time he died in 1945.

When it was over, Theo asked Ronan to hit the overhead lights. Theo dragged his stool over to the stainless steel table and motioned for the others to join him there. Grandpa sat on the only other stool; Sage and Ronan stood. Leah stood next to Sage, silent, but with a hand on his shoulder for support. And comfort. She knew what he was about to do. Sage could tell by the look on her face.

"Master Sage wishes to share thoughts," Theo said gently, as though fully aware of the emotions flooding through him.

Sage swallowed hard, pushed his shoulders back, and looked hard into his grandpa's eyes. "You've always said you'd never lie to me. Never. Ever. Is that true?" His stomach did a flip, and he felt as if he might throw up again. There wasn't a person walking the earth whom Sage respected more than his grandpa, and it cut him deeply to ask such a question.

But he had to. It was time.

Grandpa, his eyes soft and kind, his mouth drooping just a little, nodded. "That's right. I'd never lie to you."

"OK." Sage bit his bottom lip to keep it from trembling. He pointed to Leah and asked the most important question of his life. "Can you see her?"

Grandpa folded his hands on the table. "You're referring to Leah, the manifestation from your younger years?"

Manifestation? Sage's heart sank. If he could see her, he wouldn't have to ask.

"Just describe her, Sage," Grandpa said. "I'd like to make sure we're seeing the same thing."

Sage flinched. *What?* He started to say something but just shook his head.

"I'll describe her," Ronan said. "Theo, care to join in?"

Theo nodded. "Splendidly."

"Girl," Ronan said. "About Sage's age. Maybe a little older."

"Golden hair," Theo said. "Secured with headband."

"Clothes that glow. Heavenly, I'd say," Ronan said. "Boots nearly to her knees. And a sword. Oh, what a sword."

"A scabbard unlike any I have seen," Theo said. "Would make wonderful collection piece."

"Look at the handle," Ronan continued. "Jewels worth millions if regular humans could see them."

Sage watched the exchange as both of them stared exactly at the spot where Leah stood.

"Can you feel her hand on your shoulder?" Ronan asked.

Everything suddenly went blurry as tears flooded Sage's eyes. He wiped them away, but more came, then sobs racked his body and he covered his face.

"It's Leah's wings that take my breath away," Grandpa said gently. He stood and grabbed Sage into a massive hug. He whispered into his ear, "Three sets of wings are given only to the fiercest and most capable warriors. You've been in the best of hands from the moment of your birth."

He didn't know how long he cried. It seemed forever, but he wasn't ashamed. It was a dam bursting from more than a decade of second-guessing, doubt, frustration, and anger. Fights at school and home, hundreds of skeptical looks and insults from his friends, dozens of nights crying himself to sleep, doctor visits, and lying these past three years—pretending to be someone he wasn't. Finally, silence—the years of horrible silence that grew inside him like a cancerous pressure cooker.

All of it came bursting forth in Theo's Treasure Room, and he didn't care if the three of them thought he was a crybaby. Not right then. Not ever.

Leah moved to the far end of the room to give Sage the space he needed. She wore a smile as bright as a bursting star.

"We've always known," Grandpa said. "The three of us." He pulled the corner of his T-shirt down and exposed his right shoulder. The Marking for Pathfinder. "Ronan, care to show him yours?"

So Ronan did—Might. As did Theo—Sight. Like Sage's, their Markings were a deep gold that wouldn't have been visible on Sage's dad's skin at the moment.

Sage wiped his eyes, not as shocked as he thought he'd be. He'd always known something was up with Grandpa and Ronan, and he'd never fully understood Theo's friendship, the connection between a man so old and him, a boy so young.

"Leah isn't the only one who's been protecting you," Ronan said. "You've been in good hands."

It took several more minutes for Sage's head to clear, but once it did, he separated himself and asked Grandpa to sit back down. With Leah and the others on one side of the table and Sage on the other, he looked at Ronan. "Might?"

Ronan smiled, grabbed a handful of his hair, and shook it.

"Samson," Sage said. "The only one mentioned in the Bible with the gift of Might. I should have known."

Ronan smiled. "Deep down, you probably did."

"I am certain of that," Leah added.

Might. Near-superhuman physical strength. The strength of Nephilim giants. Their fighting skills were brutal and unrefined but devastating due to the power behind each blow. Ronan was right—deep down, Sage probably *did* know. "You killed the typhon in England that night our car broke down, didn't you?" Sage asked. "When I was eight years old."

"That was I," Ronan said. He grinned. "It's why Steven keeps me around."

Sage nodded, then looked at Theo. "Sight?"

The old man smiled.

It was one of the gifts Sage most remembered from all the lessons Leah had forced him to learn. Now he was grateful she had. The ability to perceive the future—Sight was a type of precognition, but with limits. Those who possessed Sight didn't know the exact order of things, especially when they were young. The ability grew as they aged, meaning the most valuable Council members were the extremely elderly, who were generally kept hidden in utmost secrecy because of their high value. They often saw multiple possibilities of the same event but could not see the extremely small details that might influence the outcome. They must rely on faith.

"You're running a gift shop in Oklahoma?" Sage's eyes widened at the thought of it.

"He's on a field assignment specifically to help your development," Grandpa said. "You have no idea how powerful you are."

Leah had always told him how important he was, but hearing Grandpa say it hit him differently.

"Unlike Samson," Theo said, "*many* with Sight are named in Bible."

"Don't have to rub it in, Theo," Ronan said with a chuckle. "I understand where I fall in the pecking order of importance."

Theo smiled. "Will never mention again."

Sage then looked at Grandpa. "Pathfinding."

Grandpa sat for a moment as his eyes watered. "You have no idea how long I've dreamed of this moment."

Him? Sage had wondered thousands of times if this day would ever come. Did his parents have gifts? His grandparents? He'd spent years wondering that. Angelic traits could lie dormant, he knew—DNA was funny that way—but how many generations could be skipped before the gifts manifested themselves? He'd been so alone.

"Yes. Pathfinding." Grandpa gestured at Ronan and smiled. "And I have him."

Sage glanced at Leah, who nodded slightly before finally giving him a little smile. "I have Pathfinding. Well, I have the marking, anyway. I've actually not seen any other evidence of it."

"I know," Grandpa said. "All of us know."

"What is it, really?" Sage asked. "It's meant nothing to me."

Grandpa dried his eyes with the back of his hands. "It's an extremely rare gift. We can track a person or object using enhanced senses. We can track from the human world into Godspace, our name for the Light side of the spiritual realm." He shrugged. "That's about it."

Ronan laughed and slapped Grandpa on the back. "Don't be modest, Steven." He looked at Sage. "Pathfinders are the hunters, the Council detectives. They're not simply the only ones capable of seeing entrances into the spiritual realm; they also have the ability to touch an item and receive snippets of images from the past. Well, not full images. It's not like watching a movie. Well, some are, I guess. Most are mere impressions, some are simply names or pieces of personalities, but a few are actual replays of events. Finally, Pathfinders are the ones searching for entrances into the Dark side of the spiritual realm, although, as of yet, they've not found any. Just a matter of time, though. So even though your Grandpa doesn't look like much, he's quite the hero."

"Thank you, Ronan," Grandpa said. "Always love your ringing endorsement."

"So that's why you're always with him," Sage said to Ronan. "Because he hunts for entrances into the Dark realm, he needs protection if he finds one and enters?" Sage had read up on some of this and remembered a little of what Leah had told him. He couldn't describe the relief he felt to actually ask these questions from somebody besides his Guardian.

Grandpa's face turned serious. "Since the day Leif Erickson disappeared into thin air in the year 1000, the Council suspected he'd been snatched by one of the Seven Princes. They've somehow found a way to cut a pathway from the Dark realm that doesn't leave a trace behind. Since only Pathfinders can see entrances, the Council teamed them either with Might or Fighting Arts just in case we find one of the breaches."

"Gotta have somebody who can fight his way out of a wet paper bag," Ronan said. He grinned again, as if immensely happy with his little joke.

"Have you never found a breach?" Sage asked his grandfather. "Even after all these years?"

"Not a single one. Since Erikson disappeared, every Pathfinder has searched. There are only three of us now, not counting you, and we've visited every site multiple times." Grandpa looked at Ronan. "We have searched, have we not?"

"All thirty-two locations. Zilch."

"So you went to New Orleans?" Sage asked. "To the spot Elsbeth Brown was taken from a month ago?"

Grandpa looked at Leah. "Hah! You *did* Memory Share with him!"

"As instructed," Leah said.

Grandpa turned back to his grandson. "Yes, Sage, we went to the spot where Elsbeth disappeared." He shook his head.

"Maybe you'll be able to see it," Ronan said to Sage. "I mean, once you're trained. Years from now, if what Leah's saying is accurate, you might help us then." He hadn't hidden his look of disappointment.

Sage's face heated in embarrassment. "I'm starting my training again. Like, today." That sounded lame even to his own ears.

"We had to let your desire come naturally," Grandpa said. "No interference from us. It was the hardest thing I've ever had to do, to stand by and watch what you've gone through."

"Me too," Ronan said. "You're the boy of prophecy, Sage the Warrior, gifts more powerful than any other. Eventually. The kid who will one day have everything. I couldn't tell you to get your head in the game." He shook his head. "Tough, I gotta tell you."

Could they make him feel any worse?

"Water under bridge," Theo said. "We must discuss Clarity."

Ronan slapped the table. "Right. Talk about hard. Standing with Sage in the bathroom yesterday? Him scared out of his mind, and I couldn't tell him what I knew? Glad I won't have to do *that* again."

"Clarity most horrific gift of all," Theo said. "Once fully developed, deformities will show everywhere. Prepare to be much disturbed."

"Clarity normally doesn't manifest until your early to midtwenties," Grandpa said. "So you're really early."

Sage rubbed his hands together. Was his dad already one of the demon people? He refused to believe that. Not yet.

"Your father and Hitler?" Theo asked. "How similar?"

Sage described his dad, the golden skin, the worms growing from his neck, the little roots sprouting from the worms. "He doesn't have the beginning of wings yet. Or the funny shaped head, but the rest is the same."

The stricken look on Grandpa's face reminded Sage that he was describing Grandpa's son. It must be emotional for him, too. He reached over and grabbed one of Grandpa's hands and squeezed. Grandpa returned the gesture, then lowered his head.

"Which Prince is it?" Ronan asked.

"I have considered opinion," Theo said. "Greed. Mammon."

"Why?" Ronan asked. "Hitler wasn't after money."

"He sought power," Theo said. "To rule world."

"He also pillaged Europe," Grandpa said. "Stealing every rare treasure his people could get their hands on. He wanted to be the richest man alive."

"None others match," Theo said. "For six thousand years, those few with Clarity have studied most corrupted. All suspected of Mammon's influence possess the same physical changes."

They sat together, each lost in his own thoughts. Mixed feelings of relief, expectation, sadness, and hope swirled within Sage. "Then we have to stop him," he said. "We have to kill Mammon."

Nobody responded.

"*I* have to kill him. That's what Leah said. My destiny."

Grandpa squeezed Sage's hand before releasing it and standing. "You need to forget about that right now. We will help you train. That's what you need to worry about."

"But Dad might be too far gone by the time I'm ready," Sage said, his voice rising.

"There's nothing we can do about that," Grandpa said.

Sage swallowed the bile of guilt rising into his throat.

It was his fault—he knew that—but he still needed to save Dad. "How do we find them? The Princes? Doesn't anybody know where they are?"

"Nobody knows," Theo said. "History unkind to Council. Chances to find them wasted."

"If we could find one of their breach points," Ronan said, "we'd probably find at least one of them."

Grandpa looked at him, a flash of irritation crossing his face. Ronan caught it and held up his hands.

"Hey, not blaming the Pathfinders. Just saying. If we could find a breach point, we'd probably find where they're taking our people. That discovery would lead us to at least one of the Princes. Everybody in the Council believes that, not just me."

Again they sat in silence. Then Sage had a question after remembering something he'd seen in the book of missing Council members. "Grandpa, how do you get to all those places?"

"What places?"

"Where the Council members were snatched? Some of them were really remote. I saw it in the book Leah gave me. They're from all over the earth."

Ronan smiled. "Oh, you're in for a surprise, young man."

Grandpa looked at Theo and the two of them exchanged some kind of silent communication. Finally, Theo nodded.

"We travel through Godspace," Grandpa said. "Through the back of Theo's Treasure Room. That's the main reason he always keeps the door locked."

7

Theo placed a hand on Sage's shoulder. "Markings are absolute. Pathfinding *has* manifested in you. We shall prove it."

Ronan went to a bookcase, bent over, and reached beneath a lower shelf. Sage heard something click. Ronan's hands moved to the highest shelf and shifted a row of books, and Sage heard another click. Five seconds later, Ronan pulled the entire shelving unit away from the wall by grabbing the center shelf. He swung it around like a door and stepped aside. It blocked Sage's view.

"Just a brown concrete wall to me," Ronan said.

"And me," Theo said.

Grandpa pointed. "Tell me exactly what you see, Sage. I want to compare your gift against my own."

Sage took several steps forward. Grandpa gave him an encouraging nod and stepped away. Call it a rift, a greenish-blue, slightly bleached, out-of-focus shimmer. He stepped closer and felt the hint of a cool breeze against his skin.

"Well, don't keep us in suspense," Ronan said. He'd made an effort to sound irritated, though Sage knew he wasn't.

Sage stepped back and rubbed his eyes. "Wow. That's unbelievable."

"So you can see it," Grandpa said.

Sage nodded. "Oh, yeah. No doubt. And I can feel it, too."

"What?" Theo asked.

"Cool air. Feels great. Kind of hot in this room. The breeze coming out of there is cool enough to dry my sweat."

"You've never said anything about that," Ronan said to Grandpa.

Grandpa waved him silent. "Tell me what you see. Every detail."

So Sage did. He probably used more words than he needed to, but by the time he stopped talking, Grandpa's eyes had gone wide. "What?" Sage asked. "How do *you* see it?"

Grandpa looked at Theo, then Ronan. He didn't say anything for a moment. "I see an oval. About five feet tall. A few inches wide. White. That's it. I can't feel any cool air."

Sage nodded and shrugged. "Well, Leah always said Pathfinders see the entrances differently."

Grandpa turned to Theo. "You're the oldest here. You tell him."

"Tell me what?"

Theo pulled a stool over and sat down. "Pathfinders record view of entrances. All similar to Steven's. Ovals, circles, rectangles. Simple shapes. One color, mostly white. None felt breeze."

Sage shrugged. "OK. So I'm different."

Ronan burst out laughing. "You aren't thinking deeply enough, young Sage. You not only see much more detail, but you can feel the entrances. Know what that means?"

The three of them just stared at him.

When Sage didn't answer, Ronan answered for him. "It means, theoretically, that we could take you to a spot where one of our people disappeared and even if you couldn't see it, you could feel it." He slapped Grandpa on the back. "We've got hope, my man!"

Grandpa's face darkened.

"Once he's ready," Ronan said quickly.

"Want to see it?" Grandpa asked.

"Are you kidding?" Sage said. "Of course."

"How much has Leah told you about Godspace?" Grandpa asked.

"I have told him all he needs to know," Leah said. "The pertinent question is how much he remembers."

A Guardian who fronts me out? Talk about cruel.

"I think I remember enough," Sage said.

"It's so vast that a human mind cannot comprehend it," Grandpa said. "Those in the Council who have spent many lifetimes exploring it feel no closer in determining its dimensions now than when they started."

"Tell him about Haddock," Ronan said. He looked at Sage. "You heard of Haddock?"

"No."

Ronan chuckled. "Well, you know that each of us live for many centuries. You also probably know that we do not age, at all, during the time we spend in there."

Sage nodded. He remembered that.

"Haddock was the youngest son of one of the original Council members. Pathfinder. The first one." Ronan raised an eyebrow and paused.

"And?" Sage asked. "What about him?"

"He's five thousand years old." Ronan belted out a laugh. "He looks like a man in his sixties."

"Five thousand years? Where does he live?"

"No one really knows," Grandpa said. "Somewhere out there. He reports in every few years, his mind a little further gone than before. He stopped filing mapping reports about a century ago."

"What about the entrances where the Council members went missing?" Sage asked.

"He's visited all the places except the one from last month," Ronan said. "He can't see them."

"Wow." Sage looked at Leah, but she wore no expression.

"Enough of that," Grandpa said. "We'll go through first and wait for you." He offered his hand to the opening. "Ronan?"

The big man nodded, stepped forward, and put his hands together as though about to dive into a swimming pool. Theo grabbed his belt and got directly behind him.

Two seconds later they were gone. It was as if the wall had swallowed them whole.

"Because they can't see it," Grandpa said, "they enter the same way every time. Ronan just aims for the middle." He smiled. "See you on the other side."

Watching them melt into the shifting mass of color reminded Sage of a National Geographic show he'd seen about quicksand. There, then gone, the surface undisturbed.

It gave him the creeps.

He stepped forward, the cool breeze tickling his sweaty forehead. His first instinct was to close his eyes, but he wanted to see everything.

"Do not be afraid," Leah said from behind him. "Your desti— the fulfillment of your mission requires much time operating within this realm."

She'd told him once that Darks had secret sections of the spiritual realm, with entrances untraceable except to the Fallen Angels—the Watchers—and their descendants. Legend held that the Watchers had offered sections of their realm to the three evil races, and that the Seven Princes had each been given his own space.

Spooky stuff. Just thinking about it made his heart quicken.

He opened his eyes wide and stepped into a thick forest, complete with a stream trickling over sparking rocks, acres of soft moss, and thousands of colorful fall leaves rustling against a gentle breeze. A large white ball set high in the sky brightened all of it like a mid-day summer sun. Aside from it being a landscape of perfection, the sun-like orb projected a white light so pure and brilliant that colors seemed computer-enhanced; so deep and rich, so crisp they radiated warmth and peace and comfort. All of his stress and worry and anger, his pent-up frustration and the years of loneliness leached away with a suddenness that left him weak-kneed yet full of joy.

He felt at home. Finally. Godspace. Now he understood the name. A place of refuge.

Grandpa, Theo, and Ronan leaned against a tree the size of a redwood.

Sage took a step forward, speechless, and turned back to the opening. Pulsing with red, blue, and orange colors—it looked much different from this side. The opening appeared like a bright rectangle Sage would be able to see from far away.

"It's a Garden of Eden," Sage whispered to Leah.

"It is a place of comfort," Leah said.

"What do you think?" Ronan said. He smiled and held his hands out as if he'd created the place himself.

"It's amazing." Sage lifted his face to the white orb. He expected it to heat his face, but it felt cool and refreshing.

"I spend much time here," Theo said. "We all do."

"More than I care to admit," Grandpa said.

Sage knelt and dipped his hand into a nearby stream. The water made his fingers tingle. "Is it all like this? The entire spiritual realm?"

Grandpa leaned in next to him. "Similar, not exact. There are mountains and rolling hills, great pastures and beautiful lakes. I guess only Haddock could say for sure, but nobody knows where he is."

"None have ever found the end," Ronan said. "Well, maybe Haddock has by now. Now you know why he's spent five thousand years in here."

"It's paradise," Sage said.

"That's what I thought of when I first saw it," Grandpa said. "The temperature never changes. We don't age. Food is plentiful."

"Many within Council spend final days here," Theo said. "Many wish to come before their time."

"But they can't," Ronan said, with a little hardness in his voice. "Because their destiny is out there. In the jungle. Trying to rid the world of the Seven and their ilk."

Sage nodded, not about to argue. "What does the evil realm look like?" he asked. "The Dark side?"

"None have seen the areas occupied by them," Grandpa said.

"The captured Council members have seen it," Ronan said. "We've spent our lives trying to see it." He clenched his fists and turned away.

Sage had never seen such fire in Ronan's eyes. The pain the man felt for the captured Council members was obvious. So was the frustration of his and Grandpa's inability to find the breaches through which they disappeared. Sage wondered if any of the missing thirty-two had been friends of Ronan.

"We need to get back," Grandpa said.

Ronan pointed at Sage. "Start training. Today. Got it?"

Sage suddenly got an idea. "Will you help me? All of you? Leah will. That's her job. But I need all of you, too."

"Certainly," Theo said.

"Wouldn't miss the chance," Ronan said. "It won't be some middle-school gym class. So be ready."

"Anything you need," Grandpa chimed in. "Don't hesitate to ask."

"Who else can help? Can the Council send anyone?" Sage remembered Leah had told him few from the Council were available to help, but he wanted to hear it from them.

Theo shook his head. "Sadly not. World too big. Evil too prevalent. Too few of us."

"Our ranks are thin," Grandpa said. "When they took Elsbeth Brown a month ago, they took one of our most powerful weapons against them."

"It's why you must train," Ronan said. "Once you're ready . . . well, that'll help. A lot."

They all headed toward Theo's storeroom. Sage thought he understood the game now and knew they expected him to play by their rules. He got it. However, his dad's life was on the line, and he'd be too corrupted to save by the time Sage was ready.

He'd have to write *new* rules for the game. He had everything he needed to start. "I'm headed to my dungeon right now," Sage said. "It sounds as if I've got a lot of work to do."

Ronan slapped him on the shoulder. "Ha! You don't know the half of it."

Nor do you, Sage thought. *Nor do you.*

8

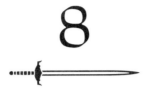

With Grandpa's assistance, Sage convinced his mom that she wouldn't see much of him over the next week. He hated leaving her with the impression that he'd be spending the week running around with Ronan, but at least he *would be* with Ronan most of the time. Grandpa gave her Ronan's cell number in case she needed to talk to Sage.

Mom wouldn't miss Sage much anyway. She planned to spend most of her time getting Grandma's backyard ready for the big cookout on Saturday—weeding flowerbeds, hanging baskets of plants, repainting three picnic tables and several chairs, strategically positioning outdoor lights high and low, locating large tubs for icing drinks, cleaning the smoker, and all the other chores she claimed needed to be handled before Aunt Sally and her family arrived.

Nick was with a buddy of his in town—a fellow gamer preparing for an online tourney—who wanted Nick to help him sharpen his skills. Stacks of pizza, buckets of ice cream, bags and bags of chips and cookies, all washed down with more caffeine-laced soft drinks than any human should ever consume over a five-day period meant Nick would be in his preferred nutritional wheelhouse until hotdogs, burgers, and more ice cream were on his menu on Saturday. Nick wouldn't notice Sage's absence.

Sage's dad was finalizing the funding for the big merger in New York City. Due back on a Saturday morning flight, he'd arrive home about the time Aunt Sally got there.

Not that Sage necessarily wanted to see his dad. With the stark physical changes that had taken place in just a few hours on Sunday, a deep, throbbing dread had already placed itself solidly in Sage's gut as he considered what Dad would look like by the weekend.

So with no interruptions, Sage spent nearly every free moment in his dungeon. When he wasn't swinging his sword, he was either studying the new books Leah had given him or exercising under Ronan's watchful eye. He quickly memorized the faces of all thirty-two missing Council members, as well as the pertinent data of their lives, especially the gifts each possessed.

On Tuesday afternoon—after spending an hour reading and jotting some notes—Sage looked up at Ronan, who wasn't even breathing hard after completing a series of offensive swings with a two-inch thick, six-foot-long solid steel bar weighing just under two hundred pounds. Now that Ronan didn't have to hide his gift of Might from Sage, the big man took pleasure in showing Sage just how strong he was. It was beyond description.

"Want to hear something interesting?" Sage asked him.

Ronan leaned the steel bar against the wall. "Sure."

Sage looked at his notepad. "There are thirty-two missing Council members, right? Has anybody ever told you how they're broken down? I mean, what gifts are represented?"

Ronan shrugged. "All the gifts, is what I've always heard."

"Not all. Not quite. They haven't captured anyone with Sight or Memory Share." Sage pointed at himself. "Of course, since I'm the only one with Memory Share, we knew that. Nobody with Sight has ever been caught. Do you think they've somehow seen it? Avoided being at certain places at certain times?"

"You'd have to ask Theo. Makes sense that they'd be hardest to take by surprise." Ronan pointed at the book. "How many with Might? Just the boy?"

"Yeah."

Ronan nodded. "David Brock. Only sixteen when he went missing during World War I."

Sage found David's page in the book. "He was English. A soldier. Disappeared somewhere in France." Brock's brown hair flowed thick and straight like Ronan's.

"He wasn't a real member of the Army," Ronan said. "He just fought alongside them. I warned him not to get involved, that human wars were not our concern, but he said he needed to sharpen his skills against real foes, not tree trunks in the middle of a forest. His specialty was demolishing the tanks the Germans had captured from the British."

Ronan told him that when Brock went missing, it had somehow galvanized his own determination to find the others. Not that he didn't care about them before, but Brock—even among those gifted with Might—was special. The boy was stronger than anyone Ronan knew, including himself. The fact he could be snatched without a trace, without a single sign of a struggle, didn't compute in Ronan's mind. "Been puzzling over that for the last ninety-five years."

Sage looked at his notepad. "They've taken four Fighting Arts, three Bell Makers, three Chain Makers, three with Voice, and three Pathfinders." He frowned. "Sixteen of them represent five gifts. The other sixteen represent fifteen gifts."

"Besides Persuasion, those are the gifts most dangerous to them," Leah said. "Pathfinders can find them. Bells and Voice physically weaken them. Chains and Fighting Arts can destroy them."

"Might can destroy them," Ronan said. "I'm not giving an inch to Fighting Arts." He grinned at Sage. "I've fought side-by-side with Fighting Arts, and they're good. Ain't saying they're not. But you give me my steel rod over there . . ." He shook his head and laughed. "Well, you just can't imagine it."

Tuesday bled into Wednesday. More sword fighting with Leah, more torturous exercise with Ronan, more book review, except it was the little book this time, the one about the history of the Council. It detailed descriptions of gifts; their ancient Elioudian ancestors who lived in Tartarus; and outlined the three evil territories, the underground world where remnants of the evil races still lived and waited for one of the Seven to release them.

Grandpa brought food on Thursday and promised to help Sage train by allowing him to Memory Share with him later in the week. Thursday's book was the *Encyclopedia of Dark Creatures*. He studied as many creatures as the day allowed, even Leviathan, the great water beast, but it was so thick and full of information, Sage knew he'd need weeks to digest it all.

On Friday, Theo spent the morning watching Sage spar with Leah and afterward discussed in detail all of Sage's gifts: Memory Share, Fighting Arts, Pathfinding, and now Clarity, because it was beginning to manifest. The old man knew many of the missing and told stories about each. It was a great break for Sage, because he was so tired from the week that he could barely lift his arms above his head.

The information he'd absorbed by the time he collapsed into bed Friday night had not only transformed his attitude, it had boosted his confidence one hundredfold. Although he was still years away from being able to actually battle one of the Princes, he felt totally ready to carry through on the plan he'd developed to find the missing Council members.

He slept late on Saturday morning, the first indulgence all week. By the time he came downstairs for breakfast, Mom had already left for Grandpa's house. The note she left on the kitchen counter asked Sage to start the dishwasher before he and Nick joined her.

Nick had already eaten breakfast and dumped his dishes in the sink. Typical.

Twenty minutes later, Sage was ready. "Nick, let's go."

Nick came out of his room, headphones on, with a look on his face that announced how much he was dreading the visit with Aunt Sally's family.

Sage locked the back door, and they headed toward the path in the woods leading to Grandpa's. Sage pulled the ear buds out of Nick's ears. "Hey, haven't seen you all week. How'd the gaming go?"

Nick laughed. "I should be the one entering the tourney. I wiped the floor with him."

"Not surprised. Why not enter?"

"Ha! Funny. Cause it cost two hundred dollars." Nick turned his iPod off and stuffed everything in his pocket. "This is a big-time tourney, Sage. Payout for first is ten grand. And a trip to Vegas to compete in the internationals."

"Should've asked Dad for the money," Sage said. "If there's anybody around here who understands return on investment, it's him."

"I did. He laughed. Told me to get a paper route."

"Paper route? Who even subscribes to a paper anymore? He's living in the 1990s." Sage laughed.

"That's what I said. Then he told me to cut lawns and save up my money." Nick shook his head. "He's got money to burn, and he's still a tightwad."

Sage smiled. "Just trying to teach you a life lesson. Work, then play."

"Got it. Thanks for that."

They walked in silence for a bit, neither of them walking any faster than they had to. Thinking about spending the weekend with the extended family was making it the longest mile of their lives.

"Hey, why is Addison such a jerk?" Nick asked totally out of the blue. He'd asked their mom this question about their cousin at least five times that Sage knew of, and each time, she always changed the subject.

Sage smiled. "You want the adult answer?"

Nick shrugged. "Whatever. The truth would be nice."

"Well . . . she took it really hard when Uncle Rick died. She's seventeen, which is a hard time for a girl as it is, or so Mom says."

"Maybe she just hates Duncan," Nick said. "Why did Aunt Sally marry him anyway? Seems weird to me."

"Weird, how?"

Nick looked at Sage. "Well, he's this giant businessman. Worth millions and millions. Maybe a billion. He just happens to meet Aunt Sally in a grocery store in Podunk, USA? Shopping for pork rinds? Then they get married after dating just a few months? You don't find that weird?"

"It does seem kind of odd." Sage said. "On the surface. Duncan told Mom he was out scouting a piece of property and got a sudden urge for pork rinds. So he grabbed the chance and pulled into the first supermarket he saw and bumped into Aunt Sally. Said it was fate. Destiny. Whatever."

Nick snorted.

"Mom said Duncan is a good guy. That Aunt Sally had to move on. That Addison will come around. Duncan gives her space, because he knows how hard her father's death was on her." Sage wasn't sure he bought all of that, but it sounded good. "Remember, Nick, Mom ordered us to be nice this weekend. Keep our opinions to ourselves."

"Addison's even worse since she got her black belt." Nick said. "One of these days I'm gonna break a board over her head."

Sage smiled. "Can't argue there, but until the day comes that you can get away with it, I'd suggest not making that threat to her face."

"Whatever," Nick mumbled.

There was something creepy about Duncan, although Sage couldn't fully verbalize it. True, he knew a couple of other adults that also gave him the creeps. No surprise there. Duncan was a nice guy, and he *had* gone out of his way not to barge into their family. Maybe it was his wealth that bothered Sage. Sometimes rich folks had a certain air that set them apart from other people. Pampered, maybe. Entitled. He wasn't sure. He figured really rich people like Duncan couldn't be squeaky clean, or they wouldn't have gotten so rich. He talked to Leah about it once, but she just stared at him as if he had a nose growing out of his forehead. She wasn't much help when it came to normal stuff.

Since his Clarity was starting to manifest, Sage wondered if he'd see Duncan with some demonic traits. He didn't know if he could stand seeing two people like that in the same place.

What about Dad? Five full days had passed. Sage's sour stomach seemed to grow with every step toward Grandpa's house.

Even before he saw her, Sage knew Addison had arrived. He heard a forced, shrill laugh that was unique in the entire universe.

Sage looked at Nick. "They got here early."

Nick rolled his eyes. "Great."

"Just be nice. It's only for two days. Addison's still having some adjustment issues."

"Yeah, adjusting to being human." Nick shook his head. "Let's go."

Sage saw his cousin from across the clearing near one of the picnic tables next to Grandma, who held Addison's younger sister Myla in her lap. Addison was tall and sported brown hair cut just above her shoulders. She was lean and athletic, with muscular legs and solid shoulders. She'd earned her black belt by defeating three other black belts at once. She was a fearless fighter who loved to mix it up. Sage had often looked at the calloused knuckles on both of her hands and wondered how many hours pounding a heavy bag it had taken to get skin that tough.

Sage's mom was speaking to Aunt Sally near the big ice tub. Sage hadn't seen her for a few months, and it looked as if she'd lost weight. She resembled Sage's mom a lot since she had trimmed up. She'd even cut her strawberry-blonde hair into the same style as his mom's. They were laughing about something.

Nick headed left, around to the front of the house. "Be out in a minute. Gotta hit the head."

Coward. Running away from Addison even before she had a chance to harass him.

"Hey, Sage," his mom said.

Sage waved. Mom and Grandma had fixed up the yard like a couple of pros. Well, Grandpa and Ronan probably did the heavy lifting, but Sage knew the two ladies were the brains behind it. It could pass for an outdoor scene in a fancy movie.

Addison looked over, saw Sage, and started toward him. Grandpa and Ronan hovered near the BBQ pit. Grandpa gave him a hand motion to remain calm. Ronan gave him a slicing hand motion across his throat and smiled. Sage almost smiled back, but didn't want Addison to think it was meant for her.

Addison stopped in front of Sage. Her eyes traveled over every inch of his body. Her large brown eyes had a hint of challenge; a film of sweat glistened on her forehead. She wore bright red spandex workout clothes that advertised her athletic figure. They'd last seen each other three months ago.

"I've been practicing my kali," she told Sage. "I'm pretty good."

Sage didn't say anything.

"I brought two sticks," Addison said. "I want to see if my kali can defeat your old-fashioned samurai swordplay. You game?"

Leah floated into Sage's line of vision and shook her head. "No," she mouthed.

"Do you even know what kali is, Loser?" Addison said quietly.

"It's a Filipino style of sword fighting," Sage said. "You can use it for knife fighting. I didn't just fall off a turnip truck."

"I want to spar," Addison said. "I've been waiting for months to put you in your place."

"And where's my place?" Sage asked.

"Humiliation, Oklahoma. It's a small town full of idiots in Loser County, just south of Desperation."

Sage had to laugh. "You are amazing, Addison. Is this how it's going to be all weekend?"

"It is until you prove you're not a girl."

"Are you sure it's not about proving that you're really a guy?"

Her face changed from smug challenger to furious fighter. "You better watch your mouth."

"Do not let her bait you, Sage," Leah said into his ear. "The first victims of emotion are logic and reason. Ignore her taunts."

"Well, I'm a little out of practice," Sage said. "So I think I'm gonna pass."

She snorted. "Figured you'd say that. I don't think that's it at all. I think that deep down, in the very depths of your pathetic soul, you're a coward. Despite how you look, all big and strong, you're afraid of real people. It's why you spent years making up a story about having an invisible friend. So you wouldn't have to actually interact with anyone. Pathetic. Loner. Loser. Coward." She spat the words, and Sage saw her eyes turn green.

Sage sucked in a quiet breath and took a half step back.

Addison leaned in closer. "I know what you are," she whispered.

Sage watched as the edges of her hairline turned just as green as her eyes. Then the rounded tops of her ears changed into points.

Clarity.

It was happening again. And she was still so young.

"What am I?" Sage asked.

She stared at him, her eyes growing ever greener. "You're a conceited know-it-all. The laughingstock of our family. Your parents are ashamed of you. Your grandma and grandpa are embarrassed. You're the kid we should lock away in the basement."

The strangest sensation came over him. Her words should have should have sent him flying off into a rage. As he watched the green skin grow even thicker around her hairline, as scales developed on her neck and cheeks like some freaky lizard in a science lab, he felt no anger at all. One of the Princes had her. Fully. As her ears grew as large and pointy as a Great Dane's, he felt sorry for her. The madder she got, the worse her condition became.

He made a decision. "I'll make a deal with you. A one-time shot, take-it-or-leave-it deal." He gave her a slight smile.

She was immediately suspicious. "What?"

"I'll spar with you, right in front of everybody. Right now. No warm ups, no practicing, no time to prepare. If you win, I will be your slave the entire weekend. I'll call you Queen Addison, serve you hand and foot, agree with everything you say, laugh at your stupid jokes, and feed you grapes while you lounge around like the Queen of Bathsheba."

"And if you win?"

"If I win, you will be nice to Nick. All weekend. No exceptions. No smart-mouth remarks, no teasing, no bullying, no touching him in any way, no jokes about him, nothing. You will be nice to Nick—and only Nick—all weekend. You can still be your dirty rotten self to everybody else, but if you so much as look at Nick sideways, I'll crack one of your sticks across the side of your head."

They stared at each other. Leah had floated in front of Sage in an effort to get his attention.

"Deal?" Sage asked Addison. "We can keep the details of our agreement to ourselves so nobody will know what's going on."

Sage could see the calculation going on behind Addison's eyes. She was weighing the pros and cons of possibly losing, for two days, her greatest pleasure in life: taunting and terrorizing Nick.

"Or is Miss Black Belt afraid?" Sage asked her finally.

Sage watched Leah's warning to him come true: Addison's emotion made quick victims of her logic and reason.

"Deal," she said. "I'll get my kali sticks." She spun around and stalked away.

Leah whispered in Sage's ear. "You cannot reveal your gift, Sage. Your superior speed will be difficult to control."

He looked at his Guardian and then glanced around to see if anyone was watching him. Sure that no one was, he whispered back to her, "I've got this."

Sage walked to the middle of the clearing and held up both hands. "Can I have everyone's attention? Hello, attention please."

Everyone stopped what they were doing and looked at him. Nick was still missing. "Nick," Sage shouted, "come out of the house. I have an announcement."

Addison looked like a thunderstorm coming around the corner of the house. She carried two fighting sticks by her side.

Nick stuck his head out the back door.

"OK," Sage said. "Addison and I will perform some pre-lunch entertainment. She's been studying the art of kali, and I've studied the art of samurai sword fighting. I'm a little out of practice, but today we will determine which of the two arts is superior. We will spar until one defeats the other."

There was so much shouting at once that Sage couldn't make out anything. He heard "no" and "crazy" and "hurt each other" and a host of other concerns, all of them coming from the three women.

Sage looked at Grandpa, who stood there smiling as wide as Sage had ever seen him. Ronan simply crossed his arms and gave him two thumbs up. Nick flew out of the house. He looked as if he'd just won a million dollars, no doubt caused by his vision of Addison being humiliated in front of everybody. Leah looked totally flat, expressionless, as though she already knew the outcome.

Addison joined Sage in the middle of the clearing and tossed him a beautiful wooden stick. Four feet long, solid and smooth, light and perfectly straight. He'd never swung one before, but he would adapt fast.

"This is not a good idea!" Aunt Sally finally shouted. "Addison, I'd never have allowed you to bring those silly things if I'd known this would happen."

"I don't like it either," Sage's mom said. "We don't need one of you getting hurt."

"I say let them do it," Grandpa said. "This might be just the thing their relationship needs."

Sage looked at his grandpa, who winked at him. He wasn't sure what he meant by that statement, but whatever.

Before anyone else could say another word, Addison stepped back and swung her stick in an overhead motion aimed at Sage's right shoulder.

"Focus on the aggression, not the aggressor," Leah said in Sage's ear as she floated beside him.

Sage parried the blow, stepped to her inside, and tagged her left arm with a solid downward-glancing strike. Then he stepped away before she could react.

"Control your speed, Sage," Leah warned.

Addison grimaced from the arm shot but recovered quickly. She set her feet and repositioned the stick in her hands. She held one end about one fist-length from the bottom. Sage knew why; it created a double-ended weapon. She could strike with the long end and use the secondary end below her fist as a bludgeon during close-quarter combat. She held the stick loosely so that she wouldn't waste energy and could keep her movements fluid. She backed out of striking range but kept the point aimed at Sage's face to skew his depth perception of the stick. She looked very confident.

Sage waited. This was her game, her art. His gift of Fighting Arts didn't just mean superhuman sword speed; it also meant he saw his opponent's movements in slow motion. There was no possible way Addison could move fast enough to catch him off guard. She couldn't swing that stick fast enough to prevent him from blocking it with ease. He waited while she calculated her next move.

She didn't wait long. In a flash, she jumped forward and moved the stick in a figure-eight motion that emphasized her downward strikes aimed at his collarbones. Her swinging hand was in front of her fighting stance, and her other hand guarded her face. It was good technique.

Sage stepped sideways, slapped her stick aside, took a strong step to the right, and put his right foot into her lower back. He pushed her forward. She stumbled and spun around, then used the same figure-eight motion in reverse, which emphasized an upward strike aimed at his midsection. She pivoted hard and used her body motion, beginning at her knees and hips, continuing through her shoulders and arms, and swung the stick flat and hard and fast, aimed right at Sage's head.

He dropped to one knee, then waited for the stick to sail past before jumping up and whipping his stick across her left hip as she completed her back swing.

Addison yelped and danced at the sting of the blow. Tears formed in her eyes, but she set her feet again and began swinging her stick in a variety of figure eight and horizontal back-and-forth motions aimed at his knees, midsection, and head.

She was trying to kill him.

He saw her aggression in super slow speed and parried each blow while fighting his urge to go on the offensive. He was content to play defense while she wore herself out. He'd already seen about six opportunities to knock the stick from her hands and end it, but he wanted her to use every trick she had in her arsenal. He wanted her to expend every ounce of energy, and he wanted her to see that he hadn't broken a sweat or been forced to breathe deeply.

Addison was in constant motion, which reduced the chances of her taking blows. But as she moved and grew tired, her swings opened up. Each wild swing was another opportunity for him to land a blow or knock the stick from her hands.

Leah floated just above Addison's head, moving as she moved, so that she could give Sage advice if she thought he needed it. It was obvious that Addison didn't possess the skills necessary to challenge him, and so Leah hadn't said anything. Even with being rusty, Sage had progressed past this level of skill as a ten-year-old.

Sage didn't know how much strength Addison had left. Being on offense was a lot more tiring than what Sage was doing, and she was getting seriously winded. She swung wide with a horizontal strike, and Sage stepped in and jabbed her hard in the ribs. She grunted and used a backhand swing to strike out at him. Sage stepped behind her and pushed his knee into her support leg. She dropped to the ground on that knee. Sage tapped her lightly on the side of the neck with his stick as he passed her on her blind side.

Addison jumped up and swung a crazy baseball-bat blow more common to a street fight than a martial arts dojo, but Sage parried it, stuck the end of his stick underneath her chin, and shoved her head back. He stepped away before she even realized what he'd done.

Gasping now, Addison belted a war cry that would raise the dead and charged and swung her stick straight down at his head. Sage gripped his stick with both hands, stepped forward, and shoved it straight up, angling it tightly against Addison's blow. Both of her wrists struck hard against Sage's stick, and she screamed from the impact. Her stick flew out of her hands and struck the top of the cooking grate of the BBQ pit before rolling off.

Sage stepped close behind her, pulled his stick tightly against the side of her neck, and whispered in her ear.

"Remember our deal. If you bother Nick even one time this weekend, I'll break this stick over your head."

He released her and she ran off, tears streaming. Sage figured she could join him as a resident of Humiliation, Oklahoma, located in Loser County, just south of Desperation.

Nick jumped up and down, whooping and hollering as if he himself had just won the heavyweight boxing championship of the world. He picked up Addison's stick and swung it around a few times. He jabbed and blocked and danced like he'd seen Sage do.

"Holy cow, Sage," Nick shouted at the top of his lungs. "Wow! That was amazing! You aren't even sweating! Grandpa! Ronan! Did you see what he did to her? And she's got a black belt? Did she get it from Target or something?"

Sage glanced at his mom, who looked disappointed in him, but Ronan gave him two thumbs up again. Grandma and Aunt Sally were stunned.

Grandpa walked over to Sage and put a hand on his shoulder. "It was just what she needed," he said quietly. "I think you knew that. You were toying with her, and I appreciate your restraint. You could have made her look a lot worse."

Sage grabbed Nick, who was still whooping around. "Listen, Nick," he said. "Addison is going to be nice to you this weekend. OK?"

Nick nodded at him, a bit confused.

"So here's the deal," Sage said. "You need to stop prancing around. Right now. Put yourself in her place and think about how she feels. OK? Don't rub it in. She's embarrassed. Got it?"

"So what?" Nick snapped. "She's been embarrassing me for years, and she didn't seem to mind that. A little payback's not such a bad thing."

Sage leaned over and got right in his face. "I just gave her payback. For both of us. So knock it off. Now! Just leave her alone and she'll leave you alone. OK?"

Nick didn't look happy, but he nodded.

"Good." Sage handed his stick to his brother. "Go put both of these over by the back door. Maybe if you ask her nicely, she'll teach you some stuff this weekend. She's pretty good."

Nick rolled his eyes. "Pretty good? Yeah, right." He stalked away.

"Want to help me mash some hamburger patties?" Grandpa asked Sage. "It's about that time."

"Sure. I know I'm hungry."

As his grandpa walked off, Sage looked toward the trees in an effort to catch a glimpse of Addison. He felt bad, but he knew he'd done what was needed. She had amazing potential, but she was letting her anger destroy any chance of developing it. Sad. Really sad.

Then Sage's dad walked out the back door of the house, and Sage forgot all about Addison. He glanced at Leah, who was staring at Dad, sword in hand, all three sets of wings fully extended. Ready for battle.

"Steven," Ronan said to Grandpa under his breath. He motioned toward Leah.

Sage heard Grandpa gasp. "What's going on with Leah?" Grandpa whispered as he stepped closer to Sage.

We're about to have a family cookout with a monster in our midst, Sage wanted to say. Instead, he looked at Grandpa as casually as he could and said, "Dad's home."

9

What do you see?" Grandpa asked softly.

It took great effort for Sage to pull his eyes away from his dad. He almost threw up his breakfast when Mom walked over and gave Dad a hug and kiss. A few seconds later, Nick, Grandma, Aunt Sally, and Cousin Myla surrounded him. Hugs and kisses all around.

"How bad is he?" Ronan whispered as he joined Sage and Grandpa.

"He's as gold as King Tut's mask," Sage said softly. He waved at Dad, who'd looked across the clearing and waved at him.

Dad picked up Myla and gave her a kiss and hug.

"His head is pointy in the back, like Hitler's, but more so. He has some kind of beak for a nose. It overlaps his chin a little and looks sharp enough to crack a coconut." Sage glanced away and crossed his arms to rub away the goose bumps.

"What else?" Grandpa asked.

"Uh . . . well, his legs below his knees are misshapen. Like a dog's. Or a large wolf. And wings are growing. They're about twelve inches. Not near fully formed but well on their way. His ears are twice the size they should be." Sage turned away and rubbed his eyes. "I can't look anymore. Not right now."

"I understand," Grandpa said. "Just act normal."

"Like that'd be a simple thing," Ronan said.

Sage told them about Addison—her green, scaly skin, her misshapen ears, her inability to control her rage. "Grandpa, is Clarity only allowing me to see family members first? Those sharing my blood?"

"I don't know a lot about it. It would make some sense, seeing how that gift has just begun manifesting." Grandpa waved at Dad. "I need to say hello to him. All of us do. Let's go."

Sage swallowed hard and followed them across the yard. He waited until everyone else wandered away so that he and his dad could be alone.

"How was your week?" Sage asked. What should have been white was red. What should have been blue was a green so stark and brilliant Sage felt as if they were drilling directly into his brain.

"Great week." Dad clamped him on the shoulder. "The deal is done." His smile revealed fangs Dracula would envy. "I'm about to transform your future, Sage. You'll soon want for nothing."

Sage nodded but didn't respond. *You're already transforming my future. More than you could ever understand.*

"Before this is all over, I might end up the most powerful businessman the state of Oklahoma ever produced."

T. Boone Pickens aside, Sage didn't argue with him. "That's great, Dad," he said weakly.

"Your Uncle Duncan's been a huge help. He here yet?"

"Don't think so," Sage said. "Mom said he might not come."

Dad's cell phone rang. He glanced at the screen and turned away. "Have to take this," he said over his shoulder. He walked off before Sage could respond.

We've got to do something! We can't wait!

Grandpa and Ronan were alone at the BBQ pit. Leah hovered in the middle of the clearing. She'd folded her wings and sheathed her sword, but she kept her eyes on Dad.

Sage joined Grandpa. "Take me to New Orleans. Tonight. Or tomorrow."

Grandpa didn't say anything, but Ronan did. "Forget about it."

"Why? What if I can see the breach where they took that girl?"

"Her name's Elsbeth," Grandpa said.

"Right." Sage leaned in close. "What if I can see it? The Council can send people through the breach if I find it. I wouldn't have to go in. I wouldn't be in any danger."

"You don't know what you don't know," Ronan said. "Forget about it."

Sage clinched his fists, furious that they wouldn't even listen to him. "Tell me why that's a bad idea. I wouldn't be in any danger!"

Grandpa took Sage's arm. "Lower your voice." He glanced around to see if anybody had heard Sage's outburst, but nobody was paying them any attention. "None of us knows anything about the dark side of the spiritual realm. Not how they're making entry.

Not how they might guard them. Not what kind of beasts might spill out the moment we step through." He paused. No one had come near them. Talking low and fast, he continued.

"Haddock, the most accomplished Pathfinder ever, has inspected thirty-one of the thirty-two breaches. There's simply no trace. Maybe your gift *is* special. Pathfinding takes no development. It will get no stronger or more refined than it is right now. So maybe you *can* see it." Grandpa held up a finger and leaned in closer. "Please understand that before you *try* to see it, you've got to be ready to fight for your life against beasts that would love nothing more than to rip you to shreds."

He'd *never* seen his grandpa like this. Never.

"You're too young to understand," Ronan said quietly. "The monsters that are out there . . . they're just . . . you just can't comprehend until you're facing them. I still get nervous, and I'm Ronan." He smiled and winked.

They stood there together. Leah put a hand on Sage's shoulder, but he ignored it.

"We have to help Dad," Sage said. "He doesn't have much time left. Pretty soon he'll be beyond hope."

Grandpa sighed and flipped several burgers.

"He's your *son*," Sage snapped.

"I know it!" Grandpa snapped back, his eyes glistening.

Ronan put a hand on Sage's chest and pushed him back a little. Then he moved to stand behind his friend.

"Everything all right over there?" Grandma asked.

"OK," Ronan said. He waved to her, a big smile on his face. He turned to Sage. "Your grandpa has to weigh the risk. The Council doesn't have a team to spare, even if we found the breach. Meaning it would just be us. Since there's no way to know what we'll face, it'd be too dangerous for you."

"You're too valuable to the future of the Council," Grandpa said softly. "Even for the sake of saving my son."

Sage's eyes teared up, so he turned away, furious. They weren't going to help. Period. If they could only see what he saw! He watched Dad bounce Myla on his knee, his budding wings moving back and forth as though desperate to strengthen themselves.

"Look," Ronan said. He motioned toward the woods where Addison had disappeared a few minutes before.

She stalked out of the trees, head and shoulders thrown back in defiance, over to Sage's dad and gave him a long hug. The sight of them, infected with evil like they were, made Sage shudder. It scared him like nothing else ever had. Would they grow closer as their respective Prince's influence became more entrenched within them? Did humans deeply infected with the seven sins form some kind of supernatural bond? He shivered again and looked away. How would he survive the rest of the weekend?

The day passed slowly as Sage skirted around Dad and Addison. He opted to play with Myla and listen to Ronan tell stories about his and Grandpa's travels while working for the State Department.

Theo came by in the early evening, and Sage spent as much time with him as he could. Sage updated him about the changes in Dad, what he'd seen with Addison, and the argument he'd had with Grandpa. Theo supported Grandpa's opinion, which Sage had fully expected.

Grandpa built a big bonfire, and everyone gathered around to tell scary tales until bedtime. Every time Sage's dad told a monster story, Sage watched with growing horror at the irony of it.

Nick and Sage walked home through the woods. Nick prattled on about this and that as he led them through the darkness along the wide trail. Sage only listened enough to grunt in agreement every now and then. He needed to talk to Dad. Not that it would do any good, but he had to at least try.

As soon as they walked into the house, Nick disappeared into his room, and Sage saw his dad in the study, bent over some spreadsheets. He heard Mom humming somewhere in the back of the house.

No better time than the present. Sage swallowed hard, walked into his dad's study, and closed the door.

This close to him, the shape of his dad's head looked even more pronounced—like one of those aerodynamic bicycle helmets. Growing from that helmet-head were thick, black, ropey tentacles that looked as if they were designed to protect his skull. His ears were twice their normal size, and his eyes, though red this afternoon, had turned nearly black. Sage couldn't stand to look at his dad's ever-growing wings.

"Keep your focus," Leah said as she stood next to Dad. "Remember who lies beneath this corruption."

"Hey, Sage." He glanced up from the paperwork spread across his desk.

120

Even his voice was changing. It now had a gravely sound mixed with an echoing bass. The hair on Sage's arms stood at attention.

"What's going on?" Dad leaned back in his chair and rubbed his cheek with his left claw.

Sage had spent the entire walk through the woods thinking about what to say. Now, all those words had left him and he felt like an idiot.

"Just speak your heart," Leah whispered.

"Can we talk about your business thing for a minute?" Sage cleared his throat and steeled himself.

"Sure. What about it?"

"Are you gonna close the Chevy dealership so you can sell the land?"

His dad's face was so corrupted, Sage couldn't tell if he was uncomfortable talking about it. Only the way he tapped a pencil against the desk, a long-held habit, told Sage he was giving it thought. "That's not decided yet," Dad said. "Maybe."

"If you *do* sell the land, will the private school close?"

"They'd have to find a new place, but I'm not predicting they would close." He glanced at his watch, then at the papers on his desk.

Clearly, he didn't have time for Sage and his silly questions. Sage tried a different direction. "We haven't had any father-and-son time, alone, in over a year. We live in the same house, but you're becoming a stranger."

Dad flinched a little and straightened up in his chair. "Well I . . ."

Sage felt a sudden flash of anger and decided to let it fuel him. "You treat Mom like she's a nuisance. You spend fourteen hours a day at your office and ignore your family on weekends. You don't pay attention at church. Everybody in town whispers behind your back—Scrooge—the guy who's about to increase the unemployment rate around here by ten percent. For what? Money? Power? You're not the same dad I grew up with." Sage kept his voice steady. "You're turning into a monster. Do you love making money more than you love me? Your family? Do you remember when you loved spending time with us?"

The room got so quiet Sage could have heard paint dry. His dad sat there staring at him, still and silent. Sage dared him to deny the accusations.

Suddenly the most amazing thing happened. Dad's eyes started clearing—from black to red to almost white. His gold skin began to fade—slowly, but for sure.

"I love . . . I do remember . . . you're my son . . ." His voice was nearly clear, almost normal. Some memories had broken through and pushed their way to the surface.

"I remember when I was eight years old. You took me camping and told me you'd always be there for me. That nothing would *ever* stand between us. Where did *that* guy go?"

Dad's helmet-head shrank; his claws reduced; his skin faded even more. "Well, I love . . . really . . ."

He's in there! He can be saved!

Sage gave him another shot. "You and Mom went to the private school. It's got dozens of kids. Good kids. They're our future. Like me and Nick."

Then something snapped in Dad's eyes. "Future," he said excitedly. "Exactly. The future is why I'm doing this. Your future. And

Nick's. My whole family." He leaned forward in his chair as his skin began to turn gold again, as his head and hands returned to their demonic shape, as his eyes turned even blacker than before. "Generational wealth, Sage. Money and status for you and your kids and your kid's kids. That's what this is about. You. I want security for all of you."

Sage leaned back in his chair as Dad's wings grew several inches right in front of him. The vision was beyond horrifying.

"Yeah, I've been a little negligent lately, but the long-term benefits are unimaginable. You just don't understand." His voice sounded twisted and dark and full of menace.

Sage stood and stumbled backward. He tried hard to keep his face from showing the emotion that nearly crippled his ability to move.

Dad waved a claw at the papers on his desk. "It'll all be worth it, Sage. You'll see. What I'm doing here will stretch far beyond the borders of this city. If you were older, I'd explain more. For now, you just have to trust me." His smile showed Sage a mouth full of fangs.

"OK." Sage backed all the way to the door. "I understand. Really. I get it. Sorry to bother you."

Only Leah's presence kept him from shrieking into the night. His dad was in there somewhere. Sage had seen proof of that. He was somewhere underneath all that greed. Sage had to stop whichever Prince had a stranglehold on him.

Mammon, according to Theo's theory. Mammon, the Prince of Greed.

Sunday was church, another big cookout, and homemade ice cream, and then it was over. Mom and Dad drove Aunt Sally's family to the airport, Nick fled to a buddy's house, and Sage escaped to his dungeon and locked himself in.

Grandpa and Ronan's words still echoed in his head from yesterday about there not being enough Council members to form a team, even if Sage were somehow able to see the breach where Elsbeth Brown had disappeared. He pulled out the book of missing Council members. In all, thirty-two warriors—four with Fighting Arts, three each with Bell Making, Chains, Voice, and Pathfinding. Two that could Teleport. Some of the others possessed Absorption, Might, Possession, and Illusion—all amazingly powerful gifts. Then there was Elsbeth Brown, the only one of the thirty-two with two gifts—Persuasion and Teleportation. Though only fifteen years old, Elsbeth's gifts made her the most powerful of them all.

What a team that would make! Since they'd been pulled into the spiritual realm, where they wouldn't age, might they still be alive? Even Leif Erickson, missing for more than a thousand years, might still be alive.

He spent two hours studying the book, memorizing everything about them. They could help him. These missing Council members. If Sage could find them, maybe *they* could be the team that could find and destroy whichever Prince had corrupted Dad.

Could Sage find them on his own? Would he be allowed? He looked at Leah, who sat quietly near the door. "If you make a promise to me," he asked, "are you allowed to break it? Ever?"

He'd never asked Leah such a question before, quite frankly because he'd never felt a pressing need for her to keep a big secret. He knew now that she had been reporting the progress of his training to others his entire life; thus, her ability to keep a confidence became critical.

"My nature does not allow me to make a promise I cannot keep." Leah moved over to the floor in front of him and sat down, legs crossed. She cocked her head. "Nor would I make a promise to keep a confidence prior to knowing what it is about."

Sage looked at her for a moment, closed the book, and sat on the floor opposite her. "If I told you I was planning on doing some stuff I didn't want anyone to know about, and I asked you to keep it to yourself, would you?"

"Possibly." She looked at the ceiling, thinking. Finally, "I have a full understanding of your destiny, which includes information I cannot reveal to you or anyone else. It is important that certain actions be allowed to occur naturally."

Sage frowned. "I don't understand."

She smiled. "There have been age-long arguments about predestination verses free will. The topic has divided churches. That is to what I am referring."

He shook his head. "I still don't understand."

"There are certain actions that will occur," she said. "Those actions are predestined. However, the actions may not occur on a timetable that is preferred. They may be delayed due to the free-will decision of the person predestined to take the action."

When Sage didn't say anything, she continued.

"It is predestined that you will train and begin your hunt for the Seven Princes. That fact will not change. It will happen. Your free will in deciding *when* to train might delay the timetable of your hunt. Do you understand?"

"I think so." Sage thought about her response in relation to his question. "So if the actions I want you to keep secret somehow fit within a predestined plan, you will allow everything to play out?"

"Possibly," she said. "Remember, I cannot make a promise before I know the details."

And I can't keep anything from her because she's with me every second of the day.

"OK, but I'm under no obligation to tell you everything, either. Right?"

"Correct. I suspect, however, that by observing your actions I will be able to determine what goal you seek."

"Oh, I don't doubt that for a minute, Leah. Not for a minute." He stood and decided what he needed for tomorrow.

Leah watched for the next several minutes. She said nothing as he gathered what few items he'd need for his trip.

The next morning, Theo stood outside his shop at just before nine, an hour before it opened to the public. Sage propped his bike against the wall and gave his old friend a hug.

"Thanks for agreeing to get here early," Sage said. "Ronan should be here pretty soon."

"Not a problem," Theo said. He unlocked the door and punched in the security code. "What do you and Ronan have planned?"

"He agreed to help me with Memory Share. Grandpa said he'd do it, but Grandma's dragging him to Oklahoma City today."

"Ah, I see," Theo said. "You can only Memory Share from inside a spiritual realm."

"Right." Sage followed him to the back and watched him unbolt the secure door. "Ronan said he'd chop wood all night so that he'd be tired enough to sleep so deeply that I could use him to train. Hope he doesn't crash his car on the way over here."

Theo smiled.

Memory Share only worked on another angelic-blooded being while in a subconscious state. Ronan's fatigue should put him out for several hours, which would give Sage all the time he'd need to find the precise memory he sought.

"Be careful inside such a head," Theo said. "Many disturbing images have collected in four hundred and fifty years."

"I'll be careful." Sage went into the secure room first and turned on the lights. "I'll move the shelves."

"That is fine," Theo said. "I will return shortly."

Sage found both latches where he'd seen Ronan access them before. The shelves rolled away from the wall with ease and he stood at the entrance with a sense of awe.

He had no time to waste. He'd told Ronan to meet him at Theo's shop at nine-thirty. Twenty minutes from now. Sage crept to the door and listened. He heard Theo banging around in the front of the shop. The old man hummed a Greek tune Sage had heard a thousand times.

He went to the back door, opened it, and grabbed the backpack and duffle bag he'd stashed there before riding around to the front to meet Theo. The duffle wasn't huge, but it was big enough to hold the short sword he'd trained with his entire life. Nor was it heavy—just some changes of clothes to last a few days. His backpack had his iPod, the small book about the history of the Council, some snacks, a flashlight, four bottles of water, bug spray, sunglasses, some moist hand wipes, a notepad and pen, and a small digital camera with a huge flash drive. Would it be enough? Was it remotely adequate? He didn't know. All he *did* know was that he was running out of time to save his dad.

Stepping into Godspace, he hid the bags behind a huge tree and made it back inside Theo's Treasure Room by the time he heard Ronan pound on the front door.

Leah had watched Sage's every move and said nothing.

So far, so good.

"I was up all night chopping wood and carrying those big rolls of hay into my back pasture," Ronan said. "Fifty rolls—a thousand pounds each, more than a mile of walking. Back and forth. Back and forth. One at a time. My back's killing me. Normally would've used a truck and trailer, but you told me to wear myself out. Mission accomplished." Ronan nearly staggered into the Treasure Room. "When I said I'd help you train, I never thought sleeping would be part of the deal."

Sage hoped his nervousness wouldn't give him away. He rubbed his hands against his legs. "Well, my Pathfinding is fine. You helped all last week with my Fighting Arts. So Memory Share is the only thing left. Leah's allowing me to Memory Share with her doesn't help me. So it's either you or Grandpa."

Ronan waved away his concern. "I know. Just saying I've never helped somebody train by going to sleep."

"I should close this door," Theo said. "Helen must not stumble upon you."

Which is exactly what Sage had hoped for. "OK," he said. "Maybe we should pull the shelves back into place."

"Not necessary," Theo said. "I will lock the outer door." He turned to Leah. "You watch over these two."

"Always. Destiny is being fulfilled today."

"True, I suspect."

Sage wondered what they meant. He sent a questioning look at Theo, who winked just before the old man closed and locked the door. Sage glanced at Ronan, but he was so focused on centering himself in the middle of the spiritual realm entrance that he hadn't noticed anything.

Theo's meaning suddenly dawned on Sage. Theo was gifted with Sight. He'd seen this. Visions of it. He knew what was about to happen and hadn't lifted a finger to stop it. That knowledge gave Sage the final bit of confidence he needed to press on.

Let's do this thing!

Ronan picked a spot of soft moss alongside the stream, underneath the same redwood-sized tree he, Grandpa, and Theo had waited by when Sage first stepped into Godspace. He lay down and closed his eyes.

"Couldn't ask for a more relaxing spot on the planet," Ronan said, already on the verge of sleep. "Sage, will I feel you inside my head? Will it feel like I've got some worm wiggling around in there?"

Sage glanced at Leah, who didn't make any attempt to answer his question. "I don't know. This'll be my first time." Sage sat down next to him. "You can tell me the answer when you wake up."

"Then it'll be a few hours before you know," Ronan said. He yawned and rubbed his eyes. "Wonder if you'll feel my gift while you're in there. Be cool for you to be me, even for a few minutes." His lips curved. "Cause, dude, I'm awesome."

"A regular Superman." Sage watched as Ronan's eyelids became heavier and heavier.

Leah sat patiently, watching with no comment. Sage took her stillness as acceptance for what he was about to do.

Sage didn't know how long Ronan would be asleep. Hours, for sure. Grandpa would be in Oklahoma City most of the day. Sage figured he'd have several more hours before Mom and Dad noticed he wasn't home and called Ronan to ask where he was. By the time Ronan and Grandpa figured out what probably happened, there'd be no way to find him.

Then again, because time within the spiritual realm moved so much slower than the human realm, he might be able to get back before Grandpa returned from Oklahoma City. Whatever happened, it was what it was.

"I think he's gone," Sage said to Leah. He gently shook Ronan and called his name, but the big man didn't move. "Ronan," he said louder. "Wake up!"

Nothing.

Sage positioned his knees on each side of Ronan's head, placed his fingers exactly as Leah had instructed, and looked at her. "Is this right?"

"It is correct," Leah said. "Remember to clear your mind. Allow the images to build. Unlike when you Memory Shared with me, you will enter Ronan's mind and be overwhelmed with flashes of experiences so vast it will appear as though you are staring into thousands of windows."

Sage fought against rising panic. "All right."

"His starkest memories will shine brightest, and you'll be tempted to step into those. Choose carefully. Choose only those involving your grandfather, for I assume you are attempting to find one of the thirty-two locations where Council members disappeared."

Enough talk. "Got it," Sage said. "If I don't do this right now, I might chicken out."

He pressed his fingers more firmly against Ronan's head, then placed his thumbs into the man's eye sockets. Relaxing, he closed his eyes and allowed his stress to drain away. He imagined a white canvas rising up before him.

It took a few seconds before anything visual materialized. He saw smoke—drifting and swirling—with some images bright and bursting with color and some dim and bleached and fragmented. He ignored the broken shards of black and white. He assumed those were Ronan's oldest and least significant memories. The very brightest was from yesterday at Grandpa's house when Ronan had watched Sage and Grandpa argue about allowing Sage to travel to New Orleans.

Memories morphed and changed. They ran like silent movies on an endless loop. Within the Memory Share, Sage imagined stretching out his hands and pushing images aside, searching carefully for snippets he knew would be important. He found memories attached to one another, grouped together by topics and similar experiences, linked by delicate threads. A flash of Ronan being attacked by a two-headed troll linked to other attacks by beasts, allowing Ronan, Sage assumed, to quickly draw from past experiences if he suddenly found himself in a similar situation.

Sage's heart quickened at this discovery. He hoped that if he could find a memory of Ronan and Grandpa searching for one of the thirty-two breaches, it would link to all of them.

He saw brilliant images of Ronan with different women and quickly pushed those away, horrified at the thought of invading such private moments. A funeral, an open grave, a woman on her knees, screaming, shoulders heaving in grief as a younger Abigail Vaughn attempted to comfort her. Then more funerals, battlefields strewn with bodies, dying monsters, ghastly images of impaled or decapitated beasts—dozens of versions of death.

Sage fought against lingering too long on any one image, afraid he'd become so entranced that he'd lose all track of time. The smoky, swirling jumble of remembrances raced by at times, which offered glimpses much too brief to inspect. Sage learned to reach out and grab them. His maneuver slowed their passage as they slithered through his fingers. Like an IMAX cinema screen, Sage had to keep his head in constant motion for fear of missing what he needed.

Then he saw New Orleans. Bourbon Street. And Grandpa, with an expression filled with desperation and fear. That image, bright and stark due to its freshness, linked to others, all with Grandpa wearing a look of despair. Sage was tempted to jump into the New Orleans scene, but hesitated because it was too obvious— he didn't want Grandpa knowing where he was about to go. The second-brightest memory in this string was a battlefield—stark in Ronan's mind—and clearly the event Ronan talked about last week: the capture of David Brock, the sixteen-year-old gifted with Might during WWI.

Sage reached with both hands, grabbed the edges of the memory, and allowed it to fully engulf his vision.

He was there, fully within Ronan's memory from almost a hundred years before. Grandpa was there, his hair a little longer, not as much gray, and he wore a moustache drooping a full inch below his bottom lip. He was bundled into a heavy winter coat and gloves.

Sage felt an icy wind against Ronan's face as he and Grandpa stood at the edge of a large field near a tree line. Three British tanks were nearby, the front of each bludgeoned into scrap metal. A dusting of light snow covered everything.

"Are you sure we're at the right place?" Ronan asked Grandpa.

Grandpa pulled a topographical map from his back pocket and unfolded it on the ground in front of them. They both squatted while Grandpa traced it with a finger. "Outside of Cambrai, France." He pointed to a ridgeline to the north. "Bourlon Ridge. The coordinates are fifty degrees, 10′ 36″ north, three degrees, 14′ 08″ east." He stood and looked around. "Witnesses said he disappeared at the base of the ridgeline right after he disabled these three tanks."

"David loved smashing these things," Ronan said.

Grandpa folded the map and stuffed it back into his pocket.

"See anything?" Ronan asked.

Grandpa took off at a slow pace toward the ridgeline in front of them. "Not yet."

Ronan followed. "Horrible way to spend Christmas. Cold, muddy, trudging around out here."

"We had to wait until the armies moved away," Grandpa said. "We couldn't search with bullets flying."

While the dead bodies had been hauled off, in addition to the ruined tanks, Grandpa saw abandoned military gear, discarded, bloody uniforms cut away from wounded soldiers, broken rifles, artillery holes, felled trees, and a destroyed farmhouse in the distance. Many lives had been lost there.

"The ridgeline isn't very long." Grandpa stopped near one end. "At least six different soldiers say they saw Brock yanked off his feet and dragged into the side of the hill." He got Ronan's attention and pointed to the rise. "You can see there's no opening."

Sage watched, through Ronan's memory, as he visually inspected the entire ridge. "You can't see anything?" he asked Grandpa. "No discoloration. No white circle?"

"Not even a hint," Grandpa said.

"I told that boy," Ronan said. "I told him to let humans fight their silly wars. That we have bigger things to worry about."

Ronan watched Grandpa walk the ridgeline. He stopped every few feet to touch the dirt embankment. When he didn't find anything, he circled around to the top and searched there. Ronan followed quietly.

By the time Grandpa was satisfied their hunt was useless, they were nearly frozen from the cold wind blasting from the north.

They climbed onto bicycles and rode into Cambrai, stopping in front of the Church of Saint Martin. "Leave the bikes," Grandpa said.

Ronan followed him into the church and headed toward the belfry. At the base of the bell tower, Grandpa opened a hidden door and let Ronan enter first. Ronan paused in front of a set of heavy drapes and waited.

"You can go ahead," Grandpa told him. "I'll be right behind you."

"Well, since I can't see the entrance, I need to follow you."

Grandpa laughed. "Still worried you'll walk straight into a wall?"

"Again? Yeah, for the hundredth time. Just lead the way."

Grandpa pulled the heavy drapes aside and stuck his left arm through the middle of the limestone wall behind it. He held his other hand out to Ronan. "Let's go."

Ronan grabbed his arm, stepped forward, and then followed Grandpa. Their mission, unaccomplished.

By the time Sage lifted his hands from Ronan's face, a truth had embedded itself into his consciousness that hadn't been there before. He looked at Leah, who sat crossed-legged near Ronan's feet. "I know Godspace. I mean, like, I know things about it. Directions. How to navigate, I don't understand."

She cocked her head. "I have been waiting many years to witness the aftermath of your first Memory Share experience with another Council member. The Council will also want to understand the full ramifications of how much information transfers to you on a subconscious level."

"What?" Sage asked.

"Many suspected that Memory Share would be more than just the ability to see another's memories," Leah said. "They felt it would also include the subconscious transfer of information." She stood and looked down on Ronan. "So you know what he knows?"

Sage stood and looked down upon Ronan. "I know how to get to the closest entrances to all thirty-two disappearances, to Council headquarters, to the Tomb of Ancient Documents. Yeah, I know what he knows." He sighed. "I also know *him* now. His fears, what drives him. His sense of humor. How much he loves Grandpa. And me." Sage paused and swallowed hard. "He'd give his life for me."

"Then you must consider carefully what you are about to do," Leah said. "Ronan's love for you pales in comparison to the love your grandfather feels for you."

Sage thought about her words. Then he retrieved his backpack and duffle bag from behind the tree. "I *have* considered it carefully. I'm going to save Dad. Or at least try. Maybe while I'm at it, I can find some of the missing Council members and send someone to save them."

He studied the sleeping Ronan and wondered if he'd ever see him again. Swallowing the emotion rising up within him, he walked away. "You coming?" he asked Leah. "It's a little bit of a walk, and the clock's ticking."

He hadn't taken ten steps when Grandpa's angry voice stopped him. "Sage Alexander! Don't take one more step!"

Sage froze and turned around.

Grandpa stood there, rage darkening his face. He pointed back into Theo's shop. "Get back in here! Now!"

10

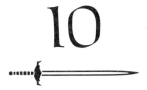

Grandpa looked from Sage to Ronan and back to Sage, his hands shaking with anger. "I know *exactly* what you're doing, and I can't *believe* you'd pull a stunt like this!"

"I just—"

"No! Do *not* make excuses!" Grandpa walked over to Ronan, put a boot on his shoulder, and shoved. "Ronan, wake up."

Leah floated quietly nearby, no expression on her face whatsoever.

"I'm just trying to save Dad!" Sage shouted.

"By getting yourself killed?" Grandpa shouted back. "Wake up, Ronan." He shoved him with his boot again.

"Dad will be fully possessed by the time you think I'm ready," Sage stormed. Since he'd made the adult decision to sneak off, the least he could do was stand there and defend his ground.

Ronan jerked awake and sat up. "What's going on?"

"Your destiny is bigger than just saving your father," Grandpa said. "The Council can't lose you. Of all people, it can't lose *you*. Get back inside. Now!"

Sage refused. He set his jaw and crossed his arms. "Come with me, then. You and Ronan. If you don't want me hurt, come with me. But I'm going, one way or another."

Ronan climbed to his feet. He rubbed his eyes. "What's going on?" He saw the bag on Sage's shoulder, Grandpa's rage, Sage's defiance, and then got angry himself. "What memories did you look at?"

"What do you *think*?" Grandpa snapped. "How could you be so careless?"

Ronan frowned. "I was just helping him train. How was I supposed to know he'd do something so stupid?"

"Sage, if you don't get back into Theo's shop right now, I'll drag you in there." Grandpa took several steps his way. Ronan did the same.

Staring at both of them, Sage knew he wouldn't make it twenty feet if he bolted. He raised his chin, stared straight ahead, and marched over to Theo, who'd stepped through the entrance at some point to watch.

Leah floated quietly beside him. She wore an expression he couldn't read. He'd never seen her gloat, so maybe that was it. It didn't matter. "I'm not giving up," he said to Grandpa just before crossing through the opening into the Treasure Room.

"Then you'd better start training," Grandpa said.

Sage dropped his bag on the floor and turned to face them. He knew they had more to say. So did he.

He'd never seen Grandpa so mad. Ever. He glared at Sage as he stepped through, stomped over to the open door leading to the back of the warehouse, and turned to face him. "You really think sneaking off is the answer?" he asked. "By *yourself!*"

Theo sat on one of the barstools while Ronan grabbed the edges of the shelving unit and started sliding it back into place.

"Do you really think—" The Darks that hit Grandpa in the back knocked him so far forward, he slammed into Ronan.

"Attack!" Leah shouted, sword in her hand, wings fully expanded.

The first of the Darks pouring into the room didn't attack anyone else. They flew past Ronan into the opening to Godspace.

Instantly, they evaporated into a puff of greenish-black smoke.

"Stop them!" Theo lurched off his barstool and grabbed a sword from a shelf behind him. "They attack the entrance!"

Swords drawn, the Darks flew into the Treasure Room four and five at a time. They blocked Leah's sword strikes, not even attempting to engage her, fully focused on the spiritual portal.

Grandpa tried closing the steel door into the Treasure room, but they knocked him back again and again. "Ronan, shut the door!" he said. "Hurry!"

Theo swung his sword, a fierce look on his face. The Darks blocked his blows with ease as they raced by him.

"Stay down, Sage," Leah shouted as she killed several.

The Darks flew head-on into the entrance, one after another, kamikaze-style, the opening getting smaller and smaller with each strike.

Ronan fought against the raging flood as he pushed his way toward the steel door. Grandpa wasn't giving up either. Despite being knocked down repeatedly, he battled forward.

Leah's sword strikes were little more than a blur as she tried stopping them before they reached the portal, but there were just too many. Over and over, they attacked, the opening half the size now, *maybe* still big enough for Sage to fit through, but shrinking fast.

Nobody was watching him. Nobody.

Decision time.

He grabbed his bag, held it hard against his chest, and went. "I'll be back!" he shouted, and sprinted forward.

"Sage! No!" Grandpa shouted from behind him.

He dove headfirst, jostled and slammed by Darks as they assaulted the opening, and landed in Godspace just before the portal snapped shut.

"You have defied your grandfather a second time," Leah said, her sword in her hands, her three sets of wings still fully expanded.

Sage didn't see how she could have *possibly* made it through, but it didn't surprise him. Nothing she did surprised him. He stood and swallowed hard, well aware of what he'd done. Grandpa might never forgive him, but if Sage didn't try to save his dad, he'd never forgive himself.

He started walking. Leah sheathed her sword, collapsed her wings, and followed. After a few steps, he looked at where the entrance used to be. "Darks can do that?"

"They believe they will eventually succeed in occupying Godspace," she said. "As you just witnessed, though, it will never happen."

A stab of fear raced down his back. "How will I get back?"

"Guardians can reopen portals," she said. "Do not concern yourself." She looked at him, but her expression wasn't pleasant.

He nodded, relieved. "We should get going."

Sage saw the bright red and purple rectangle just where Ronan's memories told him it would be. The journey was breathtaking in its beauty, familiar yet unique. The white orb that served as the sun cast a shade of light that somehow injected the colors with warmth. He would describe it to Nick as computer generated, though it was more than that. The entirety of it radiated peace and comfort. He could understand why Haddock, the ancient Pathfinder, would choose to never leave.

He didn't know how far he'd walked. Several miles at least. Time was different here, so he didn't even attempt to guess. When he came upon the red-and-purple rectangle so soon, it surprised him. The other side of this entrance was in France, several thousand miles from Oklahoma. Leah had tried explaining the concept of "folding dimensions" during their journey, but she'd used words and phrases he'd never heard of, so he dropped the subject. He didn't have to understand it to use it to his advantage.

"Are you ready?" he asked Leah once he was positioned in front of the entrance.

She nodded, her face heavy with concern.

"What?" he asked.

"You are not prepared for this. Your skills are years from being refined enough. You need more gifts to manifest. I strongly advise against this."

"I thought you knew my destiny? That you wouldn't stop me as long as my actions fit within fulfilling that destiny?"

"It is true, but the same actions two or three years from now would also fit." Leah stepped closer. "I cannot stop you, for eventually you must begin this journey. As your Guardian, it is my place to influence the timing of your free will. Now is your time to train. It is not your time for battle."

"What about Dad?" he said. "What about him? What will he be three years from now? Two years? Six months! I'm supposed to stand by and watch him ruin our family? Close schools and businesses, fire people? Kick people out of their homes? I should just stand by and watch him turn into a Dark? Claws, full wings, big black eyes? I've gotta sit across a table and look at that for the next three years? Watch Mom hug and kiss a monster? I want to puke when I look at him! I should just stand by? No! I won't do that!"

He took several breaths to calm himself. He couldn't step through this entrance, into the bell tower of a church, as angry as he was now. He wouldn't turn back. He *had* to discover if he could see the breach points.

Leah didn't respond to his outburst. She waited quietly off to the side, giving him space.

Finally, Sage hitched his backpack higher onto his shoulders and nodded at Leah. "It's time."

He stepped through and felt the heavy drapes in front of him. They smelled of dust and mildew as he pushed them aside. The small room at the bottom of the belfry looked much the same as in Ronan's memory. The heavy wooden door opened easily as he pushed it ajar to peek out. The church was empty. And dark. Really dark. No light seeped through the stained-glass windows from outside. Nighttime in France.

This would make it easier. He'd draw less attention. The centuries-old church was beautifully constructed, from what little he could see.

The street outside was also deserted, and he wondered what time it was. No moon. Heavy clouds. Pitch black. "Any Darks up there?" Sage whispered to Leah.

"A few," she whispered back. "I sent word to your squad of Archs to be waiting for your arrival here. We have you covered."

He'd never been able to see Darks at night, though he did occasionally catch flashes of Archs, who flew much lower.

The city of Cambrai looked centuries old with a few sprinkles of modern convenience. The scarcity of streetlights allowed him to stay in the shadows as he hurried along the same route Ronan and Grandpa had taken almost a hundred years before. He was amazed that so little had changed.

Bourlon Ridge sat north of the city, just a couple of miles away. Sage covered the distance as quickly as he could, ducking behind buildings three times to avoid approaching cars. By the time he reached the ridge, his eyes had fully adjusted to the darkness.

"I see it, Leah," Sage whispered. He walked to the end of the ridge.

A razor-thin line of discoloration seeped from a dark spot underneath a natural overhang in the ridge. Unlike the brilliant, swirling colors of the entrance in Theo's Treasure Room, this one was so faint and narrow, so jagged and discolored, Sage wasn't sure he would have seen it during daylight hours.

"Can you see it?" he asked Leah.

"I cannot." Leah leaned closer. "If angels could see the breaches, we would have revealed their locations to the Council."

He was such an idiot. "Of course, that makes sense." Sage placed his hand in front of it and wondered if a cool breeze would flow from within.

"Warm air," he told Leah. "Stinky." He put his nose near the line and smelled a whiff of rotten eggs. He stepped back and again inspected the breach. It appeared as though someone had sliced the fabric separating the human and spiritual realms with a sharp blade.

"I will caution you one final time," Leah said. "You are ill prepared to enter such a place."

Sage sighed. "We're not having this conversation again." He was nervous enough without Leah piling on. He'd found the breach. He knew he could go back now and report it to Grandpa, but Grandpa had already said what would happen: nothing. The Council didn't have a team to send in. Who knew how long it would be before they did? No. He would explore farther and see where it led. He could always turn back if he needed to.

From the corner of his eye, he saw Leah draw her sword. "Sage, protect yourself!"

Before he could even drop his duffle bag, he saw shadows racing toward them. Darks. By the time Sage dug in his bag and found his sword, Leah had dispatched two of them. Sage jumped to his feet to face the third.

He'd never seen one so close. Not by a mile. He gripped his sword and brought it to a battle position. Nearly seven feet tall, the Dark stood in front of him, its body blacker than the cloudless sky. Rippling muscles, wings stretched full, head sleek, narrow and bald, eyes the size of golf balls, vampire teeth, and a sword ready to kill.

It wasn't attacking. About ten feet separated them, and Sage wondered what was happening. He glanced at Leah, who still had her sword ready but was making no attempt to protect him.

A squad of Archs suddenly appeared around them, six forming a circle, two hovering just above the Dark to block its escape.

The Dark cocked its head as it looked from Sage to Leah and back to Sage. Communicating. *Leah's talking to it.*

"Uh . . . what's going on?" Sage asked, his voice breaking.

"I am allowing a chance for its survival," Leah said. "I have instructed that should it succeed in killing you, I would allow it to leave unharmed."

"What!" Sage took a step back and raised his sword a little higher. "What are you talking about?" His mouth went dry, and he'd barely choked out the last word.

"You are about to face many beasts who will desire to kill you," Leah said. "Let this be the first of many attempts. Prepare. It comes."

The Dark moved so fast Sage hadn't even moved his sword before it went flying out of his hands. He tried scrambling away, but the Dark blocked his path. It grinned, razor teeth showing, and reared its sword back for a killing blow. Sage covered his head and ducked.

Then nothing. No pain. No noise. Just nothing. Sage peeked through his arms and looked around. The Dark was gone. The

Archs too. Just Leah, who'd sheathed her sword and stood quietly, watching him.

"What happened?"

"One of the Archs vanquished it," Leah said. "That was a test. You failed."

An adrenaline dump gave Sage the shakes, and he sat heavily on the ground while it passed. Then he reached over and grabbed his sword and stood on shaky legs. "I can't believe you *did* that."

"It is a hard truth," Leah said, "to be faced with your inadequacies."

Sage sheathed his sword and pointed a finger at Leah. "You told me once that even the most accomplished Fighting Arts swordsman couldn't withstand the speed of a Dark. What did that prove?"

"It proved that your first instinct once disarmed was to cower in fear." She pointed to the breach. "I cannot enter the Dark Realm and survive. If you step into that breach, you will be alone. You are not ready. No one knows what waits on the other side."

He dug into his backpack and pulled out a bottle of water. Between the Dark attack and Leah pumping him full of doubt, he didn't have enough spit to wet his tongue. After taking a drink, he put the bottle back. "What's my destiny say? Will I live long enough to battle one of the Princes?"

She gave him no indication she would answer the question, so he tried another tactic. "How about this. I'll step through, take a look, then step right back out and give you an update. OK with that? At least then you'll know what I see."

Still she said nothing.

"Whatever." Sage stuffed a couple changes of clothes into his backpack and drew his sword. "See you in a second."

He stuck his hand out, turned it sideways, and slid it into the breach. As his arm disappeared, he glanced back at Leah one final time. Her face showed nothing. Undeterred, he stepped from France into another world.

Unlike Godspace, there were no mountains, no forests or streams, no cool air or gentle breezes. The reddish, dreary landscape reminded him of pictures he'd seen of Mars.

Scorched air—pregnant with the smell of sulfur—blew into his face and watered his eyes. Rugged, rocky ground stretched out before him and disappeared over the horizon hundreds of yards in front of him. Overhead, thousands upon thousands of circling Darks blackened a red sky.

He froze at the sight of the Darks. They were high, hundreds of feet up, but they could fly faster than a jet and could reach him in a flash. Would they see him? If so, would they attack?

The blistering wind forced him to turn away. Behind him, the breach point was invisible.

Where'd it go? Frantic, he stuck his hands out and felt all around. Nothing. He retraced his steps, confident that he would reenter the world where Leah waited. The breach was gone.

He felt thumping against his leg and looked down. His sword, quivering in his hand, had sliced a couple of holes in his pants.

Breathe. Just breathe. He looked up and saw a sky churning with what now looked like a million Darks. They were ignoring him right now, but he knew that could change in an instant.

"What have I done?" he whispered under his breath. "Why didn't I listen to Grandpa?"

The deserted landscape seemed to suck the life out of him. David Brock had disappeared through this breach almost a hundred years ago, but then what? Where had they taken him? In the distant sky, straight ahead, the Darks seemed more concentrated. Circling. Like buzzards over a dead animal. Was there something up there? Had something drawn them? Behind him, the Darks weren't as thick.

So forward. He took a few hesitant steps. He was quiet as he watched the sky. He knew if the Darks descended on him, it was over. Nobody would ever find his body.

They didn't seem to notice him. They just flew in circles like bees around their hive. With each step, he became more confident. After ten minutes of walking, sweat now covering every inch of his body, he knew for certain the Darks had seen him but were paying him no mind. Several swooped down and turned his way as they passed, but they didn't attack.

He walked on. Then he saw something. Just over a small hill, steeples rising majestically, directly beneath the mass of circling Darks. Several minutes later, he was there.

A massive stone mansion with six turrets—rugged and imposing, with dozens of windows and a front porch that spanned its entire width—towered in front of him with a ghostly, abandoned look—brooding and angry, as though daring someone to approach. The windows were covered with shades bleached white long ago. Not that this place had ever possessed any comfort or charm, but what little might have existed had been erased by a host of unclean spirits. A single, lonely wind chime—such an odd gesture in the desolate landscape—hung from a corner of the porch, its metal bars tinkling in the sulfur-filled breeze.

Sage looked behind him and saw a landscape found only in nightmares. He struggled to keep from panicking. Then he recalled something Leah told him on his fourteenth birthday: *Prophecy speaks of a great warrior sent to free his people. You are that warrior.*

Words of comfort? Possibly. Maybe the prophecy would only be fulfilled had he waited until he was fully trained to start this mission. Too late to change now.

This was it. Forward. He took a huge breath, walked over to the gate, and stepped through. The house looked haunted, home to of all kinds of imaginary childhood creatures. With every step, his anxiety increased. Total silence enveloped him, a bleak and pressing nothingness that swallowed every sound. There wasn't a single sign of life, just him and this dead house. He climbed onto the front porch. The sulfuric wind picked up and whistled through the eaves of the house, its mournful tune something only a Dark would find comforting. No doorbell. Just a large knocker in the center of the door—the head of a gargoyle with penetrating red eyes that stared at him with such intensity the hair on his arms stood up.

He reached for the knob and turned it, then pushed hard against the heavy door. It opened, creaking in protest. He shoved it all the way open before going inside. He wanted to get a good look at what awaited him.

A chamber the size of two football fields lay before him. At the far end stood one giant column flanked by six smaller ones. *How is that possible?* Still on the porch, Sage walked to the corner of the house and peered around to the back. The stone mansion was big by any human standards, but it certainly wasn't large enough to have a room a hundred and twenty yards wide and a hundred yards deep.

"What's going on here?" he said to himself. Back at the door, Sage looked in again. Still there. Furthermore, on the other side of the seven columns, at least three major hallways ran in different directions.

How was this possible? What kind of illusion was this? Sword in hand, Sage stepped through the door and pushed it closed. The odor of sulfur wasn't as strong inside, but a faint smell of decaying flesh hung heavily in the air. The ceiling, a series of rounded sections stretching fifty feet across, towered almost a hundred feet high. Sage stood spellbound at what he saw. Each circled section had paintings of great winged creatures lording over cowering humans while mighty human warriors armed with angelic gifts fought in vain to save them.

The paintings depicted the Seven Princes of Hell battling Council members! Council members gifted with Fighting Arts, Bell Making, Chains, and Might were all perishing under the wrath of the great beasts. Even a man wielding the purifying light of Persuasion had been impaled through the chest with a lance thrown by one of the Princes.

"None of this is real," Sage whispered to himself. No Council member has ever seen one of the Seven, much less one in battle.

Centuries old, the granite and gray stone chamber walls were dingy and pockmarked. A huge rectangle with windows set high allowed enough light to navigate the large expanse. Red dust had blown in through the front door, and Sage saw dozens of tracks leading toward the seven columns in the back.

He felt small and insignificant as he moved quietly through the chamber. He dried his palms on his jeans so that he wouldn't drop his sword. As he came closer to the columns, he saw what they really were: statues carved from black stone. Giant winged beasts. The one in the center stood seventy-five feet tall, half again larger than the other six it towered over.

Mammon, the name carved into the base of the big beast in the middle, stopped him short. *The Prince of Greed*. The one Theo believed corrupted Hitler and might have Dad in his grips. Mammon's wings were open wide like some glorious heavenly host, his arms spread forth as though about to direct a symphony. His hands resembled King Kong's, with thumbs as long as the rest of his fingers. The black stone glistened with moisture, giving his skin a leathery look, which glowed in the red-tinted light. A huge sword was sheathed on his back between his wings, the hilt positioned directly behind his head. His mocking grin exposed teeth that resembled short, needle-sharp daggers.

Sage took a step back, his sword once again quivering in his hand. The other six beasts—three on each side of Mammon—were much smaller, identical, all canted toward him, eyes closed, hands folded in prayer, and slightly bowed as though worshiping the Prince of Greed. Leah had required Sage to learn their names: Beelzebub— Envy, Sathanus—Wrath, Abaddon—Gluttony, Belphegor—Sloth, Asmodeus—Lust, and Lucifer—Pride.

Whoever erected these statues—Mammon, no doubt—carved the six as though they were weaker and subservient to Mammon, which Sage doubted was true. Regardless, he knew exactly what they were: Rephaim, the evilest of the three races descended from the Watchers. The Council knew that if they could destroy the Seven, the other two evil races would lose focus and be much easier to defeat.

He stepped away from the monuments and inspected the rest of the hall. From the front door, he'd seen only three hallways leading out of the main chamber. From here, he saw a dozen. The passages were straight and seemingly endless. Natural light from high-set windows illuminated the entire area. He saw doorways with heavy wooden doors, barred with sturdy crossbeams, as well as open entryways with no barriers.

The silence unnerved him. Aside from his breathing and footsteps, there wasn't a hint of a noise. He chose a hallway and started walking, quietly, just in case some beast did reside there. At the first open entryway, he peeked around the corner and found an empty room larger than most houses. The dull marble floor had a worn path in the center leading to the far side of the room.

Odd. Then Sage looked closer and saw the same discolored, jagged line he'd seen in France running down the center of the wall.

An entrance to the human realm!

Had Council members been dragged into this building? Or was it simply an entrance the Dark Beasts used that the Council didn't know about? Sage wasn't about to step through to explore the other side. At least not now.

He pressed on. At the next open doorway, he saw another large room and another portal into the human realm; more walking discovered a third and fourth. Then he came to one of the barred wooden doors. Eight feet tall and almost that wide, the door looked ancient and thick, with heavy metal brackets holding a steel bar that would prevent anything from getting out.

Which meant something—or someone—was being held inside.

His heart quickened. A Council member? Or some beast that would kill him the moment he opened the door? There were several similar doors in this corridor, probably dozens more in the other hallways.

Logic said this building was where David Brock had been taken. They'd keep him inside some kind of secure room until they killed him. Sage knew he had to check. He sheathed his sword, dropped his backpack on the floor, lifted the heavy bar on one end, and pushed until he could slide it through one of the brackets. It fell to the floor and crashed loudly enough to wake a corpse.

The door had three sliding bolts, which he opened, and a handle, which he pulled. The hinges groaned and squealed, but the door opened. He stepped back and drew his sword, careful to position himself for defense if he needed to.

A quick peek around the doorframe told him instantly he wasn't in any danger. The room was some kind of laboratory. Old. With equipment not used for hundreds of years. He didn't know the names of most of the stuff, but it was either rusted or rotten or broken apart. Bottles lined shelves on the far side of the room, and crude surgical instruments sat haphazardly on a table next to them.

In the center of the room was the body of a man strapped to a wooden table like some Frankenstein's monster.

11

The body—long dead—was encased in some sort of reptile skin, which had rotted and fallen apart and lay half on the floor. Sage did a double take at the reptile skin—diamond-shaped scales with small, barbed hooks; just like the scales from the picture of Leviathan in the *Encyclopedia of Dark Creatures*. Interesting.

Sage walked over and stopped near the man's head. He'd never seen a dead person before, and it took him several moments to compose himself. It helped that this body had mummified decades ago, or so it seemed, yet it took Sage only a second to recognize him from the book of missing Council members.

Gun Yao, a Chinese warrior gifted with Fighting Arts, disappeared from the slopes of Mount Song, just south of the Yellow River, more than five hundred years ago. One witness described Gun's disappearance as a dark cloud exploding from the side of the mountain and swallowing him up. Sage touched his mummified face and wondered how many others he'd find like this.

The lizard skin broke apart and fell to the floor in a pile of dust when Sage tried removing it from Gun's body. He looked around the room and didn't see anything that would reveal who'd done this, and so he left, determined to open more of the barred rooms.

The next room was a little easier to open, and he was careful not to let the steel bar collapse to the floor. While he didn't think anyone else was in the building, there was no reason to be so noisy.

He found Katerina Johnston next, a Swede gifted with Projection, which was the ability to project overwhelming emotions—both good and bad—into the surrounding environment. She'd gone missing in the late 1700s during a Council operation against a pack of chimeras in the slums of Istanbul. The monstrous fire-breathing creatures, composed of a lion, a snake, and a goat, had lured the Council team into a large, abandoned building. Katerina went into a room by herself and was never seen again.

The lizard skin encasing Katerina wasn't as rotten as Gun's, but he nearly pricked his finger on one of the small barbs when he tugged on it and pulled it apart. Katerina's mummified face was frozen in agony. Were they *all* dead? Had his goal of building a team to help save his father been a pipe dream from the very start? Had he risked everything for nothing?

He left the room, determined to unlock every other. He had counted thirty more, and if he could just find *one live person* to help him, he might have a chance to survive. If that one was Elsbeth Brown—gifted with Teleportation and Persuasion, missing for only a month—he'd have a real chance not only to live but to help his dad.

Back in the main hallway, Sage heard noises ahead. Voices were coming from one of the many large, open rooms, speaking a language he didn't understand. The gruff sounds were faint but getting louder. He saw the two crossbeams lying on the floor.

Some of the kidnappers? Had they returned to check on their captives? What if they saw the crossbeams? Would they search the building until they found him? Would he be locked away forever?

He couldn't take that chance. He raced back to Katerina's room and quietly lifted the beam back into place. It was so heavy he was barely able to lift it. With the voices even louder, now mixed with the clicking of their footsteps, Sage knew he only had seconds to spare. He wrestled the beam back onto Gun's door, then dashed around the corner into the nearest open room, the one with the worn path that disappeared into the breach.

He held his breath as what sounded like two men turned into the hallway Sage had just vacated. Whatever language they were speaking sounded rough and guttural, with one of the men doing most of the talking. Sage slid away from the doorway as he pulled his sword and waited.

They passed Sage's room. When their voices faded enough for Sage to feel safe enough to look, he peeked around the corner just in time to watch the two shadows turn the corner into the main hall where Mammon's statue lorded over everything.

Sage crept forward and followed them. When he got to the main room, he heard the voices down another of the dozen corridors. It took him a couple of guesses, but he found the correct passage just as the shadows turned into one of several open doorways.

He sprinted as quietly as he could and stopped at the entrance to the room just as the voices disappeared.

He waited, controlled his breathing, then quick-peeked around edge. Empty. Just another room with a worn path that led to a breach in the wall.

What's going on? Then he thought about Godspace, how the Council used it to continent jump. Was that what this place was? Some kind of intersecting crossroads that allowed Dark beasts to move around the earth instantly? This entire building was in the Dark realm—and regular humans wouldn't survive in here for long.

Council members weren't the only beings walking around with angelic blood. The evil races had it too, which meant they could survive here for as long as Haddock, the old Pathfinder, had survived in Godspace.

Sage took a deep breath and thought about the tactical advantages the Council would have if he could somehow survive long enough to show them this place. But that was for later. For now, he needed to open more of the barred doors.

Just ahead. Three more. The bar on the first was wood—solid and black and heavy. He lifted it off and slid it quietly to the floor. It took him almost a minute to pry the door open. He found nearly the same set-up as the other two, except the laboratory equipment was even more ancient—medieval.

Another body lay on a stone pallet: Norris Vickery—gifted with Animation, the ability to bring certain inanimate objects to life for brief periods of time in order to battle the Dark beasts. He had gone missing in Budapest, Hungary, in the middle 1500s, snatched while on a walk after a late dinner.

The next room was no different. A dead man, gifted with Pathfinding, missing from Spain in the thirteenth century. The one after that, a Russian from the seventeenth century—gifted with Echolocation: the ability to determine the location of Dark beasts by use of reflected sound waves. A type of built-in sonar that was specifically tuned to Dark beasts.

Five found. Five dead. Sage replaced the crossbar. There weren't any other barred rooms in this hallway, but at the far end he noticed a set of double doors tall enough to drive a 747 through.

"What is that?" he whispered to himself. When he got there, he stared up at the doors, amazed at their size. Steel columns, at least a hundred feet tall, each one twenty yards wide, met in the middle and were barred by a steel crossbeam as big as a telephone pole.

No way I'm getting in there. The crossbeam probably weighed a thousand pounds. Or more. It didn't look as if it had been opened in a long time. The doors were gray and solid and cold, huge slabs of steel that appeared strong enough to stop a missile. Whatever was behind there must be pretty valuable to somebody.

Time to move on. Sage headed back to the main chamber. Just as he got there, a hair-raising scream pierced the silence. He stopped, not sure where it came from. Then it sounded again, even more terrifying than before.

A female voice. Young. *Elsbeth?*

Sage sprinted behind the seven statues and hit a hallway on the far side of the chamber. The screams guided him. Like the others, this corridor was straight, wide, and seemingly never-ending. He held his sword as he ran and made as little noise as possible.

There! On the right. Way up ahead. One of the heavy wooden doors stood open, the steel crossbar propped against the wall. Then a wail burst from the room that was so horrifying and full of pain that it caused Sage to skid to a stop.

Slipping his backpack off, Sage steeled himself, got his breathing under control, and peeked around the corner. A beast with two heads and four arms, red fur covering every inch of exposed skin and wearing a white doctor's smock, stood leaning over a body strapped to a modern hospital gurney. The girl's head was blocked from the beast, but it was a female for sure. Jeans, pink running shoes, feminine hands, and a bracelet.

At the foot of the gurney, draped over a large metal crate, was one of the lizard skins he'd seen enveloping the other Council members. Except this one wasn't a dried, rotted husk. It shimmered and pulsed and had a tail slithering around on the floor as though searching for someone to grab.

The screaming had stopped, and the girl's body wasn't moving at all.

"That's better, little one," the monster said. "Silence is truly golden."

The beast wasn't tall or wide, no more than a head taller than Sage, but its two necks looked as if they belonged on geese. "You have been brave these past weeks," it said. "As a reward, your pain ends today."

The laboratory was as modern as anything in Sage's world. Several pieces of equipment and computers hummed and beeped. There were shelves full of chemicals and surgical instruments and stacks of sterile bandages and dressings. On the left wall was a refrigerator with hundreds of vials of blood.

They want her blood. They are harvesting her blood!

This was an Emim creature—some hybrid abomination trained to experiment on Council members in an attempt to somehow duplicate their gifts. Persuasion and Teleportation, in Elsbeth's case. The Emim race was what created every mixed creature throughout history: chimera, minotaur, cerberus, gorgon, satyr, hydra, and so many others listed in the *Encyclopedia of Dark Creatures*. Experimentation was their history—their passion and life's work.

Sage didn't know what kind of mutant this was, but at the moment, its back was to him, and it held no weapon other than scalpels in two of its hands. Double-checking to ensure no other beast was in the room, Sage cocked his sword and got ready to charge.

His hands quivered, and he couldn't still them, as he realized that everything Leah had taught him came down to this moment. She preached that he would one day battle Dark beasts, told him hundreds of stories of the centuries-long battles, insisted that he train and perfect his skills. Now the moment had arrived, and he knew that what she said less than an hour before was correct: he was ill prepared.

It couldn't matter now. It was time. He was decent with a sword. Not compared to a Dark, but this slightly built, mostly unarmed, two-headed geek was hardly that. Sage was gifted with Fighting Arts—near superhuman speed combined with seeing his opponent's moves in slow motion. He'd never come close to besting Leah, but even Ronan had commented about his advanced skills, considering his age. Yes. It was time. This beast was about to kill Elsbeth.

Sage stepped around the doorframe and charged, careful to make as little noise as possible. He stumbled just as he was within striking distance, and the beast swiveled one of its heads to check on the noise. Sage didn't wait. He struck fast and hard, like Leah taught him, and severed the first arm that reached out to grab him.

The beast screamed in pain as Sage stepped back and dodged a blow from one of the arms holding a scalpel. Sage struck again, low, and sliced the side of its right leg. He moved again just as the beast turned fully around and jumped to the side. Sage kept his feet planted and swung high. The blow struck one of the necks and severed it. The tumbling head landed on Elsbeth's lap.

Sage pulled his sword away and took three steps back, missing the blood now spraying the entire room. The beast wasn't finished. It staggered toward the door and wielded the two scalpels like a thug in a street fight. Sage couldn't let it escape. He ran forward and jammed his sword into the middle of its back. The blow drove it sideways into the refrigerator. The tip of his sword cracked the glass door.

The beast slid to the floor, arms flailing, and then it was over. It stopped moving; the eyes on its remaining head stared at Sage. A look of confusion froze on its face.

The adrenaline dump came hard and fast. As soon as the beast took its last breath, Sage began shaking all over. He found a clean spot on the floor and dropped his sword. He locked his hands under his armpits and closed his eyes as he fought to control his breathing.

Leah had told him this would happen. She'd told him several times, but like most of everything else she'd said these past three years, he'd rolled his eyes and mocked her.

He composed himself, finally, and only then did he notice Elsbeth's labored breathing. He jumped up, cringed at the sight of the decapitated head on her lap, and pushed it to the floor on the other side of the gurney.

It *was* Elsbeth Brown. For sure. Brown hair, a sprinkling of freckles, chiseled cheeks. She looked dead. Pale, eye sockets dark and sunken, her breathing so shallow and raspy he wondered how any oxygen made it to her lungs at all.

An IV in one of her arms was attached to a bag of clear liquid. He had no idea what it was or if he should remove it. Was the liquid keeping her alive or killing her?

He didn't know what to do. Could he carry her through this place, across the scorched landscape in full view of thousands of Darks, into France and a hospital? Assuming he could even *find* the breach point? Would she die in his arms while he searched? Was he even strong enough to carry her that far? He'd have the gift of Might someday, but he didn't have it now, and Elsbeth looked too heavy to carry almost a mile.

Council members had incredible healing powers and lived for centuries. He'd known that his entire life. He'd never been sick; his bumps and bruises now healed within minutes. He'd broken a finger last year that healed overnight while he slept, something he'd kept from his parents. When he was much younger, Leah told him amazing stories about the longevity of Council members. So would Elsbeth heal on her own if he just left her alone? She'd been missing for a month. By the amount of blood stored in vials in the fridge, he was surprised she wasn't dead already. What had they done to her? Had the two-headed freak pushed her to the very edge of death?

If he tried carrying her out and she died, he'd never forgive himself. If he just stood around and watched her die, same thing. If he pulled out the IV, and it was the only thing keeping her alive, he'd be killing her himself.

A thought struck him. His backpack! He ran to the door and retrieved it from the hallway. Then he carried the crossbeam into the room and closed the door. He didn't need some wandering creature noticing his presence.

He dug out the little book about the history of the Council and found the section about Memory Sharing when used in conjunction with Teleportation. Some speculated that when the "boy of prophecy"—that meant him—combined Memory Share with Teleportation, he'd be able to travel back in time.

Sage looked at Elsbeth, so close to death, and knew the only way to save her was to go back and prevent her capture. The only problem was that he couldn't Teleport.

But Elsbeth could, and she'd learned it somewhere. A Council member had taught her, and so it would be a bright memory Sage should be able to locate.

Decision made, Sage stepped behind the gurney and placed his fingers in the correct Memory Sharing position. Within seconds of clearing his mind, the images began pushing through the smoky, swirling world that filled his vision. There weren't nearly as many memories as with Ronan because Elsbeth was so young. When a memory as bright as a midday sun sucked him into its center, Sage knew it was a mistake. A big mistake! This wasn't the memory he needed, but he couldn't seem to break the connection.

Through Elsbeth's eyes, Sage saw an old Ford station wagon from the back seat as she and her dad headed toward a warehouse district north of New Orleans. He listened as Elsbeth talked non-stop about the history of the Elioudian race, the original Council—the two hundred sent to the surface from Tartarus—and about Seth, the old blind prophet whose visions predicted the future of his people. She went on and on about the Rephaim and their efforts to rule the human race.

Her voice sounded almost musical, and Sage loved listening to it. The immediate connection he felt with her was shocking in its intensity, something he hadn't experienced with Ronan. Something about that worried him, but he didn't have time to dwell on it.

"Dad," Elsbeth said after taking a pause, "can you tell me more about your operation?"

Sage instinctively knew they were headed somewhere near the French Quarter and that the trip would take a while. He felt her nervousness, her dry mouth, the slight quiver in her hands. A strand of her hair tickled the side of his face until Elsbeth brushed it away. A flash of remembrance about another of her father's operations swelled her with momentary pride as she recalled the crucial role she played.

Sage was totally and fully within her mind. He was living her moment now as she had lived it then.

Memories are filled with unspoken knowledge, he realized then. *Memories are linked to things Elsbeth had previously experienced, and all of it is transferring to me.*

"I've infiltrated a group who think they can transform humans into Rephaim through blood transfusions," her dad said. "They've been trying for a hundred years, but some new technology might now make it possible. I don't understand the science of it, but a French sorcerer named Petri is bringing in a direct descendant of Rameel, one of the Watchers."

"Where do they get humans to experiment on?" Elsbeth asked.

"The homeless," Calvin said.

The car slowed, and they entered an industrial area. He saw lights from the French Quarter in the distance. Calvin pulled the car into the shadows near a group of long-abandoned dumpsters and cut the engine. A deserted warehouse loomed over them. "We're here."

Calvin got out and went to the back of the station wagon to get his nursing scrubs. Elsbeth's earlier dread deepened.

"Remember, Elsbeth," Calvin said. "You're my prisoner. I told Petri I'd have a young girl to throw into the mix."

The plan was for Calvin to march a gagged Elsbeth past the guards and into the lab.

Elsbeth rubbed dirt over some areas of her exposed skin until Calvin told her she looked enough like a street person to be believable. He loosely tied her hands in front of her. The gag wasn't much tighter.

"OK, get in the car," Calvin said.

Elsbeth got in the back seat and leaned against the door. The car trip lasted less than a minute. Calvin spoke quickly about the layout and the plan. "Once we're in, on my signal, lose your restraints and get into action. I'll lock the door behind us after we're inside. They're solid and should slow the guards' response."

They stopped in front of a dilapidated building the size of an airplane hangar. Weeds, old newspapers, and rusted assembly-line equipment littered the parking lot. Except for several new cars parked near the door, there wasn't a person on the planet who would suspect that a modern laboratory was operating inside.

Two huge men stood at a single steel door. Calvin whispered, "Show time," just as he shut the engine off. He got out and went around to open Elsbeth's door. He yanked her out and half dragged her toward the hulking guards. They stiffened, then recognized Calvin and relaxed.

"I am very late," Calvin said. He stopped in front of them.

They nodded, unlocked the door, and let them pass.

Sage knew they were close because Elsbeth's memory was brighter and clearer than ever. He again tried to disconnect with her, but her growing terror kept him locked within her mind.

12

Elsbeth followed her father into a vast emptiness—a muggy, smelly echo chamber that magnified their footsteps tenfold. Sage rode her memory and felt her fear. Her emotions bled into his own and mixed them to the point he couldn't distinguish them. It was a strange sensation to know that when he eventually broke this Memory Share connection, a part of her would reside within him.

Sage couldn't tell what kind of factory this used to be, but the only thing that had been left behind was a gross mixture of oil and rotting fish. The odors were staggering.

"Keep your eyes pointed to the floor," Calvin said quietly as he led her to the back. "And you need to look more terrified."

Elsbeth nodded and belted a strangled cry. Her father dragged her along roughly enough to sell the performance.

"I've heard Rupert is a shock to look at," he whispered. "So we need to keep our composure."

"OK," she whispered back.

At the very back of the building, Calvin headed toward a set of double doors with two more men standing guard. He strode over with the confidence of someone important, stopped in front of them, and waited to be let in. Sage heard voices on the other side of the doors but couldn't tell how many.

One of the guards started to open the door when Calvin stepped forward, put a hand on his shoulder, and leaned in closer. "Gerald," he said softly. "It could get loud in here tonight. Rupert has a habit of shouting when speaking softly would work just fine. You know how excitable Petri gets. We cannot be disturbed. Tonight will change everything for us. Do not be concerned if you hear a commotion. Do you understand? Do not open this door."

Gerald nodded.

As soon as the door opened, Sage heard several voices at once—crying, moaning, pleas to be released, demands for someone to call the police. He also heard the quiet humming of a lot of high-tech equipment.

Calvin stepped through the door, turning sideways so he could drag Elsbeth through. He locked the door behind them.

"Sorry I am late, gentlemen," Calvin boomed.

Although Elsbeth still had her eyes downcast, she sneaked a look at her surroundings. They'd entered a big room—ballroom size—with at least thirty hospital beds lining the walls around the entire perimeter. Each bed had medical equipment beside it: IV stands, draped rolling carts holding small surgical supplies, scalpels, needles, and some things Sage didn't recognize. Strapped to each bed was a human adult, most fighting to get loose—shouting and complaining and threatening. The thirty prisoners had heavy leather straps securing their feet, legs, waists, and chests. Each had one arm hooked to an IV. All the IVs ran to a blood-processing machine in the center of the room. Several banks of computers lined a far wall, machines swirling tubes of blood surrounded the big machine in the middle. Sage didn't know anything about medical stuff, but it looked as if they'd invested hundreds of thousands of dollars in equipment.

Every head turned toward Calvin after he spoke, and most now stared at Elsbeth standing next to him.

"As I promised, Petri," Calvin said. "We need more females."

Four huge men, standing shoulder to shoulder, were on the other side of the blood-processing machine. Elsbeth tried to see around them because they were blocking an even larger man in a throne-sized chair.

Elsbeth stepped slightly to the left, then flinched when she caught a glimpse of the man in the chair: the most gruesome semi-human that had ever walked on two legs.

Sage had closely studied every beast in the *Encyclopedia of Dark Creatures,* and he hadn't seen *anything* that looked remotely like this. Rupert, a direct descendant of Rameel, one of the original Watchers, was about as creepy as they came.

Nearly seven feet tall, he had huge shoulders and arms and jet-black hair to the middle of his back. One of his eyes was situated on the right side of his forehead, the other in the middle of his left cheek. His eyes were the same round, black, silver-dollar-sized orbs as those on Darks. Rupert's nose—a bulbous mass of mottled skin—sat off-center above his mouth and was the color of a deep bruise, with nostrils pointing straight out like a pig's. Slimy mucous seeped onto the area above his lips and either ran into his mouth or dripped onto his chin. His mouth was as wide as his face, and his lips as thick as small snakes. As large and bumpy as his lips were, they couldn't quite cover his wolf-like teeth, because they protruded at a forty-five degree angle.

This is a Rephaim offspring? This is the human shape he chose to disguise himself in? Or had he somehow gotten stuck in the middle of the Transformation process?

Before coming in, Calvin told Elsbeth not to stare at Rupert. Really? How could she not?

A small, frail, elderly man dressed in surgeon scrubs bent over Rupert, trying to affix a large needle into one of Rupert's arms.

Calvin stepped forward. "I see you're about ready to begin, Petri. I'm glad I'm not late for this glorious event. What can I do to help?"

The old man turned and looked at Calvin, then waved an arm around the room. "Prepare the girl. Then check all the men's connections and open the IVs so that the sedatives can begin their work. We need all of them fully unconscious. I will be finished here shortly."

So this was Petri, the French sorcerer Calvin mentioned, the scientist who had to be stopped tonight. Rupert watched Calvin closely as he approached the center of the room, Elsbeth's arm still tightly in his grip.

"I am Rupert," the beast said to Calvin with a voice that sounded as distorted as his looks. "I have heard much about you and your work against the Council."

Sage noticed that Petri's old fingers could barely function. He couldn't get the IV needle inserted into Rupert's arm. He was either scared out of his mind or too old to do the job.

"Your reputation is also well known," Calvin said. His voice filled with a measure of respect Sage could never have pulled off. "Your blood is royalty. We are honored by your sacrifice." Calvin avoided eye contact with Rupert when he bowed slightly.

"I thank you for the respect you show me," Rupert said. "I sacrifice for us all. I believe our royal blood is the key to executing the master plan of the Seven. Our blood is pure and powerful and without equal. If we are successful tonight, many of my royal brothers will join me in this effort."

Whoa! There are more people that look like him? He's royalty?

Sage wished Nick could see this guy. He would completely freak out.

"After many years of preparation," Calvin said, "tonight will be noted in history." He bowed again, turned toward Elsbeth, and nodded slightly.

Petri still couldn't get the needle to work, and Rupert finally noticed. "What is wrong?" he snapped.

"I am sorry, sir," Petri said. "Your Excellency. Something is wrong with this needle. I will get another."

Rupert turned his attention toward Calvin. "What is your bloodline?"

Calvin began to speak.

"Wait," Rupert said. "Do not tell me. I must see you in your natural form. Then I will know your bloodline."

Calvin stood at his full height.

Sage knew that Calvin's gift was Transformation, which was the ability to change into a spitting image of one of the seven lines of the Rephaim race. The gift was what allowed them to infiltrate Rephaim offspring groups such as this one.

"Go on, then," Rupert said. "I can spot the offspring of each of the Seven."

Calvin bowed his head and held his arms out to the side. The Transformation started in his hands and quickly spread throughout the rest of his body. Sleek head, claws, black skin shining like a wet stone, muscular frame, long arms, teeth like an Irish Wolfhound. A miniature Dark. No wings, but everything else looked the same. Of course, all Darks looked the same to Sage.

"Observe my lineage, sir," Calvin said, his voice booming through the room.

"Ah, the Beelzebub line," Rupert said.

The men in the beds exploded in panic and fought against their restraints. Sage saw a couple of them actually faint.

"Quiet!" Rupert boomed. He rose from his chair slowly, his seven-foot frame nearly reaching the ceiling. "I said quiet!"

The panicked prisoners fell silent, their faces rigid with fear. Rupert stepped away from his chair and pointed a meaty finger at Calvin. "You are of the Council. You are a spy. Your daughter Elsbeth is soon to be Mammon's greatest conquest."

Before Calvin or Elsbeth could react, a great ripping sound came from their left. Elsbeth looked that way. Her memory became so bright and powerful that Sage wished he could somehow shield his eyes.

The air before them opened up, sliced by a stark-white blade that glowed red along the edges. As the breach widened, Sage saw the scorched landscape beyond and the thousands of Darks hovering above the distant stone mansion. A beast wielded the blade: skeletal, six arms with giant pincers, at least a hundred snakelike tentacles bursting from its skull, and thick, hairy legs with cloven feet, carrying the lizard skin Sage had seen near Elsbeth's gurney.

"Elsbeth, move!" Calvin shouted.

Sage's heart quickened, prisoner to Elsbeth's memory, unable to intervene at all.

Elsbeth Teleported to the far side of the room just as the beast stepped fully through the breach.

Calvin, still fully Transformed, threw his white coat to the side and pulled a short sword from a hidden sleeve in his pants. "Persuasion, Elsbeth," he shouted. "Hurry!"

"Kill the traitor," Rupert shouted. He turned toward Elsbeth and slowly transformed out of what little human form he had. His eyes and nose moved back to where they should have been as his body morphed into a near replica of the thousands of Darks Sage had seen growing up. A near replica. Not exact.

All four of Rupert's guards then transformed into their Rephaim state—growing nearly as large as Rupert and looking just like him. Clearly, all from the same bloodline. Their Rephaim skin was nothing like human skin. It was black and thick and as tough as an elephant's hide. They would be formidable opponents.

"You will not survive this day!" Elsbeth said. She raised her right hand toward heaven—palm up—and aimed her left palm at the chest of the closest beast. "From the power of heaven to the depths of your blackened heart, come with me into the light!"

It froze the entire room.

A brilliant ray of light blasted down through the ceiling, into her upraised hand, through her body, and out of the palm she had aimed at the guard's chest. The explosion of light against the beast killed him instantly. One second he was there, the next he was a puff of black dust that mushroomed straight into the air like a miniature atom bomb.

"The Persuader is mine!" the six-armed monster boomed. The lizard skin had a long tail that had curled around one of the creature's pincers. The beast grabbed it and began swirling the entire thing like a rodeo cowboy twirling a lasso.

Calvin attacked a Rephaim guard that lunged toward Elsbeth.

Sage couldn't see what happened next, because Elsbeth's attention was focused on the lizard-skin wielding monster. She aimed her palm just as the beast released the skin.

She ducked, but the skin slammed against her right side and immediately engulfed her. The pain—like a thousand red-hot knives—knocked Sage back.

Out of the memory.

He screamed as he fell backward onto the floor of the laboratory. Sweat ran in rivulets down his face. A bright light on the far side of the laboratory flashed, and he saw a round portal fading from view.

"What was that?" It was gone now, but he'd seen the laboratory in New Orleans before the image faded. He'd seen Elsbeth's dad engaged in battle with one of Rupert's guards. Was that possible?

He closed his eyes and rubbed his face, took several deep breaths to calm himself. What had he just seen?

Elsbeth gasped above him and then resumed her ragged, shallow breathing. Sage climbed to his feet. Despite the horrible memory he'd just experienced, nothing had changed. He needed to find the memory of when Elsbeth learned to Teleport so he could teach himself and Teleport into the past to prevent her capture. It was either that or watch her die.

Although he didn't understand how he'd seen the portal into the laboratory across the room, he didn't have time to worry about that now. He positioned himself next to Elsbeth's head and carefully placed his hands on her face. The powerful memory of her capture had sucked him in before, and he wasn't sure how he could prevent it from happening again.

The Memory Share connection was even faster than before. Again, her most prevalent memory tried pulling him in, but he turned fully away from it and allowed random images to float into his vision. Birthdays, quiet times with her father, a visit to the Tomb of Ancient Documents, playtime with a couple of neighborhood kids. In other images, she studied ancient books about Council history, took tests at school—but nothing about learning to Teleport.

He searched and pushed memories aside while constantly being drawn to her capture, which seemed to have its own gravitational force.

Then he remembered the hairlike strands linking memories together. He'd used that while in Ronan's memories to find the location of David Brock's disappearance.

Elsbeth Teleported just before being captured. Maybe a strand existed to the other times she'd Teleported.

Sage spread his hands out and slowly turned back to Elsbeth's supernova memory. He fought against being pulled in again and ran his hands carefully down the edges of its borders. He found a strand near the top and clenched a fist around it. He tugged it gently until an image slowly emerged from the swirling smoke.

It was of a younger Elsbeth Teleporting in front of her father, proud of how proficient she'd become. It was a peaceful time, full of warmth and happiness. Her father's smiles and encouragement, then hugs and kisses, filled her with joy and pride for her accomplishment.

A strand from there led to her practicing in her room while she recited instructions given to her by . . . Agatha-the-Old.

Sage grabbed another strand and found what he was looking for. He pulled himself into the memory, confident it was the image he needed.

They were in a one-room cabin—remote—ancient. Stone fireplace, animal pelts covering every inch of the inside walls. Sturdy wooden furniture sat on the rough floor. The smell of grease hung heavily in the air. Thick dust coated the glass of a single window.

Through Elsbeth's eyes, Sage saw Agatha-the-Old before him, leaning heavily on a cane made from a tree branch. Back bent with age, hands curled with arthritis, Agatha wore hand-sewn clothes straight from the Middle Ages. Her eyes were magnified by thick glasses and intense with focus.

"Close your eyes, dear," Agatha said, her voice creaky but strong. "Clear your mind. Imagine yourself standing on the shore of a raging river, your father near death on the opposite shore. The river is wide. Treacherous. Impassible. Can you see it?"

"I see it," Elsbeth said, her voice quiet and shaky.

Sage saw her imagination, the river, her father lying wounded on the other side.

"There is a sword at your feet," Agatha said. "Sharp, but light. You bend to pick it up. It is life, that sword, your father's life. For across the river, a beast comes. He stalks the shadows toward the smell of your father's blood. Can you see it, Elsbeth? Can you hear your father's faint cries for help? Only *you* can save him. The raging river blocks you. How can you cross?"

Sage saw the scene within Elsbeth's imagination. He felt both her desperation to save her father and her fear of failure.

"Teleportation begins with a desperate need," Agatha said. "A need that transcends the boundaries of your abilities. Your father will die, Elsbeth, unless you can cross that river. Describe the beast to me. What do you see?"

From the murky shadows, Elsbeth's imagination created a horrific monster. "It's part wolf. But still a man. Huge claws. Wings. Jaws like an alligator."

"Cross the river, Elsbeth. Save him. He struggles to escape, but his wounds are too severe. Help him. You're his only chance." Agatha's voice penetrated, and Elsbeth could envision herself over there as she fought to slay the monster and save her father. Her lower back tingled, then her elbows and the tips of her toes.

"You are floating," Agatha said. "You are moving without touching the ground, not occupying the space between where you began and where you will end. Distance means nothing. The time it takes to go from place to place doesn't exist. Release yourself. Your mind controls your destination."

Elsbeth felt more tingling, like an electric current buzzing the center of her bones. Agatha's words seeped into her imagination. She saw herself floating.

"You must center your mind's eye," Agatha said softly. "Your location is determined by your desire. Your ability to move through space is restricted only by the limits of your imagination."

She drilled her focus on appearing next to her father, sword in hand, crouched and ready for battle. Her entire back tingled now. The mental image was as clear as a summer day. She reached out for it, felt her hands gripping the sword, heard the whimpering cries of her father, and smelled the mangy stench of the approaching beast. The tingling in her bones grew stronger, vibrated outward, tickled her muscles, and then exploded to the surface of her skin.

Then she was there, outside, cool wind blowing through her hair, the sound of a raging river loud in her ears. She opened her eyes. She was outside the cabin. She had crossed the river and was running beside it.

"I did it," Elsbeth shouted. "Agatha, I did it!"

The front door of the cabin opened, and Agatha hobbled out, a wide smile on her face. She nodded and waved for Elsbeth to come back inside.

Elsbeth ran to a wooden bridge spanning the river, crossed over, and gave Agatha a huge hug.

"You did well, Elsbeth. Great need drives Teleportation. The first time is always the most difficult. Now that the gift has manifested, it will become more responsive each time. You must train heavily before using it in battle."

Sage decided to disconnect from Elsbeth when he saw nothing else from the memory that would help him. Before he moved his fingers from her face, he again noticed the portal leading to the laboratory in New Orleans.

So I didn't imagine it the first time. Calvin Brown, Rupert, Petri, the huge guards—all there. The portal—six feet tall and three feet wide—shimmered. Could somebody walk through there? Straight into the past?

Sage removed his hands and watched the images fade seconds later. The rest of the laboratory was still quiet, as was the hallway outside. He stepped away from the gurney and around the dead body of the two-headed scientist and pulsing lizard skin.

So "great need" drove Teleportation? OK. He had a truckload of great need. The greatest was saving Elsbeth, who was dying right in front of him.

13

Sage used a mixture of imagery to learn Teleportation. Allowing Agatha-the-Old's words to guide him, he pictured his dad standing on the edge of a cliff, fully transformed into the monster he was becoming. Mammon hovered over Dad, his powerful claws manipulating strings running to Dad's brain—a puppet master and his toy. Sage stood at the bottom, looking up—no way to get there without Teleporting.

Over and over, Sage changed the scene. He replaced Dad with Grandpa, then with Nick, each time using the image of the Mammon carved in the statue in the great hall. He didn't know how long it took him to feel the tingling in his bones. Hours, it seemed, though he knew it wasn't that long.

It wasn't until he used the real image right in front of him— Elsbeth gasping for breath as she slowly died—that the need became great enough for Teleportation to fully manifest. His first trip took him from one side of the gurney to the other. Three feet.

He pumped his fists in victory when it happened. It took three tries to do it again, but that time, he went all the way across the room. Then he went from inside the laboratory to outside, but just to the other side of the door.

From there, he went to the statue room, then into the room with the Gun Yao, the dead Council member. At last, he Teleported back to Elsbeth.

Ready. Making sure his sword was tightly secured on his belt, Sage downed a bottle of water from his backpack and again placed his hands against Elsbeth's face. Her skin felt cold, her pulse faint. Her breathing came in spurts now, weak gasps barely strong enough to pull air into her lungs.

Frantic he was about to lose her, he entered the smoky, swirling universe of memories and found just one—her capture, before so bright, now fading into nothingness. All of her other memories had burned away, lost to a mind close to death.

Sage plunged into her memory and held it tightly while the buzzing in his bones exploded outward. Elsbeth screamed when Sage suddenly appeared next to her in the back seat of the Ford station wagon. "Who are *you?*"

Calvin looked back and swerved the car hard to the right, just before it bounced up into the parking lot of a dark grocery store.

Sage held up both hands. "I'm Sage. Sage Alexander."

The car skidded to a stop at the same time that Calvin threw an arm over the seat and stuck the tip of a knife against the front of Sage's throat.

"Who are you and where did you come from?" Calvin's eyes, dark and full of fury, narrowed as he waited for Sage to answer.

Sage leaned as far back against the seat as he could, the point of the knife holding him there. "You're walking into a trap," he said. "Rupert knows both of you are Council members. Elsbeth will be captured, become the thirty-second missing member who disappeared without a trace. You will be killed, Mr. Brown. Rupert will disappear. And Petri."

Elsbeth gasped. Calvin stared at him, but Sage saw something working behind his eyes.

"I'm Sage Alexander. The boy the ancient Elioudian Seth prophesized about. Both of you know about me. I found the place the missing Council members were taken. I found Elsbeth. I Memory Shared with her and Teleported into this memory."

Elsbeth reached over and pushed Calvin's knife away from Sage's neck. "I'm about to be captured?"

"Not now," Sage said. "Because we can stop it." He wiped his sweaty hands on his pant legs. "I need your help. Both of you."

Calvin pulled out a cell phone. "I'll call Council headquarters for help."

"There's not time," Sage said. His panic rose, now unsure if he could convince Calvin to go along with what he had in mind. "My grandpa, Steven Alexander, a Pathfinder, has searched all thirty-two breach points where Council members have disappeared. Every Pathfinder in Council history has also. Nobody knows how they made the breach points, what kind of beast took them, how they were overpowered. But I do now. In just a few minutes, it will happen to you. We can stop it, but we have to hurry."

Sage spent the next few minutes telling them about everything he'd seen in Elsbeth's memory. Then he told them his idea.

It wasn't a complicated plan, but it was dangerous, and all of them knew it.

He tried not to stare at Elsbeth as he spoke, but it was hard. She was even more beautiful in person than in the photo he'd memorized. She gave him her full attention, holding eye contact, smiling, blushing at times. He wondered what she thought of him and knew such thoughts were distracting him. Regardless, he made his plea for their help, and much to his relief, they agreed.

Calvin escorted two bound prisoners into the warehouse instead of just one, Sage having left his sword in the car. The guards at the door paid Calvin little attention as Sage and Elsbeth both struggled enough to make the performance believable.

Calvin locked the door as he'd done before, and Rupert went through his I-Am-More-More-Important-Then-Anyone-Here routine. Sage and Elsbeth, both bound loosely behind their backs, readied for the moment when Calvin Transformed.

When the ripping sound started, Sage saw Elsbeth slip her hands out of their bindings. Sage did the same and focused on the guard most out of view from Rupert, who wore a short sword on his left hip, the pommel canted to allow for a right-handed draw.

The moment the six-armed, skeletal beast stepped through the breach, Elsbeth raised both hands, sent a blast of purifying light into its chest, and knocked it back into the Dark spiritual realm. Sage Teleported over to the Rephaim guard with the short sword, grabbed it, and Teleported next to the downed beast. Sage swung the most powerful blow he'd ever given and caught the beast just under the chin. Its head rolled away without a drop of blood.

He grabbed the tool the beast used to breach into the room and turned back toward Elsbeth. She'd sent her purifying beam of Persuasion onto Rupert. The great Rephaim, now fully transformed into his natural state, was on his knees, fully awash in white light, smoking, his body melting into a pile of mush.

"Go, Elsbeth," Calvin shouted. "Go before it closes and you can't see it."

Calvin had already killed three of the guards, and the fourth was trying to flee.

"Hurry, Elsbeth." Sage saw the breach begin to collapse.

She turned, sprinted, and jumped at the last moment. Their bodies collided. After scrambling to their feet, Sage steered her toward the stone mansion. They stepped over the six-armed beast, which still had the lizard skin in one of its pincers, its tail squirming.

Elsbeth pointed at the red sky and stopped. "Look. Darks," she whispered. "There must be a million of them."

"I know. Don't look," Sage said. He grabbed Elsbeth's hand and pulled her forward. "They didn't bother me before."

Elsbeth's breath caught more than once as she took in the bleak landscape. "So different than Godspace," she whispered. "What's this place called?"

"I don't know. We're the first Council members to see it. Maybe you can name it."

"I would call it Apollyon," Elsbeth stayed close to Sage as they walked.

"Why?"

"Apollyon is a place of destruction in the Old Testament," she said. "Realm of the dead. The Book of Revelation hints at the name of the angel of the abyss. It's sometimes linked with Sheol, another name for Hell." Sage felt her shiver beside him. "It looks like a waiting place for eternal damnation," she said.

He gripped her hand hard, not caring if she thought it inappropriate, and didn't let go until they were on the front porch of the stone mansion.

When they stepped inside, Elsbeth had the same reaction Sage had regarding the size inside compared to the appearance outside.

"I need to show you the rest," Sage said. "But let's look at this first." He pulled out the six-armed monster's breaching tool.

More than two feet long, it had the shape and color of the jawbone of a large animal. The place where teeth should go was ground into a sharp edge. It was light, but solid and unbending. The outside edge was also sharp, and both edges were tipped with a gold and reddish metal that was still warm to the touch.

"When I Memory Shared with you the first time," Sage said, "I saw a red-hot blade slicing through the fabric dividing the human and spiritual realms." He held up the tool. "This. They have some way of knowing where our people are before cutting their way in and snatching them."

Sage pointed in the direction from where he'd approached the stone mansion the first time. "That way, maybe a half mile, I came in from France. Two hundred yards away from there, they dragged you in from New Orleans? How does that even make sense?"

"I don't know," Elsbeth said, her eyes bright. "But you just stole their breaching tool. It means they can't take any more of our people."

Sage shrugged. "Assuming it's the only one. Come on. Let me show you what I found."

They stood in front of the statue of Mammon until Elsbeth had her fill. She said nothing at the spectacle, but the expression on her face told Sage everything. He again found himself staring at her. He hoped she wouldn't notice.

He told her of the two voices, how he followed them from one breach point to another, about his theory of the building being a kind of launching spot for Dark beasts to travel the globe. It took a couple of tries for Sage to remember the correct hallway, but he led her down to the doors with the telephone-pole-sized crossbeam. "I've been thinking about what could be behind there, but I have no idea."

"Well, we'll not be opening it," she said. "Impossible."

"Let's go," Sage said. "There's more to see."

One by one, he showed her the five dead Council members. Sage sat her down in the fifth room, but away from the body of Norris Vickery, snatched in the 1500s from Budapest.

"I have to tell you my story," Sage said. "I need to do it before we go any further."

Elsbeth frowned. "OK. This is about saving the Council members. I know that already. It's why my dad let me come back."

Sage sighed and looked away. "Well, I didn't tell you everything."

"What is it?"

So he told her how his dad was turning into a monster, about the old film of Hitler, the similar characteristics, and Theo's belief that Mammon was the corrupting Prince. He also confessed that Leah, Grandpa, and Ronan said he wasn't close to being ready to battle a Prince.

"I want to save any Council members I can," Sage said. "I really do, but the main reason I'm doing it is so that I can build a team to help me defeat Mammon. I can't do it by myself, but I have to save Dad."

She didn't say anything.

"You'd do the same thing for your dad," Sage said. He knew it for a fact. He'd Memory Shared with her three times. He knew many things about her. So many, in fact, that he'd never reveal what he'd learned to anyone. Leah was the only one who knew that Memory Share was more than just seeing a memory. A lot of subconscious information transferred—an embarrassing amount of information. Sage knew Elsbeth would move a mountain to save her only parent.

"Yours is the most powerful gift of all," Sage said. "Even if we don't find any other Council members alive, I think we might have a shot against Mammon."

"You're crazy." Elsbeth said. "We're not even old enough to drive. You've killed one monster in your entire life."

"Two," Sage said.

"Fine. Two." She pointed toward the great room with the seven statues. "Mammon might be the most powerful beast on planet Earth. And yeah, I'm so tough I couldn't even stop some skeletal, six-armed, super crab-man from capturing me. Some flunky beast with a lizard skin has snatched thirty-two powerful Council members over the last thousand years, and you think you and I can defeat one of the Princes?" She turned away and crossed her arms. "Get real."

Sage studied her. His feelings—magnified and then super-charged by Memory Share—puzzled him. Not romantic, really, at least not yet, but not those of a sister, either. Were his feelings real or just some kind of transference? Should he tell her about them or keep it to himself?

Easy. He couldn't breathe a word to her. Not now. Maybe not ever. Talk about freaking her out. He knew *exactly* how she'd react if he dumped that on her. He knew. Exactly. She'd think him creepy. She'd think it was a violation of her privacy, and she'd throw up a wall ten feet thick.

They sat in silence for a bit. "OK. You're probably right," Sage stood. "We have twenty-six more to find. If none of the others are alive, we'll go home. Will you help me look?"

"Of course. If we can somehow build a strong enough team, I'll help you fight." Elsbeth looked around for something she could use for a weapon but finally gave up. "Let's go," she said finally.

They ducked into the room where Elsbeth's evil scientist lay dead so that Sage could grab his backpack. The room was empty when they got there. No body. No gurney. No lab equipment. No refrigerator full of Elsbeth's blood.

"I don't understand," Sage said.

"When you traveled back in time to prevent my capture, you changed history," Elsbeth said. "What's so hard to understand?"

Sage felt his face flush. "I didn't think of that." He saw his backpack where he'd left it. They shared a snack and bottled water before heading out.

"I forgot to tell you something," Sage said. He described the portal that opened to New Orleans while he Memory Shared with her. "I saw your father. Rupert and his guards. Everything. The portal was six feet tall and three feet wide. Almost like somebody could step into the past, but as soon as I disconnected with you, it faded."

Elsbeth stopped eating. "You're saying that when you Memory Share, you create a passageway into that memory's past?"

"That's what it looks like." He thought about something. "Well, not exactly like you say. When I entered your memory, it was in the car ride. I'm not sure why your memory started there, but it did. The portal was near the spot of the breach. So if we find another Council member alive and another portal opens . . ."

"It might not be at the same spot where you enter their memory," Elsbeth finished for him.

"Right. I can't go through the portal," Sage said. "As soon as I disconnect, it fades."

"You can Memory Share and Teleport back," Elsbeth said. "You don't have to use the portal."

"Right. But if you used the portal while I Teleported back, we might not end up at the same place." Sage thought about it some more. "We don't even know for sure if somebody could go through the portal."

Elsbeth began eating again as she thought about it. "Might not be anyone else alive. So we might not ever know," she said.

Sage dug into his backpack for another shirt and changed it as Elsbeth finished eating. "First of all, don't say that. OK? We're gonna find somebody else. So . . . let's go find them."

They found five more dead Council members over the next hour. Ten for ten now. All of them were mummified, a few rotten lizard skins, laboratory equipment left behind. They left the rooms as they found them, careful not to leave evidence that they were in the building. Twenty-one left.

Sage felt himself become just a little more desperate with each door they opened.

"We have twenty-one more, Sage," Elsbeth said. Her voice was gentle, as if she could sense the distress he was feeling. "Keep the faith."

He nodded. She was right. Just keep the faith.

They traveled through the main room to hit another corridor, and Sage noticed that Elsbeth didn't take her eyes off the Mammon statue as they passed.

"I hate this room," she whispered. "I wonder how often Mammon visits so he can worship himself?"

The closest barred room was more than a hundred yards down the hallway. They walked softly, still determined to keep their presence secret.

Together they lifted the crossbeam off the door and laid it to the side. Unlike the others, this door swung open easily. The dungeon laboratory seemed like all the others, but the gloom was so deep Sage couldn't tell for sure. The body of a Council member—on a platform of rotted straw—occupied a far corner at the edge of the deepest shadows.

"What's that smell?" Sage said. He stepped fully into the room and almost gagged. The stench would peel paint off a wall.

"I have been expecting your arrival," said a monstrous voice from the direction of the Council member.

Sage stepped back and drew his sword.

Elsbeth appeared beside him and raised her hands, ready.

"Ah, I see the boy has released Lord Mammon's most recent guest," the voice said. "Lord Mammon warned me of that possibility."

"Who are you?" Sage asked. "What are you?"

The beast laughed, spewing a fresh wave of foul. "I suspect Council members know full well who and what I am." A pair of bright yellow eyes appeared from behind the Council member. Then a wolf the size of a horse stepped from the shadows. It had black fur with a hint of a red glow, yet it appeared partially translucent. Almost a phantom.

"A hellhound," Elsbeth said. "He's an abomination made by the Emim. Created to guard important locations within the spiritual realm. Given the gift of Speech by the sorcery of the seven dark lords."

"Your indignation humors me, angel-girl. Abomination? Sorcery? Dark lords? The Seven Princes are the masters of the human race, spiritual guides for weak-minded unbelievers. We have won Battlefield Earth. Soon the Council will be no more."

Sage took a step forward. "The Council is stronger now than when I ate breakfast this morning," he said with a streak of boldness. "Mammon's prison will be a pile of rubble by dinnertime."

Sage didn't know how much the hellhound would weigh since it was some kind of spiritual beast, but in the real world, it would weigh at least a thousand pounds. Its head towered above Sage's own. The glistening, reddish coat of fur didn't begin to hide the muscles that bulged magnificently each time it moved. Sage held his sword in a ready position. He'd already picked out a Teleport spot, and the buzzing in his bones was roaring full blast.

"You *are* the boy then," the beast said. "The one they call the Warrior. I was placed here to kill you in case you interfered. Lord Mammon has protection in place for all those still alive. He suspected that one day you might try to save them."

Still alive! All those still alive! If not for the beast before him, Sage might have done a dance. Some of the Council members were alive!

"Don't listen to it," Elsbeth said. "It's a deceiver. Hellhounds speak through the witchery of the Seven."

"Lord Mammon knew only the Chosen One could make it this far." The hellhound's open mouth revealed double rows of razor-sharp teeth and three-inch fangs.

"Hellhounds are fast," Elsbeth whispered so softly Sage almost missed it. "Like a blur, according to Dad." She moved to Sage's left, one palm toward heaven, one pointed at the beast.

Sage's gift of Fighting Arts included vision that showed his opponent's movements in slow motion. He wasn't that worried about its speed.

"Lord Mammon rules," said the hellhound. And then it *did* become a blur, hitting Elsbeth in the chest and slamming her against a stone wall.

Sage heard her gasp as she crumpled to the floor.

Before the beast could finish her, Sage Teleported behind it and swung his sword even before fully materializing. The tip of his blade caught the hellhound on the rump and sliced a gaping wound before it bounded away to escape another blow.

It spun around and squared off in front of Sage, a look of astonishment on its face.

"It's bleeding," Elsbeth groaned. She pointed to a spray of black, greasy liquid that had begun burning the stone floor. "The blood is some kind of hellish acid."

The beast roared and jumped at Sage, who Teleported away just before being stampeded. It *was* fast. *Whoa!* Sage couldn't imagine what it must look like to Elsbeth. Sage raised his sword high above his head and Teleported directly onto the back of the hound. But by the time he plunged the sword into its back, the creature bounded across the room again. Sage fell to the ground like a bronco rider thrown from a bull.

The hound didn't waste time; it spun and leaped again, its mouth wide enough to swallow Sage's entire head and chest. He Teleported away again, but not before one of its teeth clipped his left shoulder, opening a gash that instantly burned.

Sage gripped his sword tighter just as a beam of Persuasion hit the hound in the side. "From the depths of the abyss you came, so shall you return." Elsbeth stood bent over, obviously in pain, but she held her death ray steady.

The hound screamed as purifying white light burst from its eyes and mouth. Sage walked over and swung his sword in a crossing motion as the beast staggered on its feet. His strike lopped off half of one of its rear legs. Acid blood spewed against the floor as the hellhound shrieked and tried spinning around. Instead, it fell backward, and its remaining rear leg slipped in the blood. Sage stabbed his sword into the beast's stomach, then pulled it out and Teleported away to assess the damage. He could smell his skin burning from the acid. The pain made his eyes water.

Elsbeth stopped and lowered her hands. The hellhound attempted to stagger to its feet, its movements slow and sluggish.

"Lord Mammon will not be pleased at my defeat," the hellhound gasped. "The prophecy about you was true. I do not understa—"

Sage swung his sword across its throat, and the beast crumpled forward. He stepped forward and jammed his sword where the heart should be. After one final, violent spasm, the hellhound stopped moving. Sage pulled out his sword and rubbed it across the back of the beast, cleaning the blade on its fur.

He sheathed his sword and stepped over to Elsbeth. "Are you OK?"

She nodded and sat down. "Just need to rest for a minute. I can't believe it could move like that." She rubbed her ribs and took several deeps breaths. "Dad was right. A blur. Now I know."

Sage walked over to the Council member and recognized him from Leah's book. "He's alive, Elsbeth!"

14

H is name is Mordoc Nevingham," Sage said. "Gifted
with Elemental Transmutation." It was the ability to al-
ter chemical elements, changing them from one substance to
another by rearranging the atomic structure. They were often
paired with Bell and Chain Makers, but not always. They were
Council alchemists producing potions and poisons that killed
Dark beasts.

"He disappeared from his lab in Old London in the late 1880s."
Sage glanced at Elsbeth, who'd walked up beside him to look at the
body of the man wrapped in the lizard skin.

He was of average height with a drooping moustache and a
head of thick, brown, curly hair. The lizard skin covered his entire
body. His clothes, now rotted on the floor next to him, looked like
something Sherlock Holmes would wear.

"Look at the lizard skin," Elsbeth said. "How is he still alive
after all this time?"

Sage knelt next to him. The reptile skin was the same as what had wrapped Elsbeth: diamond shaped, brown with splotches of green and gold, and the sharp little barbs. It looked wet, glowing slightly in the pale light. The long tail, thick and solid, looked like a boa constrictor, the way it had wrapped itself around Mordoc's body.

"It looks like the skin from Leviathan, the great water beast," Sage said. "Have you heard of that?"

"I read about it. She killed humans, most believed." Elsbeth looked at Sage. "Some believe Leviathan never actually existed, that she was just a legend."

Sage shrugged. "I don't know anything about it. Just saw a picture in a book."

"Can we cut it off?" Elsbeth asked.

"Worth a try." He reached over to grab it, and his entire body stiffened as high-voltage electricity fried his hands.

Moonlight filters through broken clouds; wails of torture echo in the distance. Human bodies, strewn across a bloody courtyard, are broken and ravaged, yet survivors crawl from the terror stalking them . . .

Sage jerked his hands away from the lizard skin. "Ahhh!" Jumping up and dancing around, he watched as his fingers swelled and turned bright red. They were on *fire*. Sage blew on them, tears streaming down his cheeks. "Bad idea. Really bad."

Elsbeth giggled, then started laughing. "I told you to cut it off, not yank on it."

He kept dancing and blowing as Elsbeth laughed. "I don't see what's so funny about it," he said.

That made her laugh even harder. "It's not gonna kill you, Mr. Sage the Warrior. You'll heal fast enough."

"What *is* that thing?" he said. "You're sure you've never heard of anything like it?"

"Never."

He looked at it again, then at Elsbeth. "I got an image when I touched it."

She stopped laughing. "What?"

Sage took a moment to gather his thoughts. "Some kind of slaughter. Dead humans everywhere. Nighttime, with a full moon. Screaming. People begging for their lives." He paused. "They were running away from it."

Elsbeth frowned. "You Memory Shared with it?"

"Not by choice. A vision forced its way into my mind." Sage watched as it pulsed against Mordoc's body. His hands felt better. He looked at Mordoc's sunken face, not able to imagine the pain he must be in. "When I shared your memory of being wrapped in it, it felt like being stabbed with a thousand hot knives. It knocked me to the floor." Although he'd only experienced the agony for less than a second, the shock of it had momentarily paralyzed his entire body.

"Do you think it's the skin of Leviathan?" Elsbeth asked.

He shook his head. "I don't know. I just know I'm not touching it again."

"Try cutting it off. I'd do it, but I don't have a sword." Elsbeth attempted to be serious, but Sage could tell she wasn't trying very hard. It was the stupid little grin that gave her away.

"OK, fine." He pulled his sword as soon as he was able to grip it. "Step back."

It didn't work. He spent five minutes sawing at one of the edges. He'd take even the smallest cut, in hopes that once he had that, he could get his blade going. But the skin was indestructible.

He finally stepped back and wiped beads of sweat off his forehead. "Are you *kidding* me? What *is* this thing?"

Elsbeth closely studied Mordoc's face. "It seems as if he's breathing OK." She looked up suddenly. "Hey, let's try some of the hellhound's acid blood!"

"Yeah, sure. Whatever." Sage sat down to rest for a moment.

"You think it's a stupid idea?"

"Won't be if it works."

"Well, we've gotta do *something* to get him out of that thing." She looked at the dead hellhound and shivered. A pool of blood nearly six feet across had eaten almost a full inch into the stone floor.

"Have at it," Sage said. "The leg I chopped off is over in the corner."

The dismembered leg stank so badly when Elsbeth brought it over that Sage stood and backed several feet away. Black blood dripped onto the floor in front of her. "Hold it level," he said. "Don't waste any."

From the look on Elsbeth's face, one might have thought she held a rotting rat covered with maggots. "This is *so* gross!"

"Don't let it drip all over the floor. You're wasting it."

"Are you a sudden expert in body-part manipulation?" she snapped. "I'm trying not to get any on my hands."

"Well, this was your idea. Just giving you my two cents."

Elsbeth held it straight out in front of her and made another this-is-so-gross face.

"Hold it over his body and squeeze it as if you're making orange juice." Sage clamped his jaws shut so he wouldn't start laughing.

"Could you just be quiet? I'll do it my way." She laid it on the lizard skin near Mordoc's feet. A small amount of blood seeped out, but it had no effect. "Give me your sword."

Sage drew it out and handed it to her.

Elsbeth pushed the pommel against the hound leg and forced more blood out. It flowed easily, at least a two-inch circle, but did nothing to open the lizard skin.

They stood and watched for several moments.

"It's almost like an alien skin from another planet," Sage said. "What do we do now?"

"Memory Share," she said.

He knew it was true. "Why's everything gotta be so hard?"

"London? In the 1880s? Isn't that what you said? How bad can it be?" Elsbeth patted him on the shoulder. "Guess we'll find out."

"We?" Sage looked at her.

"If a portal opens, as it did with me, I'm going. You might need some help. That was the whole point of me coming back with you from New Orleans."

"You sure?" Sage couldn't describe the wave of relief that washed over him.

"Of course. You wanna face that six-armed beast by yourself?"

"I'll have Mordoc with me." Sage really *wasn't* trying to talk her out of it, but it seemed the manly thing to do.

"Wow. Chivalry lives." Elsbeth rolled her eyes. "Protect the weak little girl from the big, bad monsters? We need to get going on this. OK?"

As he was about to put his hands in the correct position, he said, "Remember, once I'm in the memory I won't see if a portal opens or not."

"We've talked about this. I understand the deal. I might end up miles from where you appear in the memory. I'll just wait some-place close because eventually you and Mordoc will show up. I've got it, Sage. Stop worrying."

Sage made contact and cleared his mind. He imagined a white canvas—no lines, no smudges, no wrinkles—just white and stark and crisp, waiting for an artist to craft an image of his choosing. Then he imagined the white exploding beyond the boundaries of the canvas, creeping like a fungus over everything surrounding it. Soon, his entire world was nothing but white—a blank slate waiting for an image to push its way to the surface. Then it came to him, the familiar swirling smoke, but only one image, faint and fragmented. Like when Elsbeth was close to death and only her strongest memory survived, Sage saw just one window.

He drilled his focus into the patterns, willed himself to see what shapes from Mordoc's past would rise. Buildings slowly took form, and streetlights and horse-drawn carriages and smart-ly dressed people. A distant clock tower rose high above shorter brick buildings. Then he saw a crowded city just before night fall. London. Old London.

He pulled himself close, reached for it, and pushed all the way in. When the image became three dimensional, he knew he was mentally there. Once the tingling in his bones began radiating outward, he knew he was on the verge of Teleporting. Then it happened—an explosion of electricity pushed out of his body, and he couldn't feel his fingertips against Mordoc's forehead any longer.

Sage opened his eyes in a dim, narrow, cobblestone alleyway. Fog roiled at his feet; the distant click-clop of horse-drawn buggies drifted toward him from the street. Gas-lit lanterns hung from poles along the way. A mangy dog dug through trash at the other end of the alley before looking at Sage with disinterest. The alley smelled of garbage: spoiled milk, rotten cheese, and raw fish. He could smell the open sewer somewhere close. A faint moon sat high in the sky, but clouds covered large chunks of it. It was the London from a Sherlock Holmes movie. It matched Mordoc's clothes.

A church bell sounded off to his left. The buildings on each side of the alley had back doors. To his right, none of the doors were marked; to his left was a sign that said *M. Nevingham Shipping*. Mordoc Nevingham. This was the place.

He searched for Elsbeth but didn't see her. Nor did he see the razor-thin line of a breach. Behind him, the alley was dark, the street in front nearly deserted.

Mordoc's back door was ajar. Inside was a big warehouse stacked with crates. Sage crept forward until he could see the front of the business and saw a dark shape moving around. When the man stepped near a light, Sage saw him clearly.

Mordoc Nevingham was of average height, but barrel-chested, with thick shoulders and arms. The wavy, brown hair matched his prominent moustache. He wore a suit typical of London in the nineteenth century—tweed jacket with leather elbows and a high lapel, complete with a matching vest and a pocket watch, which he pulled and glanced at.

The Council member was about to turn off the lights when Sage stepped from behind a stack of crates. "Mordoc Nevingham," he said. "I am Sage. From the Council prophecy. Here to prevent your capture."

Mordoc flinched before peering into the darkened warehouse. "Sage? From the Prophecy of Seth?"

"Yes, sir." Sage stood erect and pushed his chest out. His most commanding posture.

The man studied Sage for several beats. "They will come to-night, then?"

"It," Sage said. "I've seen the beast, but I don't know for sure when it will get here." He noticed small wooden crates stacked up along the front wall near the door. The rest of the lobby had dark wood floors, a long counter with books and ledgers and ink wells and paper stacked everywhere, and three chairs that didn't look as if they were built for comfort. It was a large, dusty room about fifteen feet by fifteen feet, with high ceilings and faded wallpaper.

Mordoc smiled tightly. "Come with me."

Sage followed him out of the lobby and into the back.

Mordoc wove through the stacks of crates and got halfway to the center of the room, when he suddenly stopped and looked at Sage.

"How did you get in here?"

"The back door was unlocked," Sage said.

The big man headed to the door and locked it. "Maybe that's how it got in when it got me. You might have prevented my capture already." He pointed over to a far corner and headed there. "Since time is short, I must show you my life's work."

Sage quickly told him about the six-armed beast and how it would cut its way into his lab from the Dark spiritual realm. "I don't think locking the door will do any good."

Then again, maybe Sage was wrong about where the breach would happen. He wondered where Elsbeth was. Had there been a portal? If so, had she stepped through it in time? He knew one thing, she wasn't gifted with Pathfinding, and if she wandered away from the breach point, she might never find it again.

Mordoc stopped in front of a stack of wooden crates that reached all the way to the ceiling. Each appeared to be solidly built but roughed up—a shipped-all-over-the-world kind of look. Mordoc removed several metal rods from hidden recesses on each side of the bottom crate, grabbed the front panel, lifted it away, and revealed a dark passage.

"Follow me." Mordoc disappeared inside.

The passageway was short, just the depth of the crate. Coming out the other side, they ended up in a blank space behind the huge wall of crates. A hidden cove. In the open area was a brick wall and steel door. On the door were three giant locks. Mordoc pulled a long skeleton key from an inside pocket of his jacket.

"They want to stop my work. I will show you the evil they have created." Mordoc's expression was grave but also a bit nervous.

He has somebody—or something—imprisoned in this room. The hair on Sage's arms stood up. He thought about all the creatures he'd studied in the *Encyclopedia of Dark Creatures* and couldn't think of one he wanted to meet face to face.

"Sir Thomas Aquinas said, '*All angels, good and bad, have the power of transmutating our bodies.*'" Mordoc opened the first lock and looked at Sage. "Have you heard that?"

Sage shook his head and swallowed hard. He hated this kind of suspense. Why didn't Mordoc just tell him what was behind the door?

"Aquinas, a medieval priest, spoke with authority on the subject, because he witnessed firsthand how the evil Emim were transmutating human bodies." Mordoc looked at Sage, his eyes intense. "Behind this door is something the Emim did not create by themselves. The Rephaim helped them. With sorcery."

Sage said nothing; his mouth had gone dry.

Mordoc opened the first padlock and dropped it on the floor. "They intended to create a Hound of Hell. Not to be confused with hellhounds. The Hound of Hell was supposed to exist only in the spiritual realm in order to protect the castles of the Seven Princes." He opened the second lock and set it on the floor near the first. "But their experiment was more successful than they intended, for their beast could also survive in our world."

Mordoc stuck his key in the third lock but stopped and looked at Sage again. "Nearly indestructible, its wounds heal so fast that cutting off its head is about the only way to kill it. Without my potion, I should add. It moves with lightning speed and can tear a man to shreds within seconds."

Sage didn't know if Mordoc was trying to scare him, but if so, it was working. The man dropped the last lock onto the floor, turned a large handle, and pulled hard on a solid, rusty-hinged door. A squeaking, fingernails-across-a-chalkboard sound only magnified the creepiness factor.

"You must understand the origin of this beast," Mordoc said. "When the Emim mixed the blood of their own bodies with the blood from a Rephaim and injected it into a human, the blood separated and refused to occupy the same host. Do you understand? When both bloods were injected into a human, the body would literally rip apart because the bloods could not coexist."

Beyond the open door, Sage saw a long, stone-encrusted hallway. At the end of it was another thick, steel door with three more giant locks. Mordoc nodded for Sage to follow as he pulled a different skeleton key from his jacket.

"The Emim had already created hellhounds to guard important locations within the spiritual world," Mordoc continued, "so they decided to mix the warring angelic blood with human blood and force it into hellhounds, who were already nearly indestructible."

When they got to the door, Sage listened for sounds coming from the other side. He heard nothing.

"For several hundred years, they tweaked the percentages of blood," Mordoc said. "When they finally determined the correct mix, they drew the demonic mixture from the hellhounds and injected it into humans. Then the only thing left was for the Rephaim to work their sorcery." He unlocked the first two locks and placed them on the floor, then looked hard at Sage. "They cast a spell so that the transformations would coincide with the cycle of the moon."

Sage watched him open the third lock, confused about what the cycle of the moon had to do with anything. Where was the man going with all of this?

"Step back," Mordoc instructed him as he prepared to open the door. With a grunt, he tugged it all the way open. A terrible odor wafted out of a completely dark room. Mordoc pulled out his pocket watch and checked the time again. "Do not speak to the beast. Wait here while I light some lanterns."

"All right," Sage said.

Mordoc disappeared inside. Sage didn't hear anything scary—no growling or grunting or monster noises—but he did hear heavy breathing, a gurgling sound of a man in great pain.

A dim light grew stronger as Mordoc turned up a lantern, then lit a second and third. From where Sage stood outside the door, the room appeared to be a laboratory of some kind. He saw a long workbench cram-packed with bottles of chemicals, boxes of herbs and dried plants, beakers and small burners, and measuring instruments. The stench drifting out of the room almost made him throw up in his mouth: human waste and urine, sweat, blood, vomit, and an overwhelming smell of some kind of dirty, nasty animal.

"Enter, Sage," Mordoc said.

He leaned around the corner. In the center, chained like the most vicious beast in all of creation, was a man. Not a monster. Not a mutation of nature. Not one of the dozens of creatures listed in the *Encyclopedia of Dark Creatures*.

Just a man. He was a big man, yes, well over six feet tall and heavily muscled. He was an ugly man, certainly, with long, shaggy hair falling past his shoulders, wild eyes, and a misshapen mouth that might have been a birth defect. He was a dirty man, with all kinds of stains smeared down both legs and across his upper torso. He breathed heavily through his nose and mouth.

Mordoc's prisoner stood chained as if he were about to be drawn and quartered: arms straight out to his side, legs spread wide. His wrists and ankles were shackled with heavy iron clamps, and the chains looked heavy enough to restrain an elephant. An even heavier chain was wrapped around his waist and attached to thick eyebolts mounted into a beam in the ceiling.

Mordoc must have read Sage's facial expression. "You were expecting more?" he asked, a grim smile cracking the corners of his mouth. "Maybe a cerberus or chimera or typhon, one of the many Emim creations we all know so well?" A sarcastic laugh exploded from Mordoc as he shook his head and pointed at the man. "No, this beast is much worse than any of those."

"Help me." The man jerked his chains toward Sage. Spittle flew from his mouth as he roared. "Help me!"

Sage took a step back.

The prisoner wore a pair of cutoff pants and nothing else. His legs and feet were filthy, as were his hands and forearms.

"The danger of this beast is the state in which you see him now," Mordoc told Sage. "For in this state, he can hide among the masses, waiting for the lunar cycle to activate its sorcery."

"He is mad!" the man shouted to Sage. "Help me, please!" He jerked against the chains again, his muscles bulging from the effort.

Mordoc walked over to the workbench and picked up a bottle of greenish-brown liquid. "It has taken me almost 150 years to perfect this, but I have finally succeeded." He pointed to the man in the chains. "Norris kindly provided the final link."

Despite Sage's warning, Mordoc didn't seem the least bit interested in protecting himself from whom or what might try and capture him later.

"This madman has kept me chained here for months!" Norris pleaded to Sage, yet again pulling hard against his chains. "I am a doctor by trade. A healer. Yet he imprisons me like a monstrous beast!"

Mordoc waved the bottle of potion at Norris and shouted.

"Doctor, ha! Butcher is more like it." Mordoc turned to Sage, still pointing his bottle at the prisoner. "He butchered five women in Whitechapel before I stopped him."

What! Sage's mouth dropped open. "He's the Whitechapel Murderer?"

"That's what I just said, is it not?" Mordoc's voice got even louder. "It is what makes these beasts so dangerous, their ability to position themselves deep within the human population before they change."

"But . . . but . . . the Whitechapel Murderer is Jack the Ripper!" Sage's voice broke. "Jack the Ripper!"

15

J ack the Ripper? Ha! A silly name a newspaper man gave the fiend
to sell papers," Mordoc said. "I pay no attention to such foolish-
ness." He pulled out his pocket watch and checked it for the third
time since Sage's arrival. "Any second now, young Sage. You will
see for yourself."

"See what?"

Mordoc held up the bottle of dark liquid. "A century and a half
of work. Imagine how often I almost quit. Yet as full of despair as
I became, these beasts continued ravaging the English countryside.
I *had* to find a potion that would stop them instantly."

Gifted with Elemental Transmutation meant that Mordoc's
blood, when mixed with certain natural elements and heated or
cooled to certain temperatures or exposed to certain chemicals,
had properties that altered the building blocks of nature. Sage
couldn't imagine spending one hundred and fifty years working to solve a single problem, yet that is what those gifted with

Elemental Transmutation did for the Council. "What's in your potion?" Sage asked.

"Liquefied silver, just hints of copper and gold, uranium, gallium, and scandium, as well as alcohol, salt water, and my blood after being boiled and frozen and boiled again." Mordoc laughed and pointed at Norris. "He provided the final ingredient, although I am certain he had no intention of doing so. Wolfsbane." Mordoc laughed again, his voice bouncing around the small laboratory.

The clues suddenly tumbled into place for Sage. He knew what Norris was and why Mordoc had secured him with such heavy chains. Before he had a chance to say anything, Norris began to groan.

"It is time." Mordoc held his pocket watch open in his hand. "The moon rises full."

Norris's eyes bulged so far from their sockets Sage thought they might pop out of his head. They turned green instead and glowed in the dim light. Red streaks exploded through the whites of his eyes as his forehead receded into a slanting, hairy slope that ran all the way to the end of his pointed ears.

Sage stepped back in shock and bumped into the doorframe.

Norris wailed and growled, his bones cracked, and ligaments popped as his body transformed into a rabid killing machine. Huge, clawed paws replaced his hands and feet; his legs grew longer and thicker. Fur shot out of his body in the blink of an eye. His entire head splintered and snapped and reshaped itself, while his mouth jutted straight forward and turned into a vicious snout with teeth three inches long. As big as Norris was as a man, he was even bigger as a werewolf.

The entire transformation took but a few seconds.

Mordoc beamed, his face a weird combination of disgust and delight. "You see now what has obsessed me for the entirety of my life's work. The Emim race's most diabolical killing creation."

Sage, frozen with terror, looked back at the werewolf. The beast pulled on its chains with every ounce of strength in its body, but they held fast. It roared and shook its head; saliva spewed from its snout in long streams of grossness.

"We can kill them now," Mordoc shouted over the noise of the werewolf. He held his bottle of potion high in the air. "I have shipped cases of my potion to Council headquarters in Istanbul. We can fight them on any continent now."

The beast snapped at Mordoc, its neck straining to reach him.

Mordoc stepped closer to the beast, clearly confident in the strength of the chains. "Just a couple of spoonfuls of my potion will poison him immediately." He turned to Sage. "Would you care for a demonstration?"

Before Sage could even consider an answer, they both heard a crash at the back door. They spun toward the noise just as an explosion of falling crates rocked the building.

"They have come for me," Mordoc said. "Quickly, over here!"

Sage looked at Mordoc, who had squatted near the base of his workbench. Then he looked at the two open doors leading to the laboratory—solid steel and strong enough to stop an armored tank. It took only a few seconds to imagine standing just inside the first door and to feel the vibrating deep within his bones.

"Quickly, Sage," Mordoc said again.

In the next instant, Sage Teleported to the first door and grabbed the handle. He was about to slam it shut, locking both he and Mordoc inside the laboratory, when he glanced out into the warehouse.

The wall of crates that created the hidden cove and blocked the view of the steel door had fallen over. Standing within the dusty wreckage were two figures. The first was a werewolf; though not as large as Norris, it looked just as vicious. It sniffed the air in all directions, then growled and drooled and snapped its jaws. The second figure was a man even larger than Norris, dressed in a black leather duster that skirted the tops of his boots. Other than having long hair and glow-in-the-dark eyes, Sage couldn't see what the man looked like.

Just as Sage pulled the door closed, the werewolf saw him. Less than a second later, the beast slammed against the door as Sage turned the deadbolt. In the next instant, the door's hinges vibrated, and then rattled against the assault . . .

How did it travel halfway across the warehouse in less than a second?

Mordoc told Sage the beasts were incredibly fast, but he never imagined *that* kind of speed. Sage ran to the second door and locked himself inside with Mordoc and Norris.

"Here, Sage," Mordoc said. "Hide in here and save yourself. It is not you they are after."

Mordoc held open a wooden trap door. Sage walked over to look and saw a hole eight feet deep. But that was all it was, a hole, not an escape tunnel. Sage would be dog food down there. Werewolf bait. He looked over at Norris. The werewolf had grown silent, as though listening to the pounding of the other beast on the first door. It was also sniffing the air but watching Sage and Mordoc.

"What's that?" Sage asked Mordoc as he stepped behind him.

"What?" Mordoc turned away from the trap door.

Sage shoved him into the hole. Mordoc screamed as he fell and landed hard on one leg. It twisted and buckled beneath him.

"Sorry," Sage looked down at him. "But *I'm* here to prevent *your* capture. Not the other way around."

Sage slammed the trap door. "Don't make any noise," he shouted. "No matter what you hear up here, just stay quiet!"

He scooted several crates and furniture over the trap door to hide it. When he stood up, he saw Norris watching his every move.

"It'll be our little secret," Sage told the werewolf, pretty certain the beast hadn't understood a single word.

He heard the first door crash open and immediately heard pounding on the next door. Sage drew his sword.

"Come out, chemist!" the man in the black duster shouted from the other side of the door. "We have no intention of killing you."

The blows against the door were so powerful they were causing the center to buckle inward, slowly pulling the deadbolt away from the doorjamb. It wouldn't be much longer.

Norris began growling again, then howling and barking and making noises that almost sounded like dog talk.

The pounding grew louder; the door bent even more.

"We will burn this place," said the man through the door. "Come out now and save yourself."

It was the reflection from one of the flickering lanterns that drew Sage's attention to Mordoc's bottle of potion, which sat on the workbench near the trapdoor. Then he saw several bottles lined up along the back of the workbench. They didn't contain much, but they would have to do. He grabbed one and moved to the far corner of the room, behind Norris, who still barked and yelped in dog speak.

The door flew open. The man in the duster entered first, his eyes glowing embers. The werewolf entered behind him, sniffing and growling and drooling as if he'd been waiting for an entire year to eat somebody. They headed straight to the trapdoor.

"Who are you?" the man in the duster asked Sage, while the second werewolf threw all the stuff off the trapdoor and yanked it open.

Sage didn't answer. He watched the second werewolf peer into the hole.

The werewolf growled into the darkness, and the man in the duster walked over and looked in.

Sage wasn't sure what to do first. Focusing on a spot directly behind the man and then at a spot near the door, he tried to plan more than one move ahead.

"I didn't think hiding was your style," the man in the duster called to Mordoc. "But nonetheless, I've come—"

He didn't get another word out. Sage Teleported behind him and swung his sword into the side of his head.

The man staggered sideways, fell against the workbench, and collapsed to the floor.

Sage Teleported to the spot near the door just as the unchained werewolf turned in his direction.

"Kill him," the man in the duster shouted as he struggled to stand, blood pouring from a huge gash on his head.

The werewolf turned and leapt at Sage. It was a brown rocket, a torpedo at Mach 5, a beast so fast Sage wouldn't have known what it was had he not seen it standing still. Sage disappeared back to his original spot behind Norris just as the werewolf crashed against the steel door.

"What's going on up there?" Mordoc shouted from inside the hole.

The man in the duster steadied himself. Sage Teleported and hit him in the head with a second blow. He went down.

The werewolf flew through the air and fell against the workbench as Sage appeared by the door again.

Norris snapped and growled and barked as the other werewolf climbed to his feet and leapt again. Sage Teleported directly into the spot it vacated. The beast crashed into the steel door again.

This wasn't working. The beast moved too fast for Sage to hit it with a sword. So he sheathed his sword, grabbed two bottles of potion, and waited. The man in the duster was out of action, moaning on the ground, blood running in rivulets onto the slate floor.

Norris barked and growled louder than ever, jerking his chains in a frantic motion that got the other werewolf's attention. They briefly looked at each other, and then Sage's world got a whole lot worse.

The werewolf walked over to the chain holding Norris's right claw, and with one unified motion, the two of them ripped the other end out of the wall. Norris jerked his head around and growled at Sage, then seemed to smile a little.

Where was Elsbeth? He needed her now!

The other werewolf attacked.

Like a bullet, the werewolf streaked through the air, caught Sage on his left shoulder, and knocked the bottle of potion from that hand. Sage screamed but disappeared just as its huge snout was about to clamp onto the front of his throat.

Pain seared through his shoulder, and his arm fell limp. The monster attacked again. Sage wasn't as quick, and the beast swiped the upper part of his right leg. He collapsed in the corner farthest from the beast and felt like he might pass out.

Norris, now able to use both claws, ripped away the chain securing his left arm.

The other werewolf came after Sage again. Sage disappeared into the hallway outside the laboratory door. He heard the beast crash into the corner. He also heard Norris rip away the chains holding his legs.

Breathing heavily now, blood streaming down his left arm and right leg, Sage had to move again when he heard Norris barking. He peeked around the door and saw both werewolves pulling on the chain wrapped around Norris's waist. He knew the wooden beam in the ceiling wouldn't hold the eyebolt secure for very long.

Sage had a single bottle of potion. Mordoc said only a small amount was needed to poison them. He might be able to Teleport over and smash the bottle into Norris's mouth before the other one could react, but it was risky. Their speed was otherworldly, and so they'd get him if he hesitated for even a fraction of a second.

He had to try. The man in the duster was out cold now, but Sage didn't think he was dead. If he woke up, it would be three against one, and Sage would have no chance at all.

He gathered his strength, then Teleported right in front of Norris and swung the bottle straight at his snout. The eyebolt exploded out of the ceiling beam, and both beasts fell backward, away from him.

Before Sage could react, the smaller werewolf charged and hit Sage in the stomach. Before Sage hit the ground, he Teleported again, this time near the door.

The beast had knocked the wind out of him. Sage fought to draw a breath, but he couldn't get any air. He looked over and saw Norris race over to the hole and jump in.

Mordoc screamed.

Sage didn't see the other werewolf until it was too late. It hit him in the chest and knocked him back. Sage held on to the bottle of potion as Mordoc's screams ended with a violent snapping of jaws.

Dead. Mordoc was gone.

Sage tried Teleporting away one last time, but the buzzing in his bones was gone. He tried again, but it was no use. This was the end. With a vicious growl, the werewolf pounced. The beast opened his snout wide; saliva dripped on Sage's face. Just before the beast ripped his face off, a blast of purifying light exploded into its chest.

"Sage, get up!" Elsbeth shouted. "Hurry!"

The werewolf, blown against the wall from Elsbeth's laser of light, tried scrambling to its feet, when Elsbeth hit it again.

"Where's Mordoc?" Elsbeth rushed to Sage to help him move.

Sage crab-walked backward. "Dead. We've gotta get out of here! There's a second werewolf!"

Elsbeth hit the wounded monster with a third blast, then grabbed Sage by the upper arm. She pulled him down the short hall and stopped at the steel door leading into the warehouse. "The six-armed creature with the lizard skin is out there somewhere," she whispered. "When I stepped through the portal I heard the ripping sound out in the alleyway." She squeezed his arm, her eyes frantic with fear. "The portal is gone, Sage. As soon as I stepped through, there was some kind of sucking sound. We're trapped here."

The fiery pain from the werewolf's attack made Sage lightheaded. "I can find the breach," he whispered back. "I can see it. Don't worry." A huge roar from within Mordoc's lab got them moving. "Norris is coming."

"Who?"

"The other werewolf. Jack the Ripper."

"Not funny, Sage." Elsbeth stepped through the destruction of the destroyed crates. She led Sage by the hand. "This is no time for jokes."

"I'm not—"

Another roar, more a scream of rage, drowned out the rest of his sentence. They hurried forward but stayed low.

"Norris must have found his dying buddy," Sage whispered. "Let's go." He limped toward the door leading to the alley, sword drawn.

The alley door exploded inward. The six-armed beast carrying the lizard skin stepped into the warehouse, its skeletal head searching. Jack the Ripper burst into the warehouse and stopped when he saw the monster at the back door.

Elsbeth pulled Sage down behind a crate in the farthest corner of the room. "We'll Teleport into the alley as soon as it moves deeper into the room," she said into his ear. He was about to respond when she squeezed his arm. "Listen."

It sounded like mumbling. "It's speaking Enochian," Elsbeth said.

"What's that?"

"Based on Enochian magic," she said. "It's a system of ceremonial magic that commands dark spirits. Used by the Rephaim mostly, but the Emim adopted it a few centuries ago. Look, the werewolf understands."

Norris watched the beast as it spoke and waved its arms around. Mordoc said the werewolf was a joint Emim and Rephaim creation. It would make sense that it could understand an Emim abomination like the skeletal, six-armed Crab Man.

"Let's go," Elsbeth grabbed Sage's hand. "To the alley."

"On three."

They appeared just outside the door. Sage immediately saw the breach at the end of the alley and pulled Elsbeth that way. "Hurry." The alley dead-ended, and the thin line leading into the Dark realm was in the deepest, darkest spot. It was much more visible than the one in France, probably because it was so recent.

Sage pulled her through and saw the stone mansion off in the distance. Like the time he'd come in from France, he turned around and saw no evidence of the breach from this side.

The sulfur watered his eyes and stung the wound on his leg. "Is this how it's going to be?" Sage asked Elsbeth. "I finally find a Council member alive and travel back and get him killed?"

"It's not your fault," Elsbeth said. She'd said it with conviction, but Sage knew she was only trying to make him feel better.

"Yes it was. Mordoc felt a need to show me his prisoner and got trapped back there. If I hadn't shown up . . ."

"History wouldn't have changed," Elsbeth said. "He'd have been captured and would have died in that prison like the others. Don't blame yourself. My question is why I got there so late. Why didn't I get there the same time as you?"

Sage didn't have the brainpower at the moment to give it any thought. He wasn't even sure he could remember his name.

"We also know something else now," Elsbeth said.

"What?"

"That the portal you create when you Memory Share is different than the breach made by Crab Man. I thought I might be stepping through the breach, but I didn't. I stepped into his memory, too, but at a later point." She looked at him, confused. "Do you understand it?"

He sighed and shook his head. "Leah always said the spiritual realm is a dimension unlike anything else in existence. Normal rules don't apply here. I think that's why stepping into the past is even possible."

They walked in silence. Sage limped while looking at the swirling mass of Darks concentrated over the stone mansion. The landscape appeared even more desolate than before. Either that or it was a reflection of the depression that had settled onto his shoulders. He might never build enough of a team to battle Mammon. If he and Elsbeth had barely defeated a single werewolf, how would they *possibly* have a chance against one of the most powerful Princes of Hell?

16

Sage didn't even look at the statue of Mammon as they passed, though he noticed Elsbeth studied it every moment it was within view. They hit a corridor they hadn't yet been in and saw several barred doors.

One by one, Sage was able to solve the location of the missing Council members listed in the book Leah had given him. All seven rooms they opened revealed another body.

Sage nearly collapsed in disappointment after finding the last one on that hallway. "Seventeen dead," he said. "Plus Mordoc and you. Thirteen left."

Elsbeth sat down beside him and stared blankly at the body of Roman Modesto, a Greek Fighting Arts master who'd gone missing during the first Crusades. "Don't lose faith, Sage." Despite the encouragement, she hadn't sounded like she believed it.

"The hellhound said Mammon put protection on those still alive," Sage said. "Maybe his information was bad."

"Hellhounds are notorious liars," Elsbeth said. "I told you that."

He didn't argue.

"How do you plan to lure Mammon here?" she asked. "Have you thought about it?"

He hadn't given it *any* thought but was too embarrassed to admit it. "I've thought a *lot* about it." She waited patiently, but he didn't say anything else.

"You're flying by the seat of your pants," she said after a minute. "You haven't planned *anything*. You've got nothing."

"I've got a little something," he said.

"Yeah? What?"

Sage stood and turned away. He'd think of something soon. It was hard to look at her and stay irritated. Since she'd saved him from the werewolf, he didn't know if he'd ever get angry with her. His confused feelings for her were even more jumbled now. "We need to keep looking." He headed for the door. "There are still some hallways we haven't checked." She chuckled behind him, but he ignored her. "We should just Teleport over to the next hallway. I'm tired of walking."

"Uh, no. Bad idea," Elsbeth said.

"Why?"

"You never Teleport into unknown areas if you can help it. Besides that, you've seen all these other hallways. I haven't. We might think we're going to the same place, but it won't end up like that. We can't just hold hands and arrive together unless we both know *exactly* where to land. Got it?"

"Yeah. Guess so. It'd be easier, though."

"Sure," she said. "Until the first time you Teleport into a fiery furnace. Or into the middle of a den of vampires. Or land inside some Nephilim cyclops's boiling pot of soup. Then you won't think it's so easy."

"OK, Elsbeth, I got it. We'll walk." Sage sighed and opened the door. He looked both ways.

"You're new at Teleporting," Elsbeth said. "Just trying to keep you from making a mistake."

Sage didn't say anything. He waited while she stepped into the hallway. They replaced the heavy metal crossbar and headed toward the statue room.

"I know you are," he said finally. "Just worried about Dad. That I won't be able to save him."

They walked for a while before Elsbeth replied. "I lost my mom when I was eight," she said. "Not to the influence of one of the Princes, but it was horrible."

"What happened?" Sage had shadows of images of what had happened from his Memory Shares with her, but he couldn't tell her that. He also knew how much her mom's death upset her and how closely she'd kept those feelings guarded. The fact she'd decided to talk about it at all made him feel good. Closer, somehow.

Elsbeth seemed to gather her thoughts for a few moments before speaking. "She was gifted with Illusion. Teamed with two Fighting Arts masters. Assigned to subterranean Rome. Specifically, the maze of tunnels running under Vatican City." Elsbeth spoke quietly, the emotion still strong.

"What were they hunting?"

"Do you know what a manananggal is?" Elsbeth asked. "They're most well known in the Philippines."

"Kind of a vampire?" He'd seen one in the book of weird creatures but couldn't remember the exact details.

Elsbeth nodded. "Yeah, that's close. They generally take the form of a beautiful woman with large, leathery bat wings. The lower halves of their bodies root to the ground while the upper parts detach to search for food. They have a taste for human blood. Young blood. They stalk at night and confuse their victims by making sounds that become fainter the closer they get." She looked at him. "Mom got attacked inside the catacombs. By at least a dozen of them. They took so much of her blood she couldn't survive. If it wasn't for the support of my dad . . ." She wiped some tears away and didn't say anything else.

"I'm sorry, Elsbeth. Really. That sounds horrible." Sage knew why she'd shared the story: to tell him that she knew what it was like to lose a parent. If he did lose his dad, she'd be there for him. He felt bad for her, but it didn't change the urgency he felt or the disappointment in his failure to build a team.

They got to the statue room and hung a left, heading down a corridor Sage hadn't been in before. There were fewer barred rooms this way but many more open areas with worn paths on the floor. A heavy-traffic area, Sage thought. They needed to be quick.

"Look at this." Elsbeth stopped at the first door. Steel instead of wooden, it had four crossbars instead of one, and each was twice as thick and four times as wide as what they'd seen so far. The top bar was above their reach.

Sage tried to lift the lowest bar. It wouldn't budge. "It must weigh five hundred pounds. There's no way we're getting in there."

"What's so powerful that it takes that kind of security to keep it inside?"

He hadn't thought about it like that. "Are you talking about what beast they might have guarding the Council member?"

"It sure wouldn't take that kind of door to keep any Council member inside."

"We need to Teleport in," Sage said. "I know what you said a few minutes ago, but we're not getting in otherwise."

She looked doubtful. "That's really a bad idea, Sage. Really a bad idea."

"We could just Teleport right back out if we need to."

"If we're able." She shook her head. "You just don't understand."

He pointed to the door. "I'm going in there. Stay out here if you want. I didn't come this far to stop now."

"Then let me do it," she said. "I've been Teleporting for years. I can flash in and out of a place so fast you'd miss it if you blinked."

"I'm good enough. I can do it."

"You're *not* good enough!" Elsbeth said. "That werewolf shouldn't have gotten within three feet of you, and I don't care how fast it was. You almost got killed because of your poor Teleporting skills. Now don't argue with me! I'll go in and assess. Then I'll come back out. Just stay here!"

She disappeared without another word.

"'You almost got *killed*. That werewolf shouldn't have gotten within *three feet* of you.'" He slapped the blade of his sword against his leg while he stalked back and forth in front of the door. "Three feet. Whatever."

When Elsbeth appeared in front of him, her face had drained of color. "You need to get in there. And fast. He's almost dead. Hurry!" Then she was gone again.

Sage Teleported into the middle of a slaughterhouse. There was no laboratory like all the other dungeon cells. No gurney or scientific machines or equipment. There were bones of dozens of creatures, big and small. Blood stains smeared so much of the floor and walls it appeared they'd been painted red. A lizard skin was ripped down the center as though something had exploded outward from the inside.

"Over here." Elsbeth knelt in a shadowy corner over a body so skeletal it could have been a Holocaust survivor. "He's so close to death I can barely feel his heartbeat."

Sage couldn't see his face, but his long, flowing hair told him who it was. "David Brock. Roll him onto his back so I can make sure."

"I'm afraid to move him."

He was in a fetal position, curled so tightly Sage wondered if *rigor mortis* had already set in.

"Let me in." He edged next to Elsbeth. She moved away and Sage leaned over to look at his face. "It's him. How's it possible he's still alive?"

He barely recognized David's face. Scraggly beard, pale skin covered with sores, skin stretched so tightly against his bones it appeared ready to rip apart. The stench coming off his body was indescribable.

"I think he's got pneumonia," Elsbeth said. "His lungs sound full of fluid."

Sage was thinking the same thing.

"He ripped himself out of the lizard skin, Sage. You can tell by how it's torn. Then he killed the beasts they sent in here to guard against his escape."

"There's a whole herd of beasts," Sage said. He recognized the skeletons of chimeras and minotaurs, a hellhound, and some breed of small Nephilim giant. At least one cerberus lay crumpled on the floor, although it was hard to tell with so many bones.

"I don't understand it either," Elsbeth said. "Maybe they conducted an experiment once he broke out of the lizard skin. Decided to find out just how hard he was to kill."

Sage glanced around the room for a weapon but didn't see anything. He knew the fighting skills of those gifted with Might were brutal, unrefined, and devastating due to the power behind each blow, but he couldn't imagine surviving some cage match to the death—with no weapon—against the fiercest of the Dark beasts. Then he remembered what Ronan said about David Brock—that he was half again stronger than anyone else gifted with Might. Ronan called him special and never understood how he'd been captured.

"Maybe they kept sending different beasts in here to kill him," Elsbeth said, "but when nothing worked they decided to let him starve to death. The bones are picked clean. He ate all these beasts."

Now the man was little more than a breathing bag of bones. As indestructible as Council members were, to survive in this cell for almost a hundred years was crazy.

"Look at the door," Elsbeth said. "Now we know what they were keeping inside. Him."

Sage turned to look. The steel door looked like a hydraulic jackhammer had pounded on it. It was so dimpled and beaten it hurt Sage's fists even thinking about it.

"You can see his knuckle prints," Elsbeth said, full of awe. "David's bones must be made of titanium."

"Maybe," Sage said, "but right now he's so close to death that if I don't Memory Share with him in the next few minutes, he might die in front of us." He knew he sounded desperate, because he *was* desperate. He *really* needed David Brock on his team.

"Then do it," Elsbeth said. "I'll wait for the portal and be right behind you."

"It's a battlefield during WWI," Sage said. "In France. It's the breach I used to get here."

"OK. I'll be ready for it."

"Help me roll him onto his back," Sage said. "I can't connect with him like this."

As gently as they could, they rolled David over and found his entire left side eaten away by gangrene and giant sores. The putrid smell of rotting pus almost caused Sage to vomit right there.

"Hurry, Sage. He can't be on his back like this for very long. His lungs are too full of fluid."

Sage placed his hands, cleared his mind, and connected quicker than ever before. The swirling smoke held one memory, and it was so faded that Sage almost missed it. He reached out and grabbed it and let the image build. As soon as it was full enough to support him, he let the buzzing in his bones ramp up to full throttle, and away he went.

The battlefield was dark and loud, full of screams of agony, gunfire, yelling, and tank engines. The sky, a lightshow of muzzle flashes from mortar rounds and cannon fire, seemed to rain ash and dirt and the smell of burning flesh. Fires burning on a distant horizon contrasted a lone bugle playing "Amazing Grace" somewhere behind him.

Within seconds the familiar red blade began ripping the air in front of him. He saw the skeletal head of the six-armed Crab Man first, then three of its arms, as it pushed its way through the breach.

"Who's this nutter?" said a British voice from the darkness beside him.

Sage didn't have a chance to answer before the beast fully materialized, the lizard skin clutched tightly in one of its pincers.

"Dark beast from the Other Realm," the voice said. "And maybe I'm the one it wants."

Sage couldn't see exactly what happened next, but he heard a *swoosh*, saw a flash of silver, and then the monster was blown back into the breach. David Brock dove headfirst in after him.

"Holy smokes!" Sage was about to jump in to follow when Elsbeth stepped out of thin air beside him.

"Where is he?" she shouted over the noise of the battle.

"In the breach! He knocked the Crab Man back where it came from and went in after him."

"Where is it?"

"Right there!" Sage pointed to the opening.

"I'm not a Pathfinder, Sage! Show me!"

He grabbed her hand and dragged her into the Dark realm.

"There!" Sage pointed to the right.

David Brock was in full battle with the Crab Man. He wielded a six-foot-long steel pole similar to what Ronan had trained with in Sage's dungeon. It was two inches thick and probably weighed hundreds of pounds. The long-haired teenager swung it as effortlessly as Sage swung his sword. He wore a British army uniform, boots to his knees, the sleeves on his shirt rolled up over his impressive forearms. He was so different than the living skeleton Sage had Memory Shared with. Just under six feet, David Brock's entire body was thick and solid—a linebacker, Sage thought, with superhuman strength. His hair was tied back into a ponytail that reached the middle of his back.

With both feet constantly balanced as he moved, David swung his steel rod with speed and grace as he defended against the blows of the Crab Man. The beast advanced and tried overwhelming David with a flurry of blows, but David held him off.

Sage was about to run over when Elsbeth Teleported behind the creature and raised her right hand to the red sky. "Experience the cleansing light of the Almighty!" she shouted.

Nothing happened.

She frowned just as the beast turned on her.

"Elsbeth, watch out!" Sage said. He Teleported beside her, swung his sword head-high, and blocked the wide-open pincer that would have snipped Elsbeth's head off.

Sage pushed her away and ducked another of the pincers. Then David hit the beast with a solid blow that sent it reeling backward.

"Now, mates," David shouted. "Let's give it a real go!" He swung his rod toward the monster's head, but it blocked the blow and scrambled away.

Sage Teleported into its path and sliced low. It leaped high over his head and took off at a dead sprint.

David gave pursuit, and Sage looked for Elsbeth. She hadn't moved. She stared at her hands, confused.

"Elsbeth, come on!" Sage ran after David, who'd fallen well behind the beast. "It's getting away!"

Suddenly it was gone. With one smooth motion, the Crab Man sliced a rip into the human realm and disappeared. David skidded to a stop as the red breach began to close.

Sage kept moving. He sprinted forward and jumped through the breach and into a desert area, sand as far as he could see. Distant mountains. Remote. Not a sign of life anywhere. A few feet to his right was another breach point. The beast had cut its way back into the Dark realm and disappeared.

He wouldn't chase it any farther.

When Sage stepped back into the breach, he found David, steel bar in hand, with a confused look.

"Who *are* you?" David asked. "Who is she? Where did you come from?"

"Sage," Elsbeth said. "My Persuasion didn't work. Did you see that? It didn't work!"

"You're of the Council, then," David said.

"Is it because of the Dark realm?" she asked Sage. "Will it not work in the Dark realm?" Her look of desperation worried him. "How can I help you fight Mammon without my gift?"

"Mammon?" David said. "One of the Princes? You lot are fighting one of the Princes?"

The red sky was still full of Darks flying in unison over the stone mansion. "We need to get going," Sage said. He looked at David. "Ronan Barrister told me about you. I'm Sage Alexander. This is Elsbeth Brown."

"He's Sage the Warrior," Elsbeth said. Her distress was still evident, as she continued to study her hands.

"We've got a lot to tell you," Sage said. "Later. Let's move."

"Where?" David asked. "I've got a war to fight. The Krauts keep nicking British tanks and using them against us."

"That war's been over for almost a hundred years," Elsbeth said. "Germany lost, so you can relax. England is strong."

"We can explain most of it," Sage said. "Just don't ask how we can step out of your past into the Dark realm and immediately be in my present a hundred years later. OK? Just don't ask me to explain that."

"A hundred years?" David grabbed one of Sage's arms. "But my family . . ."

"I know," Sage said. "I know."

Sage and Elsbeth each took one of David's arms and led the stunned sixteen-year-old toward the stone mansion. The relief Sage felt at having such a warrior on his team nearly brought him to his knees.

17

Sage and Elsbeth allowed David to soak in everything at his own pace. He asked very few questions but took a long time inspecting everything as they trekked back to the dungeon cell where he'd been rescued. David stopped and stared at the statue of Mammon even longer than Elsbeth had, but he finally turned away, a look of rage heavy on his face.

The door leading to his cell wasn't steel any longer, but wooden like all the others. There were no crossbeams, no skeletons, and no blood-painted walls. Only Sage's backpack and the breaching tool he'd captured from the Crab Man were there. Like the trips to save Elsbeth and Mordoc, history had changed, and Sage had never been more relieved.

They sat in a circle, door closed, and spoke quietly. Sage started his story at the beginning. When he got to the part about Elsbeth, she joined in until David had the entire history.

David Brock's heavy British accent bore a mixture of Scottish, and Sage found it difficult to understand at times. The Boy with Might mostly listened and gazed off into the distance.

Getting David caught up had given Sage and Elsbeth a chance to rest. There were twelve Council members left to find, and Sage was exhausted.

"Both you mates looked knackered," David said. "It was brilliant how you rescued me from my cock up, but I think I'll go explore a bit while you rest."

Elsbeth jumped to her feet. "That's a big N. O. We're not splitting up. None of us are going wandering around by ourselves."

Sage also stood. "She's right. We stay together. Period."

"Think I'm dodgy, do you?" David asked. "That I might slip out of here and head home?"

"Weren't you listening?" Elsbeth pointed to Sage. "He's a Pathfinder. He's the only one who can lead us out of here."

"Well, don't bite your arm off, lass," David said. "Just wanting to stretch my legs a little." He sat back down. "Just letting you know that I'm ready to go."

Sage looked at Elsbeth. "You hungry?"

"That's an understatement."

"How about you?" Sage asked David.

"I could eat. They have grub somewhere in here?" David picked up his steel bar and rested it in his lap. He gazed off and sighed heavily. "My mam's dead by now," he said softly. "My pap was as mad as a bag of ferrets, so he'd be long passed." He looked at Sage. "Nobody to go home to, I guess. You say Ronan's still knocking about?"

Sage smiled as he opened his backpack. "Full steam ahead. He's gonna freak when he sees you." He pulled out three PowerBars—the last he had—and gave each of them one.

"That's ace, Sage," David said. "What is it?"

"Protein bar." Sage tore his open and took a bite.

"Never seen covering like this." David pushed the foil around with his fingers.

"Chocolate," Elsbeth said. "Eat up and we'll head out."

David tore it open and took a bite. "Um, tasty. This wrapping is peculiar."

"I'm thinking a lot of things will seem peculiar to you once we take you home with us," Elsbeth said. She looked at Sage. "We continue on this hallway? There are two doors left."

"That's what I'm thinking."

They found dead bodies in both rooms, one so decayed Sage couldn't identify it. Probably Leif Erickson, missing for over a thousand years.

Ten left.

The next hallway over was the one with the massive double doors. "Elsbeth," Sage said, "let's show him the big doors. We're close."

She shrugged. "That's fine."

When they got there, David let out a low whistle. "Could drive five tanks side by side through these. What's in there?"

Sage frowned and glanced at Elsbeth. "How should we know? We couldn't get in there."

"Then let's find out." David placed his steel bar on the ground.

"You can't be serious," Elsbeth said. "It'd take at least twenty men to lift that crossbar."

"Or just one of me." David winked at her. "Stand back, now, lass. Wouldn't want you to muss your hair." He laughed and pushed by Elsbeth. "I'll just move it enough to get one of the doors open. Can't weigh as much as the tanks I've been busting up."

Sage watched, his eyes not believing, as David went to one far end of the crossbeam, lifted it about twelve inches, and began walking toward the center of the door. The steel beam squeaked so loudly against the metal brackets that both Sage and Elsbeth grimaced and held their hands over their ears.

It was over in less than thirty seconds. The beam now crossed only one door, which would be easy for David to push back into place. Elsbeth stared at the brash British soldier and just shook her head.

"OK, mates, let's see what's so valuable." David grabbed one of the brackets and pulled. Either it swung easily on its hinges, or David simply overpowered the gravity holding it shut. They stepped way back as the huge door slowly opened.

The three of them stood and stared until David finally broke the silence. "What is this, then?"

Sage would describe it as a force field of some kind—tinted black, like the windows of a dark car, but with a hint of silvery reflection. There was no structure to it; rather, it simply existed—not too different from the portal into the past created during Memory Share. Shadows moved behind it, or at least something was morphing or churning. Sage glanced at Elsbeth and shrugged.

"Shadow Manipulation," Elsbeth said. "Used by the Rephaim to hide or protect places of value."

"I've heard of that," David said. "I think." He looked at Sage. "You?"

Sage shook his head. "Never, but I haven't studied at the Tomb yet."

"There's not a lot known about it," Elsbeth said. "At least I don't know a lot."

It resembled a gigantic piece of smoked Plexiglas, Sage thought. Yet not solid in that way.

David chuckled and pointed, but then frowned and suddenly turned serious. Elsbeth noticed.

"What?" she asked. "What is it?"

"I thought I saw some bloke's face." David pointed again. "There, another one. Did you see that?"

Sage and Elsbeth were a full step behind David, so Sage stepped closer. "I didn't see anything."

"I'm probably going loony, but they looked like faces to me."

Elsbeth also stepped forward, but she didn't stop next to David. She went all the way up and put her face next to the veil.

"Oh!" she screamed after a few seconds. She jumped back, her face a sheet of white. "What is . . . oh . . ." She turned away, her eyes full, her hands shaking.

"What is it?" Sage swallowed hard, afraid to look. "What is it, Elsbeth?"

She couldn't speak. She fanned her hands in front of her eyes, her bottom lip quivering.

David stepped up and looked for several seconds before turning away, also as pale as a corpse. He rubbed his forehead and stared at Sage, about to say something. "A dungeon of souls, lad," he said finally. "A dungeon of souls."

Sage looked at the wall of tint. The churning motion couldn't be defined from where he stood, so he got closer. He cupped his hands against the sides of his head to block the light and put his face within an inch of the barrier.

A face stared back at him, pleading eyes, mouth open in a silent scream.

Sage jumped back and took a breath, panic rising in his throat. Then he realized that he'd seen more. A lot more.

Not just one face. Not a hundred. Or a thousand. Hundreds of thousands—a white, ghostly tether coming from the backs of their skulls, leading toward the center of a room fifteen times larger than the great hall where Mammon's statue ruled over the other six.

Sage stepped back, unable to catch his breath. He closed his eyes and rubbed away the goosebumps that had popped up on both arms.

"What is it?" Elsbeth asked. "What's in there?"

David stepped forward and looked again. "There's another statue. Mammon. Like the one in the front room. Look at its hands, mates."

The statue was at least as tall as the one in the entrance chamber, but it was hard to tell because it was so far away. Its wings were spread wide and its claws stretched high in the air. Each ghostly tether protruding from the back of every head led to those claws.

"Floating heads," Elsbeth whispered. "Hundreds of thousands."

"All in pain," Sage said. "Agony. All races. All ages." He looked at Elsbeth. "What is this?"

"I just saw one disappear," David said. "There's another one. Vanished."

"I just saw a head pop out of one of the claws," Elsbeth said. "Again! Look, Sage, watch the claws."

"More are disappearing," David said. "At least ten in the last few seconds."

Sage watched the claws of the giant statue, and a head *did* pop out, with a white tether trailing behind it. And another. Then two more.

"They've noticed us, mates," David said.

As hard as it was to look away from the statue, Sage did. Thousands of heads had turned their way, eyes wide, faces terrified. They all mouthed the same two simple words.

Help me!

"They can see us," Elsbeth said. "They can see us!"

"There must be a million in there," David said.

Sage's mouth was so dry he couldn't offer an opinion. Then he saw something weird happening. Directly in front of his face, the crowd of heads began to separate, dividing themselves as though making way for something to approach from the opposite side of the chamber.

"What are they doing?" Elsbeth asked. "Can they communicate?"

"Probably, lass," David said. "Since they're all tied together with telegraph wire."

"Something's coming," Elsbeth said.

The pathway was closing now, led by single head on a direct path toward them. It wasn't until it stopped inches from Sage's face that he recognized it.

Sage, it mouthed. *Save me!*

Dad.

Sage screamed and reached through the black veil, desperate to reach him, but Elsbeth shouted as David yanked him back.

"Let me go," Sage screamed. "That's my dad!"

"He's not in there!" Elsbeth said. "You can't save him by going in there!"

Sage fought, pounding against David's strong grip, but the Boy with Might pulled him away from the black veil without comment. Sage watched his dad's face disappear.

"Let me go! I can help him! I can cut that cord!"

David pulled him well beyond the massive door and stopped.

Elsbeth grabbed the sides of Sage's face and forced him to look into her eyes. "That's *not* how you can save him, and you know it. We kill Mammon. That's the way." She squeezed his face and put her nose almost against his. "Sage! Leah told you what had to be done. Your grandpa knows it. So does Theo. And Ronan. You told me that. OK? We're going to do this. When we kill Mammon, we'll free everybody else in that room. Right?" She jerked his face, and he finally looked into her eyes. "Right?"

He nodded and took a deep breath. "Yeah."

"Let him go, David. And close that door." Elsbeth grabbed Sage's arm and led him away. She did not allow him to look back.

He took several deep breaths and wiped his eyes.

"A dungeon of souls, David called it," Elsbeth said. "The smartest thing he's said so far."

"The disappearing heads were humans who died within the human realm," Sage said quietly to Elsbeth. "Dead before they could free themselves."

"New ones popping out of the statue's claws are Mammon's latest victims." Elsbeth wiped tears off her cheeks. "Dozens every minute."

"Do you think every Prince has a place like this?" Sage asked.

Elsbeth didn't have to answer for Sage to know what she thought.

Yes. Of course.

Every Prince.

Sage shuddered.

"I'll not be opening that place again," David said. "So don't bother asking." He looked at Sage. "You all right, then?"

Sage nodded, not sure if he'd *ever* forget what he just saw.

"Then we've got rooms to search," David said. "I'm itching to hit something."

The next corridor was the farthest from Mammon's statue. They walked in silence, Sage leading the way. They stopped once when they heard faint voices, but the sounds faded and disappeared seconds later.

"There are five doors down this way," Elsbeth said. "I'm thinking positive. We'll find somebody else alive."

"Have you come across Harvick Bloomingale?" David asked. "I met the bloke when I was a lad, but he went missing after that. Had Fighting Arts."

"I did find him," Sage said. "He's gone. I'm sorry."

David didn't reply.

The crossbeam guarding the first door looked thicker than normal, and Sage started to lift one end when David reached over with one hand and plucked it off the door with about as much effort as it would take Sage to lift a broomstick.

Elsbeth pulled the door open and saw another wall of black. More Shadow Manipulation. Sage had a flash of panic but knew his dad's floating head wouldn't be on the other side. He took a breath to calm himself.

"Hiding a beast?" David asked. He swung his bar up onto a shoulder.

"Most likely," Elsbeth said, "but you know what that means? Somebody's alive in there. Protection for those still alive is what the hellhound said."

"Then let's gobsmack that thing." David started forward, but Elsbeth grabbed his arm.

"We don't just rush into things," she said. "We need to be smart about it."

"Is that right, lass? What's to be smart about? We either go in or we don't." David looked at Sage. "Am I off my trolley here? Or is there something you're not saying?"

"I'm saying we need to think about the order we go in," Elsbeth said.

David laughed. "No offense, lass, but without your gift, you might want to stay out here. I go in first, hit the beast, and if the bloke in the lizard skin is alive, either I rip it off or Sage does his memory thing."

Elsbeth's face reddened so quickly Sage wondered if her ears might bleed. "First of all, stop calling me lass! Second, my Persuasion didn't work out there, but it works in here. I used it against a hellhound earlier. Finally, we *all* go in. If Sage *does* Memory Share, you and I *both* go through the portal. Got it?"

David grinned and nodded. "Clear, miss, but I should go in first. I have the most battle experience. We all agree?"

Elsbeth nodded, her face as hard as Mammon's statue.

"I agree." Sage drew his sword. "Ready when you are."

Sage watched both of them step through the Shadow Manipulation. He waited a beat before following. He'd give David a chance to engage whatever beast awaited them.

Sage took a breath, moved as closely as he could, and peered into the room to see what he could see. Which was nothing. So he took one bold step forward—and fell on his side. He slammed against the ground so hard his sword dislodged and skidded out of sight.

The walls, ceiling, and floor were covered in thick ice. It was so cold that Sage's fingers and toes went fully numb after a few seconds. The fog from his breath swirled around his face in great puffs. His lungs hurt with every breath. He shoved his hands under his armpits and crossed his arms. He wouldn't last long dressed as he was.

Elsbeth tried to stand, but the howling wind kept pushing her down. David was on his feet, hunched over, his back to the hurricane force.

"We need to get out of here!" David yelled and charged the black veil. He slammed against it, bounced off, and landed on his back. His steel rod rolled away.

"I can't Teleport out!" Elsbeth shouted to Sage.

Sage barely heard her over the roar of the wind, but her voice sounded weak.

In the corner was a body wrapped in the lizard skin. Sage staggered that way. Through the frost covering the man's skin, Sage saw a lean, hatchet-faced black man with a large scar running from the corner of his left eye across his left cheek and both lips and ending on the bottom right of his chin. It looked as if he'd been attacked with a sword that had all but cut his face in half.

David hit the doorway again, but it was useless. "We're trapped in here!" he shouted.

"Open the portal," Elsbeth yelled. "Hurry!"

The cold had already penetrated to the depths of Sage's bones. By the time he skated over to the body, he was fighting an overwhelming urge to curl up in a corner and go to sleep. They'd all freeze to death within the next couple of minutes.

It took almost thirty seconds to place his stiff fingers in the correct Memory Sharing position. He couldn't feel the man's skin at all, and he couldn't see his face because of his own foggy breath.

Sage turned his head and closed his eyes, tried imagining the white canvas that helped the Memory Share process. He couldn't concentrate. The icy temperature had gripped him so solidly that freezing to death was the only thing his mind could focus on. He opened his eyes to try again.

"Hurry, Sage," Elsbeth said. She reached a hand out, her voice fading. "Please . . . hurry."

He tried again, but nothing happened. Panic gripped him. Another failure. He wasn't going to make it out of here, let alone be able to save anyone else.

He tried stuffing his hands under his armpits to warm them, but it didn't work. They were blue and curled inward, totally useless. His vision faded, and his nose ran freely, the mucus instantly freezing on his upper lip.

Elsbeth collapsed beside him as she reached out in a silent scream.

David lunged away from the door, grabbed Elsbeth, and lifted her into his body. "Stay warm, little lass," he said. He glared at Sage. "Fight! Open the portal!"

Lungs frozen, Sage couldn't take a deep breath. His joints stiffened. He lost balance and fell over onto his side. The icy floor began sucking heat from his body the instant he made contact.

So sleepy . . . so tired. He rolled onto his back. He'd read once that people who froze to death simply went to sleep and never woke up. The ceiling looked like a crystal winter wonderland, something you'd see inside an ice cave in the wilds of Alaska or Greenland. The ice sparkled and shimmered, so out of place inside this godforsaken place.

"Hurry, Sage," David shouted over the wind, his voice raspy and weakened. He'd dropped to his knees, Elsbeth still clutched tightly in his arms. "Get up! Open the portal!"

Sage nodded off, then jerked awake. He fought the cold lulling him into death. He turned his head and saw the Council member's frozen face and wondered why it wasn't also encased in several inches of ice. The lizard skin had no ice on it, either. Not even frost. It looked exactly like the one in Mordoc's dungeon cell.

Then he remembered touching it and would have shouted for joy if he had the energy. The lizard skin could save him!

With every ounce of his waning strength, he rolled onto his side and tried pushing himself up onto one elbow. He slipped and landed on a shoulder. His second effort got him there. Vision almost gone, he fought to his knees and slid up next to the man. Then he leaned forward and threw his entire body onto the skin.

———†———

She stepped through the bodies of the slaughtered, her feet wet from the blood. There was no one left to kill—all slain from a rage she didn't understand. A scent floated on the breeze, human mixed with an animal she didn't recognize, drifting down the mountain just ahead of black smoke from a raging fire. The screams of the dead had faded by the time . . .

———†———

Intense heat rippled through Sage like the flame from a blowtorch—jerking him from the memory and warming his body in an instant. Relief overwhelming him, he stayed where he was until he felt himself roasting and then stayed a few seconds after that. Finally, unable to bear it another second, he rolled off, his skin smoking like a Thanksgiving turkey. His frozen flesh had absorbed the shock of the sudden heat, and he felt none of the burning he'd experienced in Mordoc's cell. Wasting no time, he scooted over to the man's head while flexing his fingers and then planted them squarely on the man's face.

He focused on a white landscape, but not on a painter's canvas. This time he imagined a snowy field, a blizzard of epic proportions, virgin snow unbroken by human or animal tracks and stretching as far and wide as his vision would take it. The swirling smoke materialized, and images formed: mountains, forests, a village, and a hideous flying creature.

Then he had it—a mountain range outside a small village— summertime—waves of heat radiating off a wagon track of hardened dirt. He concentrated on a spot near a large tree before finally Teleporting.

Sage arrived on his knees, hands in the Memory Sharing position. He shivered from exhaustion, terrified from near death. Birds chirped overhead, and strange jungle noises sounded all around him, but he didn't have the energy to inspect any of it. With quivering hands and heart pounding, he collapsed to the ground. He'd almost given up. Almost died. Quit. Just another few seconds—just a few—and surely he would have closed his eyes for good.

He didn't understand the memory from the lizard skin. Was it Leviathan? Had she killed the humans or arrived afterward? He sensed something different this time. Confusion. Anger. Sadness. Weariness. In just those few brief moments, emotions raged through him, pounding and relentless and real. How? Why? Was he the only one receiving the messages because of his Memory Share? He wished Leah were here to ask. He missed her, he realized for the first time. He really missed her.

He closed his eyes and took several cleansing breaths, felt his body healing and gaining strength. Had David had the strength to carry Elsbeth through the portal? Had they made it? If so, where were they?

The hot sun on his skin felt heavenly. After several minutes he felt better, rested, fully alert, his werewolf wounds mostly healed.

The sounds of the jungle were strong—dozens of insects, birds of all types, howling monkeys, and at least one big-game cat growling at something far away.

Then he sensed something else, something big and dark and dangerous, something high and far away but gaining fast. His skin began to crawl, literally, like a jar full of insects had just been dumped into his hair. He jumped up and looked around.

The crawling sensation grew stronger and spread down his neck and onto his shoulders, down his forehead and into his eyes. His vision changed, just a little at first, and then more. The world went gray in his peripheral vision, but his center vision became bright and brilliant, the colors so stark and rich he could see every detail for what seemed like miles. Then he turned his head, and his vision jumped back to normal.

"What the . . ."

He turned his head back to where the vision thing happened, and it happened again: gray edges, brilliant colors in the center. Sage kept turning his head in the same direction, almost to the side now, and his vision popped back to normal.

Meanwhile, his entire body tingled, but not like when he was Teleporting. Only the very surface of his skin felt funny, like a gentle breeze was blowing along the hair on his arms.

A feeling of complete dread washed over him, a virtual blanket of creepiness. He kept turning his head back and forth. Just by moving his head, his vision changed from colorful flashes surrounded by gray to normal sight. Finally, his eyes settled on the direction with the clearest vision. He hoped that would lead him where he needed to go.

He could see a village in a valley below him, a least a quarter mile away, surrounded by mountain peaks on three sides and a lake on the fourth. He saw thatched huts, chickens and goats running loose, villagers hauling water, clothes drying on wooden racks; Sage didn't know what year it was, but he saw nothing modern or convenient.

The sky above the mountain peaks appeared bright blue, almost computer enhanced. Just as the feeling of depression, dread, and darkness seemed too heavy to bear, Sage heard a high-pitched screech that drove nails into his eardrums. He covered both ears and saw the village explode with frantic activity.

The screech sounded again, louder this time. Sage doubled over and pressed his hands harder against his ears. He believed his eardrums might burst if the heinous sound continued.

People in the village poured out of their huts and grabbed hold of every living thing they could. As a third screech ripped through the sky, several villagers pointed in the direction of the mountain.

Skimming over the treetops, soaring as gracefully as a giant eagle, was a hideous monster straight from the pages of the *Encyclopedia of Dark Creatures*. The beast was larger than the biggest horse, with wings stretching at least ten feet across; short, powerful legs with claws as big as butcher knives; and a flat, demonic, lion-looking face.

Gargoyle.

Like a missile shot from a jet fighter, the beast tucked its wings and headed straight for the village. Sage broke from the trees and sprinted hard. He was weaponless, his sword having skidded away on the icy floor of the dungeon cell. It didn't matter. He was a quarter mile from the nearest villager, and he didn't really know what he would do when he got there, but he was here for a reason—and it wasn't to stand around and watch.

Halfway there, Sage saw a man with a sword strapped to his back and two long knives sheathed on each hip running into the center of the village, pointing and shouting and ordering people to seek shelter.

The gargoyle screeched again. Dizzy, Sage stumbled, then went sprawling across the ground in the midst of a full-on sprint. His right shoulder took the impact, followed by his right hip and leg. He rolled at least three complete revolutions before stopping.

The gargoyle landed, snatched a child, and took flight. The man with the sword jumped and sliced at the belly of the beast, causing the child to drop into his waiting arms. The child's mother grabbed her and fled into the nearest hut.

Sage staggered to his feet and ran forward, instinctively grabbing for a sword that wasn't there. The gargoyle streaked high into the sky, but didn't fly away, obviously repositioning for another attack.

It was then that Sage recognized the man with the sword—Kato Hunter—missing from his African village in the mid-1800s while tracking a gargoyle. He was the only person left on the village street by the time Sage got there. Kato wore leather boots laced to his knees, brown pants, and an animal-pelt shirt. Besides his sword and knives, he had a looped bullwhip tied to a leather belt at his waist. Then Sage noticed why Kato hadn't been affected by the gargoyle's screeching—his ears were filled with some kind of solid, milky substance.

Sage hid in the shadow of a hut, out of view from the soaring monster, and watched. The gargoyle tucked its legs and wings tightly as it twirled high above them and then dove, rocketing straight toward Kato.

Kato didn't flinch. He stood ready: body rigid, sword back, eyes fixed upon the beast with a hatred that seemed to generate heat. The beast bared the claws on its front legs and opened its mouth wide. The war cry that rained down on them drove Sage to his knees and toppled him onto his side. Gritting his teeth, he fought with every ounce of strength not to scream and give away his location. He wanted to squeeze his eyes shut, to block out Kato's capture, but he couldn't. He had to watch. He had to watch his own failure play out before him. Again.

18

As the gargoyle was about to rip him to pieces, Kato dropped to one knee and swung his sword in an upward arc, nicking the beast on its left hind leg. It veered off sharply, an earsplitting cry of pain filling the air, then soared high again, circling. Kato watched and slowly turned his body to match its movements.

Several goats and pigs wandered through the streets; a few cows and young calves were corralled off to Sage's right. A number of dogs and cats were out and about. Chickens ran free everywhere. In the center, unbeknownst to all of them, was Kato, a one-man army protecting his flock.

With the sun behind Sage's back, he was able to see every move the gargoyle made. Sage didn't understand how the clarity of the gargoyle was so crisp and bright and vivid.

High above, the gargoyle continued to hover. With no advanced moves or indicators, the beast dropped from the sky in a flash and headed for a hog rooting around in one of the villager's vegetable gardens. Kato wasted no time. He sprinted to intercept, sword raised, his face emotionless. The gargoyle got there first. It clamped its claws—front and back—directly on top of the swine's back and shot into the sky.

Kato didn't give up. He jumped at the last possible second, raised his sword high over his head, and thrust it forward, driving it into the gargoyle's left shoulder.

The beast screamed again, a wail of agony that again drove Sage to his knees. Kato's sword stuck solidly in place, blood gushing out of the wound. Still the gargoyle held on to its prize. It wobbled as it flew toward the mountain from which it came, but its retreat was fast and sure. Kato watched it fly away, a satisfied look on his face.

Sage came out from the shadow of a hut and walked over to Kato. He noticed his eerie new vision was fading as quickly as the gargoyle had flown away. The warrior heard Sage's approach and turned his way. He frowned at the sight of him.

My clothes, Sage figured. *And maybe my race.*

"You are Master of the Fighting Arts, Kato Hunter." Sage bowed deeply. "I am honored to have witnessed your skills. I am Sage. Of Council prophecy." He paused, unsure if he should say the rest of it. He did. "I'm here to prevent your capture from a Dark beast."

Kato's eyes narrowed to mere flints of coal—dark, hard, and cold—but a sense of understanding softened them almost immediately. He looked away, closed his eyes, and after saying nothing for a long time, finally looked at Sage. "I have studied the prophecy. Time must be short. You have many gifts?"

"Some. I have trained in the Arts, although my sword is . . ." He touched his empty scabbard. "Well, I lost my sword." He admired

258

the rugged beauty of the leather rigging that kept Kato's weapons secured around his waist.

Kato was slightly shorter than Sage and leaner through the shoulders and chest. His ropy arms sported virtual roadmaps of old scars from past battles.

The warrior stared at him for several moments before glancing to where Sage's sword should have been. He shook his head and began inspecting the ground where the gargoyle's blood led into the mountains. "I am not surprised by your arrival. It is wise of the Dark ones to capture me. I have slain many." He pointed to the glistening trail of blood. "That beast guards a nest I have searched many weeks to locate."

"That's why you jammed your sword in its shoulder? You're going to follow the blood trail?"

"A tracking method my grandfather once used. I grow weary wandering the mountains. I must leave now to hunt the beast, before the blood dries and becomes difficult to see." He turned away, then looked back. "I must gather supplies for our journey. Wait here." He walked off and mumbled under his breath, "I, Kato Hunter, rescued by a boy with no sword."

Sage felt his face go hot with embarrassment. The sun beat down on him while he waited for Kato's return, but after nearly freezing to death, he wasn't about to complain. Villagers came out of their huts, alternating their stares between him and the distant sky. In just a few minutes, most of the livestock was rounded up.

The weird vision thing was gone now. Sage thought it was somehow connected to the gargoyle. He'd sensed its arrival a full minute before the creature arrived.

Sensing, described by the small book Leah gave him, allowed one to feel the approach of Dark beasts or hybrid angelic-human creations, with a heightened sense of sight, smell, and hearing.

But how? Why so suddenly? Had almost freezing to death done something to accelerate it?

Kato returned with a new sword strapped to his back and a hunting pack slung over one shoulder. He carried a slightly wider sword and sheath in one hand.

"You are trained in the Fighting Arts?" Kato asked. "Your gift is true?"

"I am," Sage said in his most confident voice. "It is."

"Then you will put this on. I must witness your skills for myself." Kato handed Sage the wider sword and sheath. "Follow me."

Sage followed him out of the village and across a field, stopping near a tree line in a large shaded area.

Kato set his pack on the ground.

"We will battle," Kato said.

"What?" It came out sounding like a croak. He assumed Kato just wanted to see how he could handle a sword in the most rudimentary way.

"We will not fight to the death, young Sage. Do not appear so alarmed." Kato grinned, but the scar running diagonally across his hatchet face only made matters worse.

While Sage nervously attached the sword sheath to his belt, Kato cut the air with his sword like a man who'd been wielding it for three hundred years.

Sage had a decision to make. Should he fight Kato fair and square, using only his gift of Fighting Arts, or should he also throw

Teleporting into the mix? He was confident in his sword skills and his years of training, but Kato had probably been hunting gargoyles for centuries, given the number of scars he wore.

Sunlight flashed off the edges of Kato's sword as he practiced his swings, blocks, and parries. The blade looked sharp enough to slice a hair down the middle. Sage tried not to think about it.

"Warm your arms and shoulders, young Sage," Kato said, after Sage had secured the sheath.

Sage nodded and drew the sword. The small, checkered grooves on the wooden grip were nearly worn smooth from use. Both the pommel and guard were made from a tempered iron so smooth and shiny Sage saw reflections of the clouds on their surfaces, but it was the blade that grabbed his attention. From the guard to the very point, including the fuller, it shone like crystal and reflected sunlight like a mirror. Both edges were razor sharp. It was light, weighing half that of the one he'd dropped inside Kato's frozen cell. Written just above the guard was the same strange writing as that on the patu and bell Theo had given him.

"That sword was crafted by the ancients," Kato said. "It was given to me by my Fighting Arts instructor. I have kept it hidden for many years."

"It feels so fragile," Sage said. He compared it to the solid sword Kato held. "As if it will snap in two the instant you strike it with yours."

Kato laughed. "Do not fear, Sage. That sword is indestructible. Trust me. Swing it a few times so that we may begin."

Sage did as he was told. Like Addison's use of a figure eight motion against him in Grandpa's backyard, Sage used it now to loosen up. He worked through a series of basic sword katas. When he was ready, he nodded to Kato and positioned himself in a battle-ready stance.

Kato walked over and stood in front of him. "I must know that you are able to defend yourself against the flying demon."

"I understand," Sage said. He made his decision about using Teleportation. "I will allow you to begin." He bladed his body, raised his sword, bowed slightly at the waist, and fixed his eyes on a rock ten feet behind Kato. Tingling signaled the beginning of the Teleportation process.

Kato also bowed, took a step back, and swung his sword so fast and so suddenly at Sage's head that he almost didn't have time to imagine himself standing by the rock.

But he did. He appeared behind Kato in time to see his sword slice the air where Sage had just been. Kato controlled his sword on his backswing and spun around.

Sage moved before Kato could get his feet set, then unleashed a series of strikes and blows with a speed he'd only used once with Leah. High, low, across the body, Sage worked the sword so fast that Superman would have been proud. He drove Kato backward, not giving him time do anything but work defense.

The warrior finally jumped away to put some distance between them, then set his feet and went on the attack himself. But Sage disappeared again just as Kato's sword got within a foot of clashing against anything solid.

Sage attacked from behind—moving and sliding and dancing ever forward, his sword a blur of motion. The fact that Kato could see Sage's sword and react fast enough defensively to block each blow was amazing. Just as Kato recovered enough to go on the offensive, Sage Teleported away and attacked from the man's weak side, then from behind again before coming at him from the other side.

Sage swung twice and disappeared. Three times, then he was gone. The tingling ran so strong now that all Sage needed to do was give half a thought about being someplace else and he vanished and appeared there instantly. He was careful to always Teleport far enough away to avoid getting hit by Kato's long reach. It wasn't long before the great warrior was so confused about where Sage would appear next that his technique began to crumble.

It wasn't a fair fight, Sage knew, but he had to make Kato understand that Fighting Arts—combined with Teleportation—was more than enough to face a gargoyle.

Sage didn't know how long they sparred, but it left both of them gasping for breath. Kato finally dropped to his knees and placed his sword on the ground beside him.

Sage sheathed his sword, dropped to his knees a few feet from Kato, and faced him. In addition to the one noticeable scar on Kato's face, he also had two lesser scars of equal length—one on each cheek.

They took several moments to catch their breaths. "You have noticed the wound from my first fight with a flying demon," Kato said. "I thought I had killed the beast. As I gloated about, dancing like the fool I was, it rose from the ground and attacked with its last remaining strength. My disfigurement serves to remind me that even one drop of blood still flowing through their veins makes them dangerous."

Sage was too tired to speak. He wiped at the sweat running out of his hair and down his face.

"Your sword skill alone needs much development," Kato said. "You have a solid foundation but need work on foot placement, swing angles, and maintaining balance while moving. However, when you combine what you have with Teleportation, you are a formidable competitor. I studied all the gifts during my time at the Tomb, but I have not seen Teleportation used in such a manner until today. Nor have I seen such natural Fighting Arts skills since Beowulf."

"You knew Beowulf?" Sage asked. "For real?"

"He was my instructor," Kato said. "Never, until now, did I believe I would see such skill again. Especially in someone so young. I must admit my doubt regarding the truth of the Prophecy of Seth. But today I stand in awe of what I just witnessed." He bowed his head in Sage's direction.

Sage felt embarrassed by the attention. Leah was light years ahead of him, and he wouldn't last fifteen seconds against an Arch, so all of this praise coming from Kato Hunter left him wondering where in the middle he really was.

"A friend of mine has a store called Beowulf's Loft. I've done some reading about him. About his death. He must have been a great warrior."

Kato smiled. "Beowulf is not dead, young Sage. His reported death was to allow him to live the rest of his days doing special assignments for the Council. The grendels would have hunted him for eternity had his death not been staged."

"Grendels," Sage whispered in awe.

The grendels were large and powerful monsters with superior intelligence. They descended from the original Grendel, whom Beowulf killed while protecting the small village where he grew up.

Almost a mix between a bigfoot and a troll, they were lean and quick and possessed undocumented powers. Grendels were among the purest bloodlines of the Emin race. The *Encyclopedia of Dark Creatures* had five full pages dedicated to them.

"Beowulf isn't dead? Wait until I tell Theo that!" Sage laughed out loud and shook his head.

"Theophylaktos Alastair?" Kato asked.

Sage's jaw dropped. "Yes! You know Theo?"

"Gifted with Sight. The most accurate in all the Council. It is Theo who foresaw Beowulf's future and Theo who devised the plan to stage his death. You know Theophylaktos Alastair and know nothing of this?"

"I don't know *anything* about this. Theo and I have talked about Beowulf a lot of times, but mainly about his sword. He buys stuff to sell in his shop and gives me old weapons when he finds them. Junk mostly, I assume, but he gets a lot of ancient weapons and allows me keep them in my secret bunker. Anyway, he's told me stories about Beowulf's sword. It's supposed to have magical powers against evil creatures. Have you ever heard of that?"

"Indeed," Kato said. "It was forged by the ancient Elioudians in Tartarus from an unknown mixture of metals and the blood from the prophet Seth. After being blessed by Archangel Gabriel, it was given to a descendent of Seth for safekeeping until Beowulf's birth. Those gifted with Sight instructed the Council to again hide the sword after Beowulf's death was staged. Legend says that when used by a descendent of Seth, it wields power of such purity that the flesh of no Dark beast can stand against it."

"That's the same story Theo told me," Sage said. "So it must be true."

"It is true, young Sage. For Theo is the one who arranged it all."

"Does he know where the sword is?" Sage asked. "Do you? It's been lost for centuries."

"Certainly." Kato smiled.

"Where?"

"You have just used it to make me look foolish."

It took a second for Sage to understand, but then he got it. He looked at the sword by his side, speechless.

"It was created for you, young Sage," Kato said. "Beowulf's Fighting Arts skills were tremendous, it is true, but he would not have defeated the original Grendel without that sword. The prophet Seth foresaw Grendel's battle with Beowulf while using a normal sword. The great warrior was killed, as was then everyone in Beowulf's small village, including a young girl whose ancestry was key to your birth. So the sword was forged and hidden for Beowulf's use against Grendel. He saved the village and the girl, ultimately giving rise to your birth.

"The sword was again hidden, by me, for this very moment. I must confess that I doubted Theo's instructions. Your presence has restored my knowledge that the Almighty controls all things."

Sage thought back to when he had told Kato who he was. Kato's eyes had narrowed in suspicion, but he really hadn't looked surprised. "You knew you would be captured?" Sage asked him.

Kato climbed to his feet and sheathed his own sword. He walked over and grabbed his pack. "Theo's Sight showed him your arrival in my village and me handing you the sword. He told me nothing else. He instructed me to secure the sword in such a manner that it would never be found. He did not mention my capture. Nor did he mention what year you would show up to retrieve it."

Kato motioned for Sage to prepare to move out. "So every time Theo and I talked about Beowulf's sword, he knew you had it and would be giving it to me." Sage shook his head. "I'm gonna have a long talk with him the next time I see him."

"Theo knew that the Sage from prophecy would have many gifts and would have the ability to travel through time in some manner." Kato stared hard at Sage. "I did not understand how you would do it until you told me you were here to prevent my capture. I knew from prophecy that some Council members would be taken, of course, but I did not connect the two events until you mentioned it. I have studied all of the gifts. You used Memory Share and Teleportation?"

"Yes."

"What other gifts have been bestowed?" Kato pointed to a far mountain and began walking that way.

Sage fell in behind him. "Those two, Fighting Arts and Pathfinding. Clarity, at least a little. So five. I think I received Sensing right after I got here." Sage described the weird vision thing, the tingling on the surface of his skin, and how the extra vision only worked when he looked toward the mountain where the gargoyle had come from.

"That vision went away as soon as the beast left?" Kato asked.

"It faded slowly," Sage said. "The farther away the gargoyle flew, the weaker the signal. Kind of like a radio too far from a transmitting tower."

Kato turned and looked at him. "What is it you speak of? Radio and transmitting tower?"

"Oops. Those haven't been invented yet." He briefly explained what he meant.

Kato nodded afterward. "If you are successful in preventing my capture, I will see that one day. I am less than three hundred years old, after all. Most Council members reach a millennium."

"Is Theo that old?"

Kato walked in silence, then asked, "What century is your time?"

"The twenty-first century. The seventeenth year." Sage held his breath. Theo looked at least a hundred years old. His mind was as sharp as anyone he knew, but he could barely get around.

"He was born around the turn of the century," Kato said. "I do not know the exact year, but he mentioned once that he was born the same year that Leif Erikson, the great Pathfinder for the Council, discovered the North American continent. That was also the year that Hungary was established as a Christian kingdom by Stephen I."

"That was in the year 1000!" Sage said. "Theo is one thousand and seventeen years old!"

Kato shrugged. "I do not understand your concern. That is not so surprising. I have met many that old. Besides, it is what makes his Sight so special."

"I do know that," Sage said.

"It should tell you how special you are," Kato said.

"What? Why?"

"Theo is the most valued member of the Council. The accuracy of his Sight is second only to the legend of Seth, the ancient Elioudian. The Council should lock him away and protect him against all harm. Yet he runs a shop in your town and collects old weapons for you. If the Dark beasts knew of his existence, he would be dead within minutes." Kato began walking again. "Come. Daylight waits for no man."

Sage followed and thought about Theo. The most valuable member of the Council was on assignment? Grandpa had told Sage how important he was to the Council, but hearing it from Kato made it all the more real.

19

Kato set a fast pace despite being weighed down with a heavy bundle over his shoulder. Sage followed, not quite believing that Beowulf's sword was actually strapped to his waist. As they walked higher into the mountains, Sage worried more and more about Elsbeth and David. He hoped they had appeared near where Kato had been captured and would be waiting for him. If not . . . well, he didn't want to think about that.

Sage explained to Kato all that had happened and that he expected Elsbeth and David to be waiting somewhere up ahead. He described the Crab Man and his tool to breach into the human realm, the stone mansion, the two giant statues of Mammon, the Dungeon of Souls, the dozen corridors with individual dungeon cells, and his theory that Dark beasts used the building to continent jump.

Kato didn't say much about any of it. Since Sage couldn't see his reaction while walking behind him, he wondered what impact his story had on the hunter.

They hiked in silence for a while before Sage asked, "How many gargoyles have you killed?"

It took Kato a moment to answer. "I do not know the flying demons by that name," he said. "I have hunted them for nearly two hundred and fifty years and have slain thousands. They are not so plentiful as when I was a boy. My father slew more than I by measures, and his father twice that amount."

"How did gargoyles come about?" Sage asked. "They look like a mixture of three or four animals. I saw pictures of them in a book."

"You must learn your histories, young Sage. The book of Genesis speaks of God looking upon the earth and seeing all flesh corrupted. The Nephilim and Rephaim and Emim befouled all that walked or crawled upon the earth. The book of Jasher speaks of them mixing animals of one species with another. The book of Jubilees speaks of their sin against all the beasts and birds and all that moved about." Kato spoke while maintaining his hurried pace.

Sage was almost forced to jog. "What about the flood?"

"The flood destroyed everything on the surface," Kato said. "Many from the evil races went underground and waited until the earth dried, then fought their way out of the underground to resume their battle against man. The Council was formed to rid the earth of these abominations. Much of Greek mythology is based upon creatures my ancestors and I have spent centuries hunting. The centaur and minotaur and satyr are beasts my father and grandfather slew. They exist to this day in the deep shadows of the great forests. The evil races have done unspeakable damage to the human race."

"I've seen a lot of that since breakfast yesterday."

"The prophecy of Sage the Warrior has been a beacon of hope for the Council since the beginning. Your appearance was to come in our darkest days and mark the beginning of the final battle." Kato turned toward him. "I must now track the beast. Watch and learn."

Sage watched as Kato used all of his concentration to track the trail of blood. Not much had made it to the ground. The majority had landed on the treetops and the rest on branches well above Kato's head. He climbed trees, maneuvered around clefts and ravines, and inspected suspicious spots of moisture on plants that camouflaged it.

After almost four hours, Kato found a large, flat rock and sat down to rest. He broke a skin of water and two large pieces of hard bread and cut off a piece of cheese for both of them. Sage ate and drank in relief.

"You mentioned a nest earlier," Sage said. "How do you know there's a nest?"

"The beasts live in family units," Kato said. "Like us. The males guard the nest while the females hunt. I learned as a boy what changes occur in the females' bodies after they drop a batch of eggs. I slew an adult female many weeks ago. There is a nest. Believe me. The attack on my village this morning confirmed it. He seeks revenge for the death of his partner."

"His wife?" Sage asked.

"I should not think a priest joined them in holy matrimony," Kato said. "He is the father of the eggs, which will hatch soon if I do not destroy them."

Sage wondered if it was right to kill other creatures that just wanted to raise a family and live in peace. He asked Kato about that.

"Live in peace?" Kato spat. "Live in peace? They eat us, young Sage. We are a source of food. It is why you can no longer find people living outside the protection of a village. My great-grandfather was raised in a mountain home many miles from the nearest village. He fled when a family of flying demons killed and ate his mother, father, and two sisters. No one has lived alone in the mountains for many decades." Kato's voice rose, and the scars on his face turned pink.

Sage dropped *that* subject. "Maybe the wound you gave it will kill it," he said. "It's lost a lot of blood. How can it survive?"

Kato sat silent for several minutes before answering. Finally, he said, "That is possible. It might die, but I must make certain. They have angelic blood, though it is evil. Like us, they heal very quickly. I do not think I wounded it enough to kill it."

Sage chewed the cheese, ate the bread, sipped his water. He really liked Kato. The guy was a true warrior. Hard, no-nonsense, rugged and extremely patient. Sage could learn tons from him. "Who protects the village when you're hunting?" he asked.

"No one right now. I have begun training a younger man. It will be many summers until he is able to defend the village. He is human, and it takes much practice to acquire such skills. Should one attack while I am gone, the people will flee underground. The beasts cannot fit into the tunnels beneath our huts."

"Tunnels?"

"The villagers are experienced at hiding. The tunnels have many heavy barricades that are bolted into place behind the villagers as they flee deeper into the mountains. The tunnel system is quite effective."

274

Sage nodded, impressed at their ingenuity. "After you were captured, how would the gargoyle have defeated your village? I mean, assuming that happened. Which, of course, I don't know happened at all. I mean . . . well . . . it could have, or not, it's just . . . I'm not saying . . . I don't know what happened . . ." He let his words fade away, feeling like a total idiot for not thinking about the question before he asked it.

Kato looked at him, his face as severe as ever, his scars almost pulsing with intensity. "The same way they have defeated many other villages. They dig them out. It takes them many weeks, but they remain at the village site and dig their own holes like moles until they find the prizes they seek. If any of my people escaped through the rear of our tunnels, the beasts would smell them. The flying demons can smell a human from nearly a half mile away. This is why I must protect the village today. It is why I must destroy the eggs in the lair."

Sage shivered at the thought of being trapped underground while a gargoyle slowly dug its way to him. He'd rather die fighting out in the open.

"Are you ready?" Kato gathered his things.

Sage nodded and stood. "They can really smell us from a half mile away?" *This was a suicide mission.*

"Yes, and they have exceptional hearing. No more talking from this point. We will be there soon."

They hiked for another half hour in total silence. Kato followed the blood trail with a greater ease because fewer trees grew this high up the mountain and allowed more to reach the ground. Finally, Kato stopped behind a clump of huge rocks. He pointed up the mountain to a spot where the trees were pushed over and stacked against one another to form a kind of crude fort. Sage saw Kato's sword on the ground, the one he'd buried into the shoulder of the gargoyle.

Kato stared at the structure and scanned the area. He leaned over and whispered. "I have been here before. Many years ago. More than a century. I should have considered this place."

"What is it?" Sage asked.

"Through the stacked trees, there is a cave opening. I remember the mouth of the cave being small, but large enough for one of the beasts to squeeze through." Kato's eyes moved from the trees to the cave opening and then back to Sage. "The wind blows into our faces. If the beast is in the cave, our scent will not be noticed from within. The odor inside the cave is strong."

You can say that again! A stench strong enough to knock him over drifted into his face.

Kato stepped behind a boulder and closed his eyes. He took several cleansing breaths. "Yes, I remember the cave clearly now. Almost a century and a half ago, before Theo came to instruct me to hide Beowulf's sword for you, I killed a large male beast inside that cave. I checked this location many times over the next few decades, but no other beasts settled here. Eventually, I forgot about it."

The gargoyle hunter found a small rock on the ground and picked it up, then scratched a diagram on the boulder near him.

"There is a main chamber about ten paces inside the mouth. It is large, twice the size of my village. On the far side, there is a small tunnel, large enough for us to escape through, if necessary, but much too small for one of the beasts to follow."

"How many are in there? I mean, I know you don't know for sure, but could there be more than one?"

"Doubtful. They live in family units. I killed its mate. Not enough time has passed for it to have found another." Kato slapped him on the back. "Do not fear. Though a wounded beast is dangerous, it cannot stand against two warriors with sword skills such as ours."

Were Elsbeth and David in there? Sage wondered. He'd seen no sign of them. If they *were* in the cave, they might feel safer remaining there. They'd just hunker down and wait. He hoped. Elsbeth would not wander off by herself, but David was such a wildcard, so macho and unpredictable; Sage couldn't predict what he might drive Elsbeth to do.

Had the Crab Man breached entry into the gargoyle cave and taken Kato there? Would they be forced to fight on two fronts?

"We will approach together," Kato said. "I will go into the cave first. Are you ready?"

"Yes." Sage drew his sword after Kato drew his.

After tugging his pack tightly into place, Kato stepped out from behind the rock and stalked quietly forward. He deftly avoided animal bones that littered the ground all around them. Sage followed behind and stepped in each spot Kato chose.

The stench was a mixture of rotting flesh, excrement, and a stale odor he couldn't identify. It drifted out of the stack of trees in waves of putridity. On three occasions, he nearly vomited.

At least fifty trees had been broken and dragged into position to cover the cave entrance. They were piled on top of one another in such a way that from a distance they looked like a humongous brush pile. Kato led him to an opening large enough to drive a car through. There, no bones lay scattered on the path leading through the trees, just smooth dirt with hundreds of gargoyle footprints leading in and out of the entrance.

The mouth of the cave was comprised of jagged rocks and large boulders, hidden in the shadow of the felled trees. It was narrow, just a few feet wide. Sage noticed black marks, maybe rubbings of gargoyle skin, along the rocks on each side.

Kato stopped just inside the entrance, dropped to one knee, and listened. Sage did the same. The smell was even worse here. The opening drew the air out of the cave like a chimney, driving it into their faces in a steady stream.

Sage looked around Kato and expected to see solid darkness ahead, but he saw a soft glow of light instead. He wanted to ask Kato about it, but he wasn't about to make any noise. The silence of the cave was complete. The absence of sound made him feel as if he and Kato were the only living things in the world. He felt a sudden loneliness and wondered if Kato, Mordoc, David, and Elsbeth had felt the same isolation inside the lizard skin.

Kato stood and crept forward. As Kato had described earlier, a hallway about ten feet long opened up into a cavern about the size of a football stadium. Dozens of burning torches were mounted along the cave walls and produced just enough light to illuminate a horror chamber more terrifying than Sage's worst nightmare.

Hanging from the ceiling were hundreds of dead bodies in various states of decay. Most were animals—horses and cows, but Sage also saw tigers and bears and various other creatures. Mixed among all of them were humans—men mostly, but not all. Sage turned his eyes away, disgusted, his rage building.

The gargoyles had dug a large pit at least fifty yards across and several feet deep. It was a virtual lake of blood and guts and bones. Hundreds of rats the size of small cats feasted there and now turned their beady eyes upon Sage and Kato.

Bones piled dozens of feet high covered a large area on the far left. There were thousands upon thousands of bones picked clean, hundreds of skulls, too many of those human. On the far right, Sage saw another chamber. Kato motioned for them to head that way.

Kato stuck close to the cave wall, where fewer bones littered the floor. Sage could hear the rats now, chewing, squeaking, splashing, and scurrying about within the bloody soup. The air was so thick with the smell of death he could hardly breathe. His eyes watered and blurred his vision. Kato stopped suddenly, and Sage bumped into him.

"I forgot," he whispered in Sage's ear. "Put these in your ears." Kato grabbed one of Sage's hands and placed two balls of a soft, waxy substance into his palm. "Otherwise the screech of these beasts will immobilize you."

Sage had almost forgotten how he'd been driven to his knees by the gargoyle's cry during the battle in the village. He watched Kato shove blobs of stuff in his ears and followed suit.

Pointing with his sword, Kato showed Sage where they were headed. On the far side of the cave, near the secondary chamber, was a passageway almost invisible in the shadows. Kato carefully placed each foot before moving. Sage wondered about the burning torches. They were long pieces of tree branches with some kind of material wrapped around one end. Had the material been dipped in some type of oil? Stopping just under one, he looked up and saw flaming bits dripping onto the ground. He couldn't smell anything over the stench of death and decay, but he wondered what substance made the torches burn so brightly. Then again, maybe he didn't want to know.

On the far side of the rat-infested pond of death, Kato climbed up several rocks and stepped into the small passage. Seconds later, Sage joined him. Up to now, they hadn't seen or heard any evidence of the wounded gargoyle.

"There you are!" Elsbeth whispered from the darkness behind them.

Kato spun so fast only David's metal bar prevented his sword from striking her.

"Hold tight, mate," David said to Kato. "We're on the same team."

Sage flinched at how close Kato's sword had come to Elsbeth. He took a deep breath to calm himself. Yet he was so happy, he fought the urge to pull her into a huge hug. "Scared me to *death*, Elsbeth." He turned to Kato. "These are the friends I told you about. Elsbeth and David. Guys, this is Kato Hunter. Fighting Arts."

"My apologies." Kato bowed slightly. "My focus was elsewhere."

"Sorry I scared you," Elsbeth said. "We stepped through the portal a few minutes ago. Where are we?"

Sage was confused. "A few *minutes* ago? I've been here for hours."

"We thought this could happen, Sage," Elsbeth said. "Can't worry about it, though. Where are we?"

"I need some fresh air," David said. "I'll never get this stink out of my nose."

They were whispering so quietly Sage could barely hear them. He leaned forward. "We're tracking a wounded gargoyle. Kato thinks there's a nest in here, and he needs to smash the eggs."

"They will discover our presence soon," Kato said. "Even this smell will not mask the odor of four of us." He dug into his pack and pulled more of the ear wax out and handed it to Elsbeth and David. "Push this deep into your ears. We must hurry. Come. Follow me."

They stooped as they walked and traveled for another minute. Up ahead, Sage saw light, brighter than from the other chamber. Kato led them to the edge of the opening, pointed to a small ledge, and motioned for them to stay behind while he looked. He crawled ahead and stared for several seconds, then waved all of them forward. Sage scooted up next to Kato and saw terror on his face—stark, raw terror.

It was a nest. A community. A virtual small town. Gargoyleville. Although this chamber was less than half the size of the other one, it was filled wall-to-wall with gargoyles. And directly in the center, being treated by three others, was the gargoyle Kato had wounded.

Sage heard Elsbeth gasp. *Her* horror-stricken face didn't worry him so much as David's. In the short time Sage had known the Boy with Might, he'd sensed a confidence bordering on punishing arrogance. David looked for chances to crush his enemies, to demoralize them. Now his fearless superiority appeared shaken to its foundation. His trembling lower lip somehow frightened Sage more than the beasts gathered below them.

Positioned along the edges of the cavern were huge stacks of straw, each with at least ten eggs. Sage did a quick count and figured at least three hundred eggs. Then he counted the gargoyles. Thirty full-size adults and eighteen smaller ones. They had walked into a hive of almost fifty beasts.

Sage could hardly breathe. They needed to leave quietly before they gave themselves away. They might be able to take on a few of the beasts, but an entire herd? Not happening. So much for Kato's prediction of there being just one gargoyle and one nest.

Kato began backing out. Just as Sage was about to turn around, he noticed one of the gargoyles stand on its hind legs and sniff the air. It belted some sort of garbled alert, and several more stood and sniffed.

Not good. At all!

Somebody tugged on his arm, and Sage looked behind him. Kato was already gone, and Elsbeth was disappearing into the tunnel. David tried pulling Sage that way, but he fought it off. "Let's watch," he whispered.

In a sudden explosion of excitement, nearly every gargoyle in the room began communicating at once. In a flash, half of them fled out of the chamber and headed for the Cavern of Death.

Kato and Elsbeth! "Go to the end of the tunnel," he whispered to David. "See you there."

Sage needed to stop Kato and Elsbeth. Now. He thought about being at the other end of this small passage—really focused on it—and a second later appeared directly in front of Kato, who skidded to a stop and blinked in surprise. Elsbeth stopped behind him.

Sage whispered, "We're trapped." He nudged Kato into the shadows and pointed to the large cavern.

Below them, more than two dozen gargoyles fanned out around the chamber and blocked the main exit. They prowled around and sniffed the air like bloodhounds. Surely they would find them soon.

David arrived just as Kato pulled Sage back deeper into their passage. He leaned closer to his ear. "Can you Teleport us out of here?" Kato asked.

Sage looked at him. The man's face, hard as it was, still showed the raw fear Sage had seen a moment ago. Sage turned to Elsbeth. "Can we Teleport them out of here?"

She shook her head. "Impossible. It doesn't work that way."

"Have you ever tried it?" Sage asked her.

"No. But it's not possible. Agatha-the-Old must have told me that a dozen times. Forget about it."

"But Sage might be special." David edged close to them and kept his voice down. "The bloke's got some specialness to his game."

Elsbeth shook her head harder. "Just forget about it."

"I can try," Sage whispered. "Nothing to lose." He sheathed his sword, stepped close to Kato, and wrapped his arms tightly around him. He closed his eyes, his head pressed hard against Kato's chest, and chose the spot near the boulder where Kato had drawn the diagram of the cave. The tingling grew strong, and then he felt a breeze blowing against his cheek.

He opened his eyes. Kato wasn't there. He glanced at the entrance to the cave and saw three gargoyles sniffing the ground and heading his way.

Sage Teleported back into the cave. Kato stood in the same place as before.

"Glad we got that settled," Elsbeth said, more than a touch of impatience in her voice. "Now, can we talk about getting out of here?"

"No problem for you Teleporters." David raised his heavy steel bar and snapped one end into an open palm. "Time for a little potty knocking for Kato and me."

"Some what?" Elsbeth asked.

"It's the Barnsley version of knurr and spell." David said. "Old-fashioned cricket? Hit flying things out of the air? You need to get out more."

"Can you be serious for even *one* minute?" she said.

Sage whispered, "Kato, what about that escape tunnel you talked about?"

Kato pointed to the other side of the cavern. Sage peeked out of their small passage and looked that way. On the far side of the family cavern was a black hole about twelve feet off the ground. *Only about thirty gargoyles to fight through. Sure. No problem.* Meanwhile, a group of ten of the beasts was sniffing closer to their hiding place.

Sage dropped back into the shadows while he thought about what they should do.

"Hedgehog Defense," David said. "Perfect warfare for these flyers."

They all stared at him as if he'd just grown a horn out the top of his head.

"To defend against a mobile attack," David said. "Won some battles against the Huns using it."

"Some details might be nice," Elsbeth said. "We didn't smash tanks for fun like you."

"Kato and I fight with our backs to the wall. Fortified that way. Good defense. Hedgehog positions. They'll surround us, but it will keep a large number of the blokes busy. Then you two counterattack from the far side. Not the perfect definition, but I was never *actually* in the cavalry."

"So we flank them," Sage said. "Well, I can't leave Kato's side. Crab Man could show up anywhere, anytime."

"You think I can't protect him?" David said with an evil grin. "I'll take *that* challenge."

"I do not need *protecting*," Kato said, "by a bunch of children who have yet to battle a *single* flying demon."

"I'm not talking about protecting you, Kato. I'm talking about the breach," Sage said. "I need to see where the breach is made."

"Can we stop *talking!*" Elsbeth said. "It's time. They're coming."

"You saw the remnants of my breach after a hundred years," David said. "If Crab Man breaches into this cave, shouldn't be a problem seeing it. Stick with my plan. You and Elsbeth wait until Kato and I draw their attention, then Teleport over behind them."

Sage drew his sword and stepped closer to David. "You listen to me. *I will* distract them. *I will* get them to chase me out of the cave. As soon as it's empty, all of you run across and go out the small exit."

David's face darkened, and he grabbed the front of Sage's shirt. "Listen to me, Warrior Boy, *nobody* orders me to run away from a fight." He nodded toward Kato. "This bloke's probably killed thousands of these things. I'll bet the little lass here got her light-from-heaven thing back, now that we're out of the Dark realm. So follow my plan, and we might actually survive this."

Sage didn't back down. "I can Teleport instantly. Hit and run. I will strike and disappear, strike and disappear. Just like when I sparred Kato with swords." He turned to Kato. "You know these beasts. You have the most experience. You decide." Sage pushed away from David, who didn't look happy that Kato was about to take charge.

Kato's eyes drilled into Sage's, then he turned and stared at David. Sage could see him mentally processing their options, which weren't many. Finally, he spoke. "Both plans could work, but David's idea would allow us to kill more beasts faster, which would create panic within their ranks. Prepare yourselves."

Sage bristled at the look of triumph David shot his way, but the Boy with Might didn't say anything.

"Give me enough room to swing my bar," David told Kato. He turned to Elsbeth and Sage. "When I hit them, they'll go sailing, so peel your eyes for that. Everybody ready?"

"Push the wax deeply into your ears," Kato warned. "The flying demons can disable you with their screech."

Sage took a cleansing breath and peeked around the corner again. David motioned at Kato and took several huge steps into the open. "It's your lucky day, mates," he shouted at the top of his lungs. He swung the steel bar in a figure-eight motion and smiled widely. "Come and meet your daddy."

Kato hadn't gotten ten feet out into the open before the first gargoyle launched itself at David, who was ready and hit the beast with a swipe so fast and powerful that Sage actually felt the reverberation from twenty yards away. The blow hit the beast square in the chest and drove it back over the ledge.

"That's a run scored," David shouted.

Then it sounded as if the world exploded. Every gargoyle in the cave screeched at once. Sage staggered and fell against the wall. Elsbeth covered her ears, her eyes wide with panic. Sage looked out at David. His face showed pain, but he still swung his bar with enough power to punch the next beast off the edge of the small cliff.

Only Kato seemed unaffected. He killed the next one with a series of sword strikes so fast it was little more than blurred motion.

"I'm crossing the sludge pond," Elsbeth shouted into Sage's ear. She disappeared before Sage could comment.

Sage pushed the wax even deeper into his ears and stepped out into the open. Beowulf's sword felt so natural in his hand he wondered if it would wield special powers if used by a direct descendent of the prophet Seth, as Theo claimed.

Time to find out.

As he maneuvered into a position to view the entire cavern, more than just a flicker of doubt washed over him. The formation wasn't stacking up like David predicted. They weren't all converging on him and Kato, which would allow Sage and Elsbeth to attack them from the rear. Only one or two beasts at a time charged David and Kato. Probably because they saw the result each time one of them got close. Sage counted six dead beasts already, and the fight wasn't even a minute old.

A sudden flash of light and a small explosion of gargoyle flesh on the far side of the sludge pond caused every beast in the place to suddenly quiet. Elsbeth had gotten their attention.

"The little lass *can* fight!" David shouted from the ledge.

The gargoyles were spread out evenly across the huge room but had positioned a cluster at the cave entrance to prevent any humans from escaping. Sage's Teleporting buzz was running full blast. It was so strong, in fact, that as soon as he fantasized about landing on the back of one of the closest gargoyles so that he could drive his sword straight down through the back of its head, he was there, his legs spread wide across its back.

"Whoa! I gotta be careful!" Before the gargoyle could even react, Sage did exactly what he'd just imagined. With two hands on the pommel, he shoved the blade straight down through its head and felt it exit through its throat. The sword vibrated in his hands and burned the monster's flesh.

He Teleported back to his original spot on the flat rock even before the beast collapsed to the floor of the cave. Sage looked at his sword as the blood sizzled off and disappeared, leaving it even brighter than before.

The downed gargoyle jerked, moaned, and died within a few seconds. The beast closest to it stepped back and belted a wail totally different than the war cries the others had made. The sound ripped through the cavern at a different pitch, and almost instantly, the cavern erupted again.

"Now *that* will earn you the title of warrior!" David shouted at Sage. Then he whooped a war cry and hit a gargoyle so hard with his steel bar that the beast burst open like a watermelon.

Sage didn't waste the momentum. He raised his sword, picked a spot near the dead gargoyle, and Teleported. This time, he landed close enough to a second one to lop its head off.

His appearance back on the flat rock a second later sent a ripple of confusion through the herd. Another mournful wail lifted from the floor of the cavern as several other gargoyles scrambled away from their two dead brothers.

Another flash of light, another war cry from David, and a flurry of sword strokes from Kato dispatched three more beasts.

Sage found a spot where two beasts were huddled together, their heads close enough to converse in quiet conversation. He gave them something else to talk about. He Teleported directly onto the larger one's back, drove the sword through its head, then repeated the move with the other one. By the time he got back to the rock to watch, full pandemonium had set in.

Several gargoyles fled the cave; several more ran back into the secondary cavern where the eggs were stored. Panic mode overtook the rest.

"Kato," Sage shouted. "Can they talk to each other?"

"Yes. They are smart. Remember, they are creations of the Emim race. Bred to destroy the Council, but they have seen nothing like this. They do not know what to do."

Below him, one large gargoyle took flight and turned directly at Sage.

"Beware of their speed," Kato warned. "No bird can fly faster."

Kato was right. The beast rocketed toward Sage, all four claws spread out, ready to rip him to pieces. Several others lifted themselves from the cavern floor, eager to join the fight. Elsbeth blasted two out of the air while Sage picked a spot on the ground near a smaller beast, who watched the older ones engage first.

Fatal mistake. Sage waited until the attacking gargoyle was within just a few feet and Teleported directly beside the young watcher. He lopped its head off just as the large one crashed into the full force of David's steel bar. "Another score," David shouted while Kato ran over and cut its head off.

Sage glanced at the entrance to the cave. Only one beast guarded it now. He landed on its back and finished it off while Elsbeth Teleported away to another position.

Back on the flat rock, with Kato, David, and the headless gargoyle behind him, Sage saw three hovering directly over the blood pond, snapping gargoyle words to one another. Probably deciding whether to stay or go. Two gargoyles dragged their dead friend away from the entrance to the cave.

More of them had escaped into the chamber with the eggs. Sage had a thought. "Kato, what are they doing in the other chamber?" he yelled.

Kato headed toward the outer chamber.

After exchanging gargoyle words, the rest of them in the main cavern took flight. There were eight hovering in battle formation between Sage and his team and the cave exit. Two moved back and forth like guard dogs and protected the exit. The other six were staggered with three high and three low. They weren't screeching at all; they simply chattered back and forth and constantly altered their position.

"They have moved all of the eggs into one corner," Kato announced when he returned. "They've surrounded them five layers deep."

Protecting their young, ensuring their continued existence. Sage didn't really care about that. He just wanted Kato and everybody else out of the cave.

"Here comes Crab Man," David shouted.

Sage glanced over. The air sizzled between David and Kato, the red glow of the monster's tool easy to see in the gloom of the cave. "Handle it, David, but don't chase it into the Dark realm."

"Kato and I can handle him," David said. "Ready, mate?"

"Sage, watch out!" Elsbeth shouted as one of the gargoyles from far across the canyon rocketed at him like a silent missile.

He Teleported away just as a burst of light exploded into its side and knocked it sideways into the wall nearest David.

Sage landed on a small patch of dry ground on the edge of the slush pond. The stench nearly gagged him.

Crab Man erupted from the breach, and a second later, David swung his steel bar like the bases were loaded and he was aiming for the fence. The six-armed monster flew backward into the breach twice as fast as it entered. Sage heard the sound of crushing bones above the noise of the chattering gargoyles. *How could it have possibly survived such a blow?*

"Sorry, mate," David said to Kato. "Didn't mean to pipe his clogs with just one swing."

Kato smiled and saluted his respect.

Elsbeth shot another one out of the sky, and it splashed heavily into the pond. "I'm getting tired, Sage," Elsbeth shouted. "I don't think I have many bursts left!"

"Get next to Kato," Sage shouted.

She Teleported over to Kato and David, and the three of them stood facing the remaining beasts, all of which seemed hesitant to attack.

Sweat soaked Sage's clothes. It'd be risky to Teleport onto the back of a flying gargoyle. If he couldn't plunge the sword through their heads as soon as he landed, they could spin over and dump him straight to the ground. He joined Elsbeth by Kato's side.

"David," Sage said. "Guard that breach. If that thing comes back, give it another shot."

"I can't see the breach, mate," David said, "but I'm watching the air where it appeared."

Sage nodded and turned to Elsbeth. "You OK?"

"Tired. Need to rest. I'm useless at the moment."

They stood and looked at the hovering gargoyles in front of them. The beasts clacked back and forth, unsure, it seemed, about what to do.

Sage saw the breach, a jagged line a few feet from David, and knew they'd accomplished their mission. He didn't think the Crab Man would return.

During the hike up the mountain, Kato had agreed to return with them to Mammon's prison to battle the great Prince. They could keep fighting here or call it a day. "Kato," Sage said. "We've got beasts left to kill and hundreds of eggs. I think we should go, but you're making that call."

"Part of winning a war is knowing when to retreat from individual battles," Kato said. "We are uninjured. If we try to destroy those eggs, we might not remain so. Lead us out of here."

"I vote to stay," David said with a wide grin. "After all, I am who I am."

Elsbeth nodded. "We have nine more rooms to check and need to rest before we can continue there."

"It's settled, then." Sage walked over to the breach and put a hand into the opening to show them the way. "David, how about the home-run hitter leads off today?"

He nodded. "Baseball's not cricket, but I like the way you think." He disappeared into the opening.

Kato went next, then Elsbeth. As she passed, Sage whispered into her ear, "We're building quite a team. Don't you think?"

She gave him a thumbs-up sign. "Never lose the faith."

20

Unlike the short distance to the stone mansion when Sage entered from the other three breach points, the four of them hiked a long way through the Dark realm after Kato's rescue. The swirling mass of Darks hovering over the mansion was so far in the distance that, after nearly an hour, Sage wondered if they'd ever arrive.

Once there, Kato said little as Sage showed him the same things he'd shown Elsbeth and David, including the massive doors of the Dungeon of Souls. They hid themselves in the room from which they'd rescued David. Kato shared all the food and water he had in his pack, Elsbeth rested, and David told stories about the tanks he'd smashed fighting the Germans.

Sage didn't know for sure when he fell asleep, but when he awoke later, he found Kato guarding the door and David and Elsbeth hunched over the breaching tool Sage had taken off the Crab Man during Elsbeth's rescue.

"I am not barmy, Elsbeth," David said softly. "I feel something when I hold this."

"Like what?"

Sage heard the skepticism in Elsbeth's voice, despite the fact she whispered her reply. He stretched and rubbed his eyes. He had really needed that nap.

"It's hard to describe," David said. "A connection. A power. I sound like a nutter, but I think this thing has attached to me."

Sage sat up. "What's that mean?"

"Oh, you're awake," Elsbeth said. "We tried to be quiet. You've been asleep for hours."

"What do you mean, attached to you?" Sage asked David again.

David held the tool in front of him and showed it to Sage.

"What does this remind you of? The shape? The material?"

"A bone," Sage said immediately.

"A jawbone," Elsbeth chimed in.

"Brilliant!" David said. "Yes. It's sharp where the teeth should go and along the outside edge, but it's a jawbone."

Kato walked to where they were seated on the floor. He sheathed his sword and spoke to David. "Ramath-Lehi?"

David beamed and pointed at Kato. "Nice one! Leave it to the silent types to surprise you."

"You're not serious," Elsbeth said to David.

"About what?" Sage asked. "What's Ramath-Lehi?"

"I'm deadly serious," David said to Elsbeth. "It was never found after the massacre. Many thought it had special powers. Why not?"

"Why not what?" Sage asked.

296

"Many thought it could have been seized by the Philistines," Kato said. "Hidden. And feared. Some theorized that Goliath possessed it for a time."

"Which would mean the Nephilim had it," Elsbeth said. "They could have given it to the Rephaim or Emim. From there to here . . ." She shrugged. "I guess it's possible."

Kato nodded. "God's power could breach between the Dark and Human realms."

David looked at Sage and beamed. "Brilliant, wouldn't you say?"

"If I knew what you were talking about, I might have an opinion." Sage looked at all of them and was embarrassed about his lack of knowledge of Council history.

"He thinks this is the jawbone Samson used to slay a thousand Philistines," Elsbeth said.

"What?" Sage said.

"If possessed by someone gifted with Might—like Samson—that someone might feel a similar kind of connection." Kato nodded and looked at Elsbeth.

She shrugged again. "We've seen stranger things."

"I feel something when I hold it," David said. "The bones in my arms, a charge through my muscles. A feeling of . . . of well-being. Confidence." He grinned and looked at Elsbeth. "Not looking to get all mushy or anything, but somehow, a power flows through this and gives me strength." He looked at Sage. "You captured it. So you own it. Can I . . . can I keep it?"

They all stared at Sage and waited for his answer. He remembered Beowulf's sword vibrating in his hands when he stabbed and cut the gargoyles, how the blade burned their flesh, and how the blood sizzled away and left the blade brilliantly clean. How could he say no to a tool that might be linked to someone gifted with Might? Besides, the look on David's face convinced him that he wanted the jawbone just as badly as Sage had wanted Beowulf's sword.

"It's yours," Sage said.

"You're the bee's knees, Sage. Just brilliant." David stood and rubbed the jawbone several times before sliding it into his belt. "Well then, are we ready to go open those other nine doors?"

They were about to head out when Kato, first to reach the door, held up a hand and stopped them. "Voices," he whispered.

Sage couldn't hear anything.

"A language I do not understand," Kato said. "Many voices."

They waited, pressed against the closed door, with David holding hard against it in case something tried to enter. While traveling through the Dark realm, the four of them had discussed how they needed to avoid engaging any beasts passing through the building. The last thing they wanted was to draw attention to themselves and be forced to fight for their lives before determining if any other Council members were alive. Even David agreed that hiding was the best plan. Surprising, but true.

Several minutes passed before Kato stepped back and nodded. "Gone. I think we can move."

Kato led the way, his honed hunting skills on display. Only two corridors remained unexplored. They found six barred doorways in the first, with dead bodies in each room. Sage fought against the sinking feeling that they wouldn't find anyone else alive, and it didn't help to know that each of the bodies had surely been dead for centuries.

That left three doorways in the final hallway. The lizard skin and body were so decayed in the first room that Sage couldn't tell which was which. In the second, they found nothing but a half-eaten corpse that had been torn from the lizard skin with such violence that remnants of body parts were scattered halfway across the room.

Standing in front of the final room, Sage knew they had a formidable team but wondered if they had even the slightest chance against Mammon.

"It's time, Sage," Elsbeth said softly.

He knew she was right. David had been surprisingly quiet over the past hour, probably sensing just how deeply Sage had sunk into a funk.

"I will go first this time," Kato said.

David lifted the heavy crossbar off the door and stepped back. Elsbeth pulled the door open. A black veil filled the chamber.

"Not another one of *these*," David said.

Sage noticed a flash of fear in David's face and a look of horror on Elsbeth's. He felt the same way.

"What does this mean?" Kato asked.

Sage told Kato about the freezer inside the cell where they'd found his body and how difficult it had been to escape it. Kato stepped close to the veil and squinted his eyes.

"That won't tell you anything, mate," David said. "Won't know what's in there until we step through."

The four of them stared at it for several moments. Finally, Elsbeth spoke what was probably on everyone's mind. "We have to go in."

"She's right," David said.

"It's the last room," Elsbeth said. "Because Shadow Manipulation is in place, somebody's probably alive in there."

"Maybe someone important," David said.

"They were *all* important," Elsbeth said. "Even you."

David stared at her, started to say something, but didn't. Kato spoke instead. "I will go first." He looked at David. "I will move left, if possible. You follow close behind and move right. Sage and Elsbeth, go to the center. If there is a beast, we will give it too many targets to focus on."

Everyone nodded, and Kato stepped into the veil with David on his heels. Sage drew his sword, took a deep breath, and followed Elsbeth into the unknown.

No laboratory or hellhound. No ice storm or slaughterhouse or two-headed scientist. Just a body wrapped in a lizard skin in the middle of an empty room. Well, empty except for a spiritual being standing guard duty near the body's feet.

"What in the Queen's Name is that?" David asked.

"A dullahan," Elsbeth said.

The creature was medium height but broad through the shoulders and arms. He wore the clothes of a frontiersman, like he'd been dragged off of Lewis and Clark's expedition team and whisked into the spiritual realm without proper invitation. There were grass stains on his pants, blood spatters around the collar of his deerskin shirt, and stains from what appeared to be horse manure on his moccasins.

The head—propped underneath its left armpit—had longish brown hair and a moustache commonly seen in photos of Daniel Boone–era explorers. Its eyes, glowing red like the last time Sage saw his dad's, rotated around in its head like loose marbles in a jar. Sage actually shivered at the creepiness of it.

"Dullahans," Elsbeth whispered, "are headless corpses in the spiritual realm that carry their heads around, searching for a soul to take." She looked at all of them. "Don't get any closer."

Sage saw a flash of fear in Elsbeth's eyes, which matched his own racing heart. He remembered seeing a page about dullahans in the *Encyclopedia of Dark Creatures* but had just skimmed it because it didn't look all that interesting. Or dangerous.

"The Rephaim's preferred method of collecting souls is to drag a human into the spiritual realm, decapitate them, and capture the soul as it escapes the body. It leaves the corpse desperate and hunting for anything it can find." Elsbeth stepped back a little.

The only thing that *really* concerned Sage was the large bull-whip hanging from a loop on the dullahan's leather belt. It wasn't a whip you'd see in a cowboy movie, either. It had a reddish glow, as if it might catch fire any minute.

David looked at Kato. "Ever battle one of these blokes, mate?"

Kato shook his head. "I know nothing about them."

"Are they dangerous?" Sage asked Elsbeth. "Do you know how they attack?" He pointed to the glowing bullwhip hanging from its belt. "Should we be worried about that?"

The dullahan hadn't moved at all, but its eyes rotated constantly. They never focused on a single spot for more than a second or two.

"The histories speak of bursts of fire from its eyes," Elsbeth said. "The bullwhip is soaked in Rephaim blood and heated by the fire from the mouth of a chimera. Poison to us. Not fatal, but we'd get really sick. It cracks the whip around the neck of those who still possess a soul, but only after it determines the soul will not be freely given."

"You are a walking, talking history book," David said.

"I dove into my studies after my mom died," Elsbeth said.

I was too stubborn to take anything serious, or maybe I'd know some of this, Sage didn't say.

"There's not a lot of documentation at the Tomb about how to defeat them," Elsbeth said quietly. "Don't stare at its eyes though. Legend says that if you do, you'll hear its voice inside your head and willingly relinquish your soul."

Sage avoided looking at the rotating eyes, but it was hard not to. *It's not every day you see a corpse holding its head under its armpit.*

"Will it just stand there and let us destroy it?" David asked, his voice full of suspicion. "What kind of guard is this?" He looked at Kato. "When it feels like I got a million ants crawling down the middle of my back, that tells me the fight is about to be a lot tougher than it appears. This bloke just standing there isn't natural."

Kato nodded. "I also question the wisdom of placing an *apparently* weak guard to protect such a valuable possession. I too suspect there is far greater danger than it appears." He looked at Elsbeth. "I have seen, on more than one occasion, information from the Tomb to be inadequate or wrong. Might this be such an occasion?"

She shrugged. "Only repeating what I read."

They were all standing well away from the dullahan, though Kato was the closest. Except for its eyes, it still hadn't moved at all. It was almost like a robot switched in the off position. Sage wondered what actions on their part would activate the thing.

"Washington Irving, living in England at the time, wrote *The Legend of Sleepy Hollow* about a dullahan," Elsbeth said.

"Funny little story," David said. "I read that." He looked at Sage. "Do you recognize the man in the lizard skin? The Council member?"

Sage had known who it was before they entered: the only one they hadn't found. "Klauss Cohen. A rabbi. Disappeared during a midday Sunday celebration in Hanau, Germany, in 1797. Angelic Chains. The best chains against Dark beasts the Council ever had." The rabbi's white hair and beard blended smoothly against his pale skin. He looked dead.

"I think I can rip that skin off," David said.

Elsbeth glanced at Sage and raised an eyebrow. Sage shrugged. He wouldn't put much past David's strength, but he wouldn't envy how his hands would feel after he tried.

"It would save us a trip into the past," David said. "Any of you blokes have comments about that?"

"Beware of the whip," Kato said.

David laughed. "Caution is my middle name." He took several steps forward, his steel bar held out in front of him.

When he got within ten feet of the rabbi's body, the dullahan came alive. Its eyes locked onto David, and the body turned in his direction. "Do you offer your soul?" asked the head propped under the armpit. "Do you give it freely?"

The voice sounded creepy because it echoed, even though the dungeon cell was not that big. The voice also came from somewhere inside Sage's own head. It was faint, but there, the words already present inside Sage's ears as the pale, bluish lips spoke them.

"Be careful how you answer," Sage said. He suspected the polite nature of this thing probably wouldn't last long if David misspoke.

Elsbeth also stepped forward, hands in position, ready. The dullahan shifted toward her. "What is your name?" she asked. "What soul do you seek?"

The dullahan's eyes blinked. "I seek the soul of one willing to give."

Again the voice played inside Sage's head. "Does its voice sound funny to anybody?" he asked.

"Like it is already in my thoughts," Kato said.

Both Elsbeth and David agreed.

"What is your name?" Elsbeth asked again.

Its eyeballs rolled all the way back and disappeared. Sage frowned and looked away. He couldn't continue to watch. "My captor promised a soul would enter here and freely give. Do you *not* freely give?"

The voice was definitely inside their heads. It was getting angry, loud, and more demanding. Losing patience. Everyone frowned and rubbed their temples.

Sage felt sorry for it. Whoever this guy used to be, he hadn't asked for this. He'd been cursed by the Rephaim and left to wander for all eternity.

"Would you make good use of my soul if I offered it?" Elsbeth asked.

After a couple of seconds, the mouth on the dullahan's head smiled just a little, its lips peeling away from teeth caked with a yellow film that seemed to glow in the grayscale of the dungeon.

"Your soul would make me whole." Its eyes locked on her and glowed brighter than the bullwhip on its belt.

Again, Sage felt sad for its predicament; the dullahan was somehow forcing him to pity it. He broke eye contact and glanced down at the rabbi's body, wrapped tightly within the lizard skin, his ghostly face frozen in an expression of pain.

"Who is your captor?" Elsbeth asked as she stepped forward and turned slightly to the right.

David stepped closer, his steel bar raised like a baseball bat. The dullahan didn't seem to notice.

"The All and Powerful holds my soul," the dullahan said. "The Wonderful. Giver of All. Always and Forever."

"What is his name?" Elsbeth insisted. "Who promised you a new soul?"

"Is it Lord Mammon?" David took another step forward.

The monster turned suddenly toward David. "You dare speak my master's name?" the voice echoed everywhere—a train whistle bearing down upon them.

Sage blinked, and that was how long it took him to miss what happened next. One moment, the dullahan was empty handed; the next, the glowing whip was in its right hand and cracked toward David's head.

David flinched and leaned back while he moved his steel bar in front of his face to block the blow. The whip wrapped around the steel and melted it like a blowtorch through ice cream. Two feet of steel clanked to the floor.

Kato surged forward and used the superhuman speed of his Fighting Arts to strike, but he wasn't fast enough. The dullahan stepped left, twisted, and snapped the frayed ends of the whip against the side of his face.

"No!" Elsbeth shouted. "Kato, move!" She shot a blast at the dullahan, but it stepped out of the way and hit her with a beam of his own. The fire that came out of its eyes hit Elsbeth's left shoulder and knocked her off her feet.

David threw the short end of his steel bar and hit the beast in the chest. It staggered back but stayed on its feet.

Sage Teleported behind it and swung his sword low, but the beast moved again, turned, and swept half the room with a stream of fire. David dove to the floor, Sage ducked, and Kato got raked across the chest.

Kato screamed and staggered away, his face already swelling from the poison in the whip. He patted his chest to put out the flames but kept hold of his sword. Elsbeth, on her back with a smoking hole in her shirt, grimaced and Teleported to the far side of the room. She raised her right palm toward heaven, her other toward the monster, and sent another wave of purifying light. The dullahan moved yet again and narrowly escaped Elsbeth's blast.

Sage tried a second time, appeared beside the beast, and swung high. He caught it in the left arm, severing it just below the elbow, and almost hit the head underneath its armpit. He Teleported away just at the dullahan rotated his head and raked the room with another blast of fire.

David stepped in close and swung his shortened pole, but the whip caught it again and shortened it even more. The end of the whip scraped David's knuckles, and he yelled and jumped back.

"Elsbeth, distract him." Sage saw an opening. "Do it now!"

"Lord Mammon will die a slow and painful death." She stepped boldly forward as she shot another wave of light.

The dullahan again moved, but not before Sage Teleported behind it and swung his sword down through the top of the disembodied cranium. It fell from the dullahan's armpit into two pieces. It was hollow, like a gutted coconut—just a dry husk. The monster's body fell slowly forward and landed on its face. Well, on its chest, because its face was in two pieces off to one side.

"Look," Elsbeth said.

The two pieces of skull disintegrated first. Soon the rest of the body crumbled into a big pile of gray dust. The bullwhip remained as it was and glowed red like embers from a dying campfire.

Sage nearly collapsed from relief. Elsbeth limped over to him and put a hand on his shoulder. "Good move." She rushed over to Kato, who'd fallen to one knee, his cheek and one eye swollen to twice their sizes. Angry red streaks ran in all directions across his face and down his neck. His shirt still smoked from the blast of fire, and the smell of burned flesh hung heavily in the air.

"You came out worse than I." David walked over and cradled his hand, which was swelling and getting bigger. He also had red streaks traveling up his arm.

Kato nodded and shakily sheathed his sword. Then he hurried over to a far corner, knelt over, and puked.

Elsbeth looked at Sage, worried.

"How sick will they get?" Sage asked her.

"They?" David grinned. "I've never tossed lunch in my whole . . ." His face suddenly went pale, and he also headed for a corner.

"They'll get really sick," Elsbeth said. "We will be in here for a while." She rubbed the burned spot at the top of her chest and winced.

"How are you?" Sage felt a bit of survivor's guilt, but he was glad he wasn't hurt.

"I'll be OK." She walked to a wall and sat down on the floor.

Kato and David were still heaving. Their streaks of infection had grown twice as wide and three times as long and had turned a shade of red so dark they looked black.

"Did you notice your sword?" Elsbeth asked Sage.

"What? When?"

"During your battle." Elsbeth looked at it, her eyes bright with excitement. "It shone like an Arch's sword. I caught a flash, and it nearly blinded me."

"What?"

"It glows," she said. "It did the same thing in the gargoyle cave. Where'd you get it?"

Sage realized then that he hadn't told her about Beowulf. So while David and Kato puked until they were dry, he told her the story of the sword. He told her about Theo, whom she'd heard of during her studies at the Tomb, and the instructions he'd given Kato.

She sat quietly for several moments after he finished. "So you're saying," she said finally, "that the ancient Elioudians, our ancestors, seventy-five percent angelic, beings of supernatural intelligence and ingenuity, extinct for several millennia, crafted a special sword just for you? That the only reason you are alive today is because Beowulf also used that sword to kill the original Grendel so that his village would be saved, thereby preventing the death of a young girl, who's probably your fifth great-grandmother?"

Sage nodded. "That's what I'm saying. Kinda freaky, if you think about it."

She reached over and touched the sword. "It's about more than that. It's about your battles with the Princes. It has to be."

David stood on shaky legs and hobbled over. His entire right arm hung limp at his side. "I'm feeling better."

He still looked horrible. He was pale and had vomit on his chin, sunken eyes, and chapped lips.

"You need to sleep," Elsbeth said. "Lay down somewhere. The rabbi has lived this long in that lizard skin, he can wait a little longer."

David was in no shape to rip off the lizard skin. Sage didn't think he could do it anyway, but he had no chance in his weakened state.

Kato was already asleep. He'd crawled out of his puking corner and found a place farther up along the wall. His back was to them, and Sage was glad about that. Given the condition of David's arm with the little cut he'd suffered, Sage had no interest in seeing what Kato's face looked like after getting his entire cheek ripped open by the poisoned whip.

"We could all stand a little sleep," Elsbeth said. "If David can't get the hide off, we need to be full strength before passing through the portal."

Sage agreed but wasn't sleepy. He'd just taken a nap. "I'll keep watch," he said. "Both of you get some rest. OK?"

Elsbeth nodded and spread out on the floor. David curled up into a ball, his ruined steel bar beside him. They were both asleep within minutes. Sage moved next to the black veil and sat down, back against the wall, sword across his lap. Should anyone notice the open wooden door, they might come to investigate, which might mean them stepping through the veil. He needed to be ready in case that happened. His team was in no position to fight right then, and so it was on him to keep them safe. Team members bled for each other. They all had so far. They all would again. For he suspected that this journey was far from over.

21

Angelic-humans healed fast, especially when compared to regular humans. Although Sage would have predicted they'd be cooped up for a full day while Kato and David got better, it ended up being less than six hours.

Elsbeth's burn was gone by the time she woke up from her nap. David was next, fully recovered in two hours. He'd taken in substantially less poison than Kato and was nearly crazy with cabin fever by the time Kato declared himself fit four hours after that.

In Kato's last hour of recovery, David tried every method he knew to rip the hide off the rabbi, but nothing worked. It was simply indestructible. Only David's burned hands reflected his efforts. Unlike Sage, David hadn't reported any flashes of memory from the hide, which told them that Sage's gift of Memory Share allowed only him to receive those images.

So that left Sage Memory Sharing with the rabbi and the others stepping through the portal. David was sick about losing his steel bar but hoped he could grab something else once he got to the rabbi's village in Germany. They'd argued about whether it was safe to touch the dullahan's whip and use that. They had decided to keep it, knowing it wouldn't be there if they changed history by preventing the rabbi's capture. David carefully picked it up by its handle and grinned when it didn't poison him. He tied it to his belt and then hefted Samson's jawbone in his hand. He would use that until something better came along.

Elsbeth explained everything to Kato about stepping into the portal, then motioned for Sage to proceed. He appeared in a village with cobbled streets and pitched rooflines. A cool wind blew from his left, but the day was clear and bright and fresh.

In front of him was a small synagogue, to the right a marketplace with dozens of people shopping, bartering, and leading their livestock to and from an auctioneer, whose voice carried over the sounds of the crowd. The smell of fresh bread and sheep dung filled the air.

The synagogue was small but solidly built, with stone walls, heavy wooden shingles, and a thick front door. Iron bars guarded windows too small to crawl through. As uninviting as the building looked, the front yard displayed a colorful stand of flowers. A sign near the front door announced the rabbi as Klauss Cohen.

Sage stepped into a small entry lined with stone benches and coat racks and heard a man's voice from somewhere inside the building.

"The beautiful girl with flowing hair could not believe she had been captured and thrown into a dungeon," said the man. "For she did not know the old woman from the wood had captured many other young maidens."

"Was she to die?" whispered a boy's voice.

Sage peeked around the doorway and saw Rabbi Cohen—a skinny Santa Claus lookalike—standing in front of two boys not much older than ten or eleven. Brothers, for sure, close in age and almost identical.

"Ah, she was not to die, Wilhelm," Klauss said. "For the old woman did not know that a bird had flown into the dungeon and whispered into her ear a way for her to escape."

"Was the bird an angel?" whispered the second boy, who sat in awe of the story.

"Good question, Jacob," Klauss said. "The bird was not an angel but a great prince."

"A prince?" asked Wilhelm. "But how?"

"An evil sorcerer had cast a spell upon him," Klauss said, "but the sorcerer could not prevent the prince from flying away and finding just the right princess to break the evil spell."

"Was the girl in the dungeon a princess?" asked Jacob.

"She was. She had gone into the wood to pick flowers for her sick grandmother." Klauss leaned forward and looked intently at both boys. "The bird prince followed the princess and saw the old woman give the girl a poisoned apple, one bite of which put her into a deep sleep. The prince flew high above the trees and witnessed the old woman carrying the sleeping princess to a horrible, haunted cottage deep in the wood."

"How was the old woman strong enough to carry the princess such a long distance?" asked Wilhelm. "For old hags do not have such strength!"

"They might if they are witches!" Jacob told his brother. "She may have only disguised herself as an old hag."

Wilhelm rolled his eyes. "Maybe she *was* a witch, Jacob, but it takes great strength to carry a full-grown princess through the wood!"

"Now, boys," Klauss said. "How many stories have I told you this past year?"

Both boys dropped their heads as though embarrassed about their bickering. Their slight grins, however, betrayed what little guilt they might have had.

"And how many times have you allowed me to finish before you begin your disagreements about how each story should end?" Klauss smiled at them. "That is the wonderful thing about telling tales. Each of you can decide the ending you believe is best." The boys glanced at each other. "My endings are always the best," Jacob said. "Wilhelm does not imagine with enough possibilities."

"That is not true," Wilhelm said.

"It is. You are—"

"Now, now, we will finish this tomorrow," Klauss said. "I promised your mother you would be home in time to wash up for the town feast. Off you go."

The boys jumped up from their chairs and turned toward the door. They stopped when they saw Sage.

"Hello," said Wilhelm. "Are you here for a story?"

"No," Sage said, "but that story sounded really good."

"I can make it better," Jacob said. He puffed his chest a little. "I will write it down tonight. I am not so sure that a bird can whisper, even if he *is* a prince. Also I do *not* think that an old hag witch would be strong enough to carry a princess through the wood."

"She would use a huntsman to help her," Wilhelm said. "She would cast a spell over him, and he would carry out all of her evil orders."

The boys walked past Sage and headed for the door. "And a bird *can* whisper," Wilhelm said to Jacob. "Because in a story such as this, anything is possible."

"Who might you be?" Klauss asked Sage after both boys had left. "Have the Grimm brothers been repeating my stories and you have come to partake?"

Sage started to tell him why he was there, but then Klauss's words registered. "Did you say the Grimm brothers? Like 'the Brothers Grimm'?"

Klauss nodded. "They are Wilhelm and Jacob Grimm. After their father died of pneumonia last year, they began coming here after their studies to hear my stories." Klaus laughed. "They both have quite an imagination."

"They will become *great* storytellers," Sage said. He could hear the awe in his own voice. "*Cinderella, Sleeping Beauty, Rumpelstiltskin, Snow White, Little Red Riding Hood, The Frog Prince.* There are too many to name!"

Klauss stared at Sage. Deepening creases formed at either side of his wide mouth. "How can you know what is yet to happen? Who are you?"

"I am Sage, from Council prophecy. Here to prevent your capture."

Sage watched the man's face go pale. He staggered back slightly and sat heavily in a chair. "I know the legends, what is taught at the Council. So it is true?"

Sage sat down next to him and took several minutes to explain everything that had happened thus far. Crab Man, the breach, the three other Council members who would arrive through a portal, Mammon, the giant structure in the Dark realm where his body had been kept. Most importantly, Sage told him about the Dungeon of Souls. The rabbi said nothing as he listened, his face somber.

Klauss asked a few questions about Sage's dad, the effects of greed, Sage's gift of Clarity. Then he sat quietly for a moment before asking a question that made him red faced. "I don't want this to come across as vain or self-important, but . . . Were my efforts recorded in the histories? I should hate to think all I have accomplished thus far went unnoticed by the Council."

"Yours were the most effective chains ever produced," Sage said. "The Council needs you back." *And I need you on my team to defeat Mammon*, he didn't say.

Church bells rang in the distance, and a loud cheer sounded seconds later. "What's that?" Sage asked.

"The beginning of the town feast," Klauss said. "Come. I suspect this Crab Man will attack from there?"

"I think it's probable," Sage said. "I'll be on the lookout."

The rabbi led Sage out of the synagogue and to the left, toward the street Sage noticed earlier, where they turned left again. The village could have been a postcard with its steeply pitched roofs, cobblestone streets, bright colors, and dozens of formally dressed citizens happily milling around a huge spread of food set up in a grassy area in the middle of the square.

"Is it a holiday?" Sage asked as he stepped around people while trying to keep pace with Klauss.

"It is Sunday," Klauss said. "The villagers come together each week for a midday feast. It is their way to give thanks for the blessings of harvest." The rabbi stopped and shook a man's hand, then shook another and nodded a greeting to a third. "The feasts last until the weather becomes too cold."

Sage estimated at least two hundred people, a third of them children of various ages, were in the square. Their faces radiated happiness and joy. The smaller children played tag and hide-and-seek, the older boys chased girls, and the teenagers flirted with each other but acted as if they weren't. It was so different than what existed in his time with smartphones, tablet computers, satellite television, and cars clogging the streets.

"My work for the Council has sent me to many villages across Europe," Klauss said. "The Dark beasts know no boundaries."

"Rabbi!" a man shouted and waved from across the square.

Klauss waved back as he maneuvered through the crowd. "Some have noticed your peculiar clothing," he told Sage under his breath. "And the beautiful sword on your hip."

Sage had also noticed the stares. Most turned away quickly when he looked at them, and he smiled at those who made eye contact with him. He saw one girl about his age who was so beautiful he found himself staring. She reminded him of an actress whose name he couldn't remember: blonde, a dimple on each rosy cheek, slim but not too skinny, a narrow nose, and a high forehead. Suddenly she turned gray. Completely gray. So did everything else around her.

It was that weird vision thing again. The Sensing. As it had been outside Kato's mountain village, the center of his vision was extra sharp and color saturated. He turned his head and every-thing popped back to normal.

So some kind of beast was in the direction of the pretty girl. He looked that way again, found her, smiled, and then focused his attention on what hadn't turned gray.

Across the square, standing at the edge of the crowd, a man wearing a black robe with a cowl covering all but a portion of his face stood by a low wall. The head of a lance in his right hand contained a green stone held in place by thin strips of copper. At least a head taller than everybody else, Cowled Man made no effort to conceal his sole interest in Sage.

The man stood statue still. People flowed around him as though they couldn't see him at all. A sudden breeze moved the hood covering his head, which allowed Sage to catch a glimpse of his face.

Besides eyes that glowed as red as burning embers, Cowled Man's face appeared to have been entombed inside a mummy's case for ten thousand years. Onion-thin skin, bleached gray by decay, was stretched so tightly across his face Sage wondered if his features might crumble into a pile of dust if the man opened his mouth. Yet despite his appearance, tremendous power radiated from him. It could only be described as a force field of evil.

"Uh, Klauss," Sage said. He tried getting the rabbi's attention without sounding totally freaked out. "I think we might have a problem."

Klauss didn't hear him because of the crowd of children that had gathered, shouting for him to tell them a story. Sage glanced back at Cowled Man, whose mummy face was now totally hidden within the shadow of the hood. He'd moved the lance into his other hand and raised his right hand toward the sky.

"Hey, Rabbi Cohen," Sage said louder, but without taking his eyes off the man. "We've got something happening here."

As the man across the square raised his hand higher, the sleeve of his robe slid down and revealed a hand and arm comprised of little more than a skeleton with skin.

The noise near the table of food meant Sage would have to yell to get the rabbi's attention. Sage didn't want cause a scene. No one noticed the man in the robe. Could they even see him? Was he some kind of Dark? Maybe a demon? What if Sage raised a panic over an invisible man?

Cowled Man raised the lance high in the air, tipped his head back, and spread his feet wide. The hood dropped away, exposing a head only half covered with skin. He bellowed something unintelligible and slammed the lance hard into the ground.

Nothing else happened. No fire flashed from the sky, no creatures rose from the ground, no gargoyles or other flying beasts attacked.

Sage saw that Klauss had a mouth full of cake and was laughing with a group of children, including the Grimm brothers.

Could Sage Teleport to Cowled Man without being noticed? He cut his eyes to the pretty girl, and he knew it wasn't possible. She'd moved closer and hadn't taken her eyes off him.

Sage couldn't understand what the skeleton man was shouting to the sky over the noise of the crowd, but whatever it was, he was putting forth great effort. His head shook, his neck veins bulged, his hands vibrated, and the green stone on the head of his lance began to glow.

"Rabbi Cohen!" Sage shouted. "Rabbi!"

The rabbi stopped in midsentence, another piece of cake in his hand, and glanced at Sage.

"Look!" Sage said. He motioned to the man in the cowl.

Waves of vibrating air flowed from the green stone and mushroomed out over the village. The skin on Cowled Man's leathery face pulled even tighter against his bones, exposing large yellow teeth that looked sharp enough to bite through solid bone.

Sage glanced back at Klauss. The rabbi had dropped his cake and stepped away from the feast table, his eyes affixed upon Cowled Man as he moved toward him.

Yet not a single villager noticed the evil transpiring around them. A group of women only a few feet from the green stone broke out into song and began to folk dance.

"You must follow me," Klauss told Sage quietly. "Quickly."

"What is it?" Sage asked, as they moved away.

"I do not know his name, but I have seen his kind once before. Hurry, there is no time to waste!"

Sage followed Klauss as he pushed his way through the crowd toward the synagogue. "Nobody can see him except us," Sage said. "It looked as if he were calling for help."

The rabbi said nothing but began running once they broke free of the crowd. He ran behind the synagogue and stopped in front of a small stone building with a heavy door and large padlock.

"Where have you seen someone like him?" Sage asked. "What is he?"

"He is a scout," Klauss said. He pulled a heavy key from one of his pockets. "One of the lieutenants of Abigor, the ruler of six legions of hell. We are warned of them during our studies at the Tomb. They locate Council members for the evil races."

The rabbi unlocked the door and pulled it open. The only item in the small building was a huge wooden chest with two padlocks as large as the one he'd just opened. "I saw one many years ago, more than two centuries, in a village outside of Rome. A great attack descended upon the village soon after the demon acted in the same manner as this man."

Klauss unlocked both padlocks and grunted as he opened the heavy lid. An orange glow burst from the chest and filled the small building. The rabbi stepped aside and allowed Sage to look.

"My chains," Klauss said. "Able to bind any Dark beast. Grab several, for I fear a great fight awaits us."

Before Sage could utter a single word, a monstrous roar arose from the village square, followed by the horrific sound of people screaming for their lives. The screams went beyond mere fear. It was the sound of collective terror, a fear so animalistic that the hair on Sage's arms stood up.

The roar was beast-like, but with a human element. Sage heard what sounded like a guttural laugh, then a bark and a *harrumph*. "What is that?" he asked Klauss.

"A troll," Klauss said. He looped several chains over his head and arm. "I have dealt with his kind before. Quickly, grab several chains. Let us empty the chest. We may need them all. The demon scout might lure more than just one beast."

Dozens of coiled chains, each glowing pumpkin orange, filled the chest. Sage lifted one out and couldn't believe how light it was. "It weighs nothing," he said.

"What do you expect? I am an old man." Klauss stepped out of the building and turned toward the street. "We must hurry!"

Sage looped as many as would fit around his head and left shoulder. It might be a trick having the chains and trying to use his sword, but having extras couldn't hurt.

"I do not like carrying my chains in public," Klauss said. "They tend to draw attention, but I will make an exception today."

"I've got my sword if I need it," Sage said. He helped Klauss close the door to the shed and lock it.

"It is not much longer than your arm," Klauss said. "It would be unwise to fight a troll with such a short weapon."

Sage decided not to mention Teleportation and what a deadly combination that and Fighting Arts could be. If he ended up using them to battle the troll, Klauss would see Sage's gifts for himself. Besides, he figured, a troll might be a tougher fight than a gargoyle, and the last thing he needed to do was brag right before getting the snot knocked out of him.

He stayed directly behind Klauss as they skirted the edge of the synagogue and turned toward the chaos. Frantic, screaming people ran by them. Klauss dodged this way and that, around hysterical mothers clutching their children. He and Klauss were the only people heading *toward* the beast.

"Prepare a chain," Klauss shouted. "Just throw it at the beast, the chain will do the rest."

"I am here for the rabbi!" a monstrous voice bellowed. Just then, Sage saw a wagon fly through the air in front of them and explode against a building. "We will not be denied the rabbi!"

We? Sage didn't like the sound of that.

Klauss stopped at the corner of a building overlooking the square. Sage got behind him, dropped to his knees, and stuck his head around to see. Standing in the center of the deserted square was a fifteen-foot-tall, thousand-pound, muscular beast with an oversized head, long arms, and thick brown hair that covered his body. He was a giant version of a Neanderthal man—Goliath on steroids.

"Holy mackerel," Sage whispered.

The beast had a mouth full of food and a roasted turkey in each fist. A massive club leaned against the feast table.

Cowled Man still stood with his hand raised in the air. Waves of energy blasted from the green stone in the lance.

"Look at the demon," Sage whispered to Klauss. Though Cowled Man still stood in the same position as before, he was staring directly at them. "He knows we're here."

"He will have to be dealt with," Klauss said. "Other beasts will come unless we stop him."

The words had no sooner left his mouth than Sage heard a ripping sound and saw the familiar red blade cutting through the atmosphere between the troll and the man with the cowl. Crab Man burst through carrying the lizard skin in one of its pincers.

"There he is," Sage whispered. "That's the guy who's here for you."

Klauss stared at the beast. "I would have been overtaken by three of them," he said. "When will the other Council members arrive?"

"I'm not sure. They'll arrive at some point. Let's hope—"

"Glad we could make it, mate," David said from behind them.

Sage spun around. David, Kato, and Elsbeth all stood there, David the only one wearing a huge grin.

"I am Klauss Cohen," the rabbi said. "I am pleased to see all of you."

Kato looked even better than when Sage last saw him. The dullahan's poison was totally out of his system, and the burn across the front of his chest looked fully healed. Elsbeth's steely eyes told Sage she couldn't wait to engage.

David pulled Samson's jawbone from his belt and slapped it against an open palm. "If it worked against a thousand Philistines, might work against these blokes, eh?"

"Can you guys take some of these chains?" Sage asked. "I've got so many I can barely move my arms."

All three looped a few around their shoulders.

"Just throw them," Klauss said. "The flesh of Dark beasts attracts them."

"Lasso them like an American cowboy?" David asked.

Both Kato and the rabbi frowned.

"I'll explain it later," Sage said. He looked at his team. "Klauss thinks the demon with the lance is here to draw other beasts our way. We've gotta take him out. Oh yeah, we've got Crab Man and the troll too. Any suggestions?"

The square was totally empty of villagers now. They could hear the troll crunching at the food table, Crab Man's pincers snapping, and Cowled Man's indecipherable muttering as he called others to join the fight.

"I'd take on the troll one on one with my steel bar," David said. "Might be a little trickier with the jawbone, but I'll give it a spin. Elsbeth, can you take the demon? Kato, the pincer man? Sage, you and the rabbi evaluate and help anyone who looks to need it."

Sage felt like rolling his eyes at David's supersized helping of overconfidence. *One person each should fight these beasts?* Before he could object, someone else did.

"I disagree," Kato said. "Eliminate the beast with the lizard skin first. He is the biggest threat to Klauss. We attack him with vengeance and handle the others after."

Elsbeth nodded. "I agree. Remove that threat, and Klauss will be safe. We need him to help with Mammon."

The rabbi nodded. "I also agree. We must keep an eye on the troll. Elsbeth, a blast of Persuasion might distract him enough to give him pause. The demon isn't a threat to attack us, though we must stop him soon."

"Then let's do this." Sage pulled his sword and looked at Elsbeth. "I'll Teleport to Crab Man's left, you to his right. Klauss will hit him with a chain from the middle. Ready?"

They all nodded.

Elsbeth arrived first and launched one of the rabbi's chains. It was halfway to the beast by the time Sage appeared and planted his feet for battle.

Sage saw a shadow, just a brief flash of movement before the lizard skin slammed into him. It slithered around his body with such speed and strength not a single scream escaped his lips. His sword pressed against his stiffening body as it fell hard against the ground. Like a million needles dipped in acid, the fiery explosion of pain crippled his mind. He saw Crab Man deflect Elsbeth's chain, heard David and Kato shout, felt a thunderous roar of the troll vibrate the air around him. But his world was swirling into an abyss of pain and horror and sacrifice.

She swam, Leviathan, skimming the top of the water as she neared the shore and gained the speed necessary to explode onto the surface and launch herself to the very top of the jagged cliff. The wails from the humans propelled her; the evil from the Dark beasts drove her.

When she hit the sandbar at just the right spot, she pushed with all her strength, sailing high into the air. The typhon, this one larger than others she'd slain, breathed fire from more than a dozen of its heads. The village burned with an intensity she'd not encountered before.

She landed behind the typhon and spun. Her tail whipped with the force of thunder and struck the beast in the side.

"Leviathan!" villagers shouted. "Finish it!"

She roasted the beast. Then she broke its back and crushed it before it could right itself.

The memories swirled. Another village, another time, deep in the forest miles from the shore. Winter. Frozen ground. Goat-headed men with wings, stringing humans up for sacrifice to their gods of the Emim race.

Spring. A swampy area in a country not yet settled under human rule. A secret compound hiding Nephilim One-Eyes who had traveled far from their mountain homeland.

Winter again. Rome. A young city, but growing in importance. Targeted by the Dark beasts. The pain she suffered, the wounds, so close to death on one occasion. But she'd kept the city from being overrun.

Summer. Athens under siege. Giants. Gods in their minds. Death. Destruction. She killed human abominations there, offspring of the Fallen. She attacked for more than a year before finally cleansing the city.

Istanbul. She approached through the Black Sea and traveled over land under the cover of darkness to raid the stronghold of Mammon, the Prince of Greed. She missed him but killed all that dwelled in that place.

Years later. The Dark Beasts came by the hundreds, fueled by hate, flowing from the mountain in a wave of death and destruction. The city was under full attack by the time she dove deep and changed direction. Sensing human anguish this far from shore had happened only once before—when millions perished in the Great Flood. But this explosion of torment was different—more concentrated and focused, drenched with raw terror, and so powerful she felt weakened by its intensity.

Adjusting course again, she swam faster, heading directly toward the slaughter. She caught images in her mind's eye, flashes of the creatures she'd spent her life battling as they tortured and murdered innocent women and children. Faster still. She closed her eyes and allowed the visions to envelop her, guiding her ever closer.

She burst from the sea and landed on the beach, narrowly missing hundreds of villagers fleeing into the water. Taking careful aim, she spat a stream of fire and roasted several dozen creatures giving chase. She then jumped forward and spun around, whipping her spiked tail against another group of beasts storming toward the sea.

327

The path from the beach to the cliffside city lay strewn with bodies. Why this place? A city filled with fishermen and farmers? What was so special that hundreds of Dark Beasts would slaughter an entire city?

Giants! There! Just ahead, lying in wait for her to pass.

Instead, she attacked. One of them grabbed the gut she had ripped open at its waist while searing another next to him.

"The water beast!" another of the giants bellowed into darkening sky. "The She-Beast has arrived!" Leviathan finished him before he could shout another warning, then moved farther up the hill.

"Save us!" screamed some as they ran past, heading away from the city. "Help us!"

"Bless you!" shouted others as they fled in all directions.

A herd of bull-headed men nearly ten feet tall, armed with spiked clubs the size of small trees, sprang from the shadows and fell upon her. She jumped and spun and landed in the middle of them. She crushed several and killed three more with a swipe of her right claw and the rest with a sweeping spew of flame. Minotaur, she'd heard them called, a curse against nature.

With another powerful leap, she landed at the edge of the city and took an account. The buildings along the right edge of an expansive courtyard were fully engulfed. Many on the left side were crushed. The courtyard itself had been the primary killing ground. Blood ran an inch thick and now trickled like a small stream between her feet and over the edge of the cliff. Most of the bodies had already been dragged into the mountains, but many were scattered amongst the wreckage.

She caught a glimpse of fliers silhouetted against the cloudless sky, moonlight glistening off their black skins, screaming bodies dangling from their claws. Ahead, beyond the flames, a collection of shadows waited for her. A gentle breeze carried the stench of One-Eyes.

More than ten times the size of ordinary men, One-Eyes were from a tribe of Nephilim giants. They were few in number but fierce warriors that lived alone in mountains many leagues away. At least twenty separated from the dancing shadows of the burning city. Each held a harpoon fashioned to a thick rope. "Surround her," the largest commanded.

She heard noises behind her. A wall of creatures, all armed with clubs or spears or harpoons, had closed off her escape back into the sea.

"You took our bait," the same giant said. "As the Princes predicted you would." He bellowed a laugh and drew his weapon back.

The Princes. Now she understood. The Seven. The Rephaim. Masterminds behind the war against God and the people He loved.

All humankind had fled the city, been carried away, or been killed. Only the monsters remained. She had walked into an ambush. She studied the One-Eyes and saw fear in a few. Though she couldn't speak to them with her mouth, she could make them hear her thoughts.

No beast can stand against me, One-Eye. Go back to your mountain home and die of old age. *She looked up and saw dozens of flying beasts circling overhead. They'd dropped their human cargo and returned for the fight.*

"Your day has come, water beast. You will torment us no more." The One-Eye leader raised his harpoon. "Attack!"

She jumped high into the air, which caused many of the harpoons to miss. Several didn't. They slammed into her belly, legs, and thick tail. The fliers hit her all at once and drove her back to the earth. More harpoons flew. Some were as large as small trees and were thrown with such force the spearheads sank deeply into her body. She tried to stand, but they yanked the ropes and pulled her flat against the ground.

"Tie her mouth!"

She released one blast of fire before a boulder drove her head against the blood-soaked courtyard. At least four giants landed on her back and worked their ropes against her mouth and legs.

"More rope! Hurry. To the beach!"

Shouts and jeers and celebration erupted. They dragged her back the way she'd come. "Start the fire! Prepare the site!"

"Sacrifice," *someone shouted.* "The Seven rule!"

They pulled her over the cliff and down the path to the beach. She struggled against her restraints, but there were too many. The wounds were draining her strength.

You cannot do this, *she projected into their minds.* God will not allow this to stand.

"The false one is not in control," *belted the leader.*

He will not allow the Seven to rule His chosen people. He will—*But she hadn't finished the thought before something slammed against her head and everything faded to black.*

"None wiser, Dark Lord, we offer her. None stronger, Dark Lord, take her. None more prized, Dark Lord, we give her. The Seven will rule, Dark Lord, in your name."

The chant woke her as the Seven pushed it into her mind. Flames snapped and popped, the heat from a bonfire overtook the chill of the evening. She struggled to move, but dozens of ropes held her fast. An army of beasts stood in a circle around the fire and watched the Seven as they moved in unison, wings fully spread, claws raised to the sky.

She tried pushing the chant away, but the combined power of the Seven was just too strong. Then a single voice broke through.

"I am Mammon. I will use you against them. Behold my power. Behold my curse."

She meant only to save them, the poor humans so tormented by the beasts of the Fallen. Her creation, the purpose given to her, was to battle, constantly, the Fallen Ones, those defilers of purity and goodness and sanctity. For centuries, she'd loved the humans, though they feared her through their misunderstanding; she loved them and slew the creatures created to enslave them.

Pain now. Pierced by harpoons, hooks, and stakes the size of trees, her vision darkened by pain. But the Seven—their leathery, black wings spread in full glory—claws raised to the heavens as though offering their sacrifice to the One True Almighty, moved as one, circling their much-hunted prize with a confidence born of victory.

Attacked, bludgeoned, harpooned, and bound for sacrifice, yet no human came to her aid. She studied the Seven and burned each likeness into her memory. A Chosen One would live within her mind for the briefest of moments, feel the pain of her death, and know these evil ones in their natural form.

Sage was back. He was lying in the village square, the hide of Leviathan ripped away by David's burning hands.

"Watch my back!" David shouted. Then, close to Sage's ear, asked, "Sage! Are you hurt?"

Sage tried to speak, but his mouth couldn't form words. He grunted, tried to communicate, but gave up as he drifted in and out of consciousness. Strong hands gripped him, lifted him high, and flung him over a broad shoulder.

"David, move left! Hurry!" the rabbi shouted. "Kato, stand aside. Elsbeth, get back!"

A great roar jerked Sage awake, and he struggled to defend himself, but David's grip held him tight. "Easy, old boy," David said. "You'll need a few minutes."

"We can't let it get away," Kato yelled above the roar of the troll.

"Crab Man is gone," Elsbeth said. "Into the breach."

Sage lifted his head off David's shoulder, so weak he could hardly move. The troll, grunting and dragging one leg behind him, was trying to escape. One of his hands was missing, as was one of his feet. The chains lay smoking on the ground where the troll once stood.

David flopped Sage down on the ground near a building. "Be right back, lad."

"Hit it, Elsbeth," Klauss shouted. "Kato and I will throw a chain."

Sage rolled over onto his side to watch. His strength was returning, but he was still too weak to help.

David joined the other three, who'd surrounded Cowled Man. Waves of energy radiated off the lance, and the beast didn't appear concerned that he'd been surrounded.

David pulled the jawbone from his waistband. "We need to take this bloke out of service. Anyone care to give it a go?"

Kato stepped up and swung his sword. The demon tilted the lance toward him and redirected the waves of energy. The blast hit

Kato in the chest and sent him flying backward into the side of a building. His head slammed against the wall.

"What do we have here?" bellowed a second troll from the far edge of the square.

Elsbeth and Klauss spun around. The beast had approached from a different direction.

Kato climbed to his feet. He rubbed his head and repositioned directly behind Cowled Man.

The troll took a step forward. Unlike the other one, he used a sword, not a club. It was longer than a pickup truck.

Cowled Man moved its lance back to its original position, his leathered, ancient face impassive. David jumped at the demon and swung the jawbone. He aimed for its head, but the demon again repelled the attack and knocked David through the wall from which Kato had just stepped away.

Sage struggled to his feet but had to grab the building to keep from falling. A second later, he grimaced as he raised his shaky sword to a battle position.

Klauss stepped forward and faced the giant. "You are not needed here," he shouted. "Go back to your cave, and live to see the sun set."

"Ah, there is the rabbi," the troll said. His shoulders stretched fifteen feet across; his head towered above some of the rooflines. With arms long enough to reach his knees and a sword at least that long, Sage knew they needed to stay well away.

Elsbeth, several feet from the demon, shouted at the troll. "Experience the purifying light of the Almighty!" She hit him in the chest with bolt of light just as Klauss launched a chain toward his head. The chain wrapped around the troll's neck and sizzled against his flesh. The beast screamed, staggered back, and crashed into a building as Elsbeth's gift burned a two-foot hole in the center of its chest.

Sage covered his ears at the gagging roar of the troll, who pushed away from the building. He stumbled around and then tripped over a hay wagon.

Klauss and Elsbeth turned back to Cowled Man.

David exploded out of the building he'd been pushed into, his face scarlet with rage. "This bloke just might get interesting." He picked up a wagon loaded with lumber, lifted it high above his head, and let it fly.

Once again, the demon adjusted his lance. The wagon bounced off the energy waves and went careening back into the building next to David.

"From the depths of Hell you came; into the abyss shall you return!" Elsbeth shot a steady stream of energy at the demon, who tilted his lance toward her.

"Attack now!" Sage shouted weakly as he crept forward. "David, hit it from behind! Kato, now!"

The clashing rays of energy lit up the town square like a solar flare. Sage dropped to his knees from the blast.

"I can't hold it much longer!" Elsbeth shouted. "Hurry!"

The rabbi swung a chain over his head then let it sail. It flew flat and straight and fast, but the demon saw it coming and tilted the lance just slightly. The chain hit the wave of energy and ricocheted violently. It slammed into a far building. There, it crumpled into a pile of orange metal and lay harmlessly on the ground. Its orange glow faded and totally disappeared.

David shoved his jawbone into his waistband. "Hold it just a little longer, lass," he shouted. Then, without another word, he put his head down and charged the beast, coming in low and fast—a supercharged linebacker at racecar speed. He bounced off the invisible field with such force, Sage wondered if he had broken his neck. David groaned as a knot the size of a baseball formed on his forehead.

Sage turned at the gurgling cries of the troll, who jerked and thrashed on the ground. The troll's claws desperately ripped at the sizzling noose around his throat. The chain continued to tighten and eat through the meat of his neck. The beast uttered one final scream before the chain constricted again and the troll's head flopped onto the ground and rolled away.

"I'm losing it!" Elsbeth shouted. Sweat drenched her face. She leaned heavily forward and concentrated on the beam with a fury that gave Sage goose bumps.

Kato attacked the demon again, and Klauss threw another chain. Nothing worked. Sage staggered forward, steadied his sword, and focused on the piece of ground directly in front of the demon.

"Keep holding it, Elsbeth," Sage shouted, louder now. "Just a few seconds longer." The vibrating in his bones took longer than normal in his weakened state, but it finally got there. He grabbed the pommel of his sword with both hands and crouched, ready.

Just before Sage Teleported, the demon straightened his lance slightly and swung its head all the way around. He locked eyes with Sage.

It knows who I am.

The demon stood there—head on backward—and glared at Sage. Then its glowing eyes fixed upon Sage's sword, but its face didn't register it as a threat.

Sage Teleported in front of Cowled Man, inside the force field of energy, and as soon as his feet hit solid ground, he shoved his sword straight up. The demon had just turned when the point of Sage's sword pierced his chin, traveled through his face, and exited the top of his head. His sword vibrated so violently it was all Sage could do to hang on to it. Then he saw what Elsbeth mentioned earlier—his sword was as bright as the morning sun. He squinted his eyes just as the beast used his free hand to grab Sage's throat and lift him off the ground.

Sage tried to scream for help but couldn't. Desperate, he pushed the sword sideways, twisted it, lifted it up and down, felt the blade cut through leathery skin, heard bones breaking, and felt the monster's grip loosen.

Then Elsbeth's gift broke through and hit the demon's arm holding the lance. Immediately, one of the rabbi's chains trapped that arm against the staff. Skin sizzled.

When Kato's sword crashed through the demon's neck and struck Sage's sword, the pressure on Sage's throat relaxed even more. A second later, David grabbed Cowled Man's arm, ripped it out of its socket, and pried his hand off Sage's throat. Sage dropped to the ground, still gripping his sword, gasping for breath.

"Grab the lance," the rabbi shouted.

"Got it!" Elsbeth said.

When the demon disappeared, the village square was as quiet as a Sunday afternoon should be. Sage coughed and spat and slowly climbed to his feet.

"Show us the breach, Sage," Elsbeth said. "Time to get out of here before anything else shows up."

"Food," Sage said. He coughed again and looked at the town feast, most of which still sat undisturbed on multiple tables. "We need to bring as much food as we can carry. And water."

"Use baskets," the rabbi said. "There are several."

As Elsbeth, Kato, and the rabbi began filling baskets, Sage intercepted David, who'd thrown a keg of water onto a shoulder. "Thanks for saving me." He coughed again.

"Team effort, mate," David said.

After a couple of minutes, still without a single villager having returned to the square, they had gathered enough food and water to last a couple of weeks. Sage led them to the breach, stuck a hand in, and watched them all step through.

It took most of the long trip to the stone mansion for Sage to get his strength back. Being wrapped inside the hide of Leviathan had completely drained him.

A team of five to fight Mammon. He just hoped it was enough. His dad's life depended on it.

22

They set up shop in the dungeon cell where the rabbi had lain captured. Black veil gone now, there was no evidence the dullahan had ever been there. Sage and Elsbeth had Teleported to each corridor to confirm that the crossbeams were in place on every door where a Council member had been found. They'd set the beam in place on this room last before joining the others. They were well hidden and would remain that way until it was time for their next move. The food was spread out and organized, and Sage believed they had enough for a couple of weeks at the very least.

Upon arriving at the stone mansion, Klauss, like the others, spent a lot of time studying the statue of Mammon, speechless at the evil it represented. Sage and his team gave the rabbi a quick look around a couple of the hallways but were anxious to get hidden away. They showed him the doors to the Dungeon of Souls from a distance but didn't dare open them again.

Now they ate in silence. They had Cowled Man's lance, which leaned against the wall next to Elsbeth, its green stone dull and lifeless, no longer projecting energy waves. Could they activate it somehow? If they did, would it draw Dark beasts to them?

There were other questions, the most pressing being how they would draw Mammon to them. Sage had something he needed to share before they got into that discussion. An important something. "The statue of Mammon looks just like him," he said quietly. "Exactly like him."

The other four looked at him in silence before the rabbi spoke. "How can you know? No Council member has seen a Prince in his natural state and lived to talk about it."

"I saw her death," Sage said. "Leviathan's. She showed them to me."

"While you were in her hide?" Elsbeth asked.

He nodded.

David whistled low and long. "You've seen the Seven Princes of Hell in all their blustery?"

"Leviathan saw them clearly," Sage said. "She heard their voices, memorized the incantation as they worked their magic." He shivered involuntarily.

"What did they say?" Elsbeth whispered.

Sage closed his eyes and saw them, claws held to the sky, their leathery wings spread wide, their black, bottomless eyes reflecting the moonlight. "'None wiser, Dark Lord, we offer her. None stronger, Dark Lord, take her. None more prized, Dark Lord, we give her. The Seven will rule, Dark Lord, in your name.'"

Sage opened his eyes and found all of them staring at him.

"There is little known about the great sea beast," Kato said. "Some believe she was a protector of the humans, others say that she was the Fallen's greatest warrior." Kato stared at Sage, his face every bit as intense as Elsbeth's. She sat forward and listened intently to Sage's every word.

"What do you know of Leviathan now?" she asked.

"I saw more than just her murder," Sage said. "She protected human villages against Nephilim giants. She slaughtered Emim abominations and destroyed hidden laboratories creating human hybrids. She waged war against all the offspring of the Watchers." Sage lowered his voice, his gaze lost within the images seared into his mind.

"She lived for centuries, according to literature," Elsbeth said. "Either that or there was more than one. Some believe that, but I don't."

David looked at her and raised an eyebrow. "That's not what I was taught, but . . ." He shrugged. "I'm finished arguing with you about things."

"Leviathan was the most powerful beast in the entire world," Sage said. "The greatest example of size, speed, and strength. She ruled the seas but could live out of the water for hours at a time."

"How did they kill her?" Elsbeth asked.

Sage sat quietly and said nothing for a moment. "Ambush," he said finally. "In a coastal town in southern Italy. The village was small but crowded with people. The mountains were close and made the perfect place for an ambush."

David had placed the whip and jawbone on the floor in the middle of the room, and the whip glowed in the gloominess of the dungeon. "They bound and beat her," Sage continued, "and drained her blood to the edge of death before handing her over to the Seven. Her sacrifice was long, the pain unbearable. She fought to the very end and tried to resist the ancient spell cast upon her."

"What spell?" Elsbeth asked, her voice breaking with emotion.

"The spell that turned her hide against those she loved the most: the Council."

They sat in silence. Sage looked at David's hands, just now back to normal after ripping the hide off of Sage in Klauss's village, something he still couldn't explain how he'd done. "The curse caused the outside of the hide to burn the skin of humans with angel blood."

"They got that part of the curse right, mate," David said as he rubbed his hands against his pant legs. "Hope to never see one of those things again."

"You shouldn't have to," Elsbeth said. "Sage and I killed the Crab Man, and you have its breaching tool."

"No guarantees, Elsbeth," Kato said. "Answer this question, Klauss. Of those of us Sage found alive, you were captured first. Had Sage killed the Crab Man and taken his breaching tool in your village square, would it have changed history for the rest of us?"

They all looked at each other. "I assume so," Klauss said after a moment. He pointed to David's jawbone. "I also assume there is only one of those. Without that, maybe it wouldn't have taken any of us."

"My capture was last," Elsbeth said. "Since we killed it and took the tool, we might have stopped any future attacks."

"I want to say one more thing," Sage said.

"Spill it, mate. I think you've earned that." David grinned at him. "I'd give you a medal if I could."

Sage returned David's smile, then turned serious. "Leviathan knew it was her last battle. Mammon said he was about to use her against Council members, use her for evil. I don't know how she did it, but she created a link between her mind and mine, through her skin. It was her final attack against the evil of the Seven. They couldn't have known her hide would send me images of their true nature, but she did."

He paused for several moments before speaking again. "She showed me how to kill them."

They spoke for nearly an hour and finally came up with a plan on how to slay Mammon. The problem was getting him here.

"How do we do that?" Elsbeth finally asked. She looked at Sage and raised an eyebrow because they'd had this conversation before.

Sage had a pretty good idea now, thanks to the nuances he'd picked up from Leviathan while wrapped in her hide. But he wanted to hear their ideas first.

They all looked at each other, then David spoke. "We could give them a target-rich environment. Make it so attractive for them that several of the Princes would come." He gave them an evil grin. "I'm seeing an epic battle."

"Explain," Kato said. He touched his face, and the scars there seemed more intense than Sage remembered.

"We gather several dozen Council members here and let them know we're ready for war."

Sage's face heated up. "Yeah, and how long would that take?"

David shrugged. "Don't know, mate. I've been gone for a hundred years. I don't know how spread out our people are."

"Too long," Sage said. "I'm not losing my dad while the Council sits around and discusses the pros and cons of twenty-five different plans. It'd take weeks to gather everybody. Dad might be gone by then. You saw those disappearing heads in the Dungeon of Souls. Dozens of people are lost every minute. Maybe hundreds. Besides, we can't fight seven Princes at once. That's what we'd get if they thought they could wipe out most of the Council in one battle."

"Horses for courses, mate," David said. He raised his hands in a peaceful gesture. "Don't chew your arm off. So you don't like the idea. Fine. Just a thought." He shrugged and crossed his arms, his face turning red.

Rabbi Klauss put his hand on David's shoulder. "No need to feel bad, son. We're a team, and each one of us is valued here."

Everyone agreed. Sage, especially, was mindful of the rabbi's words. He mouthed "sorry" to David.

"We could attack the next group of monsters that travels through here," Elsbeth said. "Let one of them go. Tell it to get word to Mammon that we're waiting for him."

Both Kato and Klauss shook their heads at the same time. "What would stop Mammon from sending three hundred beasts in here to slaughter us?" Kato asked. "We might escape before being harmed, but we'd be no closer to Mammon."

Elsbeth nodded, a somber look. "Good point."

David cleared his throat and looked at Sage. "I have another idea. Mammon is the Prince of Greed, yes? The bloke's got hundreds of thousands of souls in his dungeon. Hoarding them. Very greedy, indeed. Maybe we should take them away. As soon as he begins losing them, he'd come running."

This was a point Sage had been debating with himself for the last few hours. He was glad David had voiced what he was thinking.

"You're talking about going in there and cutting the connections to the heads?" Elsbeth asked. "Like Sage wanted to do to save his dad?"

David's face got hard, his eyes bright with the challenge. "That's right. Snip, snip, snip. I'll bet if we cut a connection, that person's soul would be free."

He was probably right, Sage thought. He'd been convinced of that the moment he saw his dad's floating head. Now, though, he had some real worries about David's suggestion.

"Kato," Sage said. "If you were Mammon and somebody attacked your Dungeon of Souls and released your prized possessions, would you come?"

Kato nodded. "It is a certainty."

"*How* would you come?" Sage asked. "David's suggestion isn't bad. I've been thinking about that myself. I'm worried about *how* he'd come. Alone, or with an army?"

"Ah, I see your point," Klauss said. "You view Mammon as a great general. A tactician."

Sage nodded. "I think he'd come. No doubt. Wouldn't he bring many warriors with him, send them in first to see what was going on?"

"I cannot argue with that," Kato said. "If he were so careless as to walk into a potential trap, the Council would have found him centuries ago."

"Who else would release his captured souls other than the Council?" Elsbeth asked. "I agree with Sage. Mammon would send others in to check things out, and we'd be slaughtered inside that room."

They all sat in silence for several moments.

"We could wait for a Rephaim offspring to come through," Klauss said, "and follow him out, which might lead us to a group of them."

Sage knew there was some merit to that. The Seven could produce children, but those children could not. Their bloodlines couldn't develop roots, which meant the offspring never veered too far from their respective parent.

"We might wait weeks for a Rephaim offspring to come through," Kato said. "Possibly months. There would also only be a one in seven chance he would lead us to Mammon."

When nobody else offered an idea, it was Sage's turn. "We need to lure him *here*. We've planned our battle for the big statue room. It's too risky to do it anywhere else."

Elsbeth cocked her head at Sage. "You have a funny look. Almost as if you know how to do it."

Sage shrugged. "Maybe."

"Well, spill the milk, you bloke," David said.

He took a deep breath. "We deface his statue."

They all stared at him in silence. Then David laughed. "That's your plan?"

Klauss held up a hand and motioned for David to be quiet. "Explain your idea."

Sage stood and started pacing. "All right, here's what I'm thinking. We've all seen how the statues were built—Mammon towering over the others, who appear to be worshiping him. Arrogant, right? Conceited. He made himself twice as big as the others, which is not true. He's bigger, yeah, but not by *that* much." He steered around the glowing whip, then looked at Elsbeth. "Whoever carved that statue made it the most detailed thing I've ever seen. It looks as if it could step off its podium and walk out of here. The others? Not so much."

"Prideful," Kato said.

"Yes. But it's more than that," Sage said. "It's beyond pride. His greed for power—power over the other Seven, power over Leviathan, power over the Council—it consumes him."

"Where it is located is also important," Klauss said.

"Yes!" Sage said. "Every corridor leads to that room. Meaning every beast that uses this place and goes from one hallway to another sees his image."

"An image that reminds them of his power," Elsbeth said.

"Right," Sage said. "Except for the Dungeon of Souls, I'll bet there's not another statue like that anywhere on Earth. It's important to him. Very important."

"So we bugger it up," David said. A huge smile spread across his face at the thought. "Word will spread. Fast."

"Mammon will *have* to come see for himself," Elsbeth said.

Her eyes brightened. "And we'll be here waiting for him."

Sage nodded. "That's what I'm thinking."

Everyone agreed except for Klauss, who looked deep in thought.

"What are you thinking, Rabbi?" Sage asked.

"I'm thinking it's a great plan, Sage, but we must be selective in *how* we deface it. We must send the right message."

Sage grinned. "I know."

"What?" Elsbeth asked. "You've got that look again."

He told them his plan.

They slept for several hours because they knew it might be a while before they'd get another chance to rest. Once the deception was set, they would take turns keeping watch around the clock until the Prince of Greed arrived.

And he *would* arrive.

Sage and Elsbeth Teleported into each dungeon cell that had a hide of Leviathan still intact enough to use. Of the twenty-eight, ten were rotted beyond use. The remaining eighteen gave them enough coverage to do what Sage envisioned.

Klauss drew the design, while David crafted the tool he needed to make the changes in Mammon's statue. Kato, the great hunter and trapper that he was, sewed the hides together using long, narrow strips cut from the backpacks a few of the Council members had had with them when captured. The hides, in their reduced and nearly rotted states, weren't much tougher than leather. Sage assumed that once the Council members died, the hide died also and slowly lost its strength. Once he'd sewn them together, Kato took measurements and cut the patched quilt into the shape they needed.

It took them two days of work and planning before they were ready to launch the project. On four different occasions during those two days, Sage's team dodged travelers moving through the facility. They were usually small groups of two or three, but one group contained a dozen or more. Elsbeth was the dedicated scout due to her ability to Teleport in and out of a space so quickly that she was gone by the time an eye caught movement. They kept their voices low at all times and only spoke when absolutely necessary. At the end of the second day, Kato suggested they sleep again, and so they did. Hours later, they huddled up one last time before putting into place the things they'd prepared.

"We need to make the changes in two stages," Klauss said. "In the manner that will draw the least amount of attention, should a group of beasts walk into the main chamber before the defacing is complete."

"I agree," Kato said. "The small change first."

Before they did anything else, they moved their food and water to another hallway, to a dungeon cell closest to the main hall. The body inside was that of Council member Fredrick Hosmer, a Swede gifted with Possession, snatched in the 1650s while on a mission to possess a Rephaim offspring. As gently as possible, Kato and Klauss moved Hosmer to one corner and covered him with a dusty cloth they found folded beneath a wooden table.

While spreading their food out and setting up shop in a cell with a body in the corner gave Sage the creeps, it had been the right move. Now the slowest runner they had, Klauss, could move from Mammon's statue into the new safe room in less than twenty seconds, which was important should their work be interrupted.

During the two work periods, Sage and Elsbeth would serve as the primary lookouts. They'd position themselves near the mouths of the two busiest corridors, which also happened to be the farthest from the safe room. Being gifted with Teleportation eliminated the concern that they would be caught out in the open. Having a safe room closest to Mammon's statue was the most important thing—rotting body notwithstanding.

"So are we ready to begin?" Klauss asked.

Sage, Elsbeth, Kato, and Klauss all stood guard while David quietly slid the six smaller Dark Prince statues farther apart. This left a wide space in the center. Then he turned them around so they faced away from Mammon. Sage couldn't have begun to guess how much the blocks of granite weighed. To see David's gift of Might truly displayed again left him spellbound. Ronan had said David was half again as strong as any other gifted with Might, and now Sage believed him.

Once completed, David jogged back into the safe room, sweat pouring off him. The other four followed and fanned him with anything they could find.

"Hear anything, mates?" David asked.

"Nothing," Sage said. It had taken David less than thirty minutes to move the statues. Unless a beast happened to really focus, he'd never notice the changes. The statue of Mammon was so magnificent and so overpowered the others, one's eyes just weren't drawn to the other six.

David crammed a bunch of food into his mouth and washed it down with several cups of water. "OK, now the tricky part."

Yesterday, using a pair of pants from one of the dead Council members to protect his hands, David had used the dullahan's whip to melt one end of the longest piece of his steel bar into a wedged shape. He now had a hundred-pound chisel, perfect for what he needed to do.

After Kato tied together all of the ropes and straps he had found in the thirty-two dungeon cells, they had a rope almost a hundred feet long. David looped that around his head and arm, secured the giant-killing chisel inside a sword sheath, and climbed to the top of Mammon's statue.

As quickly as he could, he tied the rope around the top of one of Mammon's wings, tied the other end around his waist, and began pounding with the chisel.

This was the most nerve-wracking part of the project. They'd never hear voices of approaching beasts with all the racket, and they didn't have enough people to cover every corridor. So once David started chipping away at the base of Mammon's wing, he worked as hard and fast as he could. Once again, Sage was absolutely mesmerized by the power of David's body.

The first wing broke away after a couple of minutes. David sheathed his chisel and grabbed the rope just as the wing fell. Sage's stomach nearly came out of his throat when he thought the weight of the wing would pull David off the top of the statue, but the Mighty Man of Might held on and gently lowered it to the ground.

Kato untied the rope once the wing was on the ground, and David quickly repeated the process for the second wing.

Elsbeth whistled softly and held up a hand. She pointed down the corridor she was watching.

They all froze. They'd decided yesterday that if a small group interrupted their work at this stage, they would attack and kill them and hide their bodies.

Elsbeth watched, her hand raised in the air, the signal to not make any noise. Then it was over. She turned and waved and nodded.

David tied the rope around Mammon's granite head and dislodged it with only five blows of the chisel. He lowered it to the floor, untied the rope, and climbed down.

Kato and Klauss ran to the safe room to get the patchwork hide of Leviathan. By the time they returned, David had dragged the two wings into the open space between the six other statues and stacked them atop one another. Then he placed the head at one end and carefully wrapped the hide around the wings, leaving only Mammon's head exposed.

Sage stood amazed at the finished product. It appeared Mammon had been wrapped inside the hide and that the other six Princes were bowing in awe of the great Leviathan.

All of them stood there for several moments before Kato finally got their attention. "Let's go. The bait is set."

They were ready. Time to wait. David took the first shift of sleeping. He'd earned it. Without his gift of Might, none of Sage's insulting message could have been delivered. If having Mammon wrapped inside the hide of Leviathan didn't draw him here, he could think of nothing that would.

23

Elsbeth shook Sage awake and put a finger against his lips. "Listen," she whispered. "It's happening."

Sage sat up and rubbed his eyes. David, Kato, and Klauss were standing near the door, ears close to the hinges, trying to make out words. A great rumble of voices sounded close.

"How many?" Sage asked her.

"I Teleported out to our watching post," she said. "There's at least a dozen creatures there. Some look terrified. Some look furious."

"Show me," Sage said. He stood and rubbed the sleep from his eyes.

It was a risk, Teleporting out, and all of them knew it. But they'd selected the lookout post carefully. It was a small corner with shadows so deep they wouldn't be seen unless a beast was standing next to where they were hidden. Any Dark beast inside the statue room would be staring at their display, not looking for them.

Sage and Elsbeth joined hands and squatted before Teleporting. They appeared to a near riot of confusion. A great winged werewolf shouted the loudest. Two minotaurs, one cyclops, a hellhound, a pack of four ahools, two satyrs, two trolls, and a chimera all stood well away, fiery expressions on some, looks of horror or disgust on others. Sage heard more than one language and didn't bother trying to decipher what was being said.

Despite their outrage, they hadn't come within fifty feet of the exhibition. The ahools flew off first, down the corridor that led to the cell where they'd found David. Then the hellhounds left, their tails high in the air.

Fifteen minutes later, all of them were gone. Sage nodded at Elsbeth and took her hand. They arrived in the safe room and Elsbeth gave them the update.

"Those blokes don't know what to think," David said. "Shouldn't take long for word to spread."

"Assuming any of those beasts know where Mammon hangs out," Elsbeth said.

"I'm still concerned about this place being wall-to-wall monsters when Mammon finally arrives," Klauss said.

His fear was valid, Sage knew. Klauss believed that once word spread, beasts from all over the globe would come to stare at the spectacle. If that happened, they would have no chance to slay Mammon and save Sage's dad. It was the worst possible scenario.

Having been wrapped in Leviathan's hide gave Sage an understanding about Mammon that none of the others could grasp—that Mammon's greed for power had also made him prideful—not to the level of Lucifer, but probably not far behind. Sage didn't think Mammon would stand there in front of hundreds of beasts and be humiliated. Sage believed the Prince of Greed would clear the facility before seeing for himself what had been done. It was then that they would attack.

However, Klauss's point was valid. It wouldn't take many Dark beasts to outnumber Sage's team. The last thing Sage would expect them to do was hang around to be slaughtered.

They waited for the next four days. Every time they heard an uproar, Elsbeth Teleported out to investigate. She didn't need any help, so Sage used that time to work with Kato. The great Fighting Arts practitioner taught him foot movement, balance, steps and swings, angled sword strikes, blocks, parries, and defensive maneuvers. Kato drilled him relentlessly, always whispering his instruction to keep the noise level down.

While resting, Klauss showed all of them better chain-throwing techniques. They'd brought all of the chains from the battle with the troll. Klauss explained how they could be melded together by squeezing the links together in a certain way, which created an almost unbreakable weld. *Magical,* Sage thought, *and useful.* Now they had one long strand of six in case they needed something lengthier against Mammon.

David played with Samson's jawbone. He experimented with different ways to swing it around for the best advantage. He described the sensation he got when holding it as a joining. Elsbeth explained the term fusion, not used in David's 1917 England, and he agreed it more closely defined what he felt. He didn't believe that any beast on earth could dislodge it from his hand during battle.

"I'd still like to know how the Crab Man used it to cut a breach into the human realm," Sage said.

Despite how sick he'd gotten before, Kato was the one who took the plunge and picked up the dullahan's whip. He took a few cracks over on the far side of the room and nodded, certain he could use it later. Swords weren't the only weapon the great hunter had mastered.

Since Elsbeth was the one who brought back the lance with the green stone, she spent the most time examining it. When none of them could get the stone to activate, David had an idea that led to an hour-long argument. He suggested she push a stream of Persuasion through it to see what happened, which was just the kind of reckless behavior Sage would expect out of him. Despite David's insistence that it was worth a try, Elsbeth's cooler head prevailed, and she flatly refused.

It was Kato who heard the noise first. He held up a hand and cut off one of David's tank stories.

"What is it?" Elsbeth asked

"One voice, but many footsteps." Kato frowned. "Human footsteps."

How he could tell the difference between footsteps from behind a wooden door that weighed at least a thousand pounds, Sage couldn't have guessed. But he hadn't been wrong yet.

"I'll go out," Elsbeth said.

"Me too." Sage strapped his sword around his waist and grabbed Elsbeth's hand.

They appeared in the shadowy corner, curled into tight balls. The great room was completely empty, and though they could hear the voice, Sage couldn't tell from which corridor it came.

"Kato was right," Elsbeth whispered. "I can hear several footsteps."

"Can you tell what he's shouting?" Sage asked her.

She shook her head. A door slammed. Then another a few seconds later. "Are they opening and closing the dungeon doors?" Elsbeth asked. "That's what it sounds like."

"That's what I was thinking." The footsteps grew so loud Sage finally knew which hallway they were in.

"That's my hallway," Elsbeth whispered.

"It means they've probably found your empty room. There were only a couple of other rooms on your hall with captured Council members."

"If they look long enough," Elsbeth said, "they'll also know that David, Kato, and Klauss were rescued, because those are the only rooms with missing bodies."

Sage shook his head but didn't say anything. Then he thought of something. "If they check every room with a Council member, they'll eventually open our safe room."

"It'll be a slaughter if they do," Elsbeth said.

A slaughter in which way? Sage didn't ask. "They can't get there until they pass through here," he said. "We'll get a look at them."

They got that look a few seconds later. Men. Nine. Eight of them were average sized and huddled together. They held on to each other in single file and followed a large man who was more than a head taller than the rest. They were all dressed in jeans and boots and loose-fitting shirts. It was the man in the front, clearly their superior, whose voice had carried so clearly. He barked an order Sage couldn't understand just as the group fully entered the main hall.

"What's with the group of eight?" Elsbeth asked. "Like they're afraid to lose contact with one another."

He shrugged. "Yeah. Weird." Almost timid, he thought. Afraid.

The leader saw the desecrated statue of Mammon and came to a complete stop. He stood there for a few moments and shouted something else.

"What'd he say?" Sage asked.

"I couldn't make it out," Elsbeth said.

The other men felt their way forward, hands out like blind men, then stopped near their leader. They turned away from the statue and separated just a little into a formation that protected their leader's back.

"Are they blind?" Elsbeth asked, her voice pregnant with incredulity.

Sage stared at them for several moments. He knew Mammon wouldn't want any other beasts to witness his humiliation, but bringing blind guys to protect him while he checked it out? Talk about a bridge too far. "Can you find out what they're doing without being seen?"

Elsbeth frowned at him. "What?"

"You can Teleport in and out so fast, they'd have to be looking right at you to see you. It'd help to know if they're blind." Sage pointed to a spot off at an angle to the group of eight. "You'd be hidden in the shadow of that hallway. See it? Right there?"

"I see it. It's risky, Sage."

"Not so much. You'd be well behind the main guy, and the others aren't looking that way. I think you should do it. We need the intel. I'd do it, but . . . well, I'm not as fast as you. By a mile."

Elsbeth blew out a breath. "Be right back."

Sage watched the spot. A fraction of a second after Elsbeth disappeared, he saw a flash and then she was back beside him, her face was as pale as a sheet of paper. "What?" Sage asked.

Elsbeth started to say something, but just shook her head, her bottom lip quivering. "I just . . . I've never seen . . ."

"What is it, Elsbeth?"

"Their . . . their eyes . . . they've been gouged out." She swallowed hard and kept her voice steady. "There's still blood running out of the sockets. I saw mangled flesh. Slices on the tops of their cheeks, like . . . like somebody used a sword five minutes ago. The looks of pain on their faces . . ." She shivered and rubbed her arms.

Sage didn't say anything for a moment. He couldn't believe the ego of this guy.

The leader stared hard at the display, his body as still as the granite in front of him. The chamber was so silent they could have heard a cricket tap dance. The eight blind men kept cocking and rotating their heads as though desperate to sense some hidden danger.

"Could those guards be gifted with Echolocation?" Sage asked. "Is there a Dark beast version of that?" It was a Council gift but perhaps not impossible for a Dark to possess.

"I don't know," Elsbeth said. "Sage, he blinded them just for *this* trip!" She shook her head, disgust wrinkling her face. "Nobody would do that, would they?"

"Are you really asking that?" Sage said. "Really? He's one of the Princes of Hell."

"But . . . but . . ." She turned her face away again, her jaw muscles grinding. "Just to protect his *ego*?"

Sage watched for a bit as the man stepped forward and slowly circled the display. "Does he look familiar?" he asked.

"I can't see his face well enough," Elsbeth whispered. "He's too far away. But it's him. I'm convinced of it. The Prince of Greed. Rephaim in the form of a human. I'll bet all the others are his offspring. His guards."

"My Clarity doesn't show me anything," Sage said. "Wouldn't I see him like I see my dad?"

"Rephaim can shield their true nature," Elsbeth said. She frowned at him. "You know that, right? It's why the Council has never found them."

Even her speaking in a whisper made him feel stupid. He felt his face heat up. *Yeah, Leah probably taught me that at some point,* he didn't say. *But I was too thick-headed to listen.*

"Oh, yeah. I forgot." He changed the subject. "How fast can they transform?" Other than Rupert, he'd never seen a Rephaim offspring transform but knew that Elsbeth and her dad had dealt with several.

"Rephaim offspring? Almost instantly," she said. "An actual Prince? We'd probably miss it if we blinked."

They were on the far side of the great hall, too distant to make out any real details about the man. The guards were there to keep any travelers out. It was exactly what Sage believed would happen. Mammon would face the desecration of his image alone. His pride wouldn't allow otherwise.

Sage still worried that it *might* not be Mammon. "If we attack and it's not him," he said, "we'll never get him."

They'd discussed this point a hundred times. The moment the Dark beasts knew Sage and his team were in there, word would spread, and it would be raining monsters.

"How do we confirm it?" she asked. "You'll only know for sure if he transforms. Right?"

Thanks to Leviathan. "How far will a beam of your Persuasion travel?" he asked. "We're about seventy yards away. Will it reach from here?"

She looked at him as if he'd just grown three extra noses. "Yeah, but so what? The purity comes down through the ceiling and out of my palm. I can't just shoot a bolt of energy like a fireball. As soon as the light comes from heaven, the room will light up like Christmas time."

Sage leaned in closer. "Lower your voice. I know all that. I also know we spent an hour on our battle plan. It didn't include fighting Mammon *and* a bunch of flunkies."

"You want a diversion?" she asked. "To start it?"

"I want you to hit the main guy with a blast," Sage said. "If it's Mammon, he'll transform so he can fight. You're far enough away to keep them at bay. They'll converge on you, but you can Teleport and stay out of their reach. If it's Mammon, game on. While you're creating a diversion, I'll pop in and tell the others."

Elsbeth thought about it for a moment, then shook her head. "Go tell the others now. I'll wait. When you come back, I'll light him up. The shouting will start, and David can break the other two out of the room so that they can join the fun."

"Be right back." Sage appeared in the safe room and found the other three huddled against the door. He gave them the update and told them what he and Elsbeth had discussed. "Any concerns or questions?"

They looked at each other, and then Kato spoke. "So when we hear shouting, we come out fighting? And if it's not Mammon?"

Sage shrugged. "We can't let anyone leave. We've talked about this. But I think it's him. Human form. Leader. Isolated himself to inspect the statue. Not allowing anyone else to see him humiliated." He paused. "The biggest point? No other beast can transform into human form except a Rephaim or his off-spring." A werewolf could, he knew, but full moons didn't exist in the Dark realm. He looked hard at all three of them. "It's him. Bank on it."

"I agree with Sage," Klauss said. "We take the battle to them." He began looping the chains around his head and shoulder. "Kato, I'd leave the dullahan's whip in here. Wouldn't want one of them to use it against us."

"Just a last resort, Klauss," Kato said. "With it being dipped in Rephaim blood before being roasted by the fire of a chimera, I'm not sure it would affect them anyway."

David grabbed his jawbone and held it high. "Sage, get out there and get those blokes moving. I'm going as mad as a bag of ferrets sitting around in here."

Sage nodded. "See you all in a few."

"That was quicker than I thought it'd be," Elsbeth whispered when he got back. "Any hesitations?"

"None," he whispered back.

The man—Mammon—had walked around the entire hide and now stood staring at the message painted on the floor. "Has he said anything else?" Sage asked.

"Nothing. He must have glared at the headless statue for a full minute just before you came back." She looked at Sage, her eyes bright. "It's him, isn't it? One of the Princes."

Sage took a deep breath, trying to keep his heart rate under control. "Yeah. I'm sure of it."

"Then let's do this."

Sage placed a hand on her arm. "We need to time this right, OK? From the moment you call on your gift, how long is the delay between the purification coming through the ceiling and streaming out of your palm? Five seconds? Ten?"

She shrugged. "One. Two at the most. Why?"

"If I can get him before he transforms .... or at least hurt him, good for us. He'll see the light from heaven before he gets hit with a blast, right?"

"Yeah. Probably."

"He might know what it is immediately or he might not," Sage said. "If he does because he saw it centuries ago, he'll react immediately. But he'll still hesitate just a little, I hope. I want to Teleport over and hit his kill spot as soon as the light appears from above."

Elsbeth nodded. "Get your sword ready. I'll tell you exactly when to go."

Sage dried his sweaty palms against his pant legs and practiced the breathing techniques Kato showed him yesterday.

All five of them now knew about Mammon's kill spot—a small area directly in the center of his back, between his shoulder blades. It was the most valuable piece of information Leviathan had passed along while Sage was wrapped within her hide. When he was fully transformed, the spot was between Mammon's wings and was covered with a nearly impenetrable shell. They could kill the beast in other ways, of course, but the quickest and surest way was to penetrate the kill spot with nearly any instrument at all. They didn't even have to stab him that deeply.

Sage pulled his sword and focused fully on the solitary man across the great room. The other men still faced away; their heads were moving, as if they were listening for noises of someone's approach. Sage leaned over, tightened the grip on his sword, and whispered, "Let's do this."

The blow would be for his dad, for the corruption he'd been subjected to, and for how that exploitation of greed had affected his mom. The blow would be for all the dead Council members now rotting within these very walls, for the horrific experimentation on them, their torture, agony, and murder. The blow would be for everything up to this point: the battles with the gargoyles, the mad scientist, Rupert, the hellhound, the dullahan, Crab Man, and the trolls; the brush with death by the werewolf; the pain and anguish from the hide; and for the murder of Leviathan, the greatest weapon against the Dark beasts. Finally, the blow would be for the hundreds of thousands of souls trapped inside the Dungeon of Souls.

He would end it here. Now!

He would stop the Prince of Greed and watch his dying body fall upon the obscene monument he'd created for others to worship. Soon *all* would know that Mammon had died upon his own graven image.

Elsbeth stood fully erect in the deep shadow of their corner, raised her left palm toward heaven, aimed her right palm at Mammon, and whispered, "May the purifying and cleansing light of grace be magnified through me in His name. Amen. Go, Sage!"

Sage appeared directly behind the man just as Elsbeth's light lit up the room like a falling star. He plunged the sword directly into the center of the man's back with every bit of strength in his body. Using the leverage Kato had shown him, pushing with his shoulders, arms, back, and hips, he screamed and released his pent-up rage and drove the sword with a fury summoned from the most closely guarded depths of his soul.

The blow reflected off some kind of steel plate the man had placed between his shoulder blades under his clothes. Sage's sword bounced away and carried his weight and balance with him. He stumbled to the side as the man spun around.

Eyes so black they appeared as chunks of shimmering onyx magnified Mammon's scowl of rage. Just as he was about to say something, a blast of light hit him in the back and knocked him flat on his face.

Sage scrambled to his feet as the man belted a scream from the deepest pits of hell and exploded into the beast from Leviathan's dying nightmare. Feet almost set, Sage saw a massive claw bearing down, and he jumped sideways. Other roars erupted around him. The blind guards transformed into smaller versions of the Prince. The flesh around their eye sockets was gouged and mangled, empty of the black orbs so prevalent on Mammon.

A blast of exploding wood and debris sounded from the safe room, and Sage knew David, Kato, and Klauss were on their way.

Sage Teleported away, just forty yards or so, to create enough distance from Mammon to survey the battlefield.

Mammon's bodyguards assembled around the great Prince, who stood near his decapitated statue like some glorious heavenly host, wings opened wide, arms raised high—the same pose they'd seen inside the Dungeon of Souls. He was twelve feet tall and towered above his offspring; his leathery, gold skin shimmered as if gilded with the precious metal. A huge sword was sheathed on his back between his wings, the hilt positioned directly behind his head, covering the hard shell protecting his kill spot.

Elsbeth appeared next to Sage. David, wide-eyed and wielding his jawbone like a crazed axe murderer, stormed around the corner and skidded to a stop when he saw the collection of monsters surrounding Mammon. Behind David were Kato and Klauss, who were older, slower, more cautious in their approach. The three of them immediately fanned out in a half circle, Kato with his sword in battle position and Klauss with a chain in each hand.

"I'll fill the hole." Elsbeth Teleported away.

And so they were set—five Council members against Mammon and his crew. Many would die in the next few minutes. To save his dad, Sage was willing to risk being one of them.

24

The battle plan they'd spent hours developing wasn't worth ten cents now that Mammon had a team of killers protecting him. Two of his offspring stood near his back, facing away, swords drawn, ready for an attack against Mammon's kill spot. The other six circled to his front and sides, near enough to protect, far enough away to give themselves room for close-quarter combat.

Sage's team now surrounded them completely, with little idea of what to do first. Well, that was not totally true. They'd come up with a carefully prepared script that Sage was supposed to use to enrage the Prince of Greed. Sage had memorized and practiced it in front of the group, but it didn't appear as though Mammon needed to hear a taunting speech to get his blood boiling. Either the Rephaim was already enraged, or his face was permanently stuck in that menacing, infuriated grimace.

"Proceed, Sage," Klauss shouted. The rabbi was spinning chains so fast they looked like airplane propellers. Kato, sword cocked and locked, looked ready to spring the moment Elsbeth unleashed her gift. David stood loosely, the jawbone dangling in his hand, a goofy grin on his face, confidence oozing from every pore.

Sage glanced at Elsbeth, who gave him a thumbs-up sign. Sage cleared his throat and spoke with as much authority and domination as he could muster. "Your arrogance is so predictable, Mammon. Your pride so disgusting. Leviathan has won and used your greed for power against you. Today . . ." And Sage stomped his foot against the floor. "Today, the Council will have its revenge. You have walked into our deathtrap."

Those were Klauss's words, and Sage had spoken them well. The beast offered no hint of anger. In fact, he smiled and slowly reached above his head and grabbed the hilt of his sword, drawing it out in slow motion. The sword was solid black, double edged, with a seven-foot blade. With arms at least that long, Mammon's reach created little room for error.

I *have walked into* your *deathtrap?* Mammon's voice sounded within Sage's head, but the beast hadn't spoken. Like Leviathan had projected her thoughts onto others, the Prince of Greed was speaking only to him.

Mammon belted a laugh that sent a wave of stench roiling across the great hall. *You are the boy of prophecy. Sage the Warrior. Your arrival has been much anticipated. Tell me, how is your father?*

Sage flinched.

The beast smiled a mocking grin that spread wide across his face. His teeth were short, needle-sharp daggers. *Your angels never allowed for a direct attack against you, and so I developed a subtler plan. Your weak, puny father made the perfect bait.* He stepped forward and waved his claws as though showing Sage the facility. *Welcome to my collection site. I trust you have seen my growing assortment of souls?*

Sage's sword vibrated in his hand, a slight pulsation that fused them together. The sensation radiated power into his arm. He didn't know exactly what was going on, but he couldn't risk looking away.

"What's happening, Sage?" Elsbeth shouted.

Sage tried looking at her, but he couldn't take his eyes off Mammon. He physically couldn't turn his head away.

You defeated my researcher experimenting on the girl. Not an easy task. His voice was a mixture between a growl and a clap of thunder. It reverberated through Sage's head in waves of crawling terror. *You see, since I cannot collect the souls of angelic-humans, I collect their bodies. Then I break their spirit.* He laughed again, a short burst filled with hate. *However, your father, boy, your father is all mine!*

"Don't let him into your head, mate," David shouted.

I can release your father, Sage. And I will. For a price.

Tears leaked out of Sage's eyes, and he tried blinking them away.

Join me. Mammon stepped forward and offered a hand. *Become a god. Serve alongside me. Rule the Rephaim. Rule the world. Ensure the safety of your family forever.*

"He's a great deceiver, Sage," Elsbeth shouted. "It's what they do. Stop looking at him! Don't look at his eyes!"

They were pools of purity, Mammon's eyes. Dark and rich and full of wonder. Sage saw perfection in them. Power. Endless possibilities. Friendship.

You'll never be alone again. No ridicule. No tormenting from others. You will be loved. Respected. Endured by all. Join me, Sage. Lay down your sword and take my hand. Save your father.

Sage took a step toward him and reached out with his free hand. Mammon's eyes were a bottomless ocean of love and respect.

"What are you doing!" Elsbeth screamed. "Sage! Stop!"

He didn't want to stop. He turned toward her in a rage and pointed his sword in her direction. "Stay away! Get back!" He looked at the rest of them. "All of you. Get back. Leave us!"

Come, lad. Join me. Free yourself from the confines of human bondage. Use your budding gifts to transform the world into our image. We, the Seven, seek you. You will become immortal!

Sage smiled and stepped closer, a joy so pure he felt he might fly.

Mammon walked toward him, flanked by his blind guards. He reached out a hand and smiled.

"Sage, stop!" Elsbeth shouted again. "I'm warning you, Sage. Stop right now!"

"Go away, Elsbeth," Sage said. Perfect joy radiated through his body. Never had he felt this peaceful, this loved.

Touch me. Give willingly, and all will be yours.

"Yes. I want to," Sage said. He felt he could step right into those eyes. He saw freedom inside those pools of black perfection. He *finally* understood his destiny.

"Now, Elsbeth!" somebody shouted. "Do not hesitate. Do it now!"

Come, my son. Let us rule together. You. Me. Your father.

Sage bent to place his sword on the ground as he reached out with his other hand. Just a couple more steps, and his life would be complete.

The blast hit him in the chest. A searing, white-hot shot of Persuasion that sizzled his nerve endings and knocked him backward across the room.

"Noooooo!" Mammon raged.

The Purity, bright and hot and cleansing, skimmed across the surface of Sage's skin like wildfire, scorching temptation, boiling fantasies, blistering visions of grandeur. Sage rolled over onto his side and gasped for breath. He felt fire in his blood, his muscles, and bones, even on the surface of his eyes.

"Attack now!" somebody shouted.

Sage heard screams and shouts, the clash of swords, David's boasting, sizzling skin from the rabbi's chains. A great roar erupted as the final effects of Elsbeth's blast faded. Sage raised his head and found his entire team in front of him, a blockade against Mammon and his blind warriors.

Sage climbed to his feet with a surge of strength he'd never felt before. "My father will soon be fine," he boasted. He laced his voice with as much confidence as he could and gripped his sword tightly.

Mammon backed away and waved at his beasts to join him. He paused near the defaced monument. Sage took a quick assessment. Two of Mammon's guards were down—one dead with the two chains that had bound him, scalded his skin, and then cut his body into thirds. The second was also dead, sliced by Kato's sword and smashed by David's rage.

Kato was hurt, barely able to stand, one arm hanging limp, huge cuts across his upper body. David, jawbone in hand, had also taken a beating. His shirt was in ribbons, and blood flowed down his face from three gashes across his forehead. His right leg and arm were missing chunks of flesh, and his left hand looked mangled. The rabbi was fine, as was Elsbeth, though she appeared fatigued and slightly stunned.

Sage's sword melded itself to his hand. His arm felt so strong and solid, so full of power he thought it might be possible to chop a tree down with a single blow. Then he remembered the Beowulf legend that his sword did magical things if wielded by someone of the bloodline of Seth.

Sage pushed his way in front of his team and, remembering the script Klauss had come up with, recited: "*You* do not lead the Seven," he boomed. "You betrayed them! It was *your* idea to imprison the Council against Lucifer's orders! You wanted us only as your toys. You wanted to hoard our gifts, despite the danger to the Seven. Greed poisoned your sense of reason, Mammon. You should have just killed us!"

David suddenly belted a war cry and sprinted straight toward Mammon, jawbone held high. Mammon turned, but two of the beasts stepped into David's path.

"David! No!" Elsbeth screamed.

Klauss let his chains fly and hit one of the two in the neck and waist. The beast screamed as the chains tightened and sizzled its flesh. David hit the other one with such power that both of them crashed in a tangle of arms and legs into one of the six smaller statues.

Then Kato moved, sword a blur, and advanced on the closest guard. The beast was dead in seconds.

Mammon watched the battle unfold, then turned his attention to Elsbeth, who raised a hand toward heaven and shouted something Sage couldn't hear over the animalistic cries of the beasts. A blast shot out of her palm just as Sage Teleported to Mammon's side and swung his sword the instant he materialized.

Elsbeth's blast hit one of the guards who'd jumped high in the air to sacrifice himself in protecting the Prince. The beast belted a roar that vibrated the air around them before falling to the ground.

Sage's blow was meant to cut off Mammon's sword hand, but the mighty Rephaim spun and met Sage's sword with his own. He used speed Sage had never witnessed before, even from the most battle-hardened Arch. Mammon's blow nearly sent Sage's sword sailing across the room.

Sage fell on his back, then Teleported away when Mammon took a step in his direction. Shaken by the power and speed of the beast, Sage repositioned himself for another attack. Mammon roared as one of the rabbi's chains hit his sword and skittered away. The great beast burst forward in one leap, his body moving so fast he was little more than a fuzzy shape. He landed next to Elsbeth and hit her in the side of the head with the pommel of his sword. She collapsed immediately and didn't move.

The Rephaim beast didn't boast of his small victory. Instead, he opened his mouth wide and spat a blob of black mucus that hit Klauss in the front of his neck. The rabbi fell back, his face frozen in a silent scream.

Sage grabbed one of the rabbi's chains and let it fly. Mammon saw it coming and flicked it away with his sword. Mammon charged him, sword raised high, but Sage Teleported away and appeared on the far side of the decapitated monument.

Kato grunted as he battled one of the three remaining blind beasts. Despite having no sight, they wielded their swords with the skill and precision of veteran swordsmen. They *had* to possess some kind of sixth sense. Kato was weakened, slowed by injuries that would have crippled Sage.

Sage was about to help Kato when Mammon jumped next to the great warrior. Kato had just landed a killing blow through the gut of the blind guard and couldn't get his sword free to block the blow from Mammon. As he had done to Elsbeth, Mammon hit Kato in the head with a strike that sent the great warrior flying back, unconscious before he hit the ground.

Sage Teleported over to Mammon again, this time appearing directly behind him. The beast launched into the air, his powerful wings beating the air around them. Sage swung his sword and caught the inside of Mammon's right forearm. The beast dropped his sword and fell back to earth to grab it. He landed with the agility of a cat.

Sage swung at Mammon's midsection. With a speed Sage didn't believe possible, the beast lifted a leg and kicked him in the chest. He fell back and knocked his head against the stone floor.

"Sage, help!" David shouted.

David had killed three blind beasts by ripping their wings off and crushing their heads with the jawbone. Now he was badly hurt and cornered by the remaining two. Mammon stood over them, sword raised in victory, as David, clearly too hurt to fight off his attackers, tried his best to survive.

Sage Teleported to them and jammed his sword through the back of one of the beasts. It screamed and tried one last thrust, but David crushed its head with the jawbone.

Mammon swung his sword at David, but the Boy with Might ducked and pushed the last blind guard into its path. Mammon's blow cut the beast in half.

Sage Teleported behind Mammon and stabbed the beast in the back. The kill spot! He had to hit it! The beast raged and spun and slammed Sage in the chest with a claw.

David belted a war cry and hit the Prince in the center of the back with the jawbone. His direct hit crashed into the Prince like a crack of thunder. The beast screamed and spun on David. He hit him in the chest with the pommel of his sword. David grunted and fell back.

As Sage stood, he saw what had caused the cracking sound. The hard shell covering Mammon's kill spot had broken in half and fallen to the floor. The impenetrable shell hadn't withstood the blow from David's jawbone.

Mammon knew it. He attacked David again, this time slamming his head with the hilt of his sword and knocking him out.

He's trying not to kill us! He believes he can turn us! Because he almost turned me, Sage realized.

The rabbi had gone still, black poison now covering his neck and face. His chains still glowed orange in the murkiness of the giant hall. Sage grabbed the long one made of six melded together and looped it around his head and shoulder before turning to face the beast.

Just him and me. The blind guards were dead. Sage's team was down. Mammon knew he couldn't let Sage behind him, although Mammon couldn't know Sage knew that. Sage stepped forward and raised his sword. "You cannot have my father, Mammon. His soul will not remain in this place."

Mammon, his only wound the one Sage inflicted on his sword arm, also stepped forward. "The Seven choose carefully the souls we take. We do not relinquish them. Ever."

"Then I will take them," Sage said. He raised his sword above his head.

"Shadows converge," Mammon shouted. He waved a clawed hand in a circle above his head. Darkness spilled out of the corners of the room and swirled and morphed into a thick rope of blackness that hovered at the edge of Mammon's fingertips. He grabbed it, flung his arm, and whipped it at Sage.

Shadow Manipulation. As Sage focused to Teleport away, the far end of the ghostly bullwhip hit him in the chest and sent him flying across the room. His skin burned from the impact.

Mammon whipped it again, but Sage appeared behind the beast and stabbed him in the back a second time, just missing the kill spot.

The beast roared and spun. His giant sword cut the air above Sage's head. Sage moved into Mammon's blind spot over his left shoulder. He grabbed one end of the long chain, wrapped it around Mammon's ankle, and squeezed the links, melding them together. Skin sizzled. Mammon swung a claw and knocked Sage away, but Sage had the other end of the chain tightly in his grip. He Teleported to Mammon's decapitated statue and melded the chain together after wrapping it around the base.

The beast howled and grabbed the chain to pull it free from his ankle, but it burned his hands, so he flung it away. He crouched into a deep squat and shot into the air, a mixture of pain and rage bellowing from his mouth. The shadow rope disappeared. He fought to escape high into the air, but the chain jerked him short. As big and powerful as the Rephaim was, it wasn't strong enough to either break the chain or lift the granite statue.

The mighty beast spun and fought against the rabbi's magical chain, but it held fast. He was caught.

Sage glanced around at his team. The rabbi was moving his head and shoulders; the black mucus from Mammon's mouth was now fading. Elsbeth, still out, was breathing easily. Kato, cut up as he was, had stopped bleeding and appeared to be asleep. David was moaning, and his hands and feet twitched with life.

The chain would soon cut all the way through Mammon's ankle, which would allow him to escape. Sage couldn't let him fly away. All would be lost. He sheathed his sword and grabbed the chain. He pulled it toward him as he walked around the base of the statue. When he completed one circle, Mammon was a few feet closer but still too far to hit. Sage would never get him reeled in fast enough. Besides, the beast was so powerful that every flap of his wings nearly jerked Sage off his feet.

The wings!

Sage sprinted over to Klauss and grabbed several more chains. He spun one, twirling it overhead just like Klauss had shown him yesterday, and let it fly. It flew straight and true, but the beast jerked away at the right moment and it sailed past him. It landed harmlessly on the floor across the room.

Sage tried again. Mammon screamed and reached with both hands to the chain around his ankle. His movement exposed his entire back. Sage let another chain fly, and it struck home, wrapping itself around the base of Mammon's right wing.

The orange metal squeezed ever tighter around the wing. Mammon tried grabbing it but couldn't. He raised his sword and attempted to pry the tip underneath.

Seeing slack in the long chain, Sage Teleported to the base of the statue. He completed four complete revolutions before Mammon realized he'd been pulled closer to the ground.

Sage spun another chain and threw it as soon as Mammon's back was to him. It hit his left wing about a foot from Mammon's back and wrapped itself tightly. The stench of burning flesh and feathers filled the air.

The beast roared as he dropped closer to the ground, his wings now immobile. Sage yanked out some of the slack, which allowed him to wrap the chain yet another time around the base of the statue. The smell of Mammon's burning flesh nearly overwhelmed him, but he pressed on. Twice more he circled the headless edifice as Mammon's struggles got weaker and weaker.

Mammon's feet were only twelve feet off the ground now. His mouth opened as he screamed and fought against the strength of the chain. His ankle was nearly severed. Soon the beast would be free. Sage didn't want to touch him—the beast was no gargoyle—but he had no choice.

He landed on Mammon's shoulders, his feet dangling on the chest of the great beast. He looked down. Elsbeth lay directly beneath them. Sage plunged his sword into Mammon's golden chest before the beast jerked forward to throw him off. This wasn't a rodeo; Sage had no intention of riding the mighty Rephaim. He Teleported to Elsbeth, picked her up, and carried her to David, whose eyes were still glassy as he slowly regained consciousness.

Sage couldn't tell what, if anything, the stab to Mammon's chest had accomplished. The beast still screeched and fought to pull free. Sage noted the extra slack in the chain since both of the Prince's wings were now restrained. Sage ran to the statue and coiled the chain twice more around the base.

Mammon's right wing fell away. The mighty beast dropped to the ground. His feet landed where only seconds before Elsbeth had lain. Within moments, the chain that wrapped his ankle would sever his foot.

There is time. You can still rule with me, Mammon projected into Sage's mind. *Power. Wealth. Unimagined respect throughout the world. Come, join me.*

Sage avoided the Prince's eyes and felt no bond between them. "Your reign ends today, Mammon," he said. "Defeated by a boy who walks with the Almighty."

Mammon spewed another glob of black mucus, but it floated as though in slow motion. Sage sidestepped it, and the blob dissolved.

With sword in hand and Mammon still chained to his decapitated graven image, Sage swung at Mammon's left ankle. He severed the foot not attached to the chain.

Mammon roared and brought down his sword with such speed and power it rocked Sage when he raised his to block the hit. But the beast was crippled now and fell backward against a statue.

Sage backed away, shoulders and arms aching from the mighty blow. He picked up the chain and yanked, severing the beast's right foot as the beast was struggling to rise. Mammon screamed and tried rising but slipped in his own blood that gushed from his body.

Sage pulled the end of the chain to him. He Teleported near the head of the beast and wrapped it around Mammon's neck. He disappeared before giant claws could swipe him.

At that moment, sizzling, burning flesh was the most beautiful sound in the world. The chain tightened and ate into Mammon like a hungry, rabid animal. The beast dropped his sword and clawed at his neck, desperate to free himself. As quickly as he could, Sage popped next to Mammon, grabbed the huge sword, and popped out.

Sage heard moaning behind him and looked back. Both David and Elsbeth were trying to stand. He rushed over and helped both to their feet.

"Can somebody shut that bloke up?" David shouted. His wounds were healing now, though blood still dripped onto his hand and covered most of the jawbone.

"It won't be long," Sage said.

David stood and held his ears against the wailing of Mammon. His expression hardened, and he raised the bloody jawbone. "I will shut him up for good!"

"David, no!" Sage shouted.

The warning came too late. David sprinted to the Prince and began beating its head with the jawbone. One of the blows got stuck, and David had to yank out the jawbone. The beast fell silent and limp, but David kept beating it.

Sage ran over and pulled him away. "Stop! He's gone."

And he was.

"Look at the jawbone!" Elsbeth said from behind him, her face a mask of pain. "Look, Sage! Look at the jawbone!"

David held it up, his eyes wide. It glowed red, as it had when Crab Man cut his way into the human realm. "It's buzzing in my hand, mate."

The black blood of the Rephaim had mixed with David's red blood.

Elsbeth hobbled over, wonder on her face. "Was that the key?" she asked. "Mixing your blood with one of the Seven?"

David shrugged. "Beats me, lass. You're the bookworm, not me."

"Sage," Kato grunted from behind him. The great hunter was on his knees, his wounds markedly better. "Is he dead?"

"Gone," Sage said.

Elsbeth walked over to Klauss, who was trying to sit up. "Are you OK?"

"The souls," Klauss said. "Are they free?"

The souls! Sage couldn't believe he hadn't given them any thought. "We've gotta go check! David, put that thing away. We can't open the door without you."

"All of us will go," Elsbeth said. "Kato, Klauss, can you make it?"

The rabbi stood on shaky legs and nodded. He turned toward the Prince of Greed and studied the scene.

The beast was dead, the chain in the final stages of decapitating him. Its wings lay several feet away, gold and shiny, near the hide of Leviathan.

"You got your revenge," Sage whispered under his breath to the hide of the great water beast. "The Seven will not be allowed to rule this world."

"What's that, mate?" David asked.

Sage shook his head. "Nothing."

In his weakened state, it took David longer to slide the telephone pole–sized crossbar off the Dungeon of Souls. When he swung the door wide, Sage knew it had been worth the wait.

The veil was gone, and the room was empty. The image of Mammon and the million heads was now just a memory for future nightmares.

Elsbeth grabbed Sage's hand and pulled him into a hug. "Your dad's free," she whispered into his ear.

Sage squeezed her tightly and laughed. "So let's go see him."

25

They wasted no time grabbing their stuff and getting out of the building. Kato wore his pack, Elsbeth carried the lance with the green stone, and Klauss handled the dullahan's whip with great care. David's jawbone continued to glow red, and Sage wondered if he'd be able to use it to cut into the human realm.

Sage brought up the idea of simply walking through one of the many breaches used by the Dark beasts inside the building, but none of them wanted to risk surprising a nest of monsters on the other side. The decision was made to go the spot Sage had entered from France. He believed he could find it, or at least get pretty close.

They stepped out of the stone mansion, and Elsbeth pointed to the sky. "Where'd the Darks go?"

Sage looked up. Gone. All of them. There was now just a red-tinted sky and the smell of sulfur.

The rabbi looked at Elsbeth. "I once read in an old text that Darks flee from sustained blasts of Persuasion."

"I can't figure out why they were here in the first place," Sage said. "They didn't do anything except hover above the building. What was the point?"

"Preventing an attack," Klauss said. "My studies as a rabbi included more than your typical Judean biblical history. I wrote a thesis on Darks and their hive-like behaviors. I suspect other structures in the Dark realm are protected from attacks by angels of light. They let us come and go because we caused no threat to them or the structure. They might have assumed the five of us were Dark beasts."

"Good thing, then," David said. "How much farther, Sage? The jawbone is making my hand numb."

"How do you turn it off?" Elsbeth asked. "Will it glow like that all the time?"

"Let's find out *after* he cuts our way back into France," Sage said.

They walked through the bleak landscape, the sulfur stinging their eyes. All of them limped and rubbed their wounds but seemed to get stronger with each step.

"The world has advanced," Elsbeth said. "Especially for the two of you, Kato and Klauss. There are things that will seem like magic. Just stay close to us and don't talk to anybody or ask any questions. OK?"

The three of them nodded. Sage was surprised David didn't have a smart comeback. "I will need more modern clothes," Kato said. He motioned toward his torn and bloodstained African warrior garb.

"I doubt British army uniforms are still in style," Klauss said to David.

All of them had dirty, torn, and bloodstained clothes they couldn't be seen in. Klauss still had three chains wrapped around his shoulder, and Kato and Sage wore their swords. The dullahan bullwhip would freak anybody out, as would David's glowing jawbone. They didn't have to worry about any of that until they got back into the human realm.

"We're getting close," Sage said. He looked back and tried to judge the exact spot he remembered from several days before.

"Everyone stop," Kato said. They did, and Kato stepped to the front. "Your footsteps are easily seen," he said to Sage. He pointed to the ground. "I will track them in reverse. Everyone please stay here. I do not want our footprints to ruin the tracks Sage left when he entered from France." He inspected the ground and took off.

"I don't see anything," Sage whispered to the rest of them.

"Me either," Elsbeth said.

"It is what he does," Klauss said. "You told me how he tracked the bleeding gargoyle over many miles of rough mountainous terrain."

"The bloke can stick his nose in the dirt all he wants," David said, "as long as he can find the spot where you entered."

They stood and watched him work. Elsbeth touched Sage's arm and smiled. "I'm excited to get home!"

Sage smiled back. "Me, too. But I'm a little nervous about facing Grandpa." Truth was, he was *a lot* nervous about it. Grandpa's scream of "Sage, no!" still rang in his ears.

"How long have you been gone?" she asked.

"A week. This is day seven. Or eight. Maybe nine. I'm not exactly sure. I wonder what he told Mom and Dad?"

"Wish I had a mam and pap to tell," David said. "Whatever your grandfather said, however mad your parents got, it could be worse."

Sage didn't know how to respond to that. David was right. Whatever had happened after he left, it would all eventually work out.

"David, will you be OK after we get back?" Elsbeth asked.

The Boy with Might shrugged. "Got some studying to do at the Tomb. And the Council will help me. And Ronan. I'll survive." He grinned. "Might even move in with Sage."

"I'd be fine with that," Sage said.

It took Kato five minutes before he stood tall and waved them over to a spot less than a hundred yards ahead. When they got there, Kato pointed to the ground. "You came out, took a couple of steps forward, then walked back several feet. Is this true?"

"That's exactly what I did," Sage said. "I was surprised that I couldn't see the breach from this side." He looked at the ground and saw nothing but a few scuff marks. *Kato read all of that from those?*

Kato bent over and drew a circle in the red dirt. He looked up at David. "Stand at precisely this point."

Once there, David held the glowing jawbone out in front of him. Nothing happened.

"Move it back and forth, side to side," Sage said.

They were hopeful that the jawbone would find the previous breach. And then it did.

"Something is happening." David's entire hand and arm starting vibrating just before the jawbone jumped sideways in his hand and plunged into a crack in the atmosphere. A six-foot-tall, jagged line of red and purple appeared in front of them.

"Don't move," Sage said. "You've found it."

"I have?" David asked. "I don't see anything."

"Nor I," Kato said.

"Sage is a Pathfinder," Elsbeth reminded them. She looked at Sage. "You'll need to stick your hand in there so that we can see where to go."

Sage approached the jagged line and slid his hand in. It disappeared from view. He turned to look at them. "Ready?" A few moments later, they all stood in the dark on the same battlefield David had been snatched from a hundred years before. Leah was there along with the eight Archs that Sage had grown so accustomed to.

"Leah!" Sage stepped forward and held his arms out.

His angel smiled and placed her hands on the sides of his face. "You have brightened the world," she said. "The Thrones send their congratulations."

Relief washed over him at the sound of her voice. He didn't think he'd ever miss anything as much. "This is Leah, everybody. My Guardian. Leah, let me introduce you."

"I know them already," Leah said. She looked at everyone, a smile as bright as the North Star. "Welcome to Sage's time. The Council will rejoice at your return. For now, my instruction is to lead all of you to Theo. Once we alert the Council of your arrival, they will send an envoy to collect you." She turned to Elsbeth. "You may call your father from Theo's oddity shop."

Elsbeth nodded and wiped her eyes. "That sounds great."

Leah turned and led them toward town. Sage couldn't see everyone's face clearly, but he knew they must be feeling immense relief. As he was.

"This field is a lot quieter since the last time I saw it," David said. He lagged a little behind as he took in the sights. "I'll have to come back one day and look at everything in the sunlight."

They'd been walking for a few minutes when Sage asked Leah how long he'd been gone. "Eight days," Leah said.

"What did Grandpa tell Mom and Dad?"

"I do not know precisely how your grandfather phrased the explanation, but he told them that you and Ronan are in the same place," Leah said. "In an area without cellular service."

"Is Ronan waiting somewhere in Godspace?" Rabbi Cohen asked.

"Yes," Leah said.

"I don't know what cellular service means," Klauss said. "Something modern, certainly. So Steven told them something true."

"But meant to conceal the actual circumstances," Elsbeth said.

"Members of the Council have participated in similar misdirection throughout history," Klauss said. "Regular humans do not understand those with special abilities. Their interference after obtaining such knowledge has led to many problems for the Council."

Sage wondered what Grandpa would've told them if he had never come back. Or if he'd been captured inside one of Mammon's cells. It was a dangerous game, not coming clean about what was really happening, but he would leave all of that for Grandpa and

Theo to figure out. Maybe Theo's gift of Sight had told him how long Sage would be gone and Grandpa had gone with that.

Sage slipped into the church, led them to the storage room door, and then through the entrance into Godspace behind the heavy drapes.

The feeling of comfort and rejuvenation began immediately. Sage watched the faces of the others and could tell they felt it too.

"I did not know if I would ever see Godspace again," Kato said with a huge smile.

A river flowed in front of them. A mountain peak sat in the distance.

"I just wanna soak it in," Elsbeth said.

"We can rest if you want," Sage said.

"No," Klauss said. "You are eager to see your father. We must press on. All of us will soon feel as if we have slept for days."

Sage mouthed "thank you" and pointed straight ahead. "Then let's get going," he said.

"Is this the spot?" Sage asked Leah later. Although sure he was at the precise location that once led into Theo's Treasure Room, he was even more certain that Leah would know.

"Yes," Leah said.

"Are you sure you can open it again?" Elsbeth asked her.

Leah smiled. "Need determines availability. Please step back."

Sage hadn't doubted Leah's promise that she'd be able to reopen the entrance to Theo's shop, and so he hadn't worried much about it. Now, being so close, he found himself a little short of breath.

Leah pulled her sword and pointed it toward the white orb in the sky. All three sets of wings shot open, and Sage heard David gasp beside him. She tilted her head back, closed her eyes, and mouthed words Sage couldn't hear. Her sword glowed so brightly Sage had to turn away. When he looked back again, she'd pointed it at the spot where the entrance used to be.

"Look at that," Sage whispered. The red and purplish entrance started forming again.

"I don't see anything," Elsbeth said.

"It's there," Sage said. "Believe me."

In another moment it was done. Leah lowered her sword and stepped back. "Need determines availability," she said again. "Your future need to use this entrance is great. Welcome home."

Sage stepped forward, his heart racing. "Thank you, Leah." He turned to everyone else. He'd told all of them about the Dark attack, and while he believed that everyone was probably all right, he wouldn't know for sure until he stepped through.

"I don't know if anyone will be in Theo's treasure room, but Leah, just in case someone is there, can you go first to tell them I'm coming through?" Sage asked. "Don't wanna freak anyone out."

David laughed behind him. "Wouldn't want to surprise Ronan and get hit in the side of the head by that bloke."

Leah nodded and disappeared inside. A few seconds later, Grandpa burst through and grabbed Sage in a crushing hug. Everything went blurry as Sage's eyes filled.

"Thank heavens you're safely home," Grandpa whispered into his ear. After a minute, Grandpa let him go and smiled. "I should kick your tail."

Sage wiped his eyes. "I know. I had to do it. I had to."

"Is this your grandfather?" Elsbeth asked.

"Yeah." Sage introduced everyone, and Grandpa shook every hand.

"Thank all of you for getting him here safely," Grandpa said.

Kato laughed. "*He* got *us* here safely. You should be quite proud of him."

"Amen," Klauss said.

"Come on," Sage said. "Let's go." He guided everyone in, and found Theo and Ronan sitting on stools in the back of the room. The door leading to the back of the warehouse was sealed tightly. The room was completely clean, with no evidence of the Dark attack.

Ronan's reaction when he saw David step into the room would have gone viral on YouTube within hours. He jumped up, ran over, and grabbed the Boy with Might in a crushing hug. David's eyes bulged.

"Met your match, finally," Elsbeth teased.

"My pap always told me to be gentle with old people." David smiled at Ronan.

Klauss introduced himself to Theo and Ronan, as did Elsbeth.

"Theo," Kato said. "It has been too long."

Theo stood, and the two men embraced. "Much too long," he said. "Truly. Wonderful to have you back in the fight."

"It was the rabbi's chains that defeated Mammon," Sage told Grandpa. "You should have seen it."

Sage's team spent several minutes telling them about their adventures inside Mammon's collection site, but there was too much to go over right then in detail. "I need to see Dad," Sage told everybody. He looked at Theo and nodded toward Leah, who hovered near the entrance to Godspace. "Elsbeth needs to use your phone. And Leah said somebody will contact the Council."

"I will handle, Master Sage," Theo said. "Go and see your father."

Sage took his sword off, held it up, and pointed at Theo. "You've got some explaining to do about this. Kato told me everything."

Theo grinned. "Secrets. Old men are entitled, are they not?"

Sage nodded and set it on the table. "Nobody touch it. I'll keep it here until I get a chance to put it in my dungeon."

"Get going, Sage," Elsbeth said. "We'll all be fine."

"Just a minute," Sage said. He addressed Theo. "How did all of you know to be in here right at this precise moment?"

"The gift of Sight has many advantages, Master Sage. Especially to a man of my age. God provides."

"I actually told your parents that you and Ronan would be back in town today," Grandpa said. "Theo started getting visions of your return the moment the Darks closed the portal to Godspace."

"So you really weren't worried at all?" Sage asked.

"Oh, I was plenty worried," Grandpa said. "Coming back alive doesn't mean coming back uninjured. Even Theo's gift of Sight doesn't tell us everything." Grandpa's phone rang. "It's your mom, Sage." He took the call. "Hello?" He listened for a minute. "Sure. You bet. Yes, they just got back, as promised. Sure. Absolutely. Not a problem. See you in a little bit." Grandpa ended the call, looked at Sage, and raised his eyebrows. "Your mom wants all of us to head to your house. Your dad wants to make a family announcement about his business deal."

"So Dad's at home with Mom?" Sage asked.

Grandpa nodded. "And Nick. She asked us to hurry."

Sage's throat tightened, but he didn't lose control of his emotions. He felt proud of himself.

"Well, he can't show up looking like that," Elsbeth said.

"I was just thinking the same thing," Grandpa said.

"I have some clothes at your house. Ronan can drive me over and wait while I shower. I can be home in twenty minutes."

"Sounds like a plan," Grandpa said.

Sage turned and looked at his team, then stepped up and gave everybody a hug. Even David. "I'll be seeing you guys around, OK?"

"Possibly sooner than you suspect," Theo said.

Sage frowned. "What's that mean?"

"Just old man speculation."

Yeah, sure.

Grandpa's car was already at Sage's house by the time Ronan dropped him off. His hair was still damp from the shower, and the old clothes he'd kept at Grandpa's were just a tad too small, but he was clean and refreshed and felt great. Except for the brick that sat in his stomach when he thought about what his dad might look like.

He heard voices in the family room, laughter, when he opened the front door. "In here, Sage," Mom yelled.

His dad's back was to him when he got there. He stood and turned and looked directly at Sage. His eyes were clear, his head normally shaped, and his skin was as clear as Sage's own.

Sage bit his tongue to get his mind off the emotions swirling inside him. He couldn't just rush over and throw himself into his dad's arms. At least not without making all of them think he'd finally gone off the deep end. This was supposed to be just another summer day for Sage, a boring, early-June, what-can-I-do-to-kill-the-time kind of day. So he fought back his emotions as his perfectly normal father addressed the family.

Dad said, "Now that everyone's here, I have a big announcement to make."

Sage sat down next to Grandpa, who had an arm thrown around Nick's shoulders on his other side. Sage's mom sat next to Grandma on the loveseat. Mom already knew whatever it was Dad was about to announce. Her face radiated joy and peace; her eyes were as bright as diamonds.

"I've backed out of my acquisition deal," Dad said. "Deal's off." He shook his head, his eyes moist. "I realized I was chasing the almighty dollar, and it just wasn't worth it." He looked at everybody and smiled at Mom. "So you'll just have to get used to me being around here more, not working so much, and demanding family vacations." He pointed to Sage and Nick. "Getting some outdoor time with you guys. Maybe even learning to swordfight, huh, Sage?"

Sage smiled. "Sounds great, Dad. I've got a few things I can show you."

"And gaming," Nick said. "I've got a new one with some freaky, scary monsters. About battling the Seven Princes of Hell. Super cool."

Sage smiled to himself. If Nick only knew.

"Too scary, Nick," Mom said. "You'll ruin your brain by exposing yourself to all that violence."

"Ah, Mom, it's just a game. It's not like the Princes of Hell are real or anything."

Sage felt Grandpa elbow him in the ribs.

"Well, we'll talk about it, Nick," Dad said. "I'm just glad to be back in the land of the living. I also want to apologize for being absent these last few months." He chuckled. "Looking back now, I almost felt possessed."

Mom nodded knowingly, but didn't say anything. Neither did Sage, although he certainly could have said a lot.

"Anybody care to run into town for a matinee?" Dad asked. "I took the afternoon off, and there must be a few good movies we've missed."

Everybody had an idea of what to see first. Sage closed his eyes to give a short prayer of thanks.

EPILOGUE

They traveled through Godspace, Ronan leading the way, Grandpa, Sage, and Leah following silently behind. It had been a week since Sage's return, and he'd spent most of that time with his family. Grandpa mentioned a couple of times that the Council wanted to meet with Sage as soon as possible. This was it. Grandpa told Mom and Dad he was taking Sage out of town for a few days, although he conveniently omitted the part about *where* they'd be.

Theo had left for Council headquarters the day before, and Elsbeth, David, Kato, and Klauss had been there for several days. They'd given precise reports about everything they'd seen and heard. Now it was Sage's turn. A debriefing, Ronan called it.

They stepped out of Godspace into a thick fog behind a stand of head-high bushes in Istanbul. Even through the fog, the dome of the Hagia Sophia took Sage's breath away. The dome rose majestically over the tops of a row of trees, the four spires towering in the air around it reminding Sage of fairy-tale princesses trapped by evil witches.

"The Shrine of the Holy God," Grandpa said. "That's the English translation of Hagia Sophia, which is Greek. In the entire world, only the Pantheon in Rome has a bigger dome." Over to one side, Sage saw dozens of people lined up near a gate and pointed it out to Grandpa. "They're waiting to buy tickets to get in," Grandpa said. "Fourteen dollars each. We've come early. By design. The museum doesn't open for another couple of hours."

Grandpa narrated as they went. "There's a small door near the upper southern gallery, by the Great Marble Door, which opens into what used to be a meeting chamber. From there we'll enter the outer narthex by the eastern part of the atrium and slip through a smaller, inner narthex and into the nave. A ramp leads down to the lower galleries, and at the very bottom, behind a giant wall of bronze grills, is a doorway built into a marble wall, visible only to those of us who know it's there."

Sage was disoriented by the time they got to the bottom. Ronan must have seen the look on his face. "We're a hundred feet under the building," he said. "I got dizzy the first time I came down here too."

The stone corridor was less than four feet wide. Wall-mounted sconces jutted out far enough to crack your head if you weren't paying attention, but they offered enough light to see.

Then there were more stairs: a steep, narrow drop into the earth that took more than a minute to descend. Their footsteps echoed in the damp air. All of it reminded Sage of a scene from an old Dracula movie.

At the bottom, a long, stone-covered hallway stretched out before them. At the end of the hall, Grandpa stopped in front of a wooden door bearing the bronze Adamic lettering of a single word—*Council*. He knocked four times and stepped back.

This was it. Sage was about to meet the Council: Elioudians descended from the original two hundred sent to the surface from Tartarus.

Kato opened the door widely and grinned. He elbowed past Grandpa and smothered Sage in a giant hug. He looked great—refreshed, well fed, clean, but just a little odd wearing clothing of this time rather than of his own. He pulled Sage into a library full of people. "Sage Alexander, the boy warrior!" he shouted to the room.

Klauss gripped his hand hard and slapped him on the back. As voices merged and congratulations were made, Sage looked around at the Council's chambers. It was a library with thousands of volumes and a table large enough to sit three dozen people. A chandelier hung high over the center of the table.

Kato closed the door, and Grandpa pointed Sage to one of several empty chairs. He sat down and saw Elsbeth a few seats down. They smiled at each other. David was at the far end of the table and waved for Ronan to join him there.

Theo sat directly across from Sage. Besides the people he knew, Sage counted fifteen others, only one of whom he recognized: Abigail Vaughn, the Council leader he'd seen from the Memory Share experience with Leah. Everyone had a nameplate in front of them, but he couldn't see most of them because of the angle.

Abigail Vaughn might well be the oldest in the room, Sage thought. Her frail frame couldn't possibly weigh more than ninety pounds. She sat erectly, a beehive of white hair stacked high upon her head. Glasses perched at the end of her nose, yet it didn't appear as if she needed them. She looked at Sage for several moments and then turned her gaze upon Elsbeth.

The room fell silent when Abigail spoke, her voice surprisingly strong. "We welcome Sage Alexander to Council chambers." No one else in the room spoke or offered a welcome.

"The Council has read the full report of your actions within Mammon's collection site, Sage," Abigail continued. "Along with the details your grandfather chronicled from the reports you provided him, each rescued member has added their perspective. The book we created chronicling the event will be placed within the Tomb so that future generations may absorb the many lessons you, and we, have learned."

Wow, I'm gonna have my own book to study once I get to study there! Sage fought the urge to smile because Abigail Vaughn looked way too serious to put up with any silliness.

The old woman folded her hands in front of her and leaned forward slightly. "However, as I'm certain you know, we cannot complete the book until we have the last and most important detail."

Sage had probably had ten conversations with his grandpa about the events within the prison, and at the end of each one, Grandpa had asked him about the human form Mammon had taken when he arrived with his blind guards to inspect his defaced statue. Sage was the only one who'd seen his face up close and the only one who could help the Council now.

"Your inability to tell us the name of Mammon's last human identity has cost us a week of valuable research time," Abigail said, her eyes intense. "Do you not think the other six Princes have already begun covering up their interactions with him? Do you not think Mammon's offspring have begun destroying evidence of his existence?"

Sage leaned back in his chair but held Abigail's furious stare. "Do you think I withheld the name on *purpose*?" he asked. "That I *lied* to Grandpa over and over? That I don't *want* to help?" He silently counted to five so that he could get his breathing under control. *How dare she question him like this!* "Your concern is valid, but I've spent hours in my room every night searching the Internet for pictures of billionaires and millionaires. I can't find his face."

Abigail stared at him, but she didn't comment.

"Yes," Sage continued, "the Six probably knew the instant Mammon died. They no doubt have some kind of psychic connection. Since the Council never investigated the last human identity Mammon was living under, I'm sure the Six know we couldn't identify him, which means they may not be as diligent in covering Mammon's tracks as they could be." He paused and looked at the others around the table. "Eventually I will discover what name belongs to the face I saw. When that happens, the Council can investigate him covertly. We *will* find the other Princes. I'm sure of it."

Abigail relaxed and sat back. She closed her eyes briefly, then reached over and took one of Theo's hands before addressing Sage. "Your grandfather and Theo assured me of your veracity. I apologize if you took my inquisition in the wrong manner. As you probably are aware, the benefits of Mammon's death are already being felt around the world. Charitable donations are at record levels. Church coffers are overflowing around the globe. Rich governments are helping governments far less fortunate. Corporations have begun providing benefits to workers at rates never seen before. The Council is desperate," Abigail said as she leaned forward, "to discover the identities of the other six Princes. The world needs them destroyed."

Sage felt the weight of her words settle upon his shoulders. It wasn't until that moment that he realized the incredible responsibility he'd been given. He acknowledged her and smiled slightly. "I will continue searching to put a name with the face I saw. The moment I discover it, you will be the first to know."

"Very well, then," Abigail said. "That is all we can ask." She glanced around the table. "We are dismissed. Please take a moment to meet and congratulate Sage and his team on their job well done."

People began chattering, but once again, Abigail slapped the table to get everyone's attention. When the room fell silent, she struggled to her feet and placed a hand on Theo's shoulder for support.

"There is just one more thing to say. Welcome to the Angelic Response Council, Sage the Warrior. Now the battle begins in earnest."

Cheers filled the room. Sage glanced at Leah, who wasn't smiling at all. She probably knew her life was about to get a whole lot harder.

"Ready for a tour?" Sage's grandpa asked as he came up from behind him. "Council headquarters is more than just this one room."

"Can. Not. Wait." Sage said.

"I'll show him around, Mr. Alexander," Elsbeth said from across the table. She ran around and grabbed Sage's hand. "I know all the important facts about this place."

"I'm sure you do, Elsbeth," Grandpa said. "Take all the time you need."

"You bet," she said as she pulled Sage away from the table. He wasn't about to protest. She was the *only* tour guide he would have wanted.

They'd made it halfway around the big table, when Elsbeth pointed to a man talking to Theo. "See that guy," she whispered. "That mean-looking one with the big scar on the side of his neck? That's Beowulf."

Then she dragged Sage off before he had a chance to gawk.

ABOUT THE AUTHOR

Steve Copling has spent more than thirty-five years in law enforcement and corporate security. Over the years, he has worked in field training, crime prevention, SWAT, criminal investigations, narcotics, and internal affairs. He has also held multiple supervisory positions at sergeant, lieutenant, and captain ranks. He currently serves as a captain in the Plano, Texas, police department.

Copling's career as an author began as a favor to his sister, who happened to be writing a screenplay about a murder. Because her background didn't include police work or investigations, she asked him to take a look at it. He immediately recognized that her fictional suspect would have gotten caught within five minutes in the real world. He agreed to write the story for his sister as a manuscript that she could later convert into a screenplay.

Even though that first manuscript never saw the light of day, Copling was hooked. He went on to write two crime novels, *The Listener* and *The Shooting Season*. His professional background and knowledge of police procedurals inform his writing, and he often draws from his experiences when writing crime fiction. However, unlike most crime writers in today's marketplace, his writing is free of profanity. Appealing to a wide audience, Copling's books are clean enough for teenage fans of police narratives yet still intriguing enough to captivate suspense readers of any age. He is working on a third crime novel, titled *The Noise Before Defeat*.

Sage Alexander and the Hall of Nightmares is his first foray into young adult fantasy and serves as the foundation for a seven-book series based on the seven deadly sins. It was born out of an endearing request from his grandson Sage, who asked Copling to write him a book for Christmas. His ultimate goal with this series is simply to write stories that Sage and his brother, Nikhil, will love reading.

Copling has three sons and five grandchildren. He and his wife of nearly forty years live in Plano, Texas.